# TKEN KINGDOM

FROM INTERNATIONAL AWARD WINNING AUTHOR

## KIA CARRINGTON-RUSSELL

CRYSTAL
PUBLISHING

# Dedication

To my readers,

Wow, what a journey! When I started writing this series six years ago, I never dreamed it would turn into such a monumental world or shared community. I knew what I had was something special, but I never realized how many of you would pick up the first book and fall in love with Esmore and Chase as much as I did while writing it. I'm so grateful to each and every one of you who have stayed by my side with all the highs and lows and growing pains in my writing career. I wouldn't be here without you and as always- thank you. Words could never express how much I adore you.

I would like to shout a special thank you to my editor, Lisa Edward, who is as wonderful as she is magical and most certainly patient as she waited for this final book. My cover artist, Adrijana Cernic, who can somehow create a masterpiece out of my disjointed visions and descriptions. Thank you for bringing Esmore and Chase to life on the covers. And finally, Tami Norman, for creating such beautiful interiors. Thank you so much! You're the A team who turns this from being a pile of words to a spellbinding book.

To my support team and author friends, my goodness, we've grown so much together! There are too many to name, but you know who you are and you know I'm giving you the biggest of high fives and hugs. I'm so glad we found each other!

And last but not least, to a very special author friend of mine who was my writing buddy for the majority of these words placed. Thank you, Margaret McHeyzer, for sitting down with me every day as we supported one another in writing chapter by chapter no matter how much distance between us. Thank you for listening to me on the days I wanted to pull out my hair when the plot wasn't budging and celebrating with me on the days where words were swimmingly flowing. You're a star!

To everyone, I hope you enjoy the read and until next time!


Much love,
*Kia xx*

# Chapter I



LINCON WAS ENJOYING his rough handling of the two vampire scouts he dragged before me. I suspected he perceived it as the most excitement he'd had in weeks. They were the only members to remain. The rest, of course, had been disposed of before they were hauled into our territory and brought to me. I felt somehow privileged that he held the restraint to keep at least two alive—somewhat. From the sheer wide-eyed terror in their absent gazes, he probably tortured them all the way home. Lincon was chuffed by his prized capture, and I realized it was probably Kasey who urged him to have restraint from killing them.

He brushed his hand over his bloody dress shirt as if trying to look more presentable in the courtroom. He'd recently gone through another flamboyant shift applying thick eyeliner with wicked wings. I wasn't sure if he was creating the illusion of having them or was applying the thick charcoal-like substance every day and nor did I care to ask. Lincon always did extravagant things, and I'd learned long ago not to give him the attention he sought out but offering only enough so he wouldn't irrationally combust and erratically kill our allies for the fun of it.

Iris leaned over my shoulder. "They were sniffing around the borders, no more than a group of ten."

Lincon threw his hands in the air. "I was about to tell her that!" He stomped his foot. "I swear, Iris, you always try to take my glory." Iris leaned back into his looming position, irritated, all too used to Lincon's theatrics. The vampires shifted uncomfortably, daring to only look at me once before hastening their gaze to the ground before them. Whatever torture Lincon twisted into their minds, it'd taken hold for some time now. They were barely coherent, but they knew who I was just by glance alone. Good. Then this would make the interrogation simple—they knew what I wanted.

I tapped my fingernail on the armrest of the wooden throne I sat upon. My gift jittered around me like a miasma, keeping everyone an arm's-length distance away from me. My wings shuffled of their own accord as I stared down at the two vampires. Meek little scout members who we'd already identified to be a part of Antonio's Council.

I'd just begun to wonder if Tythian and Fier had given up on their blood lust to find my location and dispose of me. But with the advance of Antonio's Council, evidently, they still failed in their pursuit, which was irritatingly mutual because I hadn't yet located them either.

I sighed, vexed that we'd been playing this dance for all too long now. How many years had it been since we'd tried to take one another out? And around in the same circles we went. I'd only heard whispers of their separate Council locations and every scout had been misled, with not a vampire to be seen. And if I couldn't have their heads, then I made it a personal conquest to take out the Councils one by one until they decided to appear. And even then, disposing of the Council entirely was a fortunate fate.

A year after the great fight with Oppollo and the twelve Councils, I'd gathered a considerable volume of werewolves who joined our ranks. Impatiently, I'd decided it was time to confront Fier, but he'd vacated his San Francisco Council. Nothing but an empty vessel booby-trapped, deliberately waiting for our arrival, and I hadn't caught a whiff of him since.

But we were close, a knowing sensation dawning on me as I waited impatiently to stake their heads. We were in unfavorable circumstances after the great fight. Cesar had the Council's locations and I did not. When I'd returned to the abandoned institute to see what remained, the building had crumbled by flames, no doubt set alight by Tythian himself, leaving no trace or evidence of all the information he and Cesar carefully collected over the years.

"Where's Antonio's Council?" My voice spread into the darkness of the great throne room where we resided. It had become my favorite to occupy, simply because of its high ceilings that were still detailed in ancient architect and the swallowing depths of the room.

The two vampires flinched under my stern tone dictating that death awaited them. Both were too rattled from their time spent with Lincon to speak. I didn't have the patience to deal with this. I gestured for Lincon to take over in whatever fashion he deemed fit to excite them into talking again. He greedily stepped forward, and I looked away from his prominent arousal from the joy of torturing them.

"Wait!" one of the men shouted, scared out of his wits. I deadpan starred at him. When his gaze met mine, he dropped his to the ground once again. I took pride in terrifying them with a simple glance. I'd begun to identify the Councils individually when I noticed their uniformed clothing and behaviors. Antonio's Council was mostly scholars, educated vampires who lacked luster in fighting. It didn't mean they were incompetent by any means, just that they were beyond their natural instinct to kill—which was exceptionally boring.

"You'll kill us even if we do speak," he stuttered. His face was grimy from weeks, maybe even months out in the field before they were ambushed. Who knows, perhaps it was simply by mistake and chance he'd stumbled close to our location.

"Incorrect. I'm only going to kill one of you. The one who wins my favor will be set free." The two blanched, staring at one another. It was an easy enough segregation technique, and neither seemed to have the camaraderie to die together. That wasn't in a vampire's nature.

I watched as the remaining vampire flailed through our front gates. Werewolves snapped at his ankles as he fled. The moment he was amongst the trees, he'd forget of our whereabouts. It was an evolution in the gift my familiar had honored me with. Just as he had once used it when living within Fier's Council, I'd distinguished the same mental manipulation skill.

I'd set one free, the first of whom was to give me the details I sought after. Without a second thought, I'd imploded his comrade beside him, my gift casting him as ash in the stagnant air in the throne room.

By the time Antonio's vampire reached his Council, it would already be predisposed, I might not have killed him, but there would be no home to return to. His role wasn't to play hero, but to spread news of his Council being demolished, with a very blanketed memory of coming into contact with me. It would surely rattle the others as it had over the years. If Fier and Tythian didn't do something soon besides hide themselves, then I'd continue to destroy the Councils one by one.

I was in my private chambers, looking out through the small alcove window. Behind me, nothing had changed in the past ten years since Iris had refurbished it. The wooden bed was fitted with black silk sheets and a blanket I considered unnecessary considering I hardly slept. Those nights were frequented by Kyran who continued to taunt me. And other times, I was frozen in a place that I often tried to forget, with a certain person whom I blocked from my thoughts. Most of the furniture collected dust except for my wooden closet that harbored all my weapons. My room was rarely lived in, and I was already ready and waiting for the day where it wouldn't be home any longer.

Positioned in front of the alcove where I stood was my wooden chair I sometimes occupied when in thought, staring out at the night sky. It was an overcast day with a small splatter of rain. The werewolves below went about their daily business. Some trained, others refurbished the allotment, making it more homely. For the most part, I allowed them to do whatever they wanted to the infrastructure because this place was more for them than it was ever meant to be for me.

My gaze lingered on the three teenagers below. Titan shoved at Chris playfully as he made a joke. Perhaps her shove was a little too forceful, but he'd become accustomed to that. On the other side, Tori allowed a small smile to curve his lips as he watched them silently.

"Oh, come on," Titan shot at him and hooked her elbow around his neck, pulling him in closer. He was abashed, and I watched with slight disdain at their closeness. I'd become wary of Titan's changes as she came of age. Not only did she have a temper that I publicly reprimanded but privately admired, but she was also beginning to draw attention from the males of her age. And although Tori had become her personal bodyguard at my request to give him purpose over the last few years, I tentatively watched to make sure it wasn't anything more than that.

She'd turned into a beauty, a powerful force not to be reckoned with under the guidance of Fire's training and raising. She had pixie-cut short black raven hair, and her brown doe-eyes were striking against her shimmery tanned complexion. She was as beautiful as her handle on weapons. Or given any chance, when she was in wolf form too.

Fire knocked on the door, not waiting for my reply to permit her entrance. I looked over my shoulder at the ageless woman. Ten years had passed, and neither of us had aged. By now she should've had crowed lines around her eyes and a downward scowl permanently plastered around her mouth, but instead she'd remained frozen, just as I had as an immortal. And I assumed that had something to do with my venom in her veins.

"You'll be going tonight then, I presume?" Fire asked. Evidently, Iris had already spoken to her. The two worked surprisingly well together. When he forfeited his place within Tracey's Council, refusing to protect her younger sister, Patricia, he'd followed us to pursue revenge on Tythian for killing his master.

"Yes," I tartly said, closing my hands together behind my back and under my wings. My gaze dropped onto another familiar face through the alcove. Kasey was glumly walking amongst the wolves who ignored her as much as she did them. The wolves quickly pillowed away as Lincon chased after her, consistently irritating what he still deemed his 'plaything.' It had now been eight years since the absence of her sister, Kora. Her will to live became absent, and she took action to dispose of herself from this world that tormented her. It haunted me for weeks, in memory of what Lincon's mother, Sasha, had once said, *Not all of us are cut out to live as monsters. Some become the demon and others peril, either of their own accord or because they're hunted for it.*

It had taken Kasey months to adjust using her gift, as all their life they'd depended on one another. She came to despise her sister for it, despite never reaching a hand to help her when she was alive. But then again, none of us had. Surprisingly, the one who took it the hardest was Titan, who sometimes sat silently with her as a child. But she'd long been forgotten since.

"Will you require any assistance?" Fire asked distantly. I knew she wanted to come with me, but it would all be over in the flash of seconds. As if Antonio's Council had never existed. Iris and Fire were disgruntled when I left by myself. And Lincon mostly despised that he wasn't allowed to wreak havoc or at least watch me dispose of the cities at a time. But with the growing distance, I didn't want to wait on anyone. I wanted to deal with this now and send my message to Tythian and Fier.

"No. I'll go on this mission myself." My blue gemmed necklace glimmered despite no sunlight pouring in. I looked at it ominously, blocking any thoughts that it might arouse or of whom it reminded me. But I'd never had the strength to remove it from around my neck.

# CHAPTER 2

I LOOKED DOWN upon Antonio's Council. It was uneventful, to say the least. Of all the Councils who'd gathered at the last Vampire Council meeting, I recalled Antonio's to be one of the less frightful congregations. But that didn't make him any less of a threat, and he was now simply an obstacle. The unfortunate small city was beautiful, and it took me a full two days to stretch over the great sea in flight to arrive. The majority of the forgotten city was sunken and immersed underwater.

It was once called Venice, or so Lincon had informed me. I crouched atop the mainland, looking into the distance as the vampires vacantly walked around. Some held books, others with weapons, and I deciphered that they were guards of some sort. I couldn't sense any sabers within the area. Antonio was known to have a low tolerance for letting what he deemed 'lower' or 'dirty' creatures near his Council.

The sunken city might've been considered beautiful once, and it certainly did hold a certain appeal and charm. But that mattered not. I stood and took hold of the elongated pole beside me where tethers of a once beautiful flag might've flapped. I held onto the pole for balance because I would certainly exhaust myself tonight. I let my jittery gift freely ooze from me. It always encompassed me but went feverish the moment I allowed it off the leash.

It was a wrathful surge, swelling within me, filling me entirely as my center and being. It wanted everything. The world and more. It wanted to slip over the edges and eat away at the beauty of the stars if allowed, or on a day when I might not have the strength to orchestrate it otherwise. I took a hollow breath, where I found the edge of my vampire and huntress within, chemically imbalanced in all forms as they pushed and shoved within me, crafting a nauseous wave of turbulence as I tried to control my power.

"Hey, there's a figure up there!" a vampire shouted rooftops away— one of their guards. At least Antonio had that much. But it was too late. I released my power like a formidable gunshot. My force swarmed out of me, encompassing everything in its wave like a miasma of raw and unsolicited power. Everything it touched turned into ash. A quick slice destroying everything in its path. I choked on its magnitude, my knees giving way as I continued to hold myself up by the pole. I could feel its jittering fangs biting through everything it touched. What was once undead and moving was now nothing but ash. A dark atomic sweep passing over the small city.

I confiscated my gifts power, calling forward my vampire and huntress to choke down on its gnawing flame and cipher it out. As it fought against me, I felt my strength seep out of me. It was always like this when I used my power on such a massive level. Its efficiency was unparalleled. If I were to let it continue, I was certain it'd kill me in the process. It needed my strength in replacement. And that was something my vampire self certainly wouldn't allow. The nauseating roll in my stomach swirled as my gift whipped back into me, almost forcing me onto my ass if I hadn't been clinging to the metal pole. I took a shallow breath.

A shadow was falling upon me, and when I looked up, I realized it was the pole bent at an irregular angle arching over me from how tightly I'd grasped it. I steadied myself, staring out toward the mass of ash that blew amongst the night sky. Only canals remained, the buildings that once were, vanished, as did everything else that once was.

I took another shallow breath, drawing back the taste of my blood from my fangs piercing my lips. I slowly stood, certain the pole would snap in two, but it remained sturdy despite its small groans. I was ravished. My body was starved for fresh blood to replenish what was lost. It was done. Antonio's Council paid the price for the crime of being a part of the Council and it was another message to draw out those whose heads I truly wanted. The hundreds of vampires here today were simply a casualty.

The flight back would be grueling. I flew low in the dark clouds that spotted me with wet dollops. I didn't want to be seen, but I wanted to be low enough to the ground so as I might be able to find something to feast from, preferably humans. I wasn't far out of Antonio's city when a collaboration of sabers caught my attention. I circled a few times, monitoring their congressional as they tried to break into something. Inspecting the area, I circled closer and quietly dropped to the ground. The sabers twisted as soon as my light feet padded on the grass. I skittered my gift out to them in a flash, disposing of the searing sight. They erupted into ash, scattered in the wind, though their claw marks remained on the metal doors built into the ground on an angle—a bunker.

I inspected my surroundings once more, curious. If the sabers were after something, then perhaps, if I might be so lucky, they had smelt out humans. My fangs ejected of their own accord at the mere thought of delicious fresh blood. I lashed my gift out, eating away at the handles that were once solidly locked. It would only be a matter of time until my gift left me completely as it sought refuge to restore, so I was taking advantage of it while its remnants remained. I bent over, placing one delicate finger under the fresh hole. I peeled back the door and heard the click of the trigger before the human had time to shoot.

I pitched slightly to the side, avoiding the scattered shots that rung out. None of which hit their mark. There were four: three men and one woman. I couldn't understand their language, but one thing I could smell was the adamant fear they reeked of. It was all too enticing for my vampire, and I dared not ask it for restraint. I heaved forward in a massive lunge into the bunker that might've once kept them safe for years, if not their lifetime. But it was an unfortunate, miserable day anyway and I had a certain thirst to quench.

"It went well then?" Fire asked, standing behind me. Iris remained silent, taking in my not so pedigree attire with blood doused all over me. The mission itself had been easy. The feasting not so much. I was almost ashamed of the incomprehensible mess I'd left the bodies in. I'd been ravenous, and they'd paid the price with a gruesome death. But this power needed nourishment, and I'd already sold myself to whatever methods were required to put an end to this ongoing war.

Every day some werewolves who left didn't return. The human government was still on the move. The days of manufacturing the wolves were now spent, but the plague continued to spread as the humans intended. And for those who escaped, most found their way to us through rumor and seeking refuge. And due to their sense of smell and being able to communicate in a unique form of their own, they always eventually found us. I'd given them a place of security, and when I needed their strength they were forthcoming in all that they could offer. A silent Queen, they called me. If only they knew the truth of what I was and, for example, what I'd done today. They wouldn't be so willing to be at my bidding.

I had little to do with the Hunter Guilds except for the infrequent updates I would receive from my mother. But I had my scouts keep an ear out for one name in particular. Since the death of Campture, James had become a very hard ghost to find. But I knew in the pit of my stomach, he was somewhere out there, and my keen atonement for vengeance was overbearing at times. I knew he was still alive, drifting through day by day if only to be tortured by my hand for what he'd done. Ten years was a long time to develop a lifetime of hate and wrath.

"Antonio's Council has been disposed of, yes," I informed them. I would need a few weeks to months to rest from the onslaught of my power. I was tired and restless all at once as I found myself fidgeting with the necklace at my throat. "Any update on James's whereabouts?" The silence was enough of an answer.

I could hear Titan's voice narrowing down the hallway to my room. Her loud footing always a giveaway.

"I don't care if she's asked to be left alone!" Titan rebelliously spited. I could hear Tori's reprimand as he silently hustled beside her. He could physically stop her if he wanted to, but her willful spirit was something we'd all learned to work around since she was a child.

She banged against the door. When she screamed out in frustration because it didn't open, I looked over my shoulder and found a glimmer of humor twinkle in Iris's eyes. He had his lofty weight pressed against the door with arms crossed. She'd never be able to break through even if she tried full force. Fire's mouth twitched upward in amusement.

"It's fine," I finally reckoned. "Let her in. I'd rather her use the door than scale the outside wall just to get in here." And so help me, she would.

She fell through the door the moment Iris shifted his weight. Tori grabbed the back of her loose-fitted black shirt, bundling it into his fist so she was suspended above the ground before he decidedly dropped her, landing face first. I hid my humor once again, wanting to punish myself for finding a pocket of amusement anywhere. I wasn't allowed to be happy… not when *he* wasn't with me.

I narrowed my focus on the pair, trying to shake away the lingering thoughts I'd been having of him as of late. Tori, with little effort and a smirk on his face, heaved Titan back up. Her chunky knee-high tight-laced purple boots groaned at the overexertion.

"You left without even telling me! I wanted to go with you!" she demanded.

"Titan, I told you last time. You're not ready. Yes, your fighting is superior for your age group. But I've been purposefully going on these outings alone. Not even Fire has been by my side."

"Well, I don't care. I want out. You've trained me my whole life for this! I can do it!"

"Are you so quick to run to your death, Titan, and drag Chris along with you?" Fire asked in her sternest of tones. I knew she hadn't yet lectured her to be quiet because despite how menacing her complaint was, I tolerated her to speak openly. If anything, I was perhaps slightly too lenient of her unorthodox behavior. But she was a child of mine as much as she was all of us in raising. Everything she was, was partly us as well.

Titan flinched under the insinuation that she would lead Chris into harm's way. He was a natural fighter, just as she was and I'd realized long ago—like all the wolves were. But he certainly allowed Titan to lead him into too many brawls and harmless shenanigans. I feared on a battlefield it would alter his focus. He was and had been, always looking at her, just as Tori was now.

"Please, Esmore," Titan begged. "It doesn't have to be anything big. Send me out with Lincon next time he's scouting for food, wood or something—anything." Lincon was certainly the last person I'd allow her out with freely. He'd taken a particular interest in her by extension through my own, and I made sure to keep an eye on that so it didn't escalate into anything dangerous. But maybe some of the other werewolves, when they left to search for supplies would do. They were able to hunt freely. But evidently, she felt cooped up even from that.

"I'll consider it," I said, tight-lipped.

"But—" I shot an effective look her way. She bit the inside of her cheek with her brown doe-eyes throwing daggers at me. I was always amused at her daring intensity. But I had been playing at this game of wills for longer.

She dipped her head curtly, dismissing herself and pushing past the others and back out as extravagantly as she entered. The Barnett crossbow I'd once gifted her as a child didn't look so out of place now against her muscular shoulders and six-foot frame. Some days more than others she reminded me of her father, Sydney, who was a hunk of muscled human himself. I pulled away from that darting memory. And if it hadn't been for me, then maybe he might've seen it for himself.

"Tori, keep an eye on her," I ordered. It wouldn't be the first time she'd tried some form of trickery or escapism for self-adventure.

"Always," he promised respectfully. His quaint presence always reminded me of Dillian. It had now been ten years since I'd seen him, still with no word or understanding if he offered himself as tribute to save Tori or if he wanted to side with Tythian all along because he felt some kind of attachment to him for being his maker. Some were attached and others not so much.

I grimaced at the vacancy of my best friend. So many memories were stirring within me as of late. I pushed them down narrowing my focus on the two in the room, so we could discuss action plans into all hours of the night. But mostly all I wanted to do was stare out of the window vacantly, mentally washing off this blood on my hands. Not because I was regretful for taking so many lives but because the evidence of it tarnished my controlled reputation.

I rarely slept, but this seemed different, almost forced as I sat in my wooden chair beside my window, exhausted, looking out at the star-filled night. Today had taken a lot out of me, but there was a calling to succumb to the sleep which only fortified my suspicion. And yet, I could only fight it off for so long. I willed myself to stand, to make myself busy elsewhere, but instead, my head drooped to surrender to sleep. A pang of guilt shrouded me, and an image of Chase sprung to mind fortifying a singular tear to build in the corner of my eye. A lump formed in my throat at the thought of him after trying for so many years to put him in the back of my mind and focus on what I had to do to make this world safe for him again. But there wasn't a day that passed that his face didn't haunt me. It had now been ten years since I'd locked him away. Much longer than I'd anticipated this war to go on.

The draw to close my eyes enveloped me once again and this time I was pulled under like cold water. All I could see was darkness, a forever kind of sleep, but I could hear and sense the impending presence.

I was cold, so very frozen, and looking out through a glass cylinder door. I was frozen in time as voices bombarded me from the outside of my Popsicle cage.

"Oh my." A gagging noise. "It smells so bad in here. Are you kidding me? There's a wolf's decayed corpse." It was Balzar's voice.

"If only your wit was as impressive as your sense of smell, perhaps we would've thought of this place sooner," Clarissa chastised, though I could hear the disdain in her voice from the pungent smell. "Spungee, out of that!" Some adhered shuffling noises were made.

"I didn't see you coming up with any better ideas."

"Well, the fact that Jerimiah and the others were stationed outside in gargoyle form is a pretty good indicator," she spited back.

Another nauseous swirl provoked my stomach as I considered where exactly I might've been. I couldn't move, trapped in this enclosure. When Balzar's head popped in front of my glass screening, I couldn't murmur a word or tap against the inside to request he let me out. I knew this hell and was willing in the dream for them to turn back.

Balzar hadn't changed in the slightest over the past ten years. From where I stood, I couldn't see Clarissa or Spungee but knew they were close by.

"Holy shit," Balzar mouthed as he peered in at me through the glass door. "He's actually here." And sadness seemed to cross over his expression. "This plan has Yolo written all over it."

And at his suggestion, I too was certain it was his belated brother's intention for me to use the facility in such a way.

"How do we open it?" Clarissa asked. A scurry until she was peering at the gadgets no doubt hooked to the outside. Balzar pushed her out of the way with an exasperated sigh. He pulled his elbow back and smashed into the glass. I flinched within, not my body but myself as I began to forbid him to open it.

He hissed under the vibrating fallback. The glass didn't break, and Clarissa scoffed at him. "Always so quick to use brawn over brain," she remarked. It was the most lively I'd heard her before, but then again she always swelled with spirit when arguing with Balzar. She tinkered around until a small hissing began. The coldness swept out in a pillow as the door cracked open slightly.

I flashed my eyes open, jumping out of my chair. My wings pushed it back, throwing it against the wall by my startled state. My heart pounded erratically, and I had to recall my gift that began to eat around where I sat, marking the floor and walls with slow, delicate strokes of its festering bubble. No, no, no, no. I tried to count to ten, as my father had always taught me to remain calm.

*He couldn't be…It can't be right…*It was too soon. It might've been a dream, but a gnawing sensation prickled at me. But what if… If it was true, and Fier realized he was coherent and alive. He would just as quickly click his fingers and turn Chase into a saber.

I paced across the room, quickly changing my bloodstained attire so as not to attract anyone by scent, and strapped my sheathed sword and garter of daggers. I was out the door in no time, ignoring the werewolf who tried to engage in conversation with me as I walked down the hallway.

I stormed through the great hall and jogged down the few stairs at the entrance of the castle. "Esmoreeee," Lincon purred enticingly. He was lounged across the top of the wall, trying to drop grapes into Kasey's mouth as she leaned against it, sharpening her two blades. He dropped another grape atop her head. She ground her teeth in irritation, and he smirked. His eyes sparkled with excitement when he narrowed on my weapons. He flipped himself over the edge. "Ooooh, Yay! Where are we going?!"

"*We're* not going anywhere. Tell Fire and Iris I'll be gone for a few days. There's something I have to do."

"Wait, what—" His black hair blew into his eyes as I harpooned into the sky, the wind scuttling around me, welcoming as it always did. They were going to be pissed with me. But the sense of urgency was palpable, and my mouth was drying not only from thirst but the insatiable ideal that might've been more than a dream. It didn't feel like my usual haunted dreams where Kyran taunted me. No…this felt far too familiar and painful. This felt like Chase.

# Chapter 3

M Y WINGS BEGAN to tire from the large-scale commutes in previous days. But that didn't deter my speed. I was desperate to go to the place I hadn't dared go near in ten years. I purposefully stayed away in case I led Tythian and Fier to Chase's resting place. No one else but Darcy and Jerimiah knew about his location, and that was only because they were his accountable guardians.

Returning to this land and terrain brought back so many memories of our time here of what felt like a lifetime ago. I desperately scanned the landmarks until I finally found the abandoned Human Compound. I circled a few times, searching for the gargoyles that should've been protecting the place. *That should be protecting Chase.* The land surrounding the Compound had flourished somewhat. Since humans were no longer trampling in and out and the rodents had evidently lost interest, the woodland began to flourish as best it could. Perhaps some of the small seedlings would actually grow or die by the roots.

My feet silently padded on top of the crumbling wall that was once a guard post. Now it was the remains of a small civilization that was wiped out in a mere few hours. Unlike its former glory where the dome was enclosed and ensured their safety, it was open to the harsh weather that would've pushed through over the years. The inside was a mess with skeletal remains from the massacre that had happened here those many years before.

I jumped off the edge and walked through the broken internal glass tunnel, pulled toward the direction I knew was Chase's resting place. My heartbeat was gradually increasing the closer I got. The last time I was here with Yolo, the door was deactivated making it easy to step through, but I could smell it, the lingering fresh scent.

Of familiar scent.

*Of Chase.*

Before I even reached the room where they once harbored and experimented on vampires, I dreaded what was to come. Because I already knew.

I lifted my nose and gaze, squeezing my wings in tightly as I walked through layers of doors and rooms. Over the years, I'd learned how to maneuver around with my wings gracefully. I could retract them if I wished to but had no intention to do so. It was an example of my power and strength. The monstrosity that I was as I banished all obstacles in my way.

My feathers ruffled uncomfortably as I found myself holding my breath as I came to the final room. A light still flickered blue, the backup generators lasting as long as Yolo had deemed they would. They would last many years more.

My steps slowed as I circled the three freezing chambers. The middle one was busted open, still streaming cold smoke through the jarred door. It had begun to freeze the room over. I could see my reflection in the glass as if mirroring the very spot where I had dreamed Chase to be. Except he wouldn't have been conscious. For him, time would've stopped. And now he was free.

My lips curled savagely as I violently screamed, letting all the paralyzing fear and inadequacy out. I punched the glass door, expecting it to smash. Instead, it broke my hand and closed the door shut.

I growled, holding onto my throbbing hand. I wasn't fast enough, and I had no idea where Balzar and Clarissa might've taken him. I let my mind search for the unyielding link I savored to feel and taste once again between Chase and me but drew it back knowing I was undeserving of such a thing.

I had done everything I knew how to keep him safe, even at the cost of betraying his trust. It was my greatest hatred, and I despised myself for it. But the crack of time had unsealed itself and even as I stretched out my mind, seeking anything that resembled vampires who might've aided his recovery, besides Balzar and Clarissa, I was left empty-handed. They'd long gone, and I had no idea where to begin searching for him.

My gift was jittery and eager to escape, looking for some form of release, and my vampire wanted to feast, exploding in the frustration of failing and running out of time. But my huntress, always so tired and the rational part of me announced a longing. One I had silenced and paid no attention to for ten years. Because it was a deadly weakness I was too scared to narrow in on. And now I had no choice. I had to find him before Fier knew about his reappearance. I twisted out of the room, giving no chance to fate because it had never been my friend. I needed to return to my post and summon all the strength I could. I had built an army to protect him for when the time was just right, as he had once done for me. And even when he spited me and hated me, if we were ever to come face to face for my betrayal, I would only care that he was safe.

I scanned the area for half a day trying to catch a whiff of their familiar scent and mind. But nothing aroused. My guess was that my dream came to me when Chase began to coherently think once again, and I had no idea how long that might've taken after he was busted out. I ground my teeth repetitively, almost begrudging Balzar. The last I'd seen him, he was leaving the battlefield to bury his brother, Yolo. And I hadn't seen or heard of him since. Why was he in search of Chase? Sure, the two had begun to tolerate one another but to search for him? Had Balzar run out of ideas on how to seek his revenge on his brethren, Tythian, and Connor? I kept circling his ambition, realizing his reason really didn't matter or change the fact that Chase had now escaped.

Conscious of my time already away from the castle, I headed back. I was wearily tired, dipping from time to time in the sky before startling back awake. I'd pushed myself too much since annihilating Antonio's Council. And I had the inkling that a lot was about to change. Fier might've forgotten about Chase for now, but it would only last so long. I'd once been scared to dispose of him with the belief he was the only one who could restore Chase's clarity and mind. But after his betrayal, I realized his ambition had been to speed up that process. I had hoped to discard of him and find another way before waking Chase.

A frenzy was stirring as soon as I navigated toward the castle. I glided down below the clouds, noticing wolves stretching over the land beyond our territory. They were in small groups, breaking off into separate directions. I swooped low, intercepting one of them. They startled to a halt, skidding against the dirt. Their leader shifted into his human form, Claus, the alpha of the group. He was the strongest and fastest, mated with Anastasia. They'd had two pups now together.

Though he might've been alpha, he still took orders directly from Fire on my behalf. His forest green eyes were penetrating as his naked chest heaved back and forth.

"Esmore," he said, gathering his wits, and dropped to one knee. The six wolves behind him lowered to the ground in submission. I dismissed their formality, never entirely comfortable with it.

"Why are so many groups dispersed?" I asked.

He seemed to hesitate as he stood, reluctant to tell me the unfortunate news. I could smell the small undercurrent of fear. Like all the wolves had in my presence. It wasn't admiration that kept them in place, it was fear for what I was. "Titan and Chris ran away."

"What?" My tone could've curdled skin from their frame.

"Two days ago, we've been spreading out to find them since." I hissed, plunging back into the sky and guiding toward the castle in search of Fire or Iris. *That silly impatient girl.* I could feel the barrier of my mother's gift once I glided through it. It concealed our scent and location from foreigners. The moment I drifted through it the ample treetops and castle came into view. The wolves had begun building what looked like a small township around it to cater to the growing size of their members.

Wolves were positioned around the territory, guarding our location. It had only been compromised once in the ten years, of which the werewolves were able to slice through the barbaric group of twenty vampires within the hour. It had been a small coven who stumbled upon our land, and they never stood a chance.

I skirted along the edges of the fragmented wall, letting my mind reach out to Iris and Fire. They were on either side of the castle. I hitched toward Fire who was closest to me. It came to no surprise that she'd cornered Lincon and was lecturing him. Despite his power and strength, she'd never feared him but paid caution. And because of the favoritism I offered Fire, he was never daring enough to attack her…seriously.

Kasey was bored as she watched on, munching on scraps of roasted meat and potato bundled in a handkerchief. She picked at them one by one watching on with those coral eyes that no longer sparked with life or ambition. Her saber fangs had turned yellow over the years, her lips permanently cracked. She was leaning against the interior of the small bridge that Fire had cornered Lincon in.

"You encouraged her!" Fire remarked angrily. I swooped behind her, my wings stretching out in a ruffle, at ease that they would finally be able to rest.

"What's going on here?" I demanded.

"And where have you been?" she snapped, circling to face me. I befitted a glare and arched my upper lip slightly to bare my fangs. I didn't at all like her tone.

"Don't make me repeat myself," I cautioned her. I wasn't in the mood for a lecture. I allowed others to live in this place and build their species around me. But I worked for my selfish desires, and that would never change. I'd learned the hard way that compassion within this world was a weak characteristic and it often got people killed. And now and then I had to remind Fire that she was not to dictate or judge what I chose to do during my reign.

A large smile spread over Lincon's face. Had she been daring enough I'd imagine she would have his shirt bundled in her fist, shaking the truth from him. Lincon tucked his hands into his pockets and kicked a bit of dirt, feigning innocence.

Fire straightened out her long white shirt. She only ever wore one if she was in her human form for long durations. And that was only when requiring the tedious task of communicating with those of us who were vampires. We couldn't communicate the way the werewolves did, but she explained to me it was similar to a telepathic bond. And it came with age and experience to learn how to block others out enabling themselves privacy and silence.

"Titan and Chris ran off because this idiot encouraged her to prove herself." She hooked her thumb over her shoulder, pointing at Lincon. Her hands returned to her hips.

"Oh, come now, when you say it like that you make me look like the bad uncle in the family. She reprised her 'concern' that she wasn't being taken seriously. The girl has a lot of ambition. You know she wants to be alpha."

"The rules don't apply to her in the same," Fire snide in return. Because my protection over her excluded her into supremacy. I didn't want her involved with the politics of this new species, especially so young.

"I don't think that's the problem here," Kasey said nonchalantly as she munched on another piece of meat. It unnerved me how indifferent they were about her disappearance.

"How did she get out in the first place? Do we not have guards?" I growled. "Where's Tori?!"

I scanned for his mind, but he wasn't there.

"Tori informed us hours later. He was guarding outside her door in the bathing chambers, after you enforced he wasn't to leave her side. She escaped. When he realized it was already hours later and Chris had gone too."

"The two have absorbed everything you've taught them and are very sneaky. Oh, my, I hope they haven't run off to elope. What if she comes back pregnant?!" Lincon gasped gossipy. I snarled at his humorous take.

"Where's Tori now?"

"He left before any of the groups were sent out after him." Fire was grim. "He went on his own." I tsked, my vampire counterpart rolling in my stomach angrily, ready to make an aggressive appearance. It wanted to break something, anything. And I knew it was because my thirst hadn't been quenched these past few days.

"Keep the groups rolling out. I want her found immediately," I snapped and turned away from them. My wings dipped tiredly, and I pinched them higher to make sure they didn't drag, and my fatigue wasn't noticeable. I didn't have the stamina to search for her myself, and I had another pressing matter to address.

It didn't take me long to find Iris as I walked through the great halls. It reeked of the werewolves, though as of late fewer crept amongst the castle as they built their own huts about the place. The estate buzzed with life and yet I felt like I was a bystander watching on as they thrived, calculating my next move of destruction.

Iris was in the library, the third-largest room in the castle, besides the throne room and kitchen. A small group of the werewolves enforced the role upon themselves to keep the rooms clean. They often dusted the ill-lit room. The majority of the books had survived over the years prior to our intrusion, and I often found the burly sized Iris either reading or writing in journals.

Inside was a different atmosphere as opposed to the manic desperation outside. The door creaked as I pushed it open, slithering a small split of light from the candle mounted on the wall beside me to spill in. He was foraging through the books.

"What are you looking for?" I asked, leaning against the doorframe.

"I think it might've been my fault the pups disappeared," he said without so much as looking at me. I wanted to roll my eyes. Apparently, everyone had something to do with it. I didn't let her out. Lincon was a bad influence. Tori failed to guard her properly. She herself was too willful and treacherous. But I wondered what Iris felt guilty for.

"And why is that?" I prompted.

"None of them are here," he said, irritated as he threw books about at the floor behind him. I knew he'd frown upon his actions later considering how much he appreciated the books. The room was dark around him, almost enveloping him as it always did because of the sheer size and magnitude of his presence. I rarely saw him without his oversized hatchet on his back and today was no different. "There are particular journals I write in once I've located possible movement of the Councils."

"Why, scared you'll forget from old age?" I edged with humor. That grabbed his attention as he looked at me, stunned. Good. I didn't like seeing him in such an odd manic mood. As if realizing that he'd riled himself up he smoothed over one of his arms. As if reminding himself he still had colossal arms.

"Very. Funny," he said deadpan. "I always articulated them on a map in hopes to create a pattern of movement." I was aware. The Council had become fickle to trace, especially the two whom I wanted to target. My army was ready. *I* was ready to strike. It was just a matter of location and re-evaluating their numbers. "I think they've stolen them. Perhaps she means to do a stakeout and contribution?"

I sighed, that was precisely something she'd do. I ground my teeth. The girl was going to be the death of me. It wasn't the first time she'd rebelled, and it seemed to have only gotten worse when she hit puberty. "How many places had you mapped out?"

"Twenty-six including covens." Which we had no issues with unless they attempted to ambush the werewolves, and then I permitted them to protect themselves. "Take out the covens, there are six."

"Send out six separate teams to the locations. They're smart enough to keep themselves out of trouble in the woodlands." The werewolves had shown me numerous times their inept ability to treat the woods like their natural calling. They were sensitive and aware of everything that moved, even when they'd come across more powerful vampires. Where they might've lacked in the strength and stamina of an aged vampire, they had numbers. "It's when they get close to an organized group I worry." Titan always rushed into things, so eager to prove herself. And I couldn't deny it much reminded me of my younger years before I was titled as Token. However, I wanted her to understand that immediate action didn't always bring the best results. I'd been scorned many times learning that lesson.

"Yes, right away." Iris straightened and looked over the pile of books apologetically. Some of them were damaged from how hard he'd flipped them over his shoulder. "We'll find her, Esmore," Iris reiterated to me. I wasn't sure what my expression had given away. For the most part, I often hid any emotion or external giveaways. But I was exhausted and could feel my calm wavering. Of all the times for her to pull a stunt like this. No one yet knew about Chase's escape, and for now I'd keep it silent. The less who knew the better until I actually had a plan in place. But a part of me, one I hid away from in shame, was too scared to articulate one because that would involve me confronting him. And I found myself cowering away from what I had done. It felt as if this past ten years had caught up. It had been so long, and yet still not long enough.

# Chapter 4

I SAGGED INTO my chamber anticipating the knock on my door. I was starving and needed blood now. The woman who let herself in was my usual. We harbored few humans who'd had attachments with the werewolves before their lives being changed. Some opted they too wanted the change, but the werewolves weren't so giving of their disease. They knew the reality of the pain and torture, and so they kept their humans as that, instead of cursing them. And every full moon, we were bound to lock the werewolves into place so they wouldn't hurt any of them or us, or lose their way into the distance with no recollection of what had happened the night before.

"Esmore," the woman greeted when entering. She was my favored source. A woman who was ten or so years older than me. When we first met, she showed more curiosity than fear. It lessened the frenzy of my appetite. Although I would gorge on others, some even leading to death depending on how thirsty I was, they were always outsiders. The humans that were family to the werewolves were always safe under my roof. Lincon was the hardest to push that notion onto until the moment I gave him free rein to go wherever he wished and hunt whatever he wanted. "Quite the chaos out there these past few days."

I liked Jasmine because she was more daring than most to speak to me so casually. And I supposed it only courteous when I was often fang-deep in her neck to entertain her idle chat. And besides, she knew Titan all too well, especially when Titan used to steal the small bread rolls from her countertops in the kitchen.

"She'll be found soon enough," I purred. I had my best after her. Even if she was doubling back trying to confuse her tracks, she would be found before she could create too much strife. And intentionally I put Lincon onto her tail as well, advising him it was a friendly competition with the others. And by that, I meant he wasn't to attack any of the other teams, treating them like obstacles. I had half the castle out looking for her and Chris. I just hoped Tori found her soon and was talking sense into her to return immediately.

I stood from my wooden chair that looked out toward the day sky. I permitted her to sit down in case she became dizzy. She always braided her coarse brown hair for me, making the access easier, and took her usual position in my chair and arched her neck toward me. Jasmine was one of the few who desperately wanted to become a wolf, and I feared if she weren't eventually turned, she'd try to persuade someone to turn her into a vampire. She longed for the safety and strength after her village had been pillaged and taken. She'd been a part of Claus's village, they'd once been lovers, and he'd made sure to hide and secure her safety as he was dragged away. By the time they were reunited he'd imprinted on his mate Anastasia, and she was uncomfortably forgotten. It pained her in the way she was wronged, and I was certain she believed it was because she wasn't turned with him.

I plowed my fangs into her soft, dirty skin at her throat, wrapping a few delicate fingers around her chin to angle her better. The rush of her blood was always like a welcoming sad taste. I could feel the sorrow and longing perfume from her, and maybe that's why I enjoyed its company so much because it felt all too deserving. She arched further, and I considered she thought this was the way she'd be turned, forfeiting the reality and logistics that I'd have to inject her with my venom first. She'd never asked me personally, but she'd made the mistake of trying to lure some of the men into her chambers for such a thing. Both wolf and vampire.

Her metallic blood gave me strength and life, restoring what had been lost days before. It was like having the first breath in weeks and pushed away any thoughts that interfered with my clarity. The pulse of her blood flushed through me as a familiar presence dawned on our territory. I sighed in frustration. My mother's timing couldn't be any worse. I finished with Jasmine as she moaned in bliss, mournful as I detached myself from her throat. My nails had indented too harshly into her jaw leaving three pinprick marks. I bit into my wrist offering it to her, disgusted by how delicately she licked it. It would heal her but never turn her. But I didn't want to have that conversation once again. How odd it was to see someone so desperate to be turned instead of running away from the monsters of the night.

She lingered but shortly understood the silent message to leave. She left more downcast than what she'd come in. I looked down at the tips of my hair noticing dry blood from the night before when I'd pillaged the group of four. My mother would certainly notice. I sighed and left the room. Fire would direct her to the throne room, where I had most of my private conversations.

I stood beside my throne instead of sitting on it, despite my body begging for the rest. I could sense my mother judged my current reign and the different paths we respectfully took. I could sense her mind but nothing else. She was using her gift to conceal her scent, no doubt accustomed to using it near vampires. She always used it around us, considerate of Tori who was the least used to self-restraint. Some vampires built a tolerance quickly. Others weren't so lucky. And even when he did drink from the humans he was still monitored. He had considerable control for someone newly turned and had only lost it a few times. But it still wasn't managed entirely. And of course, she wouldn't realize he wasn't here.

Fire pushed open the wooden doors. My mother had accumulated a few more wrinkles over the years though her expression wasn't as harsh. She was still beautiful, an identical version of myself but aged. Her huntress blood kept her in pristine condition. Her orange eyes fell on me, sweeping from head to toe.

"What brings you here, mother?" I asked with as much tenderness as I could accumulate. Ten years had changed a lot between us. I wasn't the young woman she'd once treated me as. The few lettered messages and random home calls weren't enough to sustain a close bond. And mostly I knew I was a reminder of the sacrifice her familiar, Cesar, had made. He traded his life for my own, and though she loved him for it, I was a sad reminder and the remains of all that was left.

"Louise, actually." That came as no surprise. I wondered what the foreseer huntress prophesized this time. Though often it would be a message of caution by letter. "Michelle has fallen ill. As I'm here now, it's very likely he hasn't made it through the night." Michelle was the head of the Hunter Guilds in New York. Our kind didn't often get sick.

"What kind of sickness?" I drawled out curiously, though it mattered not. I just wanted to eliminate if his own people had imposed his 'sickness.' She said nothing, and as I suspected, I was correct. Their rebel group had been working Michelle for years, and I suspected it'd most likely be Sabe or Louise to next take his place. This unfortunate 'illness' no doubt had something to do with them. So, even the rebels were slowly making a move.

"The kind he won't recover from," my mother said. I stifled my maddening laugh. Even the hunters would turn on their own for lust of power. Though my mother frowned upon my methods and reign, what she was a part of was no different. Decidedly, I took the seat, folding my legs over one another as I watched her, the darker side of me enjoying that she was my audience. Fire had fallen to the shadows beside the doors, ensuring no one walked by to eavesdrop. "You wiped out another Council, and half a country I hear."

Rumor wouldn't have spread to her so quickly. Louise would've foretold her. That tricky thing about her comrade who kept a keen eye on my movement. "Only four days ago," I said satisfactorily. My mother grimaced. I suspected she feared this power of mine as she had from the very start. Though it was a necessary evil, she always showed concern that it was too much for one to handle. "Louise wanted me to warn you."

"As she always does," I said dryly. My suspicion of Louise's gift remained. Though I knew she had value and it certainly had helped in the past, it often turned out very differently from her predictions. In her defense, she said timeline and fate constantly changed. I believed in stepping into my power and executing the outcome. So I never depended on her stories, besides my mother's reprimand.

My mother gritted her teeth slightly, evidently not amused by my skepticism of her best friend these days. She thought the way to clear the vampires was by reshaping the hunters' future, making them stronger, and changing their ideals when addressing the human government. I considered it short-sighted and would only draw out this waging war for hundreds of years more. I believed in snuffing the problem out entirely by eradicating the Council, well until Tythian and Fier showed themselves and Chase could be freed once again.

"Your familiar…"

I stood up from my chair. My mother and I both flinched at my sudden movement. My gift rasped around me, the most energetic it'd been in the past few days. I abruptly sat back down. What did she know of Chase? Louise must've seen him. And if she knew he was alive, then who else had she told, who else could get their hands on this information?

"She saw Chase… with your gift. Annihilating all of New York, but it continued seeping and spreading until the gift devoured him whole and had nowhere else to go."

My heart stopped and my mouth felt dry. The only way he could acquire my gift was through me and if we were intimate with one another once more, which I highly doubted would ever happen considering what I'd done to him. But above all, I had no idea where he even was.

"Is he still alive, Esmore?" my mother asked her tone a coaxing purr. Most thought he was dead. The only ones who knew the truth were me and the gargoyles. The others who suspected were buried in the ground.

I studied my mother and could feel Fire's gaze on me. Brutally and despicably intense. I'd told everyone he'd died in that war. It wasn't that I didn't trust anyone, but I couldn't risk it being siphoned out of them.

"You know he died," I said in a firm voice though even I heard the wobble in my tone. The thought of him dead completely shattered me though I'd wished I'd be able to convince myself of such an outcome so I wouldn't be haunted by his beautiful face every day I lay awake.

"So you say," my mother said, disbelieving. "Esmore. New York is important to our kind."

"How would you know?" I argued. "You live a great distance away from it, in the shadows rebelling against their cause while your comrades are on the inside betraying them every day. So how would you know of its importance?"

My mother's lips went tight at the implication of my statement. Though she might've had patience and motive, she was taking too long to move and take action. To create actual change. I had never stepped foot in her rebel community and had no desire to do so.

"I'm tired from the commute and will stay the night until I'm restored," she stated abruptly, which meant she wasn't done with this conversation. I forfeited a breath. No matter how much I spited her insinuation and unraveling of my once master plan, I couldn't very well kick my mother out.

"Fire, could you please take her to the guest room and amend to her needs." I waved them both out of the room, an unnatural headache forming from my lack of rest and commotion of events. Or maybe it was something else… a physical link to a vampire who had long been asleep and was now slowly coming to consciousness. I drawled out another sigh. If that was true, it meant Chase was getting closer.

# Chapter 5

Fire insisted that I dine with my mother, enacting the importance of a mother-daughter bonding session, despite already understanding both of our indifference. The two got along well enough, and I wondered if it was my mother who pushed for her to do such a thing. My appetite was both blood and food, though the latter wasn't a common source of my nutrition.

We sat on either end of the dining table in a small separate room. Jasmine had brought in some salad and molten bread. I pushed the salad around with my fork. A singular candle was lit between us in the dark. And only because my mother insisted we light at least one because I'd become so accustomed to the dark.

"Where are Titan and Chris? I didn't see them on my way in," my mother asked. The few times she had come for a visit the two rushed for her, remembering the days when she looked after them in the institute. Titan had even pushed for her to teach her huntress moves, all of which I'd already taught her personally.

I let out another exhausted exhale not at all wanting to confess my failings of keeping the two in line. My mother would only look down her nose at my inability to control the two teenagers. I had an army, and yet the two sneaked out so easily. Besides, Fire had probably already told her. They'd be gone for two days now. My mother skirted her gaze over my large enveloping wings. She'd never asked why I no longer retracted them.

"You already know why," I gritted out. I could sense a wave of smugness amplify from her. Despite how dangerous the world was outside, neither of us conceded the idea that she would be severely harmed. The girl hadn't had enough consequence to her actions and behaviors, and perhaps that fell on me.

"She's a rather obstinate young woman. Does it not remind you of someone?" she insinuated while I speared a lettuce leaf. I bit down, the mass of leaves unappetizing after I'd had a fulfilling amount of blood and was already thirsty for more.

"Mother, I think sometimes you forget I was raised by you. Where do you think one would learn such a trait?" My mother uncharacteristically shrugged a shoulder.

"I execute patience in my practice. There's a difference." She took a mouthful of water from her glass. Well, this was going as pleasantly as I reasoned it would.

"One might condemn it as dawdling," I antagonized, unable to take the bite out of my tone. There was silence, and I could sense her grating her teeth once again. I took a mouthful of my water all too sensitive to its acquired taste. There was a river close by where we harbored our water and boiled upon its return. I began counting, as my father had taught me to calm myself. "How does Julia bode?" I asked.

My mother had joined the same group of rebels who had taken Julia in. When I saw my mother, I asked about her, in hopes of the day I might be able to extend the knowledge onto Dillian if I were ever to see him again. And if he even cared. Julia felt like the last link that bound him still to us. And I felt long forgotten and that he might've dropped the other end of that line.

"She's good. Quite the beauty still. We've become rather dependent on her gift, though she's still condemned as an oddity with her 'unique' personality." What my mother meant to say, was her inability to hide emotion and ability to empathize with others. Despite being rebels, they evidently hadn't evolved that much.

"Has she wed?" I asked, my tone rather crisp. A part of me hoped she had moved on. And then another part of me wished she hadn't, always hoping in some way or another her loyalty to Dillian was lifelong.

"She hasn't been with anyone else since." My mother and I went quiet, considering our own losses. I stared at the plateful of food that was begging to create an unnatural anxiety in my stomach, far from the appetizing appeal it might've had. I let my gift stretch out to spread it to ash and quickly blew it away so as not to offend Jasmine and her meal or raise an eyebrow from my mother. I left a few stray leaves on the plate. "Esmore, is Chase alive?" my mother asked more fiercely than before.

I looked her dead in the eye. Obviously, there was more to Louise's forewarning than my mother was letting on, and as if that premonition itself wasn't foreboding enough. "If he were…I wouldn't know where."

"Esmore!" Fire rushed in. She was naked, clearly having only shifted into her human form recently once again. "Tori's returned with Titan and Chris." I grated the chair against the uneven brick-layered flooring. One of the wooden legs snapped under the awkward force. *Great.*

"Excuse me," I pardoned dinner with my mother and made haste toward the entrance. I would have to be harsh on the girl and publicly humiliate her. Though she might've had my favor, she could lead by example that if things went unchecked, and if she was daring to do so, then who else might after her. She'd pushed it too far this time.

I could sense her apprehension as a wave of mental abuse before I even rounded the corner. Those who remained watched on. Some angry. Others shaking their heads. Others in awe of her brave escape.

Chris trailed behind her, his head sunken. He'd filled out as a man these past few years, double her width, and I had a sense that had something to do with the werewolf plague that ran deep in his blood. But his grave face offered all I needed to know. He'd yet again run along with one of her self-serving plans.

The moment she saw me, she straightened her shoulders as best as she could. Tori edged his body slightly in front of her as if to take the absorption of my wrath. I tacked him with a stare so frightening, he quickly forfeited his station. All my anxious energy stirred into one, and my vampire prickled to the surface gleefully wanting to play. I would never severely hurt her but…

"Esmore, I can explain—"

I struck her across the face, so hard Chris caught her. However, the girl would have too much pride to fall to her knees. The onlookers in the room seemed to morph back. I let the glower of my gift ominously skitter around me in a display of power. My redraw open palm was the least of what I could do to her. My favored child still had to be treated like the others, but had it been someone else, they might've endured a far graver injury.

"Do you have any idea how many have been sent out to search for you? The fact that you took the opportunity of my personal absence demonstrates your immaturity and how unready you are to be handled in a team to go beyond our borders."

"*You* were going out on missions as an apprentice at my age," she dared grit out in frustration. Though I sometimes allowed her to speak her mind I had to squash that now in front of the others.

"*I* was a different matter in a Guild built for fighting and moving in a team. You only think of yourself. That stunt you pulled risked everyone who's looking to protect you now."

"I can look after myself," she hissed, lowering her hand from the red mark on her face. Her eyes glowed like they did in her wolf form and she dared bare her canines at me, her adrenaline spiking. "I can contribute just as much as everyone! If not more! You can't blanket me in protection my whole life!" she snapped and tried to barge past me. I stepped in front of her, my purple eyes glowering over her and my black wings stretching so she couldn't pass me.

Everyone's eyes were glued to us. "Tori," I gritted out, begrudging of what I had to do. "She's to be locked in her room for two days."

"You wouldn't dare," she hissed.

In a lowly voice, for only her to hear, I glowered to her. "You've given me no other choice."

"It was my idea," Chris boldly spoke up. I flattened him with a stare. I didn't even have to read him to know he was lying.

"And lock him up as well," I instructed Tori, who was reluctant to move. Eventually, he did and tugged at Titan's arm. She eyed him as if he'd betrayed her. Chris, however, went willingly. Rolling in waves of hatred and rage that hit me far too sensitively, Titan allowed herself to be dragged along looking like she had so much more to say. I effectively eyed the onlookers who were quick to go about their daily business.

"My, hormones and a fiery temper really have overridden that one, haven't they," my mother summarized. Perhaps she considered it as some kind of karma as I tried to balance my nature and lack of nurture.

"All the teenagers inflicted with the curse go through this *independence*," Fire said, poised beside her. "Though she certainly takes it to a new level. Not even she's in control of herself." And that was what had me worried. Fire had theories that Titan was not born to be ordinary in the slightest. It might've been the ancestral huntress blood in her that offered her a heightened advantage, but combined with teenage hormones and the uncharted trial of their kind, it was becoming prominent that she wanted to dominate the older she got. An alpha, Fire had once suggested. But her age was riddled with sexual tension that even I could taste in the air, and her willing counterparts were already at her bidding, which meant I had to have a serious talk soon, especially with Tori.

"Maaaa." A foreign animal's cry called out to me. All of our gazes slid to the small goat with rope around its neck, holstered by one of the werewolves' hands.

"What is that?" I asked the dark-haired woman. She gulped, unable to reach my gaze, although she tried her hardest.

"It's a goat, mam. Titan and the others brought it back. Apparently, they stole it from a human camp so we could create milk, butter, and cheese. I was baffled. The child had absolutely stunned me. She hadn't at all gone toward the mapped-out danger…but instead went to all this effort and punishment…for a goat?

Fire let out a small, uncharacteristic laugh. I swiveled to meet her humor, trying to keep my own peculiar laugh down. That child had brought a goat into a den of wolves.

"I dare say you will have plenty more years of mischief from that one," my mother remarked, not at all finding it funny. I could see in those calculating eyes, she acknowledged Titan as a weakness in our group because anyone who acted on their own made the rest of the team vulnerable. I knew that look all too well because it was only years before she'd set it upon me.

# CHAPTER 6

I RESISTED THE sleep my body so acutely craved as I sat in my chair positioned beside my window, pining to see the near-full moon. In four days the werewolves would have to chain themselves, ensuring they didn't attack anyone on the night of their uncontrollable rampage that happened every full moon.

I'd been staring at the sky for hours, avoiding the possibility of being confronted in the dream place. Kyran's menacing grip frequented my dreams regularly but what I so desperately wanted to prepare for was if Chase reached out instead.

Mixed emotions rolled within me. I wanted to see him as much as I wanted to naturally avoid him. How could I face him after all these years? And how could I not be curious of his whereabouts so I could find another way to keep him protected? The less who knew of his awakening, the better.

I gripped the chair arm, forcing the wood to groan in protest that I don't break it. *No.* Instead of focusing on his whereabouts, I needed to articulate and fasten my haste to be rid of Fier and Tythian. I suspected it would take Chase time to recover. Selfishly calling him toward me would only resurrect the werewolves' interest. I had let everyone believe he died on that day. For whatever reason, Balzar wanted him, and he wouldn't so quickly cast him out into the sea of this suspended war.

"Maaaa." The goat's vibrated cry called out from the darkness of night as two werewolves whispered their delight and the potential of what it might bring. I couldn't see them but shook my head frowning upon the bizarre audacity of what accomplishment Titan had stretched so far for. As furious as I was with her, I also had a yearning to speak with her privately. I'd given her two days of solitude, a light consequence and in the privacy of her own room.

It wasn't a lesson I enjoyed enforcing upon her, especially when freedom held such importance to her. Howls erupted in the distance, and I knew another group was returning from their search mission. One by one the members were trickling in. Another two howls cooed from the inside of the barrier, calling to their comrades and welcoming their return. *Good.* It might've been left too close if she'd been out for any longer. She was dangerously close to the full moon to pull such a stunt. Chris's punishment was a second thought. Titan was the instigator. I'd speak with her privately, but for now, my time would be spent focusing on what I could control. And teenage cross werewolf hormones were not one of those. No matter how harshly I tried to snuff it out.

And yet somehow, I found myself tapping on Titan's door halfway through the night. I reasoned that she should be asleep but knew otherwise. The girl enjoyed being awake at all hours of the night and sleeping throughout the late morning if the opportunity ever presented itself. As if she herself were trained on a vampire schedule as opposed to a werewolf's.

Tori was guarding her door, a wave of dread oozing from him the moment he picked up on my presence until the dim light of night cast light on my apologetic expression. He stepped to the side, throwing me the key that locked her door from the outside. He and I would soon have a conversation about what had happened. But first I had to ask her personally what on earth was going through her mind when she decided to steal a goat of all things. It had been gnawing at me all night, and I needed a distraction from my other fickle thoughts.

I edged the door open, downcast about all the brightly lit candles. She had a flair for the rare bright and sunny days. She sat cross-legged on her bed, flicking through a book. The girl had adopted an interest in literature after Iris had taught her to read and write. And from what I'd heard, Lincon had started teaching her his home tongue, French, in whatever instance that might help her. On her table stand was a small potted flower vase protruding with half-dead flowers. She was still trying her hardest to keep them alive.

Upon my entrance, she hmphed quietly, not loud enough to make it insulting but enough to exemplify her arrogance and revolt. I let myself in, walking over to the tattered matt she'd found years ago in a spare room in the castle and claimed as her own. There was little in the room. And the breeze that swept through the open window might've frozen her half to death had she not already been at an irregular searing temperature.

I took a seat at the end of her single bed. She ignored me and flicked over another page. She wasn't going to make this easy, and I found myself irked that I'd come here at all.

"The punishment will remain that you stay in here for two days," I said.

"Come to rub it in?" she sassed.

"Tone." I reprimanded her with a hint of a growl that reminded her of the predator that lay within. Her eyes snapped to attention, calling to her own beast who cautioned her. She threw the book to the side.

"Yea, I know, what I did was reckless, but you don't take me seriously…I wanted to show you I can contribute."

"It was impulsive," I acknowledged. "And how did you intend to prove that with a goat of all things?"

She looked downward somewhat sheepishly, fidgeting with the edges of her long-sleeved shirt. "You're going to get angry if I tell you the truth."

"I'd be madder if you didn't." Titan had always been under the impression that I was a mind reader. The fact that I could sense one's emotions often gave away their thoughts. But I couldn't mind read. Speak telepathically, yes, if they permitted me, but I avoided it, uncomfortable by the implications. But as a child I let her believe the lie, and it made her much more forthcoming, under the insinuation I would call out her lie.

She brushed her fingers through her pixie-cut hair as if building the courage and licked her lips. "Well, when you left and wiped out the city, I really wanted to see it."

"My gift is not a trick, Titan." I don't know how many times I'd told her that. Her admiration was flattering but also misplaced. There was no need for her to be a part of and witness the destruction I possessed. I was certain she'd never look at me the same. Sure, she'd seen me implode objects and foreign vampires but never annihilate an entire Council. And I wanted to keep what strand of childlike wonder she might have intact for as long as possible.

"Yea, I know," she whined. "And then when you came back you flew off again. And I just really wanted to prove to you that I could do something. So then maybe you'd put me on a mission next time. Put me on with Claus, and you know I'll be protected," she suggested with an outstretched hand as if pointing directly at him.

I jutted my chin out. Despite her punishment, she still had the gall to be demanding. She continued, "At first, Chris and I considered staking out one of the locations Iris mapped out. But then, I heard yours and Fire's voice in the back of my head, pestering me that it wasn't just my life I was risking but Chris's too." She seemed to be mocking us now. "So I decided to go to one of the human camps mapped out instead to see what we might be able to bring back because I didn't want to come back empty-handed. And I overheard Jasmine and some of the others talking about how good they recalled milk to be. And so…yea…we stole the goat. Tori found us lingering around the human camp…and by then we were already committed so, yea… But it wasn't his fault. I went ahead with it anyway, he just lingered around to make sure we were okay."

I stared at her dumbfounded, trying my hardest not to smirk at the ridiculousness of this situation. I was so angry by the amount of search party teams sent out to find her that I was almost willed to laugh. I never recalled any teenager acting like this within the Hunter Guild. Did she lack in mental capacity for maturity or was this simply a trait in her personality?

"I don't ever want you doing something like this again," I sternly warned. "I don't take satisfaction in humiliating you in front of the others, Titan." She scornfully looked down, sulking at the implications of our exchange tonight. Right now, it seemed like she couldn't care less of what others thought. It was an admirable trait but a sheltered one. She needed to be conscious about their impressions and watchful gazes. A safe haven could only last for so long, and at any point, allies could turn into enemies. She needed to be conscious of the subtle changes around her.

"You seemed pretty eager to slap me down," she daringly said in a small voice. I took a big breath, counting to ten, calming my nerves. My gift wanted to jitter out slightly as if to give her a tiny lick in repercussion for her daring mouth. And yet my vampire self seemed to relish in her sass.

"As a huntress, if you disrespected a superior you were locked in the cells for far longer than two days. And a slap was the least of your worries."

"Well, lucky I'm not a huntress then," she added spitefully. But her emotional wave pressed with a mild hint of jealousy.

"Titan, you're a warrior. And I see you. But now is not yet your time. It's a skill to be able to kill, Titan, not a blessing. You're too eager for the fight." *And that was a deadly distraction.*

"And that's exactly how *you* led armies!"

"And that's exactly how I lost loved ones too," I corrected.

She was silent for a moment, biting her bottom lip. She was trying to hide something, and I dipped my head so I could look up into her avoiding gaze. "What is it, Titan?" She squirmed as if it was the eye contact that gave me the phantom gift to read her mind.

"I don't know how to say it. I thought…" she mumbled, unsure how to spit it out.

"With your words…"

"I thought I saw your familiar." My heart stopped, and a cold rush ran through me. "But I know he's dead, and then Tori jumped out, so maybe he scared the dear life out of me, and I was hallucinating…I don't know."

"Where?" I asked far more breathlessly than I would've liked to have led on. Her eyebrows furrowed in confusion at the seriousness of my request.

"Near the human camp," she said deliberately. "He *is* dead, right?"

"Yes, of course. I'm just concerned that someone might've been watching you, that's all." I wanted to reach out and place my hand on hers in a sign of comfort but internally retreated from the nurturing contact.

"Esmore, *please* let me go on the next mission. I know you want to keep me safe. But you and I both know my dad would've had me out on that field years ago."

The mention of her father, who she only had a few fleeting memories of shot a pang of guilt through me. I could beg otherwise, in fact he probably would've built a fortress with a barbed wire fence to keep her in—far more extreme than I.

"What?" she drawled a slow smirk as she assessed my grim smile.

"I was just thinking about how he would've locked you up far tighter than I ever have."

She groaned, but I could tell she dearly held onto the small bit about her father. "Please, Esmore," she moaned.

"You're still staying in this room for two days." I wouldn't waver my punishment, if I did it would create tension between the other werewolves in regard to the favoritism.

"I know." She moaned out loud. "But after that, please promise me." She poised her pinkie in the air. "Pinkie promise. No matter what mission it is, no matter how great or small—it's mine."

I was apprehensive to give in to her demand, feeling as if I was somehow being tricked. But I couldn't deny the warrior in her that thirsted to get out. Surely, I could give her this one adventure.

Reluctantly, I tied my little finger around hers somehow manipulated into giving in to her demand.

# Chapter 7

I STRUCK AT Tori's face which he'd always been slightly precious about. He blocked and wrapped the corded silk around my wrist, trying to throw my balance. I dug my foot into the ground, using my superior strength against him. He couldn't pull me over, but he was certainly enthusiastic to try, especially because I wasn't one hundred percent. It was always like this after I'd used my gift on such a massive scale, and it also took a portion of my focus to ensure my gift didn't take a taste of him. It was always like this while sparring.

Tori and I often rounded one another. He'd gotten a few good blows in with a sincere apology for finally having a 'win.' Today would not be that day because I was pissed.

"You let her escape," I panted. We tried kicking at one another looking as if we were playing footsies instead of training. He'd opted to have a silk thread as his weapon of choice this time. I simply knotted mine around my wing. I didn't need it to put his back to the floor.

A small growl crept out as I jutted a leg out and he dipped his thin rope underneath, taking the bait. I hooked my quad under it instead of the calf he'd expected. He wanted to throw my leg over my head, knocking me off-balance. I simply stepped my foot through and as he came down with the flow, kneed him in the face. He stumbled back, letting go of the grip and growling as he wiped his bloody nose that dripped a few black drops. Yet he was equally impressed by the strike.

"Yes, I failed at my task. But I was the first to find her and bring her back."

"And why is that do you think?" He looked at me skeptically. We were training in an open grass field, and no one else was around to overhear our private conversation. He wiped away the blood that had already stopped bleeding.

"What do you mean by that?" he asked as if I was knocking his competence.

"You know what I mean." I glowered. "You two seem to be close as of late."

"I've always been close to her and Chris, as you requested of me since they were children."

"But now she's not a child," I said coolly.

"Neither of them are," he said incredulously and narrowed his eyes on me. "What are you trying to ask me, Esmore?"

It was time to be blunt. "She's coming of age. Fire has informed me she's excreting hormones, so to speak, to her own kind. I would like to be enlightened if you're indifferent to her charm."

His eyes bulged slightly. "You think I want to *bed* her?" He was utterly baffled. Surely, he was aware of his attachment. And she'd certainly made a point to defend him last night. "Esmore, you've instructed me to *protect* her."

"I'm aware of the task I handed to you. I just wanted to ensure you were still conscious of that agreement."

He was angry. Seething even. "You've been heard," is all he gritted out. By his looks, Tori was attractive for a teenager. He hadn't changed one bit since he'd been turned, trapped in that sixteen-year-old body of his. And although he might've been a brute of a warrior, he would never fully turn into the man he might've become. Not physically anyway. "You need to give her the opportunity to show you what she's capable of, Esmore."

I raised an eyebrow. The determination in his tone was what grabbed my attention. "Oh?"

"We've been training since she was a pup. I know her skillset perhaps better than anyone else. She's ready. Had it been back within our Hunter Guild, she would've been an apprentice by now. Fighting alongside us in our raid teams. She's ready."

*And look how well your first raid went,* I wanted to point out but couldn't bring myself to be so cruel. But he was right, and I'd already promised her she'd be a part of the next mission. She deserved recognition if that's what she so deeply desired. I just had my concerns for the moment the floodgates of it happened, and she got a taste for the kill. Maybe it'd turn her entirely. Or worse, she'd realize she wasn't suited for the purpose of which we raised her.

Claus ran through the open fields toward us in his wolf form. After I'd become accustomed to wolves, I began to realize who was who even when they shifted. He changed into his human form the moment he was close enough.

"Esmore!" He gasped from how ferociously he'd run across the paddocks. "We've spotted a group of vampires on the outskirts of our border. They're not too close, but they're heading straight in our direction. We have reason to believe they're a part of Tythian's Council."

"What?" I gasped. "How can you be sure?"

"The one who leads them wears a black coat and mask. The rest are all in blue."

"Get your team ready!" I encouraged. I took no time to dash toward the Council's direction, Tori by my side. Behind us Claus howled into the day, summoning his crew. *Why now after all this time?* It was the closest they'd ever been, and also, we so rarely spotted them. Tythian had taken in the remains of Oppollo's Council and uniformed his people. Those who ranked and led were the black-robed assassins. After the last war, I assumed that few remained, and the rest he colored in blue.

We'd have to double back around them to surprise them from behind. That way if they smelled the path we'd come from, they'd be fooled into the wrong direction, deterring them from the castle.

"I'll tell the others." Tori pulled straight into rank. I nodded and took to the sky, circling to find them. I followed the two packs of wolves, each with eight members splitting from the castle, and followed the one that Claus led. They preferred to go in smaller units, depending on the size of their opponents. Fire said it was easier to coordinate their attacks telepathically when fewer were involved.

I groaned as familiar black and brown coated wolves caught my attention. I'd only just let the pair out that morning and already Titan and Chris were up to their mischief. I descended, halting them in their tracks. Titan didn't so much as flinch as she shifted into her human form, still zipping through the trees as I ran beside her. The wind whipped past our ears as I spoke to her.

"What are you doing?" I didn't have to look back at Chris who hadn't shifted, knowing I'd reprimand Titan first because he wasn't the instigator. Ever.

"You promised the next mission that I could be involved, so that's what I'm doing. Trust me," she added before I could argue. I contemplated Tori's and my earlier conversation. He'd made a fair point. Had we been in our Guild, she would've already been made an apprentice. Chris as well. They both held magnificent potential. And I couldn't ration my reasons for wanting to keep her so caged other than being protective.

"Fine," I gritted out. More irritated by my protectiveness of her than anything. I took to the sky again, noticing in my peripheral that Tori and Fire were on their way. I wondered how Iris had the power to restrain Lincon into staying. Unless Lincon hadn't yet heard the commotion. I surveyed from the sky, skin prickling as I thought about his whereabouts. Unless Lincon was already out and about, which was far worse.

I made sure to hide in the clouds and not get too close to the spot where the wolves were bottling. I didn't want my shadow falling over the group or grabbing the foreigners' attention. I lowered to the ground, pulling back further from them. I'd made it a custom to avoid revealing myself upon contact with other vampires unless intentional. If for whatever reason one was to survive and report back, then they'd only mention the wild werewolves who'd attacked them. Not the vampire behind them who watched from the trees.

Titan and Chris plowed through the cracked ground catching up. From this distance, I could just see but remained far enough away where they wouldn't focus on my scent, not while they were so preoccupied.

They circled in a formation, alerting Tythian's crew with their harrowing howls. With the glimpses of the black robe and men in blue, it definitely appeared to be members of Tythian's Council. *But what had brought them in so close?* The wolves erupted again, communicating to one another in preparation to attack. The vampires unsheathed their weapons, and I braced myself to watch on, especially by the time Titan and Chris caught up with the group.

A colliding of snapping and snarls began. The wolves were fast and cautious not to be struck by the blades and helped one another to create windows of opportunity to attack. One would act as the distraction, and simultaneously, another would bite. The vampires were fast and smooth, like a current melting between them. But they were outnumbered.

My eyes scattered back and forth, especially tracing the steps of the black-robed assassin. I'd had many encounters with them, knowing too well their specialty. Claus and his second in command circled the warrior cautiously. Tori and Iris strode up by my side, watching on with anticipation. Tori had added more weapons to his arsenal, and he intently traced Titan and Chris who jumped in and out, playing the part of the distraction.

One of the wolves finally had an opening, biting down on the vampire's arm and dragging him toward the ground. The vampire cried out, anguished with the knowledge that one bite would be the end of him. But he didn't give up without a fight. He speared his hand toward the wolf's ribcage, but Chris latched onto his arm, pulling his arm back and twisting it off with ruthless strength. The two wolves yanked, marring the vampire back and forth as he screamed until the shredding of his skin filled the air. Black blood and blue material fell to the floor as they amputated both of his arms.

Titan covered their backs, ensuring no vampire tried to impose on their victory. When the wolves left the vampire to scamper, his wounds festering from the bites, they rounded the next one. My heart pounded with adrenaline, my vampire too keenly wanting to be a part of the fight.

Claus and his second were diving in and out on the black-robbed assassin who swiftly diverted them. He was equally matched as he so fluently dodged their every ambush. He armed himself with two small blades waiting for his opportunity.

Claus jumped in, but this time instead of dodging, the assassin stepped into it, kneeing him in the jaw. He was flung through the air headfirst. The second wolf bared his fangs hoping to take a bite out of the vampire's side. Instead, the assassin flipped his weapon over his fingers and rearranged his hold. He pierced through the bottom of the wolf's jaw, sidestepped, and thrust his blade from bottom to the snout, suspending the wolf in the air. With an efficient breeze, the assassin glided his other blade across the wolf's throat.

Iris's oversized Hachette was in front of me, preventing me from stepping any further. I'd been so enthralled by the fight that I hadn't noticed his appearance. I growled in warning, but he wasn't willing to budge. I had to remind myself that this was the wolves' fight just as much as my own. This was how they gained strength, and unfortunately, loss was one of the casualties. I simply never enjoyed watching it when I could possibly prevent it instead. And I knew Iris would remind me later of the importance of why I had to stay back and endure.

Claus howled, drawing attention to his fallen comrade. A dark cloud bubbled from the ground as one of the vampires focused his gift on Claus. The ground turned into goo beneath him like a sticky substance that weighed him down. He lifted his paws one at a time, trying to pull himself out.

The assassin made his way toward Claus. I couldn't sense any emotion roll from him, not even smugness for his soon-to-be win—just a lethal blade with a mission and no thoughts. I raised my hand. This had gone on too long. But instead, Tori placed his hand on my forearm. The jitter of my gift ate away at his palm, leaving raw skin as he slowly pulled away. But his eyes were focused as if intentionally telling me to do the same. It felt as if he were saying, 'Just watch.'

Titan jumped at the assassin while Chris bit down on the scruff of his comrade and reefed him out. The goo lingered around Claus's paws but he could be dragged out when an accomplice tackled the gift-using vampire. The wolf jumped on him, biting at his jugular and thrashing his throat around.

As Titan's black fur lunged for her new prey, my heart stopped as I watched on. Tori placed his hand in front of me once again. Not that it could truly prevent me from stepping forward if I wanted to. Her shiny black coat glistened, but she left herself too exposed. The vampire reefed the blade from the former wolf's jaw and speared it toward her chest. She shifted into her human form and naked glory, rolling toward his feet and collecting a blade from the ground in the process. Her brown eyes were savage as she looked up and snarled, all wolf despite being in her human skin. The assassin was caught off guard by her shift and pivoted his blade to thrust down, but Titan had already sliced across the backs of his ankles. His body gave way under the weight, and she rolled around him, slicing up and hacking off the wrist that still held the weapon. Then Chris ambushed him, while Titan grabbed the remaining hand, pulling it back. Her chest heaved back and forth as she stood over him, looking down at the assassin with deadly intent. She speared the blade through his back and into his chest. The body sagged into decomposing sludge. Chris jumped back away, and for a moment, she looked in our direction, those usually brown doe-eyes having changed into a deathly near black. She shifted into her wolf form and was nuzzled by Claus in approval and appreciation.

She'd used her smaller size and element of surprise to her advantage. I was impressed and equally enthralled. I met Tori's gaze, and he said so lowly that even I almost couldn't hear, "She's born to be a Token."

Turns out, we had raised a killer after all.

I would've preferred to have the assassin as the hostage, but evidently, he was also the greatest threat, so instead they dragged only one away, having to circle the vampire and shift into their human forms just so they could take him. That one bite kill thing was a tricky beast. Other than an ambush, nothing seemed off. They were a scout and informant team tracking something. And the question was what exactly to bring them into these parts of our territory.

Wolves had been sent out to inspect the numerous tracks that were fresh in the outer layers of our territory. They rolled over one another numerous times, and it could take days for the wolves to establish the end route. But if these vampires had been the only ones, they wouldn't trace anything because they were already dead.

I left the torturing to Lincon, closely watched by Iris to ensure Lincon didn't kill him in the process because he got too excitable.

I waited in the library patiently for Lincon's report as I hovered over the books Iris had mapped out. This was the closest Tythian or Fier had been to our location, and I had to wonder if it was because of our recent visit from my mother who might've been followed or if it was something else that brought them this way. There was no clear pattern. From the few places we'd suspected their Councils, it was a ways from here. And although I had scouts out there now, searching for their base, none had returned with a solid conclusion. Two large circles were placed on the map. One considerably close to New York, which would be ballsy of the Council to position so close to the Hunters' lead Guild. Both of the areas were constantly being carefully surveyed. So what drew them so close to us?

Lincon skipped in, his feet almost tripping over one another as he zig-zagged happily into the room. "Oh my, it was so much fun, Esmore..." he sang whimsically. Iris stepped in after him, not as amused. "Thank you for letting me do the honors." Lincon bowed dramatically.

"Is he still alive?" I asked edgily.

"Barely," Iris grumbled out. "But I don't think he can give us any more information."

I furrowed my eyebrows. "Then why keep him alive?"

Lincon went sheepish. "Well, I wanted to have some fun with him later again. I do love to kill, but there's a certain charm about having such a rugged vampire strapped to a chair, begging for dear life." He looked off into the distance, daydreaming.

Iris looked away from him in disgust. "Apparently, they were sent out to track Balzar, Tythian's brother. They'd caught wind of him a few months ago and have been tracking him ever since."

I went quiet and still. If I interpreted my dream correctly, then it was definitely Balzar and Clarissa who broke Chase out. And if Tythian's men were attracted near us... it meant, possibly...they themselves were near.

"Do you think your former brother might be looking for you? Or stumble across us by chance?" Iris asked coolly. His sheer size was blocking the doorframe. Lincon was swinging his legs back and forth as he sat on the table watching the silence draw between Iris and me.

I could sense Iris's pause of mistrust. And he had every right to feel that way. I wasn't telling them everything. But I couldn't so much as believe it until I saw *him* with my own eyes.

"Either is possible though I don't know what ammunition he'd have to find me after all these years. But we need to keep a better guard on our territory now that the outskirts have been breached. Who knows the last time Tythian communicated with his team, their assassination will surely bring suspicion around this area. Did he give intel on their whereabouts?"

Lincon charmed a delighted smile. "Not yet, but I haven't been nearly creative enough."

I grasped onto that. This could finally be it. We could finally pinpoint Tythian's Council location assuming his vampire would betray him. "I want answers, Lincon," I gritted out, and he relished in the responsibility.

"Tomorrow night's the full moon." Which meant the werewolves would have to be locked up. All remaining scout teams who'd been out the past full moon would return from their missions. They were to be out no more than a month because this home base was their security and also where they could safely be detained. Apparently, physical reconnection with the rest of the pack was also important to their species. If they were stranded for too long, they'd spiral into a depression, so we found the month a reasonable quota. "After that, I want all scouts focusing on this area." I pinpointed my finger to the section the hunters had once tipped us off. We had to find their location. And we had to do it now. I had to tie Tythian down with a silver chain and find out where Fier had been hiding all this time. We were running out of time, and my patience was already years too thin.

# CHAPTER 8

TENSION AMONGST THE castle always arose when groups returned after being on a mission after a full moon cycle. Most of them remained in their wolf form during missions out and when they returned took time to adjust into civilization once again. Fights were more inclined to break out, and testosterone often went rabid to reassert the hierarchy. But after a few days, the attention and immersion back with their focal pack calmed them down once again, blanketing them back into human order.

Now was no different. A scuttle had broken out in the main square when I was bypassing with Fire wanting to check on the group before they were locked in their chamber as was standard procedure on the full moon. And as poor as Titan's timing was that we were walking past right in that moment, she was one of the culprits involved in the brawl. The two wolves were snapping at one another. If this was how Titan was trying to earn my favor after just being granted permission out of her room, she was sorely mistaken. Their temperaments became further heightened just before the full moon so naturally Titan picked a fight with the biggest male around her age, who was already on edge after returning from his scouting mission.

The two fought for dominance as the crowd mixed with humans and wolves stepped back parting way for them as they watched on. Claus was in his wolf form growling as he observed the two mediating and watching carefully as to who the victor would be. I was inclined to tear them apart, but Fire shifted into her human form beside me, acting as translator.

"She's come of age," she purred, watching intently. "She's not as undisciplined as you think. It's a natural instinct to find placement in her pack. Although, she might be a little more forward about it than some." Fire motioned, almost amused by her gusto. Chris watched on in alarm with a broken arm dangling. Ah, well, that explained what started this fight then.

Chris was powerful, his body turning into that of a tense male, rigid in all its forms as hormones pumped through him. But he didn't have the same killer instinct as Titan, and he was less likely to argue amongst his pack. Or perhaps he hadn't yet started transitioning to a point where he felt the urge to climb up the ranks.

It was just advantageous that Tori was inside quenching his thirst and having a short period of solitude from his duties. His inclination to be amongst the wolves heeded warning, and I worried in a scuttle like this he'd accidentally get involved trying to pull Titan back. All it took was one bite to end him, even a small nip to back off and the damage would be done.

Titan swiped the large wolf away and flipped him onto his back. Where she lacked in size, she made up for in speed. She was on him, her teeth baring at his throat as Claus intervened with a low growl and fangs bared. It was a warning not to take it too far.

Her chest heaved as she delicately got off him and sauntered off, nudging Chris in his human form. He looked back between the two, disgusted in himself, no doubt that she had come to his aide. They weren't kids anymore. Would he still be like this as a man? The wolves around howled in approval, claiming the victor. Some looked on with approval; others however, looked ashamed of the young man who'd just lost his pride. He was only a few years older than Titan, but she'd been privileged and trained by the elite. She also worked harder than most, especially after hours, to catch up on her indifferences with the males' natural advantage.

I wasn't sure where Titan ranked amongst the pack, but I was certain that fight just obtained her a new gold medal of sorts. Everyone began returning to their duties. It was late in the afternoon, the time for them to start packing into their cage for the night that was descending upon them. Parents ushered their children into their rooms for a restful sleep before all evil broke loose.

A part of me still pitied the wolves for the curse that bound them to every moon cycle in this world—forced to lash out with no recollection of what they'd done the night before and exhausted by the sinister notion of what might've transpired. Then again, maybe I pitied them so much because I understood that feeling all too well.

The extreme temperature of the scorching hot tub was delightful. It was like a giant cauldron that hung from the ceiling, flames licking beneath it that had been lit prematurely to my arrival. The atmosphere was always hauntingly eerie as the wolves chambered themselves in the self-contained bunker hidden beneath the castle and were locked in from the outside so they couldn't escape. When their numbers outgrew our expectations, we could no longer chain them to the walls individually. Now they were cramped and huddled together in the room below.

Scuffles would often break out between one another as they fought over dominance and the bunker door had endured severe damage over the years from when they tried to break out. And despite that, all and all their savage nature, especially on the full moon, they felt more secure as a unit when confined on the night of the full moon. It was bizarre to watch a pack co-exist with a warm family-orientated ideal. It was disturbing and alienating to watch.

The hot water felt as if it was softening my skin and made me feel lightheaded. The human treat that Lincon had provided me dangled limply over the edge of the cauldron. The woman's neck wound leaked a prominent trickle into the water, tarnishing its color. My wings fluttered slightly in the water, self-cleansing and producing ripples around me. My body always responded well to the hot tub where unseen mental knots had time to ease as I sagged further in. And although I tried to take this time to think of nothing, I found my mind racing with unprecedented thoughts continuously. Iris was in the library looking over the reports the scouting teams had returned with. And together, we would articulate the best form of action in the proceeding days, especially around hurrying our agenda to source Fier.

The flamboyant vampire had become very good at hiding, which was surprising considering his usual rage lust that had him acting impulsively. But perhaps and more than likely my display of power the last time we met set caution to him because he'd never dared invade one of my dreams again.

I collected the woman's wrist as she bubbled a complaint, the tips of her dry curly hair dipping into the hot water. I arched my fangs toward her wrist but hesitated when a stormy scent hit me. My entire body tensed as a dark figure overshadowed the moonlight and narrowly streamed in through the half-open window. We were on the second level, but that would be no feat for him to jump.

I straightened my shoulders, a significant weight pressing in my throat. I was too scared to turn in case it was an apparition. I closed my eyes, allowing myself to divulge in that familiar scent. *Let me at least have this- if nothing else.* It could've been an assassin for all I knew, and yet my body still wouldn't move. I didn't want to move, too scared to face its reality.

The silence was palpable, and the woman's wheezing became the undercurrent of embellishing one another's presence. I scanned my mind over his, recognizing its familiarity even though it was purposefully closed off to me—no surprise, considering my betrayal.

I swallowed the heavy lump in my throat and took precedence. "How did you get in here?" I rasped. I needed to clear my throat, but hinged on what he might next say, not willing to make another noise in case I missed it.

"I knew your wolves would be locked up for the night." I closed my eyes, relishing in that edgy, raw voice I'd longed to hear for so long. I fought internally with myself. I wanted to throw myself at his feet and apologize just as much as I wanted to embrace and kiss him and claim everything I had done—had been for him. I held myself sternly in place from doing any of that. *He shouldn't be here.*

"I don't remember locking Lincon up?" I said with a foreign raspy voice. I slowly stood up, the hot water sliding down my body in trails of condensation. I could feel his intense gaze sweep over me. For him, time might've felt like only weeks and months. But for me…it had been much longer. My nipples peaked with the knowledge that he was so close and attainable, my body blossoming with a hunger it hadn't felt for what felt like a lifetime.

"Well, as you know, Lincon's easily distracted…" His voice was velvety smooth. Aka, someone was bravely distracting him. I didn't need to ask him *how* he found me. In a world where both he and I existed, we would inevitably find one another, no matter the gifts or obstacles in place. I felt my wings cocooning around me slightly as if to protect me from him or remain in denial we were now sharing the same space and breath. If he was able to actually breathe.

Iris's relentless speed zoomed through the hall and opened the door without so much as a pardon. "Esmore we think—"

I swished the water, turning to face Chase. But he was already gone. My wings went slack. I could sense Iris's eyes scanning the room and the lingering scent instead of trailing along my naked body in any romantic way.

"I know, Iris," I said quietly. "I saw him just now."

"Cheeky buggers!" Lincon exclaimed with far too much enthusiasm. I was wrapped in a loose bandage silk robe that catered to fold around the joints of my wings easily. We were in the library, Fire still hadn't shifted out of her wolf form, but I could tell by the indignation she wasn't at all happy with the recent revelation. That and she was also sluggish from the night before. She would need to go rest for some time after this meeting. "I can't believe they got away from me. That was a very clever distraction." He seemed entertained by it all. No doubt it was Balzar who led him personally if Chase and he were working together. Balzar was one of few vampires who might've been able to give Lincon the slip.

"Your familiar's alive…" Tori said with contemplation. "But I thought…"

"We all thought," Iris corrected. There was no personal judgment. But I could see how he calculated what this would change in our course of action.

Kasey seemed indifferent as always with her back pressed against one of the bookshelves. "Another lie from our Token, what a surprise," Kasey easily said. My gift grafted toward her, falling short at her feet as her eyes widened slightly. I'd only caught it just in time. Her insinuation that I was a liar grated me the wrong way.

"I've never lied otherwise. But in this instance, I had no other choice. Those who might've known were liabilities. I did what I had to, to keep my familiar safe."

"You could've told us," Tori said quietly with a casual shrug. "We could've helped, Esmore." He had his arm slung over one of the chairs casually with his boots on the table.

"That's beside the point now," Iris reminded them. "So, what do we do now? He snuck into the castle last night. He clearly knows how to get past your mother's barrier."

"It means he was spying on us. Possibly his coven too if they've been reunited," Tori added skeptically. It was so incredulous that we spoke about them as if they were the enemy. All night, all I could do was stare out at the full moon through my window, paralyzed by replaying Chase's voice over and over again. But unable to set one foot out of premises. If he'd wanted more from me he would've stayed. And I was frightened to chase him and have the confrontation I wasn't yet prepared for. I was a coward, but also tactfully tried to think about the others as well.

"What do we do, Esmore?" Iris asked, realizing I'd become particularly quiet. I tried to push away my feelings, but how could I? It was *Chase*. And now my own were looking at me, seeking direction. I'd disappointed them with my deceit and had to offer them some kind of ruling answer instead of running off into the sunset calling upon my love. I couldn't romanticize the reality of the situation. If others found out about Chase's existence, he was in danger. And if he'd already made himself known now, it meant very clearly he'd linger around to stay which could create all sorts of issues with our territory and the werewolves.

"We bring them in and have a discussion," I said, crossing my legs. I couldn't push him away. But I feared bringing him closer, my head in a spin as it lost focus. We had a hit from one of the groups, and a chance to inspect what might've been Tythian's Council. I couldn't focus on nursing Chase's and my broken relationship while trying to destroy the one thing that was the obstacle of our being together.

"What, do you want us to go out with a letter or something?" Kasey sneered. My sharp gaze struck her indecent attitude. After all these years, I still didn't find it any less imprudent.

I hastened my resolve. "No. I'll go to them and start the negotiations."

"Negotiations?" Tori sounded baffled as he looked amongst the group. Fire's gaze carefully watched my every movement. I despised not being able to read her mind in moments like this. And waves of tense scrutiny rolled from her. "Esmore, this is *Chase.*"

"I know, Tori," I said beratingly. Trust me, I more than anyone knew. And the reality was I remained strong because I hadn't yet faced him, and it would take everything in me to keep that resolve when I stood before him. I simply had to will myself not to break before him. I had to remain strong, even for him.

"Well, I suppose that's that," Iris said scornfully. The wolves wouldn't be scouring the area for a few days yet as they recovered which offered me ample time to extend a hand in greeting.

"It was a long winter's day…" Lincon began, reading from a journal in the corner of the dark room.

"Where did you get that?" Iris snapped and charged for him. Lincon shrilled, running away with the book wavering it in the air.

"We were caught in another snowstorm—"

"Give me that!" Iris yanked it out of his hand and curled the small book to his burly chest. He looked over at the rest of us, seemingly shrinking into a smaller version of himself. A lick of insecurity fermented around him. He was silent, fighting with himself if he should offer any explanation. "I, ah, I liked to journalize memories from my days of being a hunter. It lets me relive what it was like to be…alive…you know, taste and feel things."

Very quietly, Tori mumbled thoughtfully, "Maybe I should start doing that after all of this chaos as well. It sounds like things around here are going to become a lot more interesting."

# CHAPTER 9

FOR ONCE I decided to walk. I was still tired from the previous days, and there was something refreshing about sauntering through the decaying woodland instead of missing it entirely as I flew. Because of the current season, the mist that pooled around my ankles wasn't as prominent. I strapped my sword between my shoulder blades making sure it was still quickly reachable between my wings. Though I could use my gift if I truly had to, it was limp and exhausted from the atomic explosion only days before. At most, it took me a year to restore that swell of power within me, and it always came back even stronger, almost needing to be liberated once again.

Although I suggested I go alone, Iris insisted he join. I brought him only because I knew I couldn't manage Lincon alone. He'd been following and bothering me about like a hound. And even when I elicited he wasn't to follow me, he simply stared at me with incomprehension. He now skipped in front of us, a dead flower in his hand which reminded me far too much of the ones Titan was trying to keep alive in her room. I truly hoped the two weren't befriending one another again. She couldn't choose a worse idol.

My mouth felt dry with every step I took as I instinctively followed an unseeable pull that I was certain connected with Chase. It was disheartening to be blocked from exploring the link we shared as I remembered it. Naturally, he'd closed off to me, and it felt like a repercussion to all the times I'd done it to him without understanding its pain. My head and heart fought with one another, and so I fortified an emotional wall. I was much better at balancing my emotions after my heart had been reinstated, but I still often took on the indifferent cold mask of my huntress. I was trying to treat this as transactional.

I could sense members out of sight gather around us. As I swept my mind over theirs, I could perceive familiar impressions and personalities. Jerimiah, Darcy, and his gargoyle gang. It was so nostalgic my senses coming alive with the old stimuli that shaped my path to where I was today. I wanted to selfishly reach out to them but balmed myself with the cool, indifferent persona.

Despite Chase's early appearance, I couldn't hold it against them for letting Balzar and Clarissa slip through. Clarissa, after all, was a part of their coven, and they wouldn't dishonor their pact by putting a blade to her throat for wanting to resurrect their leader.

It had taken us less than an hour to stumble across their makeshift camp. His coven was cluttered under the trees, but they were nestled in a rather open space. Chase's efforts were half-assed considering the lack of security he provided them had it not been for his assumption that I'd look for him after last night.

I felt their attention as we dawned closer, and Lincon, as always, was insensitive to the tension as he continued to skip around us in circles. I hissed at his childishness. His thick winged eyeliner was a continuous strip as he circled us quickly.

"Even after ten years, I'd hoped you would've blasted him into ash." Balzar's voice crept from the darkness, but I couldn't yet see him. I felt frozen, bombarded by all these who were familiar, but not so much allies.

"You got the best of me yesterday," Lincon cashiered happily. "I was hoping we could play tag again today." Balzar grumbled his complaint. And then Chase's rough voice broke through, drawing attention and silence.

"Leave us." It wasn't a polite question, and nobody had to query as to who he might've been referring to. Iris didn't leave until I nodded my approval. I remained on standby, ready for anything and the possibility of an attack. I could handle this much myself, though in my heart of hearts, I knew he wouldn't hurt me. Not in a physical way. But his nearing rejection and hatred for my betrayal would slice me in half more than he could ever know.

Lincon was the hardest to be rid of. But Iris somehow was able to drag him away, exploiting Lincon's weakness of having my disapproval. Lincon was flabbergasted that he used such a tactic against him and yet it still worked every time. Still, eleven years later of working with Lincon, I couldn't entirely figure him out. But we'd found our ways around his erratic behavior and dealt with the consequences of when he imploded.

Chase kept his distance so far that it was hard to study his features. His scent drifted over to me as everyone else receded into the dire and gloomy trees. I closed my eyes, once again encompassing myself and worth with the scent I'd longed for. I recalled how it made me feel and the inner stir I always felt. But time had taken away the remembrance of his smell, touch, and voice. A memory that was now taking deliberately slow steps toward me, as if he was holding himself back just as much as I. Or perhaps he was reining in his unstable temperament.

Cold gray eyes crept from the darkness, sheltered away from the glum daylight. His usual silky black hair was matted and dirty. I rubbed my cool thumb over the lock of his hair in my leather pocket that I'd inevitably carried around with me from the day of our exchanged vows. His leather ankle-length jacket was still torn and damaged from the fight we'd endured together those ten years ago. I avoided letting my shame show.

He was a shadow from the past. His slow steps were predatory-like, and he stopped thirty feet away from me. My breath hitched, and he angled his head, probably listening to the heightened beat of my heart. I steadied my breath and jutted my chin out. I opened my mouth but nothing came out. I couldn't speak. I wet my lips, inevitably dropping my gaze to his. They were parted as if panting and thirsty. How badly I wanted to throw myself at his feet and apologize. But I couldn't spoil myself so much with such a leisurely notion.

So much had to be said. And yet so little at the same time. We were on either side of a coin overshadowed by the time lost between us. My love. My familiar. My Husband. Who was looking at me with such disdain.

"Balzar told me what you did, and Jerimiah gave me the specifics," he edged. His voice was like a blade to my heart. I uncurled my fingers that lightly danced on the lock of his hair in my pocket and pulled back my shoulders as if to try and pull myself away from his potency. If I stepped closer, I was certain he'd take a step back and that rejection already felt stifling. He was okay. That was the only thing I focused on. For the most part, I had done what I'd set out to do.

"Yes," I replied in a rasped voice. Again, there was that unfamiliar tone of mine. This time I did clear my throat. "I betrayed you—for you. Fier tried to impact the final blow to deteriorate your mind, but we'd prevented it just in time." I found myself crossing my arms over my chest, adamant not to show my insecurity and not sure where to put them.

His lips thinned, and a dash of pain settled over his expression. I tried to pry into his mind and delve into the mental link we once shared, but it was so tightly shut that his pure suspicion affronted me.

"You often blocked me out," he commented distantly, knowing that I had tried to engage. And it was true. I had closed my mind to him, especially nearing the end of our time together. It was only fair that I received the same punishment. "For me, it felt like a long sleep, but so much has changed and so little all at the same time."

I was silent, my grip tightening around me. I was grateful not to have an audience to see me look so weak and vulnerable. If I had, I'd act in an entirely different way. "Why?" he rasped. "I could've helped you. We could've managed something *together*. As we'd always promised."

His raw expression and furrowed eyebrows yanked at my heart. He might as well have pulled it out and stomped on it. "You know why," I said in a small voice. But he was practically begging me to say it. "I did it so I could protect you."

"For how long would you have kept me in that box?" he asked quietly, and I knew he was scared to hear the answer.

"For as long as was needed until I'd cleared the obstacles," I said so directly that I felt my power withstanding once again. "Already it's a threat. If Fier caught a whiff of your resurrection, he could click his fingers at any time."

"But I could *help* you, Esmore. I'm not a child."

"You were losing yourself on that battlefield, Chase. What would you have had me do? Watch you until you spiraled into oblivion?"

"Like all the times I watched you lose host to your powers and inner conflict. But I helped you. That's what we do. That's what we *did.*"

I hitched on my next breath. *That's what we did.* I reinstated my walls around me, reminding myself to rule as I had. I had to dance within that cold wall I'd fortified. "Chase, had our positions been parallel, you would've done the same."

He snarled in reproach. "I'd never take your decision away from you."

"But you did! So many times!" I took a hollow breath that seemed to not feed me enough air. I needed to calm. He seemed baffled. "We wanted different things."

"We wanted each other," he corrected. And it was the truth, and for me that was still very much my vow.

"Had we successfully walked out of that battle alive, what would we have gone back to? A quarter of your coven and werewolf pups who would've never been treated as equals. A divide in how we'd walk forward and keep your sanity in check."

"You treat me as if I'm incompetent! Is this what this was about? Because we didn't see eye to eye on the werewolves?"

"No!"

"So you froze me to run away from my opinion?!" he damned.

"No! That's not fair!"

"Not fair?!" he exasperated with tears filling his eyes. I leaned back, wounded by his hatred.

"You took away my right to protect you, Esmore. Even if I had died, I would've died for you… you didn't give me a choice."

"I did what I felt was right," I said in a low voice, but now I was re-evaluating everything I'd done. I knew confronting him would be hard. But I never imagined how much it would hurt. Our surroundings seemed to morph into irrelevance. And I'd wondered how loud we'd shouted at one another and then crept to low whispers of apology.

"And it had always gotten us into trouble," he gritted out as if hating himself for throwing such a low blow. I swallowed. Hard. For all the indiscretions we had, I had let them fizzle out over the ten years, but for him, it hadn't been so long. This raw intolerable disagreement we had was bubbling back to the surface, so fresh and violent. Even worse than it might've been in the first place.

I was scorned by him, and I couldn't blame him for being so seething. He gripped onto the most hurtful thing he could've brought up, and I had no doubt there was plenty more to come. And I'd be willing to listen. But now wasn't the time, we had other pressing matters. And I painfully recognized that I was still in denial, willing to push away this discussion so I didn't yet have to face it.

"I don't know where Fier or Tythian's Councils are located," I said to break the silence. "But if Fier finds out about your existence—"

"Let me worry about that," he said forcefully. For the first time, I dropped my gaze, unsettled by the way he spoke. He'd always been so gentle, even when I'd irrationally done things he disagreed with. Now, I was faced with the coven leader others had feared. I couldn't fear him— ever. But my memories of him couldn't so easily be erased.

"Chase, please—" My voice broke. We would continue going around in these circles: beg and fight. I uncrossed my arms, suddenly remembering my men behind me. I didn't want to show weakness in my resolve and rule in case they could overhear. "Well, you sought us out for a reason. Why are you here, Chase?"

He seemed baffled. "Why am I he—" He cut himself off, allowing his expression to glaze over in the same starkness as my own. "You're not the only one who is fighting against them, Esmore. Balzar suggested—"

"Balzar…" I drawled out, so ashamed of our inability to put aside our difference and stubbornness and cater to our true needs. To simply hold one another. I could sense it from him, just as much as myself without reading his mind. I stopped myself from either hysterically laughing or crying. My vampire had slowly crept to attention, antagonizing over fight or flight mode. I didn't want to talk about Balzar or any other member of Cesar's coven.

"Yes, Balzar knows where they are. And there's no greater power than the efficiency of your gift." His voice was a sharp monotone as if he had to grit out every word.

"And so he set you free to convince me to act on his behalf? For my gift," I said impudently. Had he come himself I might've considered it, but to outright express it was to use me for my gift goaded me into feeling like a puppet even after all these years yet again.

"No, he set me free because it was the right thing to do," he sharply replied. Round and round in circles we would go. He sighed in frustration, realizing the same. "He knows their location."

That caught my attention. We'd been in search of it for the last ten years. "How?"

"You're not the only one who's changed over time, Esmore." How I'd pined to hear him say my name for years until it was nothing but wisps of fragmented memories. And now it came out more as a feral growl. "Balzar has a way to get there. We're here to ask for an audience."

I couldn't help the vicious smile that crept over my face. After all these years, he'd come for an *audience* with me. But then again, I was acting in the same stubborn fashion. I wasn't willing to admit I'd basically built this foundation and army *for him*. I couldn't stand his proximity and the vile feeling that rose. My body was heaving in mixed emotions: fight or flight. I had to get out of here.

"You can bring a few members, Iris will collect you tomorrow. No more than a few because the wolves won't welcome you to our palace," I said coldly. I needed to return and let the others know what was happening before we spoke of any sort of treaty. And on top of that, I needed to speak with my werewolves to ensure they didn't attack them on sight. They were accepting of the few vampires who walked amongst them now, but besides their exceptions, they were utterly ruthless to the vampire kind.

"We never expected to be welcome," he said darkly. "But it would be in all of our best interest that you hear what we have to say."

I didn't like his tone. Familiar aside and pining for his love, I wouldn't allow him to speak to me in such a haunted manner unless he truly was picking a fight with me. "You're not welcome because you're all the very same species who are trying to run them and their families into extinction."

"*You* are, by definition, part of that same species."

"And I gave them a chance!" I ushered harshly. We eyed one another, my heart beating for an expected fight as adrenalin pumped through me. I had to get out of here. "This is enough for today. Bring your few members tomorrow."

I spun on my heels, cutting off anything else he might have to say. I wanted to fly off into the dire sky and calm myself, but I didn't want to look like I was so evidently running away. I could feel his eyes on me as I left. Every part of me wanted to turn back and run to him, that intangible physical bond we had summoning me as we were both left cold after not touching for so long. But our battle-ready armor would prevent any of those irrational steps to flourish.

# Chapter 10

THE WEREWOLVES WERE gathered sluggishly in the town square, and unfortunately, I had to call forth the mothers and their children as well. Everyone had to be here for this announcement to ensure it didn't go wrong immediately. The only engagement they had with vampires was to hunt. So, to enable a handful to so leisurely walk into their home was going to prickle at their natural instincts, and at most, their temperaments weren't level at the best of times but would be especially on edge after the full moon. They were all in a vulnerable state not entirely restored and so their natural instinct would be to protect their young.

Titan and Chris waited patiently in the front of the crowd. Chris had his arm in a sling. It would take a few days to heal completely, not ideal with a full moon that just passed that would delay the process as his body recharged. Fire was at my side, seated stoically as I glided the tips of my fingers back and forth through her beautiful white fur.

She still hadn't shifted into human form to discuss Chase or any of the others. When we'd discussed it as a group, she remained tight-lipped and watched on which was common, unless she had a pressing matter to discuss.

Claus had his arm over Anastasia, and their two young pups were curled around their legs—one in wolf form and the other as a child. The atmosphere was still touchy from a few days ago as they'd mourned the loss of their comrade and second in charge. And now with the fluctuation of teams that had returned, barring one that hadn't made it back in time, everyone was uncharacteristically downcast. Still, a solid two hundred remained. Not an overbearingly massive army, but at least one hundred sharp warriors in their prime.

"I come with vexing news," I announced, already certain how this would go. I stood in my power which they looked upon with fear and awe. I might not have been one of them, but to them, I was the founder of their oasis. And I wondered how much this news would sway leniency for that. "Tomorrow, we'll house a group of foreign vampires as guests." Snarls and whispers erupted. Fire's low growl over reined them.

They feared her just as much as they respected her. Because of my venom that coursed through her veins, she smelt of both species. An immortal wolf bound to me. And like all creatures, something that was tainted with the unknown was always feared.

"They're my guests," I reiterated, "and could be the solution to our problem of locating the other Councils."

"We've been making progress on our own," Claus argued. Others agreed, far too spiritedly for my liking.

"And we're running out of time," I harshly flattened their debate. "If anything can help us, then I will at least hear them out. I've fought alongside those who will enter our solace. Warriors who for a time guarded my back."

The group went silent as if having forgotten that I once worked alongside the very covens they despised. They wanted the Council vanquished just so they could live less frightfully. But even they knew the reality was the vampires were not the only threat. The human government still slipped from the shadows from time to time, using their experimental wolves and soldiers to spread their plague. My group here had been forced to kill their own simply because the others were shackled to the humans' whim. And the hunters still kept a wary eye on them, fighting as they came across their packs, hedging down those who ambushed their human camps.

This war would never end for them, simply because of what they were. And my soul purpose of ending the Vampire Council had waltzed right up to my door and broken into my bathing chambers last night.

"There will be consequences to those who initiate anything. And for the next two days we will bunker within our castle so as not to draw attention from any passers-by." After Tythian's men being so close, it could be expected to find more. And also, I didn't want my werewolves running into any members of Chase's coven, unsupervised. *How many even remained of his group after the last battle?*

"You expect us to allow vampires so close to our children?" someone else yelled from the crowd. Tori shifted beside me, not to intimidate the crowd outstretched in front of us, but to remind me that I too had numbers to back up my resolve. We would be moving forward with this.

"They will not be entering your homes," I berated. "They will be led directly to me. And it's not up for negotiation. This is happening. Do not make me warn you *twice*," I hissed. Few of the werewolves groveled, seemingly subordinate. But my gaze lingered on those who might be a problem.

A too enthusiastic hand flung in the air. I snapped my attention to Titan who had a hand on her hip and the other one sluggishly waving in the air. I felt my eye twitch. This girl had no consideration for the room she was supposed to be reading. "Who is it?" she asked.

"That is none of your concern," I begrudged. But the looks on their faces said otherwise, and I didn't want to lose their faith now, especially not when we were possibly so close to confronting the Councils which we'd depended on defeating for so long. Titan was still looking at me expectantly, her pressure seeming to know that I would give in to her request. But I also knew that some of those who would walk in tomorrow might've been the reason why some of their comrades had fallen those ten years ago. "Members of the late vampire, Cesar's coven, and…" Only a few had seen Chase or even knew who he was. By scent alone, they would probably identify we were familiars, and yet a part of me wanted to still keep that information close to my chest for a little while longer. "And members of my familiar's coven, who'd previously worked together to combine forces and take Oppollo down."

Whispers began amongst the group, and I made a point not to hone in on them. I had heard many variations of my efforts in defeating Oppollo on that glorious day, but most importantly to me it was the day that I'd lost my love. I spun off the podium, not expected to give them any more information. This was enough.

Titan sidled up to me. "So, does this mean we'll be going out for more missions soon?"

"*I* will be having a discussion, that's all there is to it. Their word and information might lack any real resolve." And yet, it was possible it might've been the answer we were looking for. We walked through the wide hallway, Tori and Chris behind us, making sure to keep their distance from my wings and my jittering gift. Titan, however, always pressed too close, almost yearning for the skin-to-skin touch. I had to consciously put effort into rein it in so it wouldn't zap her. Even like now, she was brushing her shoulder against mine in a jarring effort to psyche me up and give her more information.

"But if something does happen, I can go, right? You saw me out there, and how well I did, I can handle myself. And I can help," she quickly added. I side glanced her, considering most were lethargically dragging themselves about, but she was still bountiful with much energy. I wondered if it had something to do with the lost hunter bloodline that gave her a slight edge.

"You did well indeed," I encouraged. "But I promised you one mission. This might be entirely different."

"I didn't say how many times when I forced you to pinkie promise." She wiggled her eyebrows at me. I scoffed at her eccentric expression. Chris chuckled behind her somehow managing to bring heat to my cheeks from embarrassment.

"Maybe we should go study," Tori suggested, bringing Titan's attention to him. "And let Esmore rest, she still hasn't fully recovered from events, and neither have you." He looked back at Chris, who was obviously struggling to walk around to keep at our pace. She seemed like she wanted to argue with him, but then finally, as a saving grace, she appropriately read the mood.

She nodded curtly and stopped following me. I silently thanked Tori for giving me some peace because inevitably it would be the last we would have for some time.

Claus and Fire were in their wolf form on either side of me. A consistent growl vibrating lowly through him. Even after an effective stare, he didn't cease by any means. Iris and Tori stood in the back of the room. Kasey cleaned under her nails as she acted indifferently to the change of events. And Lincon… Lincon was on the opposing side with a tantalizing smile, sitting beside an uncomfortable Balzar.

It was pleasant as much as it was strange to have Jerimiah, Darcy, Clarissa, and Spungee in the room at the back of their coven leader. Chase looked as perfectly glorious as I remembered him to be, though the stare-off we were having didn't set the tone for this comradery we were deciding on. Since we'd last spoken, he'd cleaned himself up, evidently having found the river nearby.

"Oh, wrong side," Lincon disrupted, clapping his hands on his legs and skipping over to our side of the room within the library. I resisted rolling my eyes, and Chase arched an irritated brow, no doubt thinking about how much he still very much despised the vampire.

Heavy breathing sounded down the hall as two pairs of feet crept toward our meeting. I looked over my shoulder at Tori with a sharp gaze. He shrugged his shoulders, feigning innocence.

Titan let herself in, her eyes going wide at the sight of the vampires in the room. "So it's true!" she exclaimed. "I knew it!"

"Titan," I growled out at her impudence.

"You said you'd give me a chance."

Chris scanned the danger in the room accordingly, far more aware of his situation than Titan. And it was her overconfidence that concerned me the most. "I can help." She popped her hand on her hip calling attention to herself.

"Titan," Tori psst her over, but she ignored him, studying Chase.

"You know, you're a lot more attractive than I recall." This time my deathly growl did catch her attention, and she looked as if she sank into her skin. "Like for an old dude. Good job to you is what I meant."

Lincon let out a monstrous laugh, slapping his knee at the hilarity of her gall. I could sense her satisfaction even when she'd been trained well enough to keep the sheepish smile reaching her face. She practically pranced over to Tori, Chris not far behind as he guarded her exposed back.

"You always take it too far," Tori whispered, heeding her Council. I could sense her heart beat faster as he leaned toward her, acutely aware of his closeness. I ground my teeth, oddly irked by the attention she drew toward herself, not out of jealousy but from somewhere else. Something I couldn't quite put my finger on. All I knew was I berated her maturity as not ready for sexual partners. Not yet…or ever.

I strangled with inner conflict, constricting around my throat as I tried to steadily breathe and sit across from Chase. He simply watched me distantly in the same way he had yesterday.

"How much do you know about their whereabouts?" Balzar asked when he realized Chase wasn't going to start the conversation any time soon. We seemed to simply be staring at one another across the table, consumed by nothing else.

I briefly glanced at Iris who shifted his weight over the table and hunched awkwardly over a map that elicited our circled whereabouts of where we considered they might've been. But we'd never gathered sure enough information where we could advance.

Chase's snarl twisted through the room as Iris hovered over me in a looming presence. Upon his growl, my lower half squirmed with anticipation and the very claiming response of having another male so close to me. I was both flattered and frustrated. I'd depended on Iris these past ten years, and it had never in any way been romantic in the slightest. Iris didn't stop either, ignoring his challenge. But what he did inevitably do was purposefully block my sight from Chase which felt like a suspenseful relief so I could focus because all I wanted to do was stare at his beautiful face.

Balzar circled the long table to slouch across from Iris. They were cautious of one another as they sized each other up. One of Balzar's eyebrows rose as he looked at the map. He shook his head. "This one, yes." He tapped on our suspected whereabouts of Fier's Council. "Tythian's, you're way off."

I sucked in an unsavory breath. At least we'd been close on one, but it still wasn't enough. "And how do you know this?" Iris asked condescendingly. Balzar smirked at the open challenge, and I let my gift fluctuate slightly, no matter how uneasy it made my stomach feel as I did, reminding them that this wasn't the time for fighting. My gift was like an overstretched rubber band, loosely controlled under my demand but not enough strength in it to do anything spectacular. This was the backlash of using it on such a wide-scale magnitude. And it meant that we wouldn't be able to rely on it if we were to ambush the Councils soon.

Balzar leaned back with his arms crossed over his chest as if all-knowing as he licked his lips and looked down on me. "For the first four years after we divided, I hunted down a particular hunter. It was hard considering in the end I had to use myself as the actual bait. I wanted his gift. He was a tracker—pretty self-explanatory as to why I wanted it." And how interesting that he'd finally acquired a gift. If Cesar were still alive, his ruling would only allow the four sons to have one each. The hunters were fabricated by design to harbor such power, the vampires when they adopted it, took a risk. Either they would control it, or it would control them.

"And you have his gift now?" I asked.

"Yes. All I need is a face and scent. And then it blindly leads me to them. However, as soon as I located them, no matter how badly I wanted to pay Tythian a visit, I knew I was outnumbered. Besides, when I did snoop too close his men found us and slaughtered the majority of the remainder of Cesar's coven members. Few of us barely made it out unscathed. I knew I needed numbers after that or the next strike would be in vain. So, I tracked Clarissa and the remains of Chase's coven, and then Chase."

"Why?" I said quietly. Iris leaned back from the map, filling his half of the table to match Balzar's pose. *Why Chase?* I could feel his gaze on me, and I shifted my own inevitably to match him. So much tension bounced between us. And yet he said very little. So few words and it was unimaginably killing me to not rely on that link between us to sense what he was thinking.

"Because he shouldn't have been locked away in the first place." My grip tightened on the edges of my seat. No one understood why I did it. If I hadn't, he would've been a mindless saber. I had to do what needed to be done. "And I needed *you,*" Balzar grumbled with complaint.

"Then why not come to me directly?" I gritted out. We could've prevented all of this and jeopardizing Chase. But maybe Balzar wasn't smart enough to think that far ahead, which meant he didn't entirely care about Chase's outcome. He was only working for himself.

"I considered it, but then I weighed up the likelihood of even getting through your little wolves on my own." Claus snarled at his deeming comment. "Exhibit A!" Balzar said, affronted. "But also, with total transparency, I didn't know how you would receive me. And so, I needed leverage, something that would hold you up for long enough not to blowtorch me into ash."

I considered him for a long time. He was right not to approach us of his own accord because it was likely he'd never get through the werewolves or Lincon in worst-case scenario. I looked over my shoulder at Lincon who beamed with a smile, knowingly aware of what I'd been thinking.

"So then the question is, are you willing to align with us once again?" Balzar asked.

"You want us to stay here?" Clarissa edged potently at him.

"Of course not," I was quick to elicit. We all knew how well that went last time within the institute having two covens, let alone two species who hated one another. Claus's snarl erupted again against the proposition. I slid a gentle hand over his dark fur atop his head, silently advising that I heard him. They might not have enjoyed this meeting, but I was certainly not going to jeopardize their children or members in such a way. But their offer was tempting. Not so much the power, but pointing us in the right direction.

I watched Chase at the end of the table who simply studied me. The others had become uncomfortable by his statured presence. "And what do you think of this?" I asked him directly. Had he opened his mind up to me perhaps we could have a private conversation about it.

He was reluctant to speak and only stared. Instead, Clarissa spoke on his behalf. My lips went thin as I held in my frustration at his arrogance of not even speaking to me directly now. He was able to do so yesterday. "Fier and Tythian's Councils need to be wiped out at least to remove the target from our leader's back. The rest of the Council means very little to us."

I didn't care for what Clarissa had to say, only more irked that she felt it okay to directly speak to me when I'd asked something of him. My vampire self was furious and bubbled to the surface. I slammed my will into him, almost trying to pry open his mind. He snarled and pushed back the chair infuriated by my attempted intrusion. I'd pushed my chair back the exact same time he had, matching his pose. And that's when I saw it. I hadn't seen it so clearly yesterday because we stood so far apart. But now, being so close I noticed the split of gums and veins that protruded ever so slightly around his fangs. It was only minor, but it was the first transition in becoming a saber.

He stormed out of the room, and I gaped at the spot where he once stood. My heart lurched, and I squared Jerimiah and Darcy for answers. Darcy looked away ashamed, and it was Jerimiah who stepped into the candlelight regretfully. "The serum did its job as we'd hoped. It just…"

I sucked in a harsh breath. *We'd already been too late?*

"Give him some space for now," Balzar said quietly, surprising me with his sorrowful expression. He seemed uncomfortable by my intensity. "You were the first thing he wanted to find."

I circled my gaze around the room, horrified by the pity that reflected in everyone. My heart pined and broke at the revelation, more painful than the thought of him living a long and happy life and hating me for all eternity. The desperation thrummed through my veins as I looked to Balzar for answers.

"And where do we find Fier's Council?" I asked. I spited the mournful expression on his face.  No doubt considering that it might already be too late. I knew I had to be rid of Fier the moment he tried to turn Chase completely. But even by killing him, he might not come back to me. I sucked in a breath. "WHERE DO I FIND HIM, BALZAR?"

# CHAPTER II

I WAITED UNTIL Iris had escorted out the others with Lincon, and Claus who growled and eyed off their ankles the whole time. Clarissa had to drag Spungee by the hand so he wouldn't stupidly lash out at the growling wolf, who I was certain wished he'd do just that. I could tell that Jerimiah and Darcy wanted to explain themselves to me, but the time didn't permit it. And equally, what was already done couldn't be reversed. Chase would never willingly stick himself in that frozen coffin again.

"I'll be back," I notified Tori, Fire, and the others. I wanted to find Chase. Balzar had disclosed the whereabouts of Fier's Council. After all these years, we'd been so close and yet so far. But now my mind was a jumble of priorities. How much time did Chase have left until the transition would complete? From what I'd observed, some spiraled quickly, whereas others fought it for years. Could Fier reverse his handiwork or was it already too late?

I padded out one of the side doors, excusing myself and taking flight, locking on the whereabouts of that yearning link between us. That natural calling and enticement I'd yearned to feel for years. I should've remained within the castle and with the people who I'd dedicated the years to fight for. But my natural instinct was to pursue the one person who had truly felt like home to me. And I couldn't fight against it so easily, knowing he was in jeopardy more than I ever realized because the transition had already begun. I didn't know what I would say or how I would act, but I couldn't stomach him running away from me. And oh how he'd run, close to the river where he sagged on a wet rock looking down at his reflection contemplatively.

I circled him a few times, building the courage to impose on his space and trying to think of what I might say, but continued coming up blank. I scanned my awareness out further to ensure no one was lingering close by. The reality was their group had drawn Tythian's minions our way, and there was always a possibility that another would be sent to replace the one we'd already conquered.

I could feel the hackles of his senses and urgency to run away again as I shadowed over him and dove for the ground. If he did run, then I would pursue. The canopy from my aerial view closed around me with sagging sad trees. I kept my distance, just like the last time we'd met, almost too scared of our reactions in close vicinity. I wanted to be with him, and that sense of urgency hastened as the reality of his deterioration set in.

His jacket was splayed open, endorsing his beautiful body. I tried to pry my eyes away from it, but instead my gaze dipped to the V line that continued beneath his leather pants. I cursed myself silently, disgusted in my ability to be taken over by my physical desire so easily. I knew I couldn't have him again in that way, if I did, I'd curse him with my gift. And even worse, the rejection from him would hurt forever more. Ignoring me, he picked up a small pebble and threw it toward the river. It glided, skimming the water far into the distance where I lost sight of it.

"So did you create a temporary treaty with Balzar?" he asked almost begrudgingly.

"I didn't come here to discuss that," I said quietly. He tucked his legs beneath him and leaned over his knees, almost insecurely. It was so unlike the Chase I'd remembered. His blazing gray gaze peered out over his knees as if scrutinizing me while he hid the rest of his face. Suddenly aware of how vulnerable he might've looked, he stood up in an easy swoop. His muscles bounced as he easily landed with elegant grace. His shoulders straightened, elongated his abdomen, and my gaze once again betrayed me. "Does it hurt?" I asked.

"No," he said considerately.

"Did you really think I wouldn't find out?" I growled, mortified that he even tried to hide it from me.

His lip tugged with an agitated snarl, and he looked away to try and hide it. "My objective hasn't changed. For as long as I'm functional, I want them dead." For me. He wanted them gone so I wouldn't have any opposition for the rest of my days. Bile rose from my stomach and lodged in my throat.

"Are you kidding me?" My voice cracked again, and he seemed surprised by the bubble of vulnerability. "That isn't the objective here! We need to find a way to reverse this, Chase! I didn't know I was already too late when I…"

"Had you ever checked up on me, you might've known," he said bitterly.

"That's not fair. I'd only ever done that for you." The lump in my throat was bound, unmoving as boxed emotion tingled through my body. I wanted to see him every single day, but I was too scared that if I was followed or someone caught my scent on the wind, that he'd be found. I didn't know what to do as my heart sped in defiance and I found myself hiccupping in a weird form of anxiety. I was ashamed of my emotional body. For so many years I'd found balance with my emotions and now they were pouring over, all because of this man who… "How can we fix it?"

"Fix it?" For the first time his expression seemed saddened, and I felt the slightest quiver of his mind stretch out to me. But it snapped up so tightly and fast that I felt whiplash in the process. "Esmore," the way he said my name was mournful, "there's no way to reverse this. This is the evolution of our kind. The final stage before we're put out of our misery."

"I don't believe that. I'm aware of the natural process, but this was forced by Fier's hand. A gift of all things, surely there's some way we can *fix* this."

*My love,* his voice whispered into my mind, and I savored the intimate touch even though I knew it was a regretful slip on his behalf. It didn't even give me enough time to fill myself within his walls. To be so connected with him in ways no one else knew. My Chase, my beautiful handsome Chase. He took a few more steps back as if the proximity was becoming a challenge for him.

"I've never seen him reverse his work on someone. Remember those many years ago within your Guild, just before we met for the first time. There was a vampire who was turning into a saber and partnered with a human girl. You found them on the outskirts of your Guild, killed him and took her back to be interrogated, and then put her in your local human camp. That was of Fier's doing. That saber didn't naturally spiral, it was a punishment for falling in love with that human. I've never seen Fier reverse what he's done, so I don't even know if it's possible. And even if he did have a cure, he wouldn't use it on me. And the moment he knows of my reappearance, he'll oblige to snapping his fingers and ending my sanity. My fate is completely cemented now." A hollow bleakness shimmered over us. No, this was everything I had been working so hard toward to prevent.

"Then we should shelter you somewhere until he's disposed of and then we'll find a cure and—"

"Esmore." He huffed. "You can't keep hiding me. I'm not a child to be protected. This was the path I was on long before you were even born. I was created to protect *you*. Don't make this hard on me again by taking away my right. Let me at least have this. Use me so we can achieve our last victory together."

"Use you? I did all of this *for* you?" Involuntarily, I stepped toward him on weakened legs. He simultaneously took another two back.

"I know," he said ever so quickly, almost dismissively. "But we still ran out of time, which we knew was a very real possibility, so now we make the most of the time we have left."

My mouth went agape. How could he so easily accept this? Instead of fighting until his very last breath, wouldn't he want to do anything else? A mournful part of me so wished that he would choose to spend the rest of his days with me. But I couldn't believe, even theoretically, that this was close to the end for us. I'd built the last ten years on *this*. Of the fantasy of how we might live once all the bloodshed had been put aside. After I'd slaughtered through all of the obstacles that came in our way.

"Please don't make this any harder for me. I've found my resolve, and this is what I'll do with it. Don't be the one to step in between my objective," he said coldly. I hiccupped as a tear ebbed in the corner of my eye. He was so forcefully pushing me away and by no physical means. It just felt like we were two worlds apart.

"Chase, please," was all I could manage out.

"I have to go, Esmore," he said and ran back toward his coven in the near distance. My lingering outstretched hand did nothing to pull him back. He'd vanished as quickly as I'd appeared and the anchoring rock in the pit of my stomach didn't so much as let me move my feet to follow him once again. I was simply left with a hollowness as my shoulders slumped.

I waited patiently outside the manmade hut, listening in on the woman's harbored breathing and delay between screams. The sharp metallic smell of blood filled the small village on the outskirts of the castle. Wolves ominously howled around us in anticipation of the arrival of their new little member.

"Just one more push," Fire encouraged the woman. I'd heard that natural births for humans were something once feared. The majority of the time the mother wouldn't survive. But with the mixture of their werewolf blood which gave them fast healing properties, we hadn't had a fatality for either mother or pup. But still, it sounded like the most barbaric of screams and pains I'd ever heard before. Claus waited patiently outside with me, more so as a natural instinct to protect his members than anything else. The father was inside tightly holding his wife's hand doing all that he could during the ordeal.

I took deep and meaningful breaths, deterring myself away from the smell of so much blood. The werewolves' blood wasn't appealing in scent in the slightest, but I vacated the other vampires just in case, and also to ensure the werewolves felt safe no matter what.

I was staring at the cloudy gray sky in deep consideration about Chase's and my exchange. The woman let out one more defiling scream before a new sound of cries erupted from the hut. A tear pricked at my eye at the wailing baby's first breath into the world. This dangerous, chaotic world that had little happiness to offer. Nonetheless, my heart ached at the beauty of its sound. Of new life and a bundle that would be adored by its pack unconditionally.

"Don't tell me you're getting soft," Claus said with a sheepish grin, despite the tense atmosphere throughout the village since the vampires had passed through. The husband's howl erupted from inside, parading a welcome song that was harmoniously shared amongst the pack.

I didn't answer Claus. I wasn't the same as them. Family was not a prioritized privilege, but I couldn't deny the curiosity in me of what it might've been like to live a much simpler life. One that didn't condemn me to naturally lead armies and relish in it as well. It was where I thrived and birthed the greatest version of myself. But it was cold, and a delayed sense of morality was creeping up on how much blood I actually had on my hands in what I thought was victory. Even if I was a marvelous killer in a world where one had to be to survive, did it still make me righteous?

Fire excused herself from the tent, surprisingly clean-looking considering the messy commotion from inside. She squared Claus off expectantly as she wiped over her hands with a wet cloth. "A little boy," she chimed with a glimmer of that maternal instinct I imagined she'd tried to bury with her once she'd realized she couldn't birth children herself. And yet the women in the village depended on her for all of their deliveries.

"Thank you, Fire," he said, taking my position in front of the door to stand guard. Other wolves were standing close by, naturally pulled in by the instinct to protect. She curtly nodded and began walking with me through the small quarters of the village and back toward the castle. I could tell she was angry with me as I side glanced the fearless woman. She was wearing an oversized shirt that came to her knees with a few smears of blood blotched on it. She'd only ever really worn oversized shirts because it was the easiest thing for her to fling off and on if she stayed in her human form for a period of time.

"You're angry with me," I said with great impatience on finding a private room to speak. Everyone was fixated on the newborn pup and wouldn't care to listen in on our conversation.

"Disappointed, actually," she said angrily. She was both, which made it all the worse. That unusual link between us had strengthened over the years, and I found myself dependable on her perception when I might've been blinded by personal gain. Fire didn't work with such ambitions which made her mediation perfect in strategizing, especially when Iris was known to sit back far too patiently until all options were weighed, and Lincon was fast to act and then ask questions later.

"Those who knew of my secret would be a liability to Chase," I said in my defense.

"I understand your reasoning, Esmore, but I'm inclined to question what we've really been working toward this whole time."

"It doesn't change anything. I've rightfully chipped away at the Councils imploring to dwindle them down to nothing which has helped those who have found refuge here. And when were you so quick to align with the werewolves?" She'd always made such a point that she held no alliance toward them just because they'd been made into monsters together. But she'd followed my orders unfalteringly.

She scoffed, vigorously rubbing at a clean spot on her hands. Her white dreadlocks bounced as we skirted around the corner and under the small bridge. "Don't try and twist this around onto me. I care not about your deceit but what it means going forward with our plans. Yes, we have an advantage now with Balzar's ability to track them. But the greater risk is that your familiar is a form of distraction and a liability to you, and I don't want you taking down the army we've built in the process because of personal misjudgment," Fire said coldly.

I glazed over from her scornful insinuation. I didn't plan on jeopardizing them in any other way then what they'd already signed up to from the start. "But it's Chase," I said so quietly, feeling like a child. Fire liked Chase. And in truth, it had been him who had saved her life.

"And you say that like it's an answer," she said whimsically. "As powerful and advantageous as he might be, he's also a ticking time bomb and could turn at any point."

The cold slap of her words silenced what I might've said next. This was why I sought out her Council, but it didn't make the rationality of her reasoning any less hard to swallow. It was *Chase*. "Had you been reunited with your love after so many years, could you so coldly throw him to the side?" I asked her in earnest. Her mate had been killed right beside her when we'd first found her, and she'd been guarding his freshly murdered body. If he had come back after all these years, could she so easily discard him?

"I would put him out of his misery," she said carefully. "Don't think that I do not share your respect for Chase, Esmore. But you came to me for rationality because your emotions have been compromised. You have an army to lead in a few days, and it's my responsibility to make sure you're fit for that role or you'll send them into ruin."

I ground my teeth, wanting to argue with her but self-imposed by the truth of her words. I had built this army to protect Chase, and I couldn't discard them now as if they served no purpose. Army aside, the werewolves and I still shared the incentive to destroy our primary obstacle. And that hadn't changed even with Chase's arrival. I'd simply have to find another way to cure his curse because I couldn't so easily be defeated by the woes of this being our end. There had to be another way. And if I thought with my heart, it wouldn't provide me with the answer. I had to rest my emotions so then my clever mind could acquire a sensible solution. He might've been inclined to have given up already, but I wouldn't follow the same regard.

# Chapter 12

A LIGHT TAP on my door woke me from drifting spirals of thoughts and calculations. Jasmine's musky aroma wafted, and I permitted her entry. She crept in slightly more apprehensive than usual. I had an array of weapons out on my bed as I sifted through them, deliberately choosing my favorites out of the collection. Fear perfumed off her which was enticingly delicious. I swallowed, the saliva not nearly enough as my vampire wanted, my fangs already edging for their claim to her throat.

"Why are you so fearful today?" I asked, looking up from my made bed, still with a hand on the arch of one of my many daggers.

"Oh, I'm not." I arched a suspecting eyebrow, and she quickly caved.

"Well, I heard a rumor that you'll be leaving tomorrow for battle. You and the others. I knew it would happen, but it all feels so rushed," she gushed. "Is it because of those vampires who came?" She fastened to correct herself, almost shriveling into her too-curious mind. "I'm sorry, I shouldn't have been so bold as to ask." She let her hair fall in front of her face as she lowered her gaze.

"I don't mind that you ask, Jasmine. After all, in my absence I'll be depending on you and the others to maintain this palace as a fortified home upon return."

She looked up at me admirably as if my compliment were some trick. I looked away, uncomfortable by the cold response she expected. I only had myself to blame, I'd always ensured to put distance between myself and them. I flipped some of the silk over the knives concealing them from her view. Perhaps that was also putting her slightly on edge.

"Then you best restore as much as you can before parting. You must still be famished after your last fight," she gushed, walking to the edge of the bed and showcasing her neck. I held back my irritable disgruntlement from her implication that I was weak. I didn't much like that it had become common knowledge within the castle about my recovery period from using my gift on such a mass scale. And that was no thanks to Lincon's gossipy loudmouth.

"Tell me, Jasmine." My voice was an inquisitive purr. "How do the others fare during tonight as they prepare for departure tomorrow?"

She seemed chuffed that I'd asked for her opinion. Little did she realize she was somewhat known for her loose lips, not in a harmful way, simply she liked to talk about everyone's business and I knew I'd receive a somewhat direct answer from her. "The soldiers are excited and scared all at the same time. Those who have been past the borders are staying quiet and spending time with their families. It seems very quiet, atmospherically. I mean I think it's a bit scary. It's possible not all of them will come home." I didn't have the heart to tell her indefinitely not everyone would. This solace we'd created over the years harbored refuge for a few hundred of them where they could build and grow their families. We'd lost some over the years who went past the border and were casualties in scuffles with vampires and humans. But now…this would be different. I was leading them into an actual war.

Cautiously she added, "But I think it'd be nice not to live with this looming feeling over our heads. Obviously, there's a long way to go and many others to be dealt with. But for *them,* I imagine it'll feel like a victory. And they could only do that with *you* leading them." She still felt like an outsider but spoke fondly on behalf of the werewolves.

"I thank you for your opinion and observation, Jasmine," I decreed as I flicked away a remaining piece of her hair. My vampire danced obnoxiously, ready for the kill. I had to remind it, repetitively, before I took my first bite that she was *not* to be bled dry, unlike the wild one in the bathroom only nights before. It was disappointed but concurred that it would still get a delicate taste. But my body was craving for far more than Jasmine's aromatic blood that she could offer. It was becoming aroused once again for the taste of blood in a sexually heated way, which I hadn't felt for some time now. And I had no doubt it was because of my paths crossing with one particular vampire.

Considering the recent events, I felt sentimental, as if conversations needed to be had when previously I might've avoided their uncomfortable exchange of feelings. I'd sharpened and cleaned all my blades and walked down the narrow hallway to Titan's room.

Tori, who might've usually lurked around, wasn't anywhere to be seen. Though the mild giggling coming from inside between her and Chris certainly roused my urge to protect her from running into any sexual acts in her teen years. Instead of barging into her room though, I lightly tapped. It was at her age I'd first been with a man, and perhaps it was because of my own scarring from the oppressive relationship and that terrible fated day that kept me from encouraging her own decisions. I couldn't understand why it perplexed me so, she was, after all, her own woman.

"Come in," Titan welcomed, still giggling. Cautiously I opened the door into the candle-lit room, barging in on Chris, not at all happy with the firm-fitted dress wrapped around his shoulders looking like a tight-fitted shirt. His chiseled and developing abdomen slicing underneath the material.

"This is embarrassing!" he snapped with a feverish growl. Titan rolled back, kicking her legs in the air laughing.

"Well, that's what you get for taking a bet and losing. You should be grateful I'm not making you run around wearing it in the village," Titan mused. My eyes drifted to the layout of weapons she had and the newly crafted bows she had in her quiver. Exactly as I thought.

"Chris, can you give us a second," I asked him, and he almost seemed relieved to strip the ornate clothing off. Titian moaned in disapproval, but I noticed the brief gaze she raked down his body as he stretched out his arms and very uncomfortably pulled the tight material off. Chris was turning into a man, and she was beginning to notice.

"Thank you," he sheepishly said as he gathered his shirt and threw it on before leaving the room.

"Well, that's no fun." Titan dropped her bottom lip into a pout.

"You seem to be in an awfully playful mood considering the ominous news of what tomorrow brings." Of which we still hadn't discussed if she'd be coming or not. "Where's Tori?"

"He's feasting, you know, getting his big bad vampire strength up for tomorrow," she said nonchalantly. "Look, I know what you're going to say. You want me to stay and play safe, but that's not what I'm built for! I can help, and if it's okay for the others to go then so can I. I'm of age now!" She groaned. "You saw me out there and how I dealt with those vampire assassins. I can be of help."

"It's not a matter of not being capable, Titan," I said, walking over to my old Barnett crossbow and running a sentimental finger down it. I had trained her personally to use it, waiting out the years until she was strong enough to wield it with one hand. "One day when I'm not here, I want this to remain a safe haven for you. Where you aren't hunted simply for being what you are." What a reversal in the beliefs I'd been raised on. "And so, yes, sometimes I might seem overbearing, but you'll serve a far greater role than a foot soldier." And I had no disregard for those very warriors, that's where they learned survival, killer instinct, and turned into great leaders—just as I had. That's how tokens were created, and I had no intention of keeping her away. Not anymore.

"Why are you talking like this? Like you're not going to be here for it. You're, like, going to live forever. There's no one that can beat you. Is this because of Chase's return?" Her earnest tone only saddened me, thinking of our last conversation. I had to act and be perceived in a certain way as I led them, but inside, I wanted to break because, for once, I didn't have the answers.

"Titan, my familiar's life is on the line. Which means, by extension, so is mine," I said honestly. I wasn't sure what to make of Chase's and my current predicament, but I did know that my willingness to do anything for him remained. Even if he couldn't stand me being so close to him in proximity, I couldn't change that inbuilt reasoning of his protection being my number one priority. And I wanted to make sure security was in place for Titan, no matter what upcoming challenges might prevail. We were going into another war of which she'd never seen before. I believed in her ability, but sometimes it didn't prepare the heartiest of us as we watched our closest friends die on our watch. I never wanted her to know the taste of feeling powerless ever again. A lingering memory of Dillian came to mind, and I cringed away from the sharpness of his absence.

"But you'll, like, live forever. And I just know there's a way we can help him. We won't let him turn like the other sabers do. I don't remember much of him, but what I do remember is how nice he was and how protected I felt with you both." It warmed my heart to hear such a thing even though it frosted over simultaneously. If the other wolves who came from the same Human Compound as her had survived, they would've told her he was the big bad vampire who'd taken her father's body away. And I was the standing monster who'd made the final blow. "Hey, it's going to work out," she said, sounding far older than she was. I appreciated her optimism much in the same way I blinded myself.

"You'll stick to the rules and formations. No running off on your own like you sometimes do and don't let yourself lose control to the beast," I lectured. I'd seen all of them lose to the insatiable creature within them as if it was on a full moon night because they lost their temper. Their tunnel vision aggression was dangerous, and it always threw off the entire pack. Titan had been no exception. And Tori had to knock her unconscious before she seriously hurt any of her training counterparts.

"Stop, you're starting to sound like my mom again," she complained. But I could sense the fondness pool off her in waves. I suppose in many ways, I'd raised her as closely as one could be to my own. And this would be the first time I'd ever take a child of mine into war. It brought a completely different weight onto the field.

I recalled the first time I'd ever gone on my own mission at sixteen as an apprentice within the Hunter Guild, and my mother waited for me at the gate, not so much as showing emotion upon my return but a proudness that I would be as grand a warrior if not more than she'd ever hoped for. Now I realized with dread that perhaps it was because she wasn't sure when my true beast and vampirism might trigger or if I'd return at all.

"And this one looks a little blunt." I pointed to the small blade that would fit on the inside of her boot.

"I know. I was going to sharpen them all tonight."

"And don't stay up too late," I added, now teasing her.

"STOP!" She pushed at my leg playfully, and a small smile prickled at my lips.

"Just please be safe. I won't be able to give you the same attention when we're out on the field. You'll be a soldier like all the rest."

"I know," she said sincerely. "And, Esmore, thank you for letting me come. I'll do you proud."

I reluctantly placed my hand on her shoulder, always seemingly scared of the physical touch. Skin to skin transmitted a different kind of connection than words. "I know you will. But remember all of your training has been not only for what's about to come, but all that you will be. Make sure to think out there."

She placed her hand over mine, those brown doe-eyes melting into soft amber as she sincerely thanked me. "Thank you, Esmore. We're finally going to make a difference. The day has finally come."

I offered a small smile. For her, this might've been the day that had finally come. But for me, I'd already given so much before, and killed so often that the days blurred together. It was just a fixed anxiety of who I would lose in the next battle and the many lives I'd be forced to take. The cunning death had no tip of the hand or insight until it was already too late. This was the game of war, and the only way she would learn its scorn was by being thrown into the blazing fire itself.

# CHAPTER 13

D AWN WAS AN offensive sight, and my overactive mind certainly didn't allow me to anchor any sleep. Instead, I polished my weapons vigorously, staring out my window from time to time at the passing clouds. Now that the sun had begun to creep up on the horizon, it meant only one thing. It was time for our armies to come together and march forward. From the commotion below, the werewolves were mostly packed. The atmosphere of the unknown and jittery expectation for a fight perforated the air.

There was still so much to be discussed regarding tactic and precedence, but I was certain of my role and the werewolves who were willing to fight with me—raised for exactly this. I tightly tied my leather boots, flexing my neck and shoulders as I began sheathing my weapons. My sword was perfectly positioned between my wings and shoulder blades; my golden claws were in their usual pouch at my hip, and my leather garter with daggers was strapped around my thigh. I strapped two large knives crisscrossed against my tailbone, discretely hidden by my wings but easily reachable. I wouldn't so easily be able to depend on my huntress gift, but that didn't make my ability to take pleasure in using my weapons any less. If anything, I preferred it more because it substituted closer to a fair fight.

I met with the others downstairs, who were already waiting. The only members who weren't yet accounted for were Lincon and Kasey which was no surprise. "We'll leave without them. They'll catch up." I'd learned to ignore Lincon's bizarre behavior. The times when I'd followed him personally or had others do the same brought him far too much delight in having such attention, and that was often when he'd create disaster and rifts amongst the werewolves and the few vampires who housed here. For the most part, he went off hunting for fun, and when he couldn't find it, he'd torture small animals or sabers, at the very least, just to pass the time. I'd concerned myself in the first few years that he might draw unwanted attention toward us because of his sporadic behavior, but he was never sloppy. More specifically, there was never enough to remain for anyone to trace it back. And Kasey often went with him, not so much as an accomplice but to get out of the castle herself. I still hadn't figured out the merit of their relationship, and I'd given up years ago trying to understand the incentive that bound them.

The werewolves were armed and shared the weight of bulky backpacks containing tents, food sources, water, and weapons. Some might've held sturdy silver chains, in case we were gone for longer than a full moon and we had to improvise a jail cell.

They faced me bravely, but I could sense the nauseating swirl of mixed emotions wave off them. Anticipation, anxiety, fear, excitement, darkly pitted revenge, and sadistic pleasure. I kept an eye on the few who focused on the latter, Claus being one of them. This was their time, but it didn't make them any less a liability than those who might be stunned from fear. If they were taken over in rage with their own beast they'd be just as accountable.

Titan, Chris, and Tori were discussing amongst themselves. Titan often briefed a glance my way, and I was certain she was envious of Fire and Iris who were by my side instead of her. But my comrades had earned this position through years of bloodshed and unrelenting faith in our cause.

We'd left a few of the older soldiers to remain, and anyone younger than fifteen was to stay and defend the castle if something were to arise while we were gone. The women and children remained with plenty of stockpiled food to keep them going for two months.

Women saw off their mates while children remained asleep in their huts, undisturbed by the send-off. There was a luxurious mix of male and female fighters which pleased me. It would be peculiarly quiet once we left, taking almost two hundred soldiers. And yet, it never felt quiet enough.

"We've all waited for this day," Iris said seemingly sentimental. What would happen to him afterward? Would he return to the land of ice and snow after he sought out his revenge on Tythian? Would I return? And more importantly, how many others would come back alive?

"Yes," I said, gravely aware that there would be many more sacrifices to come, as it had always been, but it didn't make it any less disheartening. Fire rubbed her head against my thigh as if to agree with my warranted thoughts. "It's time."

The werewolves made way around us, dividing into a platoon of three units. I briefed a glance noting that Titan and Chris were centered in the left row. Tori had taken his place leading the same unit. Claus was in the peak and Ruppert, his new second on the right.

Not one of the women cried as they saw off their loved ones. They had their heads raised high and just before we disappeared beyond the border of my mother's gift, their howling song began to send us off. A mournful howl that anticipated the war cry they might've supported us with on the battlefield.

Chase's gargoyle soldiers greeted us, none of whom were Jerimiah and Darcy. They remained in their gargoyle forms acting as a guard post as we walked closer to the cluster of vampires. Growls vibrated from behind me as they stalked toward the gathering. Some were in human form while others in their wolf, and yet I couldn't differentiate between where the growls came from.

The few in their wolf form were on the outskirts of the platoon, and were mostly those who had the most experience beyond the walls. They didn't carry any backpacks and were used to quickly ebbing in and out, scout and fight if we were attacked, giving the others that extra moment for preparation.

Balzar greeted us, and I raised my hand to signal the others to stop. I didn't want them merging any closer toward the group of vampires in case either party decided to become hot-headed straight from the get-go. Although Claus had given them a stern talking with about what was to happen over the next few days, I didn't have utter faith in them fighting against their natural instincts. Not when I had so often lost to my own.

The vampires hissed under their breaths, conscious of the same stern talking to I'd imagined they'd had. They had fewer numbers than I'd been expecting, maybe one hundred altogether. I would've scoffed at their size had I not been there for the near annihilation of both covens. Chase was in the distance, partially hidden behind his group with his back turned to me. I ground my teeth conducting a steely presence. Jerimiah and Darcy, however, who guarded his back, seemed almost apologetic over the exchange. Darcy couldn't hide his expression any better than he could when he was once swigging wine with Chase those many years ago, and Jerimiah, despite his cool demeanor, also seemed slightly perplexed by the change in our relationship. I had no right to ask anything of them, but it was more infuriating having them feel like strangers.

Clarissa stood from the log she'd been sitting on, patting Spungee on the head like a pet. She pointed that unruly sharpened finger at me. "Your dearest Lincon poisoned our members!" She hissed. I snarled at her accusing, disgusting finger at me. It was so uncharacteristically like her, who was always lacking in anything relative to life.

I met Balzar's gaze, ignoring Chase since he was doing the same to me. It was obvious Balzar was calling the shots, well publicly anyway. I had no doubt that Chase orchestrated his talent behind the scenes, out of my earshot and understanding.

"A handful of our members found a sleeping human in a nearby cave and didn't think before attacking. So naturally, they dove in fast, only to discover the human had been laced with poison," Balzar gritted out.

"How do you know it was Lincon?" I had no doubt Lincon was behind such a stupid ploy but how could they directly assume it was him without evidence.

"Because he laughed in our faces, gloated, and then terrorized another three members before running away, hoping the gargoyles would chase him."

Tsk.

"Where did he even find poison?" Tori grumbled his complaint from behind. Gone were the days about asking how Lincon acquired anything.

"Where is he now?" I asked.

"We don't know. We were hoping you'd know and perhaps could put a leash on your dog."

"How mean." Lincon whistled from a tree above, swinging his legs over the branch. Everyone was startled by his intrusion. He'd obviously been deflecting their attention with his illusionist gift. I wondered how long he'd been sitting up there waiting for his grand entrance. Lucky he unnaturally defied gravity, or he might've fallen. As if granting my wish, a bolt of lightning struck from the sky and burst the branch to obliteration. Lincon wobbled as he fell backward, landing like a cat and flicking his hand over his face as he stood as if flicking back a mane full of hair.

"Iris!" he squealed. "How could you?"

"I told you it'd piss them off." Kasey glowered from behind as she walked through the treetops. Others snarled at her entrance. She didn't care, and I had the sneaky suspicion that none dared to test her simply because of her close association with Lincon.

"Why?" I moaned out. Why did Lincon do anything? I could hear a slight chuckle and whipped my head around to Titan who had been so daring as to goad Lincon publicly.

"Do you really want an answer?" Lincon asked dubiously.

"Not really," I sighed out. "How do they fair?"

Balzar was infuriated, but there was nothing that could be done. The only two who could take Lincon on as it stood were myself and Iris, who could obliterate him within a second and that was if he didn't catch onto the thought first. He had a sixth sense for saving his ass. "They were vomiting up blood for half the night before it passed. They're okay now."

"See, they're okay. It was just a simple prank, you know, amongst campmates. Some might even quote it as 'shits and giggles.' We're all going to be best friends soon, so I thought I'd make an impression on my long-lost friends! I missed you guys!" Lincon anguished childishly. Kasey rolled her eyes with arms folded over her chest. She was strapped with her preferred weapons and carried a heavy dutiful bag.

"You know," Lincon perked, that brilliant, crazed gleam coming to his eyes. "Yolo would've loved this prank!"

Balzar was on top of him quickly and was able to get in one good hit before Lincon validated it'd be seen as self-defense. "Don't you dare say his name!" Balzar yelled as he raised his brazed knuckles a second time. And then he snapped into an uncomfortable daze as terror hit his expression. Lincon squirmed a smile as blood pooled from his nose and over his lips, his elongated fangs showing in delight at the easy bait having snagged his prey.

"Lincon," I let my voice whistle over the wind as my gift scattered to take a chunk out of his calf. It was a poor effort as it sluggishly went over to him and he watched it, simply taking a small step away to avoid its reach. He knew about my weakness after using my atomic gift, but he also might've considered it a half-assed threat, which it was. With the few soldiers we had going up against not one but two Councils, he was invaluable. My gift receded, tired from its expenditure. "We're not here to play games."

He looked at the horror-filled Balzar. Other vampires crept closer. He was, after all, their coven leader now. They would have to die for him unless they challenged him for his position, but they also recalled the threat that Lincon was from the times we'd housed together in the institute. "But—"

"Put him down," I said far more aggressively. "Are you here to be of assistance to me or *not?*"

He huffed, saddened he had to drop his new plaything. The moment Balzar hit the ground he snapped clear to consciousness, swinging loosely as he staggered to stand. Lincon took his position beside Iris who wearily side-glanced him. Oh, how this was a great impression of how this was going to work, set by example on the first day.

"You should've gotten rid of him a long time ago," Chase eerily said, hiding behind his people as he casually sat atop a fallen log with a leg propped as if he were some king of the jungle.

"Oh, hello, he still speaks," Lincon mocked. A low growl sounded from Chase.

Lincon sighed in boredom. "You know. I preferred him when he was much more tolerant. I don't know how I'm going to handle all this nit-picking."

"Great. This has just started off fucking great." Balzar threw his hands in the air. And I couldn't' agree with him more.

# CHAPTER 14

WE MAINTAINED THE distance between the separate units. I warily eyed the vampire covens on either side of us. No matter how spread across we were as a united wall and front, I didn't like being wedged between them because it unnerved my werewolves, just as I imagined they'd intended. We outnumbered them which was why surrounding us was a good strategy. But to request a change or move out of it would opinionate my mistrust.

I couldn't help but subconsciously reach my mind out to Chase's like a constant magnet, still disbelieving that he was here and in such cold terms. I remained visual as we moved out in case we were ambushed at any time, and my distraction with Chase was a vexing reality. I just wanted to touch and be with him, in mind and spirit. And the physical torment of having him so close heated my core more than I liked to admit when he seemingly had no reaction or looked my way even twice. Iris often guided his gaze down to me and then over to Chase. I wished he wouldn't so obviously look. And maybe that was because he was calling me out for being so obvious about it.

I half anticipated crossing paths with another group of Tythian's men, which we hadn't yet, perhaps because there'd been no one to report back or they thought they were tracking Balzar elsewhere. How would he move against his own brother? Considering he'd happily stood by the death of his youngest, I was certain a reunion wasn't in mind. But Balzar had military wit, which was enough to give him pause for thought. Or maybe I was overthinking it all. Everything was a gamble and a game. I only hoped we made a clear path to Washington DC before we ambushed Fier's Council.

Besides a few heated squabbles and near fights, the groups kept enough distance from one another to avoid any bloodshed. And I'm sure it didn't pass their notice that we would already be shorthanded in numbers when facing Fier's Council. Everyone had so much to gain from this fight, from what had been lost those many years ago and for what was to be gained for the generations to come. Or they'd die trying.

After the first full day of a consistent run following Balzar's lead, he called for a rest period, which the wolves were grateful for. They were magnificent and could match the vampires, but they still remained living and partially human meaning they fatigued. And I wanted to constantly restore their energy as often as possible before any form of fighting happened.

They steadily set up tents. I'd never understood their reasoning behind it, perhaps a lingering habit as humans. Their temperature was always warm even as humans, so maybe it was a psychological kickback of some kind, a way to feel safe in the wild. I allowed them their privacy and privilege as I watched the first round of guards step out into the trees. It was midnight, and the vampires were edgier having to run during the day as opposed to the night. But being in the dark was the best time to take shelter even with the possibility of sabers being nearby.

"Esmore, we've built your tent." Titan sauntered up to me. "Claus insisted you have privacy." Behind her was an eight-person tent, perfectly constructed in a matter of minutes. She still had hammer in hand as Chris fastened the final pieces.

"It's not necessary," I condoned. I could never sleep anyway, with or without the privacy of a tent.

"Please, Esmore," Titan urged a little more demandingly. "Claus wants to showcase that you belong to *us*. And we treat you as our queen. You shouldn't be patrolling or lingering outside, that's our job."

My gaze narrowed on her. The vampires were stationed elsewhere, far enough not to distract the werewolves from a decent night's sleep, especially with their brothers and sisters guarding their backs, but not enough so that they could see how they treated me, or I them.

I scanned the many minds, finding Claus's before I saw him physically. He was shouting orders to ensure everything was erected as quickly as possible. Werewolves were circling as guards as if we were their herd of sheep.

Fire nudged the back of my legs, insistent toward the tent. I narrowed my gaze on her as well. Or they were trying to keep me in so I wouldn't run away, leaving them behind for someone else. They were cornering me into duty, and as much as I could defy them, I knew it wasn't the morale they needed right before I took them to war. Especially seeing my heart divided in my role to lead them and my shattered one that so desperately wanted to reach out to my familiar across the grove.

"Perhaps we could have a staring match all night and see who wins," Iris said dryly as he offered Titan a grateful smile. *Would he even fit in the tent?* As he bunched his shoulders and craned his head into the flap of the door, I took that as a yes. I understood what they were doing, their antics not so sly, but equally I was grateful for their desire to 'prove' I was theirs and considered part of their pack. And they always looked out for their own. But fighting the tug of Chase's link and mine was outrageously difficult, and every step toward that tent felt like a sinking pit, even though logically I understood it was the right choice.

"Esmore," Tori summoned attention and Titan straightened slightly beside me. My fang pricked at my lip as I bit down my dissatisfaction for the way she reacted to him. "Balzar and the others would like to speak with you soon in regards to placement when we surround Fier's."

I wanted to query who was defined as 'others.' "Tell them to meet me…" I looked over the ugly-looking tent and waved my hand around it. Oh, how mighty and powerful I was, suggesting they meet at my glorious tent.

"Oh, that's nice, you get your own tent," Tori said with a sly smile, and I was sure he was poking fun of me. He vanished before I could reprimand him. Chris opened the fabric door for me. Surprisingly, the tepee tent looked far more comfortable inside, and they'd even organized two blankets and dragged in a few stumps. Considering the circumstances, I supposed it was somewhat homely but unnerved me in the way it offered comfort when we were to be on guard at all times. Where I was offered a ridiculously large one, they piled and overfilled theirs, not at all deterred by the close proximity of one another—because they were family. And ours whistled with a particular coldness as a small breeze swept through the door amongst Iris, Fire, and me.

I sat on the floor cross-legged, tapping my finger impatiently on my thigh as Fire rested her head on my other leg. It wasn't long until Tori returned with a report on our posts and who was currently monitoring them. Lincon had long gone with Kasey for another adventure, and I chastised him that if he were to play any of his 'pranks' that they'd be kicked off the 'fun' of this upcoming fight. Not that I even knew how I would do that.

"I don't like it in here," I complained about the stuffy place. "I can't even see the sky or stars."

"You know it's a rarity to see the stars anyway," Iris equally tipped. "You're just being impatient." I ground my teeth at his forward nature of calling me out. He was wrapped in a comforting blanket, which reminded me of his attire when we first met. And even now the blanket looked too small for him and besides, he didn't need it for any reason other than comfort.

"You have visitors," Chris announced. I stood up too keenly, completely forgetting about Fire who lay on my knee. She offered a small yelp from the startled awakening. She looked at me begrudgingly that I'd interrupted her sleep and sauntered off into the corner, lapping a few times and laid back down. Though her eyes were closed, she certainly was not sleeping. Her ears were flicking as she listened to the crunch of oncoming footsteps.

"Wow, what a nice tepee," Balzar mocked as he came in. "A bit cramped though," he said, somewhat guarded as he squashed his broad shoulders in beside Iris who came up to his pecs even while sitting down cross-legged. It was unbecoming of the warrior as he wrapped himself in the cozy blanket, still an arm's reach away from his oversized hatchet. Clarissa crept in afterward, indifferent to Chris who was positioned so closely toward her as she nudged Spungee in like a child so he wouldn't stand too close to the humanized wolf. They seemed relieved that Lincon wasn't here. Weren't we all, but it only begged the bigger question of what he might be up to.

I anchored myself strongly into the ground mentally as Chase's intoxicating scent filled the air. My throat tightened as my mouth moistened at its delicacy. It was ecstasy to me, and it rattled me to the core as I held myself accountable for staying as far across the tent as possible. If I didn't, I feared I'd forget anyone else was in here, and my mind would immediately be flooded with steamy memories and fantasies. I chastised myself, so irritated by my body and mind betraying my stealthy shell.

Balzar cleared his throat as if trying to help remind me that everyone *was* still in the room and could definitely suspect my arousal just by being caught in the whimsical smell of my familiar. Damn my body for betraying me so obviously. Chase remained close to the door, equally trying to put as much space between us, and yet the material of the tent could've hugged us like a blanket. His stormy gray eyes were locked on me and then my throat as I focused on steadying my breathing. Damn my body for betraying me! I looked away, focusing on the task at hand.

"Anyways," Balzar interrupted uncomfortably with raised eyebrows. "I have a few game plans for when we arrive at Fier's."

"As do I," I equally measured. He seemed to pause and then smirked.

"Now I remember why we argued so much," he said dotingly. A smile dared to prickle at my features. Oh, how Balzar and I had come a long way from our very first meeting of wanting to spike one another's heads on a post and walk away as the victor. Had I thought we'd be here twelve years later still talking tactics and warfare as comrades, I might've laughed in his face.

Balzar expressed his options and plans which truthfully were similar to those Iris, Tori, Fire, Lincon, Kasey, and I had discussed over the years. And in recent days with the additive of what they might be able to do for us.

I quite enjoyed the idea of going in for a sneak attack instead of head-on, considering our disadvantage in size. To our advantage, we did have a few key player warriors who could wipe out numerous members at once. Lincon and Iris's gifts were a spectacle in themselves. And if I hadn't used my gift those weeks ago, no one would've had to raise a hand. But that wasn't an advantage we had right now, and it killed me to admit it so publicly.

"I can't annihilate the space, but I can still use my gift in close range," I somewhat lied, and Iris's peripheral gaze told me he wasn't on board with my fib. But I wanted to be the one to assassinate Fier, and if they thought for a second I held any weakness, then they might argue to take that role away from me.

"I heard about your atomic gift." Balzar whistled. "You've been busy."

Chase didn't so much as look at me. I imagined Balzar would've already informed him about my doings in the past ten years. And I hoped it might've been impressive enough for him to give me some credit for what I'd accomplished in that time.

"You should remain hidden. The moment Fier so much as sees or picks up your presence he'll switch you over into a saber in a heartbeat."

"You can't elicit what me and my coven will do, Esmore," Chase growled.

"Oh for…I am not going to be stuck between this lovers' quarrel." Balzar grimaced, looking up into the roof of the tent. As if entertaining him, Iris looked up ominously as well, more so because he knew the avalanche of rage that was about to come. Working so closely together for ten years gave us an advantage and understanding of someone's temperament. Tori simply watched on with arms folded over his chest, not being able to sink out of the tent any further.

"Are you kidding me?" I arched an eyebrow and placed a hand on my hip. "What would be the point of any of this?" I snapped my mouth shut, tittering on wanting to slap him and throw myself into his arms. It was almost my undoing as his expression softened ever so softly. I wasn't the only one after Fier's blood, and they all had their own selfish reasons for it, but at least they were able to be guided under the precedence that we were working together as one.

"I agree with Esmore." Clarissa spoke up for the first time in her automotive monotone. "We didn't come this far to lose you so quickly."

"You're already losing me," he said in a prickly tone. "So, either one of you can challenge me now for the position, or you'll have to wait until I die out," he said nonchalantly.

"Don't say that," my voice was a quiet plea. So uncanny for my usual prestigious form.

"If you want to make it to the end game and take it up with Tythian, then you need to stay out of Fier's sights," Balzar remarked.

"My problem *is* with Fier," Chase snarled, showcasing his unnaturally large fangs. He shook with fury, condemning himself for losing face.

Balzar was unfazed by his outburst. "It doesn't mean you have to condemn yourself so quickly. You'll never even make a scratch before he sees you coming."

"You don't know what I'm capable of," Chase said murderously. Outraged by the conversation, he barged out the door. I was quick to follow, my heart pounding in fury that he couldn't so much as look or face me in the tent and now he was storming off like a child. Why was he acting so cold when everyone around him simply wanted to help?

"Are you just going to ignore me then?" I demanded of him in the unlit night. I could see an array of colored wolf eyes glowing from the trees, small growls evoking from them as they slowly stalked closer.

"What do you want from me? Everything has already been said," he said impatiently as if I was holding up his time. I scoffed, mortified that this was all he was giving me. *Lash out. Scream. Just do something.* I was internally screaming at him, banging against that link of ours that was so tightly shut off to me. I wanted to shake him, to tell him he wasn't alone and we would find a way. Chase was always so optimistic, and now he was just tatters of a man who I didn't even recognize.

"Esmore," Balzar said, stepping outside the tent and considered placing a tentative hand on my shoulder. Retrospectively, he decided it was best not to. "Just leave it for now."

"Leave it," my voice quivered in fury. *Just leave it.* I was ready to combust, and even my wings quivered with the building rage inside of me. I could feel Chase's coven members edging closer to my pack, which had them growling on guard and a few members from the tents appeared, prepared for a fight. Almost inviting it. Titan looked down her nose at him. A sight I never intended for Chase. I didn't want him feeling like an outsider or an enemy. Never against me or those I led. I built this army for him. And yet my actions would very much induce their next move and behaviors. I couldn't let them see me lashing out like this toward Chase unless I truly did want to obliterate the remains of his coven. Which how could I when all I wanted was *him*. An open and vulnerable conversation, instead of…whatever this was.

Chase's gaze lacked in empathy, not even a spark of the lover I recalled. This timid shell of my familiar that I hadn't been expecting at all. I whirled back into the tent, furious by how quickly I was coming undone. All because of him. For these last years, I'd kept it together. And now…I was left falling into pieces desperately trying to collect shards of him and me to put back together. I would give anything to have half of that. Half of him for however many days.

# CHAPTER 15

M Y DISCONCERTMENT WAS felt amongst the camps, and there was nothing I could do to bring it down besides ignore Chase but have him in my peripheral at the same time. By day three, I had to go hunting, ever so cautious not to run into any foreign forces, considering in two days time, by Balzar's estimate, we'd be at what was once known as Washington DC.

Balzar had called Fier tactless considering it was the resting place for the last human government and Vampire Council war, and more personally, it was also where Balzar died as a human and was rebirthed into a vampire at Yolo's request. Fier had built on top of the grave from the last great war between humans and vampires, shamelessly and symbolically claiming what he considered to be his.

I couldn't even focus on the hunt as my body pumped with an anxiety I hadn't known for years. I needed to kill, ruthlessly and unapologetically. The next two days couldn't come soon enough. I stumbled across Lincon and Kasey. Lincon had chained down a saber with silver. It was panting harshly, screeching under the pain.

"Ssshh," Lincon cooed to it as he knelt beside it. He held one of Kasey's daggers and was sketching into the creature's side. "See, and this is how you would spell my name in French," he said twistedly to Kasey. She wasn't even watching him as she picked at a handful of berries, bored. The saber squirmed and screeched in pain once again, moving its legs limply trying to shake off its shackles. I snarled at his cruelty and focused all my efforts of oppressed anger and agitation to hasten into my gift. Hiding behind the trees, I snapped my mouth shut so tightly my fangs pricked at my bottom lip where I began to bleed. I forced my gift out, with the wrath of my vampire behind it. It wasn't fast or gripping, but it spluttered across the saber, putting it out of its misery and ashing the silver chains that bound it as well.

"Hey!" Lincon shouted, unimpressed that his plaything had just been taken from him. My gift squirmed back to me like a sluggish rope being dragged to its master. I stepped out from behind the trees to reveal myself, tension rippling from me.

He huffed and attempted to collect the remains of his silver chain. Who even knew why he was carrying that around? "Ouch, burnies," he complained as he snaked the silver around his fingers, and then pressed a squeamish smile at the sizzling pain.

"Leave us," I ordered Kasey.

"Someone woke up on the wrong side of the bed this morning," Kasey mocked but smartly hastened her steps.

"You don't let me have fun anymore, and now you're taking away my only friend," he pouted speaking childishly, which only infuriated me more. "Ooooh, apple." He collected a half-rotten apple that Kasey had dropped when she left, dropping the now bloody silver for his newly opted toy. He was acting completely mindless, one of his crazier versions that unnerved me to no end. He began awkwardly spinning the apple on his finger as if it were a ball.

"Lincon, I need you to take me seriously for once."

The apple continued to spin on his finger unnaturally as he stared at me. "I do take you seriously, Esmore."

I closed my eyes. That was as close an admission of receiving his council as I'd ever get. "Have you ever heard of a way to postpone the rapid descent of becoming a saber or how to reverse it?"

He flicked the apple into the air and snatched it with his hand, his gaze unmoving from mine. "No."

There was a silence. "No. That's it? Don't you have anything else?" I asked, infuriated by the usual chatty Lincon who apparently now had nothing to say. He'd usually eat out of my palm by the highlight of having a one-on-one meeting and that I was asking for his opinion.

"No. It's nothing I've seen in my time. This is the natural evolution of what vampires are, Esmore. I—"

"I don't need a lecture on the vampires' lifespan, Lincon. I just need to find a way to break the cycle."

He remained silent which only infuriated me more. I began pacing, uncharacteristically uncertain of how to channel this helpless feeling. He was the oldest vampire I knew. If he didn't know, then who did? Suddenly, it dawned on me that there were older vampires than even him. "What about your mother?"

His mouth went agape. "Fuck no!" His adamant and almost sane response startled me. "That bitch is *crazy.*" I couldn't help but think the apple didn't fall far from the tree. "And besides, her research hasn't ever touched on the lifecycle of vampires, more so how she can eradicate them as efficiently as possible. Aka, like your gift would be a big fucking help. You better hope she never finds out the magnitude of it or she'll come hunting for you to conduct all new and exciting experiments."

"But what if in recent years she's—"

"No," Lincon said firmly, and his poise forced me to sag back into my unnatural pacing. How had I turned into the crazy one when speaking with Lincon?

"Look, I know this whole familiar thing has you upset, and you don't want to lose him, I get it, I do—"

"How could someone who *killed* their own familiar possibly understand what I'm going through?" I loosely exhausted myself.

He arched an eyebrow as if enjoying my tongue lashing. It infuriated me even more that I was losing myself and confiding in Lincon of all people. I tried to usher the calm of my jittery breath and the power that was throbbing to release.

"Well, yea, he was my weakness; at least I was able to identify that. Perhaps you should've considered that ten years ago instead of freezing him and dragging out the process. I'm just saying…"

I snapped wildly, crossing the distance between us and digging my nails around his throat. I flushed my hot breath on his face as I bared my fangs, and then suddenly I was immersed in a world of difference. A place that felt peaceful as much as it did unusual.

Trapped. I was in one of Lincon's illusions, but instead of painful memories, or excruciating torture, my gaze set upon something far worse.

"Well, you just need to be careful with the water, it's heavy," Chase said with that beautiful smile of his. He was helping a small child with short black hair and gray eyes that could only belong to Chase, carry a bucket of water.

"Yea, but I want to be as strong as you and Mom." He pouted, struggling with the weight of the water bucket. He was no older than four.

"You will, son." Chase placed his hand on the little boy's hair, ruffling it. The boy slapped away at his hand, irritated by the distraction to his unyielding focus. I felt a tear jerk at my eye. Here, it was light and warm. A bright unnatural day that heated my cheeks and my cold unnerving jurisdiction of the world.

I was startled into clarity like a cold slap to the face. Lincon was watching me from where I'd once stood, flicking his fingers in farewell before disappearing into the night. My shaky legs gave way, my wings awkwardly bowing as I sagged. What a cruel illusion indeed, I would've much preferred the torturous pain. My mouth became dry as I savored the remains of the illusion. If only I could give Chase such a gift. I crumbled inward, all my angsty desperation sapped out of me, only leaving the remains of a saddened woman. What if I were to become a widow? What if there really was no way? Could *I* continue on knowing that he was no longer in this world with me?

He'd once described familiars as the lover in this lifetime and the next. Perhaps this wasn't our time, and I hoped whatever life we chose next— if there was such a thing—offered us so much more than this one.

I could sense wolves move around me and quickly collected myself from the guttered earth. But I couldn't fall into ruin, not until we crossed that bridge together. Even if he couldn't so much as look at me now.

By the fourth day, whatever triggered in me from Lincon's illusion somehow also offered me clarity of mind. I had given away my hope that Chase would come to me. To speak, or ever so slightly touch. To simply be within the same room and study the crevasse of one another's every detail in that awful reality that we might never have the chance again.

I'd let that desire go. He'd made it prominently clear every day that he wanted nothing to do with me and purposefully stayed away. And now that we neared closer to Fier's Council, only one day away, I had to ensure my focus was on my werewolves and their future. Because bleakly, I wasn't sure what would become of my own. And I allowed my stubbornness to curate a sensible justification to avoid Chase. If being around me only brought him suffering, then so be it, I would keep my distance.

I rested cross-legged within the tent that werewolves had insistently erected. Instead of mocking it like I had on the first night, I now appreciated its privacy. My eyes were closed though I could still sense Fire pacing back and forth, waiting for Iris and Tori's return. They'd since gone to find Balzar and ensure there were no changes in the plan. Tomorrow we would be near Fier's Council, and the intensity of everyone being on edge was palpable in the air. More werewolves surrounded the camp, guarding rather than resting.

I tried blocking out the gentle squabble amongst the camp, trying to align myself meditatively before the fight. I had waited on this day for so long, and I had to ensure my strike was hot and fast. That, and I also tried my hardest to gain some kind of rest even if I couldn't fall asleep. But even with my eyes closed, the immediate image of Chase immerged. My mind continued to rake up the image of his body and handsome face. Of all the times we held one another and depended on one another in life and death. Of the night we exchanged our wedding vows and became husband and wife. My fingers automatically brushed against the lock of his hair in my leather pocket that I'd carried around ever since. And the searing blue gemmed necklace was a constant reminder that I was his. I wondered if he'd even noticed that I still wore it. Not that I should have to prove to him my love.

His scent was a lingering memory. It always took me to a wild place, of forest and an undertone of enticing spice, so delectable in its coaxing ingredient and his blood… My eyes flashed open as I realized not only was I getting carried away in the memory, but that scent wasn't just a memory. I took an impartial inhale and looked over my shoulder through the tent as if I might see him on the other side. Noticing my sudden clarity, I could feel him shift and walk in the other direction.

I jumped out of my meditative thoughts and crossed the tent in two large steps, throwing back the flapped door. Titan was outside expectantly and pointed in the direction where he'd left. Well, that explained how he'd gotten so close without one of my other wolves attacking him, if she'd guarded his arrival. "Wait here for the others," I ordered Fire without looking back at her.

I chased after that unyielding link between us, being intervened by Darcy and Jerimiah. I speculated whether it was to allow Chase privacy, despite that he had the nerve to stalk me after he'd made it so clear he wanted nothing to do with me.

"We wanted to speak with you before the first strike," Darcy quickly said. I'd never blamed them, and yet they'd built the courage to face me after all these years and confront the demand I'd asked of them. It had already been a week since we'd been working together, and truthfully, I'd been avoiding them. I liked the two of them very much. And there was no one else I trusted more with what I'd asked of them. And yet, I was uncertain as to where that left us now. We were on either side of a line, separated in duty.

"We couldn't attack Clarissa and Balzar," Darcy gushed defensively. A great knot in the pit of my stomach began to unfurl. *Did they think I was upset with them because of recent events? Of Chase being released?*

"We also overheard them discussing their plan to confront Fier and Tythian afterward and wanting to find you. And we thought after ten years…maybe it was a good idea," Jerimiah rationalized.

"Honestly, everything happened so quickly that day on the battlefield that we hadn't realized Chase already took on minimal features of a saber until they'd broken him out. After we drugged him, we put him straight into the icebox like you told us to. If we'd known—"

"Darcy." I quickly cut him off. And I included Jerimiah, so he knew this went for both of them. "I don't blame either of you for this outcome. I've always been indebted for what you did that day. You've never once been accountable for what happened. And even then, my only condolence is that we were too late."

Darcy's sad expression only triggered my internal mourning as if Chase were already gone. Of his coven, I'd liked the gargoyle vampires the most. And I wished we'd reunited under better circumstances. Clarissa's presence crept up on us, watching the exchange unfold with those dead eyes of hers. She, however, as Chase's second, might've had a different opinion. "I look forward to fighting alongside you again." I curtly nodded, pushing past them to ensure I didn't express the raging war internally happening. "Excuse me."

I pushed past the two and continued to follow the lingering trace of Chase. I felt his coven vampires edging toward me like I was an intruder, but none were so daring as to confront me. I jumped and heftily beat my wings, skirting along the treetops as I searched for him.

When I found him, I perched atop a tree branch, far away. The branch groaned in complaint under my weight but was sturdy enough not to break. I hunched myself into my knees, resting on the balls of my feet with one hand rested on the tree as I leaned toward him, even when we were separated by such distance.

He was alone with his head in his hands, shoulders slumped in defeat. He'd simply kept walking into the forest. I dipped my head to the side, the predatory instinct in my vampire coming out as it joyfully stalked. He was alone, so within my reach and yet a world away. I knew he could sense me, as I did him.

No matter how much I wanted to prioritize my werewolves, I'd somehow ended up here, once again blindly following, hoping for a second glance.

*Don't,* his voice within my mind was a forceful desperate plea. And as quickly as he exchanged the singular word, he snapped shut our link and internal communication. And yet cruelly, his internal growl was like a mental embrace that filled me with warmth and sadness all in one. My wings sagged, depleted. Would he really not have me? Did he truly despise me that much? Then why did he even come to my camp? Had I foolishly convinced myself it was because he reciprocated my love and anguish over lost time. Or was I fabricating my own personal ideal?

He continued walking, and somehow, I found myself dancing from branch to branch, stalking him throughout the night, simply being bound within his radius but not so much exchanging words. How pathetic I'd become.

When the chill in the air nipped harshly, I realized dawn already approached, and we'd be packing our camp and leaving. I'd been here the whole night, stalking him. It had felt like a blurry dream, one of Lincon's illusions really as I had to pry myself from the spell I'd been under and return to my people. But it didn't make it any easier as my gaze continued to linger on him and as if knowing I was about to depart he finally looked back. His gray eyes were sad as if he wanted to express something else, but his lips remained as tightly shut as his mind.

I jumped from the branch and glided low into the sky, making sure not to risk myself being spotted. I quickly found my way back to the camp. We hadn't gone far, simply rounding in circles precariously. When I landed, Iris was waiting outside the tent and Fire offered me a warning growl. I'd been out all night.

"You need to keep your affairs discrete. We're about to go into war," Iris reminded me.

"My affairs?" I hushed. "He's my *familiar.*" I had to remind him. Chase and I had kept our relationship and infused scent secret when we'd addressed Tracey's Council, who Iris was once bound to. Since and after the last war, he'd learned the truth about our relationship, under the pretense that Chase had been killed.

"Even so, your leaving doesn't go unnoticed," Iris pressured as he tentatively regarded the members of the pack. A few were looking my way unenthusiastically. Chris stepped in their path as if blocking their mismatched gazes.

"Why is it taking you so long to pack up?" Titan demanded from one of the older men. He sneered at her but surprisingly didn't reprimand her as she had hands on hips, ordering him around. I still wasn't entirely sure where she measured on their hierarchy, but her pushy attitude spoke volumes.

She exchanged a brief and sullen expression, which only tightened its grip around my heart. I shouldn't depend on a pair of seventeen-year-olds to take away their scrutinizing gazes. I owed it to them to be here, and yet my body betrayed me every time.

"Thank you," I acknowledged Iris and Fire, aware that they were doing their best in the role I'd ordained them, my personal interests and desires aside.

# CHAPTER 16

T HE AUDACITY OF Fier to take up refuge in plain sight wasn't at all a surprise. It was as stupid as it was clever. Balzar, Iris, Fire, Lincon, and I stood looking out at the city beyond from a distance. Chase kept his distance on Balzar's right, still close enough to listen but far enough to bridge the obvious gap.

Washington DC looked worse than any other city I'd come across. Its feral remains and potent fumes of war a little more than a hundred years ago lingered. It was a stark graveyard and yet somewhere amongst it, Fier thrived like the cockroach he was. Not even sabers scampered about, evidently offended by the impudent smell the city reeked of.

Balzar's gaze frantically scattered over the elevated view we had, and I wasn't sure if it was because of terrorizing memories from his past and his death as a human or if his gift was working to locate Fier precisely.

It was a dreary cold day, insufferable some might consider. But to me, every aspect of this spiked my heart rate, beating rapidly with excitement for what was to come. Bloodshed. Vengeance. A time well worth waiting for.

After our last grueling day of running, we'd had a few hours to rest, but only a few were able to acquire any form of sleep as we so edgily anticipated the day to come. We'd had to kidnap two patrol scouts who'd stumbled upon our existence. Between Lincon's and Chase's gifts, they were able to compromise their memory and recollection of ever seeing us or our whereabouts. As tempting as it was to kill them, doing so would've alarmed Fier that something was amiss.

"Ahhh, how this brings back so many memories," Lincon reminisced as if he were bathing in the non-existent sun.

"You fought in the last war between humans and vampires?" Iris couldn't help himself from asking, and I wished he'd remained silent. It would only open up another bizarre story from Lincon's past.

"Oh, goodness no! How filthy! That was all the Vampire Council's doing, like I'd step anywhere close to that. *Before* the Council moved in on Washington, I had quite the time in the nineteen hundreds and created quite the scandal. So many good times. So many presidents to play illusions on." He chuckled and dipped toward me discreetly. "It always brought me so much pleasure tormenting what was considered the most powerful human in this country. It was so inspiring for my work as an artist and how it changed their decisions thereafter." There was a bright, mischievous gleam to his eyes. And by 'artist' he meant the rows of bodies he'd creatively left behind.

"Lincon, you're rambling," I riposted. Down the line past Balzar, Chase was watching us carefully. The moment my gaze connected with his, he leaned back out of sight. "Can you sense him, Balzar?"

Balzar grunted his acknowledgment. I knew that distracted look all too well as he quickly re-evaluated our plan. "As we discussed earlier, Fier's divided his Council into three locations that are used simultaneously. So, I wasn't sure which one he'd be housing in by the time we got here."

"What are the locations?" Chase asked direly.

Balzar pointed in the direction of the shabbiest and most bombed part of the city. "The National Portrait Gallery." That particular area was in shambles and mostly rubble now where it might've once been beautiful. His leather-clad hand skirted left. "The National Cathedral." Then right. "The Ronald Reagan Washington Airport."

"And let me guess, Fier's in the Gallery," Chase said.

"He seems like the type, doesn't he?" Balzar rhetorically asked.

"I just know his tastes too well," Chase replied solemnly. They'd known one another far longer than most of us would ever understand.

Fier had been introduced to him in a bizarre stepfather-like figure, and Chase had worked under him for years until fate brought me onto his path. The heavy weight of betrayal loomed over him.

"Then nothing in the plan changes," I added.

"No, we move on as planned," Balzar agreed.

"It irritates me, knowing how quickly I could wipe out this city if I hadn't done so a week ago already in Venice," I murmured irritably.

"But where would the fun in that be?" Balzar said with a coy twisted smile. "And besides, selfishly I don't know if I want this place wiped off the face of the earth like it never existed. I lost a lot of friends that day. They fought for this space."

"And now you're on the other side," Iris reminded him. The story was probably very familiar to his own.

"And now I'm here again, over one hundred years later still fighting for my rights and vengeance for my brothers," Balzar condemned. "Prepare your teams, it's time we head out." He snaked a brief glance over to Chase who continued to blazingly stare into the distance, not giving any titbits away as to what he might be thinking.

I walked off, returning to my platoon of soldiers. "Iris, I want you to lead with Tori." The wolves had been given the go-ahead for the cathedral, the lesser of the piled vampires. Chase and his coven would take on the airport which housed the most. "Lincon and Fire, you stay with me. Kasey as well." I would be going in with Balzar as my backup. In my favor, it was agreed upon that Balzar and I would lead the remains of his coven toward the gallery. There our team would silently take out the guards while I focused on only one particular vampire. Fier was *mine*.

"And, Iris," I caught his attention, "make sure to keep an eye on Titan and Chris." I could sense his comical indifference suggesting that I was doting.

"Esmore," Chase called out to me from behind. I stopped in my tracks, uncertain if I'd heard correctly or if my mind had begun to play tricks on me. I very slowly turned to face him.

"Remember what I told you about Fier's gifts," he preluded which only irritated me more. I had, for whatever reason, hoped he'd come to say…something…anything but telling me how to fight.

"I know how to fight, Chase," I said, trying to control my tone in front of my pack. They watched on incredulously, and I harshly stared them down. Iris strode over to start throwing orders on Tori's behalf as he filled him in on the details.

Chase grabbed my forearm, snapping my attention back to him, the touch scolding and evoking all the same. "I'm serious, Esmore. Don't take him lightly. If he feels threatened, he will rely on the other gifts he can't control," Chase warned.

"I've never taken Fier lightly," I edged, but my tone was shallow as I focused on the burning sensation of his hand on my skin. Its cold touch somehow created an irrational warmth and shudder through me. Up so close, I could see those black tentacle-like veins engrossing his mouth and toward his protruding fangs.

Realizing that I was studying him instead of his warning, he released my arm as if I'd poisoned him. "I'm sorry. I shouldn't have touched you."

My mouth went agape, but I quickly snapped it shut. *Touch me was all I wanted him to do. That was our right as familiars.* I couldn't push away the hurt that scorned my expression.

"Was that all, Chase?" I said determined, though it dared quiver. "Just focus on your task and don't die," I said, burning myself with the acidic tone I'd used. I stalked toward my group only briefing a glance over my shoulder as he tucked his hands into the front pockets of his pants, his leather jacket flapping in the soft breeze behind him as he advanced on his coven, who all equally measured me with heavy looks.

"We'll move forward with our first plan. Stay within your formations and protect one another. We still have a long way to go even past this," I declared to my werewolves. Their varying colored eyes looked back at me with a loyal fierceness. They'd set aside their bags, hidden in the shrubbery for when we'd return afterward. "And parade on their greatest fears and offer each of them a lethal bite."

The smiles they returned were feral, the death now tainting their gaze. They were focused. We were ready. And it was time to descend.

"I didn't expect the bridge to be broken." Balzar grumbled his complaint as we neared the edge of the riverbank. And to avoid any delay we'd have to go straight through. The others had set out, and we didn't want any time variance when we all attacked.

"Great, we're going to smell like swamp rats by the time we come out," Kasey grumbled. They all looked disgusted as they paddled through the water. With little remorse, I collected Fire carefully in my arms and hovered above the water as I flew us across.

"That's cheating," Balzar groaned as he appeared first on the other side. The rest of his vampires snarled at the stench of the river as they hastily swam through. Balzar hastened to hide behind mounted rubble. One by one his members followed on their own outpost as we surveyed our surroundings. The space was too open. Despite the amount of debris around us, we could still be easily spotted. Beside where we hid there were shambles of rock and skeletons. Black goop stained the ground that must've once been vampires, and the skeletons' obvious remains of the humans Balzar once fought alongside.

"This used to be the Lincoln Memorial, maybe one day your wolves will craft a giant statue of you in the same way," Balzar lightly joked as he looked back and forth. His humor was lost on me. "So if we skirt along this path and twist left we'll find him. Just follow my lead, I'll take us directly to him."

He gestured a few hand signals for his vampires to spread out and they did on either side of us like great unfurling wings. Altogether there were only thirty-two of them. These were the remains of Cesar's coven, the rest had fallen to their knees in death those many years ago. I wondered how he might've felt that after all these years one of his sons had taken up his mission, but another had so evidently turned against him, despising him all this time.

We cautiously jogged beside what looked to be the remains of a long rectangular pond. The water had evaporated and the cracks and wreckage of what once might've been beautiful, made room for the weeds as cockroaches invaded the filth. Surprisingly, a few trees barely remained standing alongside what might've once been a park.

Something caught Balzar's attention as he paused momentarily. On guard, I traced his gaze down rows of streets and landed on what once might've been a mighty house. It looked like it'd been torn apart by some sizeable beast, scattered pieces of it imploded on the crevassed ground that was once lawn. Nothing grew here, the grass a stark bleakness like the cloudy day it was today. This city carried, oh so silently, the unfriendly ghosts of all those who were killed and the final efforts of the humans to take back their land. Well, until recent years anyway.

"Is that where you died?" I asked, cautiously locating the others to ensure our position wouldn't be compromised.

"That's where I first met Yolo," he said considerately. I recalled that Yolo was infiltrating as a vampire soldier so Cesar could assess if Oppollo himself was making an appearance. And when he was leaving, he'd stumbled across Balzar's broken body and returned him to Cesar, asking if he could save the young soldier and turn him into one of their brethren. "And yes. This is where I died as a human. C'mon, we don't want to dawdle."

Fire's ears were pinned back as she listened out for newcomers. The city felt inexcusably vacant considering it held a Vampire Council so close by. But perhaps that was the appeal Fier had been going for. He'd done much the same with his Council when it was positioned in San Francisco.

I was shocked to see a mighty foundation still standing over five hundred feet tall. I brushed over the filth-ridden sign. *Washington Monument.* I wondered if its spectacular size represented anything in particular, or if it once held a greater function. I couldn't help but gawk at some of the human-made landmarks, in awe of what their practicality or representation might've been about. It was completely different from the world I knew and an ancient knowledge that wouldn't rise ever again.

The ruins around us were a casting grace that we hid behind as we made it through what were once gardens and prestigious buildings. When we approached closer to the center, closer to Fier, the ruining decay began to lessen. Fire's hackles rose on her back as she darted her gaze from one building to the next, peering into the shattered windows and flickering curtains.

Balzar gestured to himself, Fire, and then me indicating we were to follow his direct lead toward the thickly pillared building at the end of the street. He gestured a few more signals, directing four members of the group to separate and deal with the few members who were closing around us. I sent a small prayer out to the others that they made it out safely as I delicately slipped on my golden claws. Because here, no one would escape our net.

# CHAPTER 17

CONSCIOUS OF THE onlookers, Balzar waited a grueling minute until one of them gave him the thumbs up from the windows above. It seemed ill-fitted that they'd overcome them so quietly, but I supposed that was the element of surprise. But even then, had Fier simply become sloppy or had his Council taken such a hit in numbers from the last war that there weren't so many to guard his fort? After all, he might've been teleported out alongside Tythian, but that did nothing for his remaining members who were abandoned on the battlefield.

Balzar led Fire and me along the crumbling buildings, avoiding walking straight up to the front with beautiful pillars. He guided us across the street and pressed himself stealthily against the side of the enormous building. The building was lined with countless windows with iron bars preventing us from sneakily breaking in. Most of the glass had been smashed in by evasive weather over the years. Despite the eerie silence amongst the city, we could hear a low pounding of rhythm and scratchy beats coming from inside.

Chase had once told me that Fier enjoyed creating a 'clubbing' atmosphere for his members where they partied as if it were their 'old days' within the technology era. Evidently, he'd somehow been able to conduct the use of power here once again. The disjointed music might've acted like a sure distraction from our intrusion and maybe, if luck were on our side, they'd be inundated with whatever concoctions they often thrived on. If memory served correctly, Fier had a particular taste for the vile substance, vodka.

"Psst." Balzar flagged me down to the corner of the building. He pointed up. On the second level, one of the windows with the metal prison-like bars folded outward. I looked at him skeptically, he seemed to know exactly where he was going, and then the dread of this being a trap dawned on me.

"How do you know where directly to go?" I asked him in a low growl. Fire didn't miss a beat as her hackles rose and she began growling alongside my suspicion.

"Woah, ease up." Balzar raised his metal knuckled leather gloves in a defensive position. "I'm not your enemy, Esmore."

I prodded my instincts. I *did* trust Balzar. For now. And we all had our secrets, but there *was* something he was hiding. It certainly wasn't now when he put his life on the line. I'd deal with that later. I webbed the edges of my golden claws on top of Fire's furred head to let her know it was okay.

"And I'm assuming you want a boost?" I taunted him. He dropped his hands and gave me a deadpan expression. No, I looked like the last person he wanted help from. But I provokingly smiled and curled my fingers together, enjoying the cool touch of my golden claws as they curved. Balzar gestured to his group to hold a few minutes before following in after us. Begrudgingly, he slipped his foot into my interwoven hands and tensed for balance as I flung him into the air. He latched onto the railing and barged into the thin-looking window.

I jerked a small smile. If he really wanted to, he could've made a small run up and jumped for it. Maybe he was already embarrassed about his sloshy rubbery shoes that he'd taken off because of the sound it might've caused. Oh, how pride was such a wonderful thing for vampires, even during a time of such peril. I collected Fire delicately cautious of my bladed nails and hovered to the second level. I dropped Fire in first and then awkwardly curled my wings in behind me, slipping through.

I fell into an overly large and dark room that was stuffed with collections of ornaments, paintings, and twisted objects. The room felt forgotten, collecting dust like the century it came from. My gaze was drawn to a magnificent painting that was barely recognizable through the thick layer of dust. It diluted what its once rich colors were. It was a painting of a battle in the clouds, perhaps of the old gods they prayed to. White-winged beings challenged those of the darkness. I couldn't help but notice the irony in such circumstances as I reflected on my own black wings. When the Descendant had first come forth, my wings had been a beautiful white. And now both had transitioned into a stark black. And as I stared at this painting, drawn in by its powerful notion, I wondered if that reflected much in my decisions and the side that I now stood with. The hunters were far from perfect, but as my birth origin, had I been born in the righteous reign and spiraled into the unforgiving madness of evil.

Fire studied the painting and then me, ominously understanding my draw to it. What was more striking was to consider that humans had time to leisurely paint, let alone stroll through and admire such things. And now I, something they considered to be a haunting evil with graphically dark wings, stalked through its remains.

Leaving the painting behind, just like its forgotten time, I followed Balzar, narrowly dodging the overfilled space and followed the heaving music of untimely beats. Balzar was at the edge of the room, flicking his gaze back and forth as he assessed the narrow hallways. The obstacle with such a building was the open space which made an assassination difficult.

When I walked past a row of paintings, my eyes were blasted with light streaming in from the next room. The music poured in louder, and I stuck to the edges of the door, remaining in the shadows. Light from electricity always seemed like a peculiar treat to come across, and it also eliminated more places to hide amongst the shadows.

To our benefit, the elaborate partying that was happening downstairs acted as a distraction from anyone picking up our presence and scents until it was too late. Balzar's team began to silently spill into the room behind us. He flicked his head to the right, suggesting I follow him, and circled his finger, instructing the others to go left.

Fire and I followed him, shouldering against the wall as tightly as we could. I scanned my mind around ensuring we weren't about to stumble into any unwanted members. We had the element of surprise, and we had to keep it that way.

The center of the room was hung with beautiful rich green plants, and I didn't dare peep over the railing to where the party was, though I curiously wanted to see what it looked like. Flashes of bright colors streamed across the room excessively, pooling into the other darker rooms. I looked back at Balzar's team of vampires who skirted around the edges much like we did. They would begin to spread out, ensuring they had fully encircled the majority of the members before pouncing. Had they been spread out through the building, the mission might've not seemed so straightforward though I could sense a few members clustered elsewhere in private rooms.

Much to my surprise and grand ideal, Fier wasn't amongst them. He was by himself in a room, perfect for the taking. We skirted into another room, dodging the mainstream light, the sign above the door stating American President's room. I'd recalled studying that these were once the leaders of this continent and now they were nothing but a painting on a wall unless they still managed such hierarchy amongst the remains of the human government. There was still so much mystery around their remaining existence which made it speculatively dangerous—especially considering their recent stunt with the werewolves, after hiding in silence for so long, no doubt waiting for their werewolf plague to spread and grow in numbers.

The paintings in here were in even worse condition than the last room. Grave slashes from what looked like someone's outbursts marred many of the men's faces. It reeked of human blood and that fumigating liqueur Fier loved so much. It didn't take me long to find the remains of shattered bottles that had been thrown against the wall with the debris never to be cleaned. Comparing to Fier's last Council, this one seemed to be a messy upheaval, and I wondered if that had anything to say about his current state and control over his Council.

I sensed two vampires approaching the room, and Balzar and I pressed ourselves further into the shadows. A staggering couple who were talking dirtily to one another slipped into the darkness of the room for privacy. The moment they stepped out of sight from their party Balzar punctured through the man's back, cleanly breaking through bone to rip his heart out. I had my hands around the woman's neck, snapping it before she could scream, and reefed out her heart just as efficiently. I stepped back, ensuring not to get any of her disgusting remains on my clothes.

Fluidly, we moved onto the next room, Fire a shadow at my back. I could sense Fier, oh so close, my fingers flexing back and forth as I counted to ten. I had to do this fast and meticulously. This day had finally come, and I couldn't so easily lose to my vampire self who bounced in joy at being unleashed.

Two vampires guarded his door. Unlike most of the other rooms that were openly available to step into, this one was heavily enclosed by wooden doors for his privacy. I grimaced. It seemed like the only way to get in, and it'd offer him those few seconds to coherently understand what was happening.

I grabbed Balzar's attention and tapped my temple. He might've grumbled his complaint had we not been sworn to silence. His mind reluctantly opened up to me, and I hesitantly spoke to him telepathically. I still didn't enjoy speaking to others in such an intimate way.

*You deal with the guards, and I'll take out the door and take on Fier.* He seemed to disagree but caved in reasonably quickly. We didn't have a better option.

*What about her?* he asked, gesturing to Fire.

*Don't worry about her, she'll know what to do,* as Fire always did. I very rarely had to give her any kind of direct command because as if an extension of one another, we fluently knew how to work optimally, simultaneously sharing an idea for strategy. And that very much was because of my venom coursing through her veins.

He curtly nodded and clenched his leathery gloves, inundated with sharp silver knuckles. Now was the time, after all Fier had done to my familiar, he would pay with his life. Balzar and I exploded into action, snaking around one another in perfect unison.

The guards were slightly more alert than the rest who were on an elevated high during their rave. Balzar imploded into the first vampire knocking him back so strikingly that he knocked into the second guard, completely freeing the door. Fire chased after them, ripping at one of their necks and shoulders as he screamed, and Balzar dealt with the second.

I twisted the doorknobs and barged the doors open. My hand slid to my daggers, and I threw three across the room. I was immediately thrown back by a gust of wind, and slammed into the wall, my wings painfully crunching behind me. The door slammed in anguish, and my daggers *thunked* heavily into the wall beside me.

In the dark room, only lit by a few side lamps, Fier had his back to me, his red velvet shirt comparatively bright to the gray and dreary room. His hands were folded behind his back as he silently hummed to himself.

"Did you really think I wouldn't sense your presence, little golden bird?" he asked in bemusement. I dropped to the floor, and loud bangs began to sound outside where Balzar and Fire were trying to get in.

A loud explosion boomed from the other side of the building, and wild screams and snarls erupted into chaos. I unsheathed the two blades at my tailbone guarding them in front of my face as I dropped to the floor. He slowly turned, those dazzling blue eyes striking me with a fierce hatred. In the tradition of Fier's flair, before him was a beautiful throne, so out of place in the large obsidian room with a wooden table and chair on the left. Large bay windows behind his throne had been lacquered with a dark screen so sunlight couldn't possibly slip through. Two couches and a wooden coffee table were on the right with a fireplace and a red carpet leading from the door to his throne. It was empty compared to his old Council, a blemish of thought in contrast.

"And after all these years, I thought you'd forgotten me," I provoked him while simultaneously trying to calm my own wild storm.

"Forget you?!" He snarled, barring those decently sized fangs at me. "You ruined me! Do you have any idea what they call me now amongst my own Council?! The 'betrayer' and 'coward' because Tythian teleported me out from that last fight, leaving my men to fight to their deaths. I was publicly humiliated because of your intervention, you stupid bitch!" He violently shook. "And you thought you'd so easily waltz into my Council and stab me in the heart." He spat at the ground before my feet. Most likely, Tythian had purposefully taken him because he knew it would jeopardize Fier's reputation and reign because they both ultimately wanted utter dominion over the Vampire Council. And yet it plagued Fier to blame only me because he wasn't in a position to vex Tythian for one-upping him. "As if I haven't been waiting for this day all these many years."

"You could've made yourself known," I retorted. "Maybe your Council members weren't all that wrong about you running with your tail between your legs." I flexed my fingers over my two blades, running my tongue along my fangs, mock smiling him to throw his temperament off.

"You bitch!" he violently spat, slicing his hand through the air and coursing a sharp blade of wind toward me. I twisted out of its way, tempted by the invite to get closer when he left an opening, but I wasn't a fool. Those slicing winds were a quick reflex. Having insight that he considered me as the villain who destroyed his world brought me great pleasure because now he knew how I had felt all these years when he'd so filthily fiddled with Chase's mind. And now, now…look at what had become of him.

Fier was on the offense without hesitation. For what little value I might've once served him to keep around, it no longer held. We were only out for blood. The thunderous bangs outside had stopped and I assumed that the others were caught up in their own fight. Fier continued striking gusts of wind pretentiously toward me as I dodged each and every one purposefully agitating him.

He was acting like a desperate madman. For all he knew, I might've been toying with him, ready to use my gift to glitter him into ashes. If only it were so easy, but besides that and before I held my knife to his throat, I had one question to ask him.

I slithered around his winds easily. When he went low, I'd hover in the air. When he'd swoosh to the side, I'd roll opposingly. I tauntingly and easily made my way toward him. "Losing your touch would you say?" I wickedly toyed. I could see the maddening craze in his eyes so easily falling into my trap.

My gift was jittering with excitement alongside my vampire but with no way to assertively strike at him. It was a mere bystander as I predatorily skirted toward my prey. My huntress part was the only thing keeping my vampire in check, making sure that we as a whole didn't so easily succumb to the anger and revenge I'd thirsted for years.

Two separate winds skirted on either side of me and boomeranged back. I flipped up and over them, training my keen eye on Fier as he continued to rile himself. "You stupid bitch! You took everything!"

Suspended in the air, I sent a hearty sense of shock into his mind, which was blocked. Usually, it would stun my opponents but whatever mental gift Fier had made him resistant against mine.

I harpooned toward him when he was distracted by his last striking wind. Now he was on the defense. He quickly managed to unsheathe the sword and small knife that resided by his throne. Blades for blades were matched, growling and snarling at one another as I descended on him and let out the wrath of the Descendant on him. My power exuded from me as the floor beneath where he stood began to crack. I thrust my wings toward him, jutting them to restrain him so he couldn't move anywhere but beneath me—in his rightful place.

My gift secreted little effort to help gain the upper hand, extending past my bladed fingers and toward him. Strips of flesh began to peel as he hissed and pulled back. He took the bluff, and I took the opening. He blocked his chest, but that wasn't what I'd been aiming for. I flipped around the back of my handle, crunching it into his once-perfect nose. I kicked his stomach so hard he tumbled across the room and hinged over his throne.

I pounced on him, unable to move away from his knife that carved up the side of my ribs as he tried to defend himself. I pinned his other hand that held the sword awkwardly over the handle of the chair, and slamming my weight into it, snapped it into a cruel crunch. He grunted in displeasure as his grip went limp and the sword clattered to the floor. I pierced my other blade through his wrist, pinning it to the seat of his chair. Black blood oozed, and I took righteous pride as I honed in on my prey, trying my hardest to remain deadly calm so I could ask my question. My wings hunched over him, all of me, my essence, looming over him like a dark hound of death.

I poked the tip of the blade slowly into his chest letting my jittery gift peel parts of his flesh. I might've been lacking in power to feed my gift, but he would be plagued with its wild calamity upon physical contact. I stared into his daring blue eyes that so very much wanted to hurt me as he thrust back and forth with little concern for his inundated hands. I would only have a few seconds with him like this. I couldn't toy for too long. "Now you're going to be a good boy and reverse what you did to Chase."

Black blood stuffed his nose, and he had the audacity to laugh in my face. "Reverse it?" he squeaked in outrageous enjoyment and threw back his head in a condescending laugh as if he had the upper hand despite his situation. "Even if I knew how to I wouldn't!"

Rage bubbled up and through me as he so callously laughed at my familiar's undoing. "He was supposed to be like a son to you!" I gritted, trying to count calmly to ten, but no matter how many numbers swirled in my mind, none were countering the simmering hatred I felt toward this hideous vampire. My blade was delicately edging in deeper as I studied his eyes, every single expression that flashed across his face as the skin peeled tormentingly from it. Red raw muscle showed from beneath as he finally snapped.

"And he betrayed me for a vile wench like you!" He cursed, and his eyes flashed a mossy blue. My body stung ferociously as my stomach felt like it was swelling from within. Unfamiliar with whatever gift he was using I was quick to slam my blade down. A gust of wind boomeranged from the side and swiped me off him before I made that satisfying crunch through his chest cavity. I rolled uncontrollably to the side as I clung to my weapons. I felt like I was growing larger as my body swelled.

I stumbled to stand, narrowing my gaze on him as I dared not look down even for a moment. His broken wrist had already healed, and he reefed my other blade out, throwing it toward me as if daring me to attempt to take it once again. His face was becoming swollen and melted on one side.

"This might hurt me, but it'll hurt you even more." He cursed as water dribbled from his mouth. He didn't so much as choke. I, however, had a heart and working anatomy. Liquid prickled my lungs, and I fought against the wheezing that aspired. Within seconds I was drowning from within. I grasped onto my gift, willing it to implode toward him. Very meekly and slowly and with the backing of my vampire self that didn't want to die, it struck out at him.

It evaporated his leg, exhausted from taking even that much. He screamed and fell toward his throne to balance. Water bubbled from my mouth as I choked. Another thunderous bang shook the building as a perfume of smoke mixed with the unnatural liquid drowning me. I could taste its vileness. Fier picked up his sword as his body appeared to sag limply. It might've been affecting him, but it would certainly kill me sooner.

A bright light broke through as the wooden door splintered into pieces. Fire burst through first, snapping and snarling as Balzar swept in behind her throwing a dagger at Fier. Fier deflected it, his movement sluggish from the toll of his gift. He still had fight in him, but not in the regal way he did ten years ago.

Four vampires barged in through a side door that hadn't been apparent before. Two of which were suited with bombs strapped to them. Despite his face being half swollen and drooping, Fier somehow managed to produce a smirk. "Goodbye, Esmore."

One of the vampires without a bomb dove for Fier. I took a lethargic step forward, and Fire gave chase, snapping at their heels as they jumped and smashed through the black hazed window. She followed after them, and I tried to call her back, but more water filled my lungs, buckling me to my knees. I felt the moment Fier vanished from range because the acquired liquid vanished as if it were never there. I took my first shaky breath. The bombers pulled the string on their garments, and I scurried to bolt for the door, following Balzar. The flash was bright, fast, and hard, much reminding me of the time in San Francisco when I first thought it was my end. Fier had used bombs even back then. And now I was certain this time it might ensnare us.

The blast peeled the back of my flesh as my vampire screeched out in pain from the ferocity of its heat. All I could think about was Chase. And how I'd miserably gone wrong not having detected those other vampires or ending Fier's life when I had the chance instead of toying with him. I'd never learned my lesson.

I hastened flight, sweeping in after Balzar to make sure he got out as well, or at the very least my body would act as a shield for his. When I scooped him up not so gracefully, we were flung to the side as a familiar figure barged me away from another blasting that went off beneath us. *Chase.* The building exploded with numerous bombs setting off, and I was only quickly able to briefly glance at the massacre below. The dance floor was inundated with black mounded piles of goop. The floor cracked and exploded in one heap as another bomb went off.

*UP!* Chase interjected into my mind as glass showered down on us from the ceiling. Without thought, I followed his direction as he scooped the weight of Balzar easily out of my hands. That's when I realized the only way he was with me right now…was because of the great black wings, rocketing him into the dancing pieces of glass that rained down on us.

Fire exploded around me as I ascended, equally measuring them in speed as we found a way through already groaning and broken beams. We burst into the sky. The building was a flash of heat beneath us as those mere seconds felt like the pinnacle of a lifetime. The building crumbled beneath us and Balzar stared wide-eyed at what might've been his resting place had we not intervened.

Chase flapped his magnificent black wings that outsized my own with ease. *And he was coherent.* I almost considered I wasn't seeing right since I had my left eye closed and bleeding from one of the showering pieces of glass. My body stung with hundreds of small cuts and some not so small. Having no time to gawk at him, I followed the link that tied Fire and I together. She was surrounded by five vampires, who intervened to allow Fier to make his grand escape. *Forever the coward.*

They might've not respected him, but by protocol they still did as he said. I swooped into the circle, picking one up by the head, and flung him across the city. I circled back to find Chase standing by Fire, slaughtering the four who remained as if they were no more than a speck of dust in his eye. I'd forgotten how daringly beautiful and haunting he was when he fought. And the presence of those wings made him look like something out of that painting I'd peered into…a god.

Black muck slickened his bare chest as he growled, unsatisfied by their weak inability to put up half a fight. His wounds from the raining glass began to stitch together easily. Fire bit into the neck of the last remaining vampire and jerked their neck, snapping it. Even when they did wake up from it, they wouldn't live long after that bite.

*Are you all right?* Chase asked me, his stormy gray eyes scanning over every inch of me.

I somehow managed a slow nod, still in disbelief as I took in the wonder of him and the giant wings that were his—and the Descendant all in the same. The very same power that had been his undoing for decades. *How?*

He was reluctant to reply, and I could sense he was ready to pull away after confirming I was okay. *We'd already dealt with the vampires who infested the airport.* And by the looks of his slicken body, by *we* he humbly meant he'd slaughtered through them making a new personal record. And he also knew that wasn't the question I was lingering on. How was he now able to control the Descendant?

It felt like time had paused, giving us this moment to finally be one and communicate through our link, even though physically we were still worlds apart.

*I don't know. There's a sudden calm and clarity before the end of my time, I suppose. Or maybe the disease is more prominent than letting any other power overtake me.* He wasn't speaking to me directly, it was a wisp of a thought he'd had, but I could hear it and understand the peril it put him under.

Balzar ran over, his wounds having healed. He, too, was marred with black blood and goop.

"Fier's gone," Balzar grumbled furiously.

"What do you mean? He only had a few minutes in front of us, surely you can track him."

"I can sense he's with Tythian now," Balzar gritted. "It means Tythian was about." Saving his ass once again. A shudder ran down my spine as I considered its implications.

I spun on Chase. *Do you think this means they know about you? What if he saw you?* And then he told Fier who would act on it.

*I couldn't sense Tythian at any point which means he wasn't in my reach. But only time will tell,* he said as an afterthought. And then as if suddenly realizing we'd slipped into our old ways so fluently, he closed himself off to me again, that great wall severing our link once more.

"Don't you dare!" I growled, angrily stepping toward him, furious after feeling its bliss to now have it taken away from me.

"It's dangerous for us to be connected, just leave it!" he snarled back just as harshly. I was wounded, staggered into a halt. *What did he mean dangerous?* "I need to check on my coven," he excused and took off into the sky. And I was left standing there baffled in a deserted city, watching him leave me behind once again.

# CHAPTER 18

THE MAJORITY OF Balzar's coven made it out before the bombings and more impressively, only a few were lost in the fight. The element of surprise really had been to our advantage which offered the bigger question as to why Fier didn't properly warn his Council until it was too late. Either he himself hadn't felt us until we were at his door, or he simply cared less for what happened to his Council. They did, after all, scrutinize him, so maybe he lacked empathy, even if they gave him numbers. He'd once been so ambitious in wanting to take over Oppollo's place, but now…he was nothing but a spoilt child on a throne.

Fire and I ran to the cathedral, coming across two vampires who were evidently confused amongst the disarray. I punctured one in the heart and beheaded the other. Smoke billowed from the area of the cathedral, and I ran faster keeping my senses attached to Titan who was still in her wolf form. I couldn't communicate with her, but as long as I felt her, that meant she was okay.

When Fire and I rounded a corner, what I imagined was once the cathedral was up in flames. In front, werewolves and those who still wore their human skin guarded the herd they'd accumulated. *Humans.* Those who had shifted back into their naked human form were directing them into a safe pile away from the blazing building.

Iris sidled up beside me with a clean slice of splattered black blood across his face. "This was where they kept their humans. Not too many vampires to squash and we only lost three." I quickly darted my gaze across the group of werewolves. *Titan. Chris. Tori. Claus. Kasey…* And there was Lincon laughing crazily with his hands outstretched at the fire before him. One of his arms was disgustingly growing back. Before I could even ask, Iris beat me to it. "There were a few bombs placed inside. We were able to get the majority of the humans out in time. For whatever reason, he purposefully remained too close and lost an arm. And now he seems thrilled about it."

I grimaced. Great, this just meant Lincon would be on a drunken high from his ample 'fun.' Fire was now with Titan and Chris and nuzzled into their necks endearingly. I watched on, sorely disappointed I wasn't capable of such empathetic exchanges.

Tori padded over, a deadly smirk on his face after a job well done. Sometimes, he still reminded me of that arrogant apprentice I first received, but I would give him this victory this once. He joined our circle, expecting to be included, which of course he was.

"Did you kill Fier?" Iris asked coolly, but it didn't hide the brazen dislike for the vampire.

"He escaped," I gritted out. "And then blasted the building to rubble and had Tythian teleport him out."

"Tythian?" Iris perked with interest. His arms were crossed in that burley way he often did. By way of my evidently displeased expression, he grimaced. We wouldn't be fighting them again today. And now we lost the edge over Tythian. He'd know we're coming. And he was now holding onto the last loose end I tried to cut. I queried how Tythian might've known we were coming for Fier, but it never escaped my mind that someone within Fier's Council might've been able to reach out to him with some stolen hunter's gift.

"That's so like Fier. Always the weasel. When things get too much and his tail's on the line, he runs away," Iris said distastefully. "So, we'll be tracking them then?"

"I believe so." I hadn't yet had that conversation with the others, but there was no other expectation other than pursuing them.

Balzar and his coven made their way over and as time permitted it, so did Chase, ensuring he kept his distance from me. I bit the inside of my cheek trying to find some kind of outlet for my pent-up frustration during the fight and irritable mixed emotions toward him.

The vampires prowled the humans looking at them greedily. They shook in fear. Oh, yes, this was the all so scary covens the Councils had raised them to fear. That they'd be plucked one by one and eaten in a gruesome way, and the only way they were protected from that was becoming a food source for them in a contractual friendly agreement.

"I haven't had a fight like that in ages," Darcy glorified to Jerimiah who silently seemed to agree. Clarissa was scratching Spungee under the chin, rewarding him for a good job. But it wasn't. We hadn't succeeded in what we'd come here for.

"Where do we go now?" I asked Balzar. Smoke blanketed the city from the multiple bombings that had gone off. Although not of our doing, it was satisfying to know we at least left such a disastrous mark. I might not have assassinated Fier, but at least we ran him out of his home and wiped out most of this Council. Less could be said about all the victories he'd managed up until this point, trying to congress his power that was being so quickly stripped away.

"North. Montreal, Canada."

"That tracking gift seems like it has some perks," Tori wistfully said. And part of me wondered if he'd consider ever asking Balzar to try and track his father or if he even wanted to reach out to him. To even gauge whether he was still alive since our fight with the Guild those many years ago. No one had found the remains of his body, but it meant very little.

"What do we do with the humans?" Claus asked as he shifted and walked toward me. Chase glared as the werewolf approached me, full-frontal. It prickled my flesh with delight that he still couldn't hide his territorial claim on me. His words might be cutting, but his actions were still prominent.

"I don't particularly care what happens to Fier's pets," I hauntingly said, looking over at the shivering humans who were stark and cold now that they were no longer in the warmth of their insulated hub.

"Esmore, you know how this works," Iris said beratingly. "Humans are desperate to keep themselves alive, aligning with the Vampire Councils is so they can survive." Even so, I'd seen that some had come to enjoy it. And besides, he was an ex-Council member. Would I be reprimanded for punishing their decision? It was no different to the humans who housed with us and fed me under a similar agreement.

"Well, we can't carry around humans," Balzar interjected impatiently. He was ready to move on and so was I.

"We could turn them to join us?" Claus's new second, Ruppert suggested.

I turned on him, raining down all the fierceness my expression could command. He shrunk in size, the wolves around him inevitably falling away from him. We weren't in the business of turning just to build our numbers. They of all people knew how cruel this curse was. Both werewolf and vampire alike. And for him to even suggest they turn them into their own brethren impacted me far greater than I thought it would. We took in the refugees for those who had already been plagued not to only spread it further ourselves.

"Why don't we play roulette?" Lincon chimed excitedly. His wound was hideous like a tiny arm growing out of the disgustingly burnt flesh that was taking longer to heal because of its severity. It would be fully fleshed out within the hour. I'd learned this from all the other times he'd sacrificed a limb simply to get a thrill. "We can either eat them or turn them?"

"Or more like a treat for all our hard work," Clarissa agreed. I had no need for more werewolves, freshly turned would only slow us down, and I couldn't be sparring with my numbers so much that I could have a group return them to the safety of our castle. These humans were nothing but a burden, and if left to their own devices, they'd be killed within the week anyway.

"Lincon, play roulette as you please. As for the rest of you, have at it." At least that way they'd be refreshed after today's fight and Lincon might be appeased for the next few days with his desire to be constantly 'entertained.'

"Esmore," Titan said, panicked. "Maybe we should spare them."

Her sullen expression made me feel guilty which only evoked my vampire self in fury for even contemplating denying what I was in part. I wanted her to rule and command attention one day. And so, I would teach her an important lesson today, my personal sense of rejection put aside. "Titan, we're at war, this was just a primary fight where we succeeded at nothing but shifting a few pieces on the board. We cannot give these humans refuge as we walk to our next battle. And need I remind you, this is who we are." To make my point, I cruelly pointed to Tori, who seemed ashamed as I spoke the words. "This is what we need to survive and build strength. If you were to deny us that then we cannot fight alongside you. Look around you. How many of us are there?"

She seemed reluctant to circle her gaze around at the few grinning vampires who were excitedly waiting for the go-ahead. Balzar wasn't remorseful in the slightest, if anything, he was bored that I had to explain this to her. Chase, however, watched me very seriously. Oh yes, how much I'd changed. No longer did I torment myself about the humans which were our food, and I didn't need him to hold my hand to realize that notion.

"We could always pass New York and drop them off with your mother and their rebel group," Tori suggested.

"It'll only hold us back," Balzar and I said in unison, startled by one another with a sharp glance. I was becoming irritated by how Chase was simply watching it all unfold. His wings had since disappeared, and great big holes remained in his favored jacket. "And we don't have time to be held back." No. I needed to figure out how to help Chase *now*. The set back of even an hour was frivolous.

"So…" Lincon crooned with a creepy smile. And it was the only time the vampires around him agreed.

"Please," one of the humans shouted, trying to break past one of the werewolves who growled at her to step back within the circle. "Please, we'll do whatever you want. Please don't kill us," she said frightfully.

I willed away the small amount of remorse that might've crawled up. This was only a distraction from the means to my end. "I'll count to thirty, giving those of you who don't want to witness this time to meet us on the outer edge of the city."

Titan tried to grab my hand. "Esmore—"

"You will learn," I said cruelly. We might've been different species, and my verdict might've seemed harsh, but it had to be made and those who fought today would need their strength. There was a means to my madness, even when she considered me wickedly cruel for it.

"One. Two." I began to count as I stared into her beautiful brown doe-eyes. She fiercely spited me in that moment.

Chris shifted from wolf to human. "C'mon, Titan," he encouraged and tried to pull her away by the shoulder, but she continued to level me, unmoving.

"Five. Six." And what would she do to stop me?

Tori crept into my peripheral. "Titan, *please,*" he said gently. And I felt the wave of devastation pool out of her. A reminder that one of the boys she shared what she might've considered a 'special' bond with, was in fact the very same monster that I was. But instead, he hid in the shadows, hiding his nature away from her. I was not so coy.

"Nine. Ten." Other wolves reluctantly ran off. Claus and a few others remained ensuring none of them escaped and honored my order. Those who remained no doubt had an understanding and grasp on what I wagered here. We couldn't have stumbling weak vampires, even when they so lucratively hated their kind. The more strength we had meant the greater chance in numbers we would leave with.

Chris grabbed her hand, urging her to leave. With a fierce expression and tear in her eye, she came to her senses, looking away and allowing the two men to encourage her departure. Perhaps she hated herself even more for being so weak not being able to watch or intervene. She might've been naïve, but I approved of her willfulness to stand up for what she considered was right. After all, it's the very reason I'd kept her alive when I stood up against the vampire covens those many years ago. If only she knew how similar we were, despite evidently sitting on either side of the coin at times.

The humans began fighting back, trying to punch at the wolves to make an escape. The mature wolves were careful not to bite them, but did enough to scare them into submission despite their fighting spirit. One man even dashed toward the flames, far more tempted to burn alive than be drained by the vampires.

"Marshmallow," Lincon said, licking his lips as he stopped the man who was brazen enough to end his own life.

"Sixteen. Seventeen…Thirty." The flames glittered behind as the wind ruffled around me by the speed in which the vampires swamped them, and the werewolves stepped back, out of place in this ritual. I walked away, and my werewolves followed me. Chase watched me, and as I passed him, he commented quietly, "You should eat too." I was perfumed by his aroma, all too intoxicated by it as if we'd brushed shoulders for the first time.

"You're past the point where you can tell me what to do," I said harshly and leveled him with a stare. "Even if thoughtfully. You'll either let me in or you won't." And continued walking. I couldn't be so close to him, so close to be painfully splintering apart and hating myself. We possibly had so little time together, so why were we acting like this? Why were we so distant as if enemies? I continued walking with my shoulders peeled back and my platoon of loyal soldiers so that he wouldn't see the tear that pricked at my eye. In memory of Titan's angry expression and Chase's oh so distant one. I could sense Fire watching me but ignored her as I focused on the horrific screams that terrorized behind me. I'd never claimed to be a hero, and it was just more blood on my hands.

# CHAPTER 19

I ROLLED MY thumb over the lock of Chase's hair in my pocket contemptibly, considering all the things I'd said to him out of hurt and anger, and all the things I wanted to say instead. I couldn't so openly say them when he had me at an arm's distance. But I so quickly wanted to gush them, knowing that any moment could be our last. If Tythian or Fier picked up that Chase was with us, then he would've done something by now, but even then I couldn't override the panic that settled in.

As soon as the remaining vampires swaggered over, I refused to ask where Lincon was. He was probably using their corpses as dolls to play house in that forsaken city. Even Kasey returned.

"Maybe he'll actually be left behind for once," Balzar said wishfully.

"He'll always return. He's much like a dog and Esmore is the bone," Kasey said with an unempathetic smile.

"Has anyone told you how ugly those fangs of yours are?" Clarissa pointedly said to Kasey as she sauntered by. She pulled out a silk serviette, dabbed it on her tongue, and began cleaning away at Spungee's messy face. The werewolves shuddered at the twisted affection.

Kasey leaned against a tree crossing her arms. "Has anyone told you how hideous your pet is? And maybe your lack of soul too, you blood-sucking demon."

A small, twisted smile uncharacteristically crawled over Clarissa's face, and I wasn't sure if it was menacing or appreciative for the just as cruel comment. Especially considering Clarissa hardly ever showed expression. Perhaps after working with Balzar for some time she had begun to gain a sense of humor. I looked over at the brooding Balzar who was impatient for everyone to catch up. Maybe not.

"We need to be more alert from now on," he said, crossing paths with me.

"You don't have to tell me that," I said pointedly. We could be intercepted by Tythian and his Council at any point. "How many days until we make it to Montreal?"

He hummed to himself. "If we include a little bit of rest. Less than three days."

"Let's hope he doesn't coward away like Fier and upturn his Council somewhere else."

"He won't," Balzar said brazenly. "Tythian's very calculating, but he's not a coward. He'll meet us head-on." He seemed so passionately assertive that it even surprised him. Even after all these years to fixate and hate on Tythian for what he'd done, and his hand in killing Yolo, he still admired him. And he particularly hated himself for it. No one here knew Tythian better than Balzar.

"And besides," Chase said, sidling up beside me, closer than I might've liked. When he was close, it lured me in and gave me a head spin. And the way he looked at me insinuated he'd almost forgotten what he was about to say. "Tythian would've been waiting for this day. Since he hasn't acted sooner it's because he's been holding out to acquire his own resources. If we know at least anything about him, it's certainly that he's a patient man. And most importantly, he has something to protect."

"Whitney," I said, savoring the taste of his words. My bloodied golden fingers twitched, wanting so desperately to slowly edge closer to his and remember how the feel of his sturdy hand felt around mine. My body was a magnet to his.

"Well." Balzar clapped, startling us. We both jumped. "We're not going to get anywhere by staring into one another's eyes. We need to move out."

Chase cleared his throat. "Agreed." And sauntered back toward his coven. I licked over my fangs, drawn to him and inexplicably thinking filthy thoughts. He turned back for a moment, sensing the insinuation of my thoughts, even when he closed himself off so deeply to me.

Fire shifted beside me into her beautiful human form. "He's able to control the Descendant now," she said thoughtfully. And I certainly know she didn't shift just to make such an obvious statement.

"So it would appear," I replied, already sensing where she might be leading with this conversation. "I know, and I'm trying to keep it under wraps." I was trying not to let myself be carried away by Chase. But it was so hard when all I wanted to do was run away with him.

"He's still a very befitting warrior," she said easily. I turned to her, uncertain of what she was trying to express, but she just as quickly shifted back into wolf form. Was she trying to encourage our feelings for one another again? But this went beyond *feelings*. This was an unrelenting divine connection and love in its purest form. And I was trying my hardest to ignore it as I gifted myself one more glance, only to find that he was looking back at me. I tried lightly knocking on our link where he might open up to me, but the moment I did he turned away. Why was this so hard? And as if that weren't so crushing, my warriors were divided in sentiment about the humans. Some overlooked the action, understanding of the reasons why I'd done it. And I could feel the weight of disgust roll off the others, including Titan who was seemingly ignoring Tori and Chris as well for pulling her away.

Half a day into our run, Balzar stopped, suspiciously suggesting we should have a short rest. My werewolves were grateful for it, but we certainly could've gone for longer before stopping. I warily watched Balzar's movement, still conscious that he was hiding something from me as we all were from one another. The groups purposefully kept their divide, so when during midday he opted for rest, I was torn between following Balzar, or Titan who was following the scent of a nearby stream. Titan instructed Chris to stay and leave her alone for the time being.

"I'll be leaving for a few minutes," I said to Tori and Iris, and surprisingly Fire stayed behind as well. Tori seemed dejected, no doubt because of how he considered Titan now might be viewing him. Claus was busy watching over his men, and Chase had also disappeared.

Darcy pointed in the direction he'd taken off, insulting my ability to already sense where he'd gone. I turned my back on them, following Titan instead.

I might've considered Titan foolish for going out on her own had it not been for the numerous members who went to self-clean as well. Naturally, she'd ventured independently toward a small dip in the stream, washing the dirt and black smear of blood from her face. She didn't so much as look over her shoulder when I made my presence known. Instead, she took a seat beside the bank in a dry patch of dirt.

She'd been avoiding Chris and Tori ever since the incident with the humans and although she might've had her reasons, going into battle with any kind of resistance toward her teammates was a problem. I knew that firsthand.

"You can't ignore them forever," I urged her. "Or even me, for that matter."

She sighed, obviously wishing she could, and then her shoulders sagged, defeated. "I know. I'm not ignoring them on purpose I just needed time to myself to think."

"About?" I asked somewhat reluctant to hear the answer. I knew what this was about mostly. But besides the act itself, I was curious as to what about it truly triggered her.

"They both keep trying to protect me. I know there are hard decisions to be made. And I don't always agree with them. And I don't agree with killing all those humans. I was a human once too, even if I can't recall those memories so easily. It just seems cruel."

"Cruel is being born as the human. Having very little power is the cruelest sincerity of this world. And they protect you because that is their duty and also their wish. So let them do so."

I was biased to them shielding her. In a situation that I might not be there to protect her, those two were my only hope. Not that she necessarily needed protection, but her temperament would indefinitely put her in dire situations, and Tori and Chris were a lot more cool-headed.

"Do you miss him?" she asked earnestly, uncomfortably changing the subject. It was relentless thinking of Chase as already gone. For so many years Fire, Tori, and Iris tried to broach the topic of Chase. To see how I felt after his 'death.' But now was an entirely different situation. Now he was here, but seemingly no less a phantom. "He still watches you, you realize that, right? I know he's turning into a saber and all, but can't you spend the time that you have left together?"

Her words churned my heart at the reminder he might only be with me for a little while yet. That all my efforts had been in vain. I didn't want to break from my stoic image I'd raised her to believe me as. Giving in to her question truthfully would make me vulnerable. But I also knew that communication amongst the werewolves was paramount and although I couldn't speak with them freely as wolves, I could at least offer her the slightest of insights. To regain her trust, an eye for an eye. A sensitive intel for the same piece in return. "It's complicated, and truthfully, I wish it weren't." Was all I could manage. I couldn't even articulate the precise feeling, too scared to give it any words or life because if I was being honest with myself, I was still in denial.

"What's it like to be in love?" she asked me quietly. My mouth went agape. And I uncomfortably lowered myself to sit on the dirt-ridden ground with her. My wings perked up gracefully trying to prevent the dirt from touching them. Titan curled her knees under her chin insecurely.

"I, ah—" I cleared my throat, surprised by my inability to speak. How could I describe such a phenomenal feeling in a few words? I felt uncomfortable by the conversation because if she was querying it, it was relevant to her. And I wondered who she had set her eyes on. I wanted to know the answer to that, feeling protective of her. Because the reality was, love was beautiful as much as it was painful. And I didn't want her yet navigating through the obstacles of encountering it, especially when it could be so distracting on missions—like mine was now. "Love is many things and comes in many forms."

"You know which love I speak of. Like between you and Chase. Your familiars, how did you know?"

Again, I felt my mouth go dry, and my wings curled in slightly as if to give me warmth when my body felt a sudden chill, and it had nothing to do with the breeze. I humbly considered her question, connecting with a much younger and innocent side of myself. "Before I met Chase, I thought I was already in love with another," I admitted and held the acid in my tone for what I now felt for James and the hideous thing he'd done to me. I hated how powerless I'd been and even when I looked into our relationship, it was seemingly the same, it just hadn't yet become so twisted. *He* hadn't yet become so twisted under the pretense of being my better and trying to fix me from the monster I'd become.

"But when I met Chase, so different to me, a natural enemy, I found myself questioning everything I'd been raised on. My values remained, but my beliefs changed. He'd never asked me to be anything else and was happy to compromise with time, keeping a space between us to make me feel comfortable and come to terms with the over-sensational grasp and pull of wanting to be together.

"And when we finally became one, it just felt right. Like I'd been lost my whole life, no matter how mighty or powerful, I felt impossibly complete. That no matter how much I despised myself or actions, or even what I'd become, he was my savior. To always be standing at the end of the tunnel to tell me it was okay, or that I wasn't alone even during my darkest deeds. That I had a partner even on the monstrous path, who loved me unconditionally and would never leave me. But he would also pull me back when I stood so close to the edge or lacked clarity in my vision. He was the least scared to tell me differently. It was a constant wave of balance where we suited one another." Until of course we were too unstable for one another, when outside powers dictated and forced our hands apart. "It's the belief that you would do anything for one another and never be left alone in the dark. A life worth living for one another—if nothing else."

I suddenly became self-conscious from the vulnerability I showed and the tangent I'd been on. I could sense Titan looking at me in awe, which only made me further self-conscious.

"I hope one day, I too can experience that," she said solemnly. I wasn't sure which of the boys she'd set her heart on. Perhaps both, but I stretched my hand out to hers and clasped it, making sure not to let my gift jitter away her skin. My hands were still bloodied, and I felt dirty for touching her freshly cleaned hands. But I wanted her to know that I was here for her. I might not have been the most maternal of figures, but I'd certainly gone to great lengths to ensure she could be properly trained to best deal with this world.

"You are never alone. And at the very least, you have me."

A small bobble in her throat flexed, and she gave me a sad smile. "I'm sorry I couldn't understand back there with the humans, I just—"

"You don't need to apologize, Titan. A vampire's thirst is something you will never understand as I will never understand the tug of shifting into a wolf. But I made that decision for all of us and what I thought was best going forward, even at the expense of your disapproval. You too will make hard decisions one day. And if I've learned anything in my time, taking the weight of each one personally will only destroy you. You need to learn to detach as best as you can."

Her eyebrows narrowed in confusion. "I don't know if I'd ever be able to do that."

"It's a journey for every individual. Once you take a life, and then another, the numbers blur but the memory remains. Each and every battle physically and internally will follow you. And you'll find a vice to block them out. Either of your own accord or it'll suffocate you for its attention, leaving you paralyzed during the events when you need to be most decisive. And all of this can only be learned over time."

"Then maybe you and Chase should speak your minds instead of dancing around one another. Who knows how much time you have left? And you can tell in the way you two still look at each other with your backs turned that you still love one another." She curled her fingers around mine, holding me in place where I might've pulled my hand away.

"One other thing about love…it can be complicated," I added with an arched eyebrow.

"Or perhaps uncomfortably simple."

I wanted to argue with her and express that she didn't understand, that I'd tried to speak with him. But she was still a child who hadn't yet known love, and I was embarrassed to even have confided in her about such a subject. But perhaps she'd never understand that my distance was also for her and the werewolves. How ironic that she be the person to ask me to speak.

# CHAPTER 20

THE ROUTE WE were taking meant that we'd be passing through the New York district near the main Hunter Guild. Although Sabe was the new leader, it didn't mean our previous acquaintanceship would let us pass through with an army of vampires and werewolves, so we ensured to round their region carefully. I couldn't help but replay my mother's warning and Louise's premonition of Chase wiping out New York City with *my* gift. My mother still wasn't aware of Chase's reappearance.

One of my werewolves doubled back, and Claus shifted into his human form to update me. His second in charge, Ruppert, quickly filled the space Claus had been standing in, fluently leading the others.

"Esmore, the wolves can smell smoke," Claus informed me. I halted the group, and it didn't take long for Balzar and Chase to join us. Tori, Lincon, Kasey, Iris, and Fire were already beside me. Claus reluctantly repeated himself to the others as well. "From that direction. It's billowing from a city."

"The closest city from here is New York." Balzar grimaced. The very place we were trying to avoid.

"Then we should just avoid it altogether," Claus suggested. Tori and I exchanged a brief glance. As easy as that would be, we both knew what else lay so close to the city—my mother and Julia amongst the rebel group. They worked as a side operative from the main Guild, having waited out their time after all these years for Sabe to take charge and slowly integrate their new beliefs into the Guild, to change their vision from the corrupt toxicity that controlled them.

"We shouldn't leave it to chance. If the head Hunter Guild is being attacked, we at least need to know why and by whom," Chase argued only just loud enough for us to all hear.

I nodded, trying to avoid his engrossing gaze. "Should we send the wolves to inspect?" Iris asked me curtly.

I considered it. "No. I'll go as well. We'll take a small inspection team. The rest standby here and don't make any moves until advised otherwise." I wanted to see it for myself. Because I was one of few who'd made contact with members affiliated with the Guild and that could give us an upper hand. I didn't like the idea of a diversion, but my instinct also pulled me in the direction of the smoke. This wasn't a coincidence that we were stumbling across chaos.

Of my group, I only took Lincon, Kasey, and Fire. Iris was to lead in my stead, and Tori had his own platoon to guide. Though I might've appreciated his eyes considering he too had wandered the city streets with me once before being turned. He might've recognized familiar faces as well.

Balzar and two handpicked vampires, Chase, Jerimiah, and Darcy came while Clarissa ordained supremacy until he returned. Claus and three of his pack members guided us toward the smoke that their keen nose could smell before we did.

However, once we came into the downwind, a hint quickly turned into a consistent smoky stream. The sky was filled with dusty black. We crept atop a hill, hunching over to watch a few of the towering buildings up in flames. It reminded me much of the city we'd just come from, even though it hadn't been of our doing from the bombs, the chaotic madness was the same. I held my breath for a moment as I focused my sight on the stream of figures that crashed into the city and hid amongst the mist until too late. I couldn't hear the disaster below but knew they were fighting inside the smoke.

"Sabers," Chase confirmed. They ambushed the city on a mission. It was too far for me to see clearly from the direction they came, but I found myself raising my arm, warning Chase not to step any clearer into view.

"What if this is Deemori's doing?" I asked out loud. "You need to stay hidden." If Deemori was directing the sabers, which was highly probable considering their magnitude, then that meant Tythian was behind it and the moment anyone saw Chase they'd report it.

"Maybe Tythian's on the offense a lot sooner than we'd thought." Balzar examined them and the direction in which they came. "He knew we'd be passing by."

"Why piss off the hunters though? It has nothing to do with them, unless he incredibly miscalculated my remaining ties with the hunters."

"Unless this is a decoy," Chase said lowly as he stood back into the shadows of the trees. Jerimiah and Darcy warily watched Lincon who for once was surprisingly quiet. And for the first time in a long time, Kasey actually seemed intrigued, if only because it was to do with hunters. I wondered how much of her still pined to live her old life, or whether she'd entirely given up on such an ideal.

"There." Lincon pointed sharply into the centerfold of the sabers. I followed his gaze, my keen sight struggling to see what only a few of us could make out. No matter how good my vision as a vampire I still strained to see. But there, hidden amidst the numerous sabers rushing out from the trees, stood Deemori, Connor, and…my breath hitched. *Dillian.*

"This is a trap," Balzar said, realizing the same thing.

"I know, how exciting," Lincon squealed, dancing his fingertips together. "Shall I go and make my presence known?"

"No," I growled. Because if they found Lincon they'd know their plan had worked to coax us in. But what kind of a trap? Surely they'd know we weren't so gullible as to try and help. But there was something I so dearly wanted to get closer to…Dillian. After all these years, I'd never understood if he'd actually betrayed us or gone with Tythian to protect Tori. Did he need saving? Tythian had leveraged one of the few things I hadn't been able to manage to get my hands on after all these years and brought it into the nightlife.

A howl erupted amongst the trees, coming from where the others waited. Suddenly, an explosion of lightning shook the ground. "Shit." We bolted back toward our group. I took to the sky, seizing an aerial view of what so quickly divided our groups into disarray. Wolves scattered amongst the trees giving chase to something I couldn't see. By the time I'd reached Iris and the others, they were fighting invisible forces.

My feet touched the ground, and I felt a wave of offensive pressure trying to overtake my mind. I found myself incoherent and sluggish like I'd been hit over the head, loosely understanding that the figures around me were fighting ghosts. I could hear my own breathing as I slowly pushed back against the pressure. This wasn't like Lincon's illusions, this was something completely different—a mental gift I'd never touched before. But the thing with mental gifts was one could fight against the other, and so I pushed, compelling it away.

I felt like I was zapped the moment Chase grabbed my wrist. I could see and hear clearly, shaking off his hand as if it were fire. "I could've managed." Had he given me time.

"What a fun little gift," Lincon mused as he watched Kasey struggle and fight against an invisible force.

"Lincon!" I growled, and he looked at me expectantly. "Hunt." His smile cracked into an embellishment of madness. One moment he was there and the next he was gone. The wolves were scattered, and Tori and Iris boded no better as they fought invisible foes. They could equally take one another out. Shit, I realized some of them were going toward the city, like a calling bell. I entrusted that Lincon of all vampires would easily find and dispose of the creature behind this, whether it be hunter or vampire.

A familiar scent acquired my taste buds and ran my blood cold. Chase and I looked at one another, haunted by its familiar greeting. *James.* I fought against my instinct to follow him. I so wanted to, but my gaze instinctually snapped on Titan who was swishing her blade at an invisible attacker, so close to Chris and Tori who fought beside her. If I left them exposed like this...

A wave of hunters circled us. It didn't make sense that the hunters would attack *us* while their Guild was under attack. The only ones who seemed unaffected by the mass mind play game were the gargoyles, Chase, and a few werewolves who evidently had a natural tolerance against mental gifts.

"Scatter out, protect the coven and Balzar's as well," Chase instructed the gargoyles. And just as Chase had helped me dispel the fog, he grabbed onto Balzar's wrist quickly influencing him and pushing away the gift that coaxed him.

"Wah?" Balzar snapped to attention straight away, realizing he'd been in a daze and what was erupting around him. My werewolves were growling and snapping at the dark figures that loomed around us, protectively circling in their pack mates who were affected by the spell. I wasn't surprised to sense James was waiting by, simply watching and evaluating like he often did. I didn't recognize any of the hunters he worked with. The last my mother reported, James hadn't been seen for some time nor had he been integrated into the New York Guild. So that led to the more significant question as to where this group came from. Chase dodged Iris's hefty attacks, clamping his hand around his neck the moment he had an opening. I guarded their backs as Iris blinked to awareness.

I searched for Fire and couldn't find her. When I reached out to her mind, I felt her running toward the city. I bit the inside of my mouth. Shit. Shit. Shit. Three arrows shot toward us, and I quickly glided my sword across, splintering them into two. Iris and Chase growled at the weak attempt while their backs were turned.

Chase's attention was fixated on the group storming toward us as he said, "Go! Find her, we can handle this." I reserved a look toward Titan, Tori, and Chris. "I'll look after them," he promised. Reluctantly, I nodded and took to the sky. At least they were protected in numbers. Whereas Fire was purposefully being compelled toward the city most likely into a trap.

The moment I took to the sky, I could sense I was being followed. I equally distributed my attention toward my stalker and Fire. She'd only just made her way into the outskirts of the city, still minutes away from the fiery action. Only one saber trailed her amongst the dirty outer suburban area that had long been abandoned. From above it looked like a maze, but eventually, it would lead her toward the chaos in the center which I had to prevent. I noticed another saber coming from a street on the left. And then the right. Shit, they were simultaneously surrounding her. It seemed too orchestrated, coming from the handler who could manipulate their minds and coax my second in command straight toward the belly of the fight.

I swooped low amongst the disarrayed suburban area housing multiple apartments. I silently scanned them with my mind to ensure sabers weren't following from inside the apartments, my gaze still intent ahead. The stark night acted in their favor, but I would summon it into mine as well.

I dove for the saber that trailed Fire. Before he could even sense me, I swooped in on him like a bird would their prey and torpedoed into the sky. The saber scraped and tugged away from my grip, trying to vulgarly bite at me. I loosened my grip, satisfied by the giant drop as it splattered behind me and I focused my attention ahead.

Fire had stopped, her head swiveling in disarray from side to side, trying to shake off what I imagined to be the remains of the spell. I could feel her mind clearing from its grogginess which meant Lincon had succeeded, but it left Fire in a vulnerable position.

With sword in hand, I dove toward her, my leather boots skirting along the cracked street as I intercepted the first saber on her left. I swished my sword over its crinkled hands, slicing them off before they so filthily touched her. It screeched, heaving over with momentum as I side-stepped and punctured my sword into its chest from beneath. It slummed into a decaying mass.

I flipped over Fire, blocking with my sword the saber that tried to attack her face. It clamped down on the edge of my blade biting it instead. In a clean sweep, I cut through its skull. I followed my momentum countering the last one who tried to step around me and to Fire. I pierced my sword into its side, its screech rippling through the once quaint streets. I delicately grabbed hold of the loose strands of what might've been thick hair. This saber had only turned in recent years, her features less defined and feral than the rest. I lifted her, watching her squirm, her legs scraping the ground. I pulled my sword out, hissing at her hideousness. *How could I ever imagine Chase to look like such a thing?*

A dagger swooshed past me and impaled into the chest of the saber. She sagged into a decaying mass. Revolted by the gooey mass on my hands, I dropped her and flashed my purple gaze toward my newly announced prey.

A bald, pale, lanky man with a baseball cap turned backward flashed a toothless smile. The only teeth he harbored were his two ambitiously large fangs. The only reason I knew about baseball was because Chase wouldn't shut up about the game on one of the nights we spent together when we'd first met in Fier's Council. This vampire looked as if he'd been cracked out of a long-ago sealed wall. He was overbearingly pasty white against his gray tee shirt and tight jeans with an unworldly filthy appeal to him. "He said you were pretty." His voice was like nails down a chalkboard, and my spine straightened to a newly heightened attention. *This vampire was dangerous.*

"I prefer the term *deadly,*" I said in a no-nonsense tone.

His insincere smile didn't slip. He was gangly and meek-looking, but my vampire self was fluttering into a wild dance, excited to see how it'd fare against someone so old. "Tythian said I'd get a promotion if I bring your head on a plate."

*Of course he did,* I bitterly thought. I side glanced Fire who was almost fully coherent. I brushed the tips of my fingers amongst the fur on her forehead to comfort her transition. I wanted to whisper for her to stay back but knew as soon as she was with me mentally, she'd understand her role. My gaze darted about at the sabers who collected around us, as if we were boxed in an arena to be watched. To either keep us in or attack the moment he did.

In moments like this, I realized how easy it would be to use my gift had it not been exhausted already. Instead, I let my vampire spring to the surface, an arsenal in itself as it so eagerly begged to be freed. An unwarranted thought prickled at me. I hadn't for so many years had to consider what might happen to Chase's mentality if I were to go berserk. But neither could I hesitate now, or it might cost me my life. And besides…I wanted to be set free. I could feel the vampire cooing within me, coaxing me to relinquish all power over to it. Only a killer could face a gummy, toothless killer with the charm of death oozing from his every pore.

"Well, I don't really know you, and I hope you don't take this personally, but you won't be walking out of here alive," I promised.

"Not even going to ask for my name before we dance?" He arched an eyebrow with that clown-like smile remaining. I'd seen that glimmer of madness in his eyes before. It was the same that Lincon held. He unsheathed his own sword with an edgy satisfaction.

"There's no need," I said and swallowed. Who he was, was irrelevant. He was only an obstacle in my path.

# CHAPTER 21

I LINGERED FOR only a few more seconds, long enough to catch the glimmer of coherency in Fire's eye before I sprang into action meeting the vampire in the center. Cockroaches scattered amongst the debris as if they too sensed the danger that beckoned.

We met front on, our swords grinding against one another in dominance. His lanky build did nothing to affect his strength as I gritted to match him. He purred over our blades as if he had all night to play. "I'm surprised you haven't tried to pulverize me with your harrowing gift."

I twisted a foul smile. "Now, where would the fun be in that?" Only a madman would be crazy enough to take me on if he knew I harnessed the gift to obliterate him within seconds, and how true I wish that were now.

The harnessed control that kept the sabers at bay snapped, and they burst into action making a beeline for Fire. Instead of having to worry about her fighting behind me, she was smart enough to leave me to my battle and coerce the sabers further into the city. I didn't like being separated, but at least she wouldn't be outnumbered and cornered because she was trying to stay close to me. She would more than likely loop and trail them back toward our pack, trapping them.

The vampire's strength increased, pushing me back and off-balance. He sliced his blade across where my stomach once was. Where he might've had the upper hand in strength organically, I had the advantage of speed. "Don't be focusing elsewhere," he chided.

I charmed him a violent smile. "I have nowhere else I'd rather be," I lied. These games and taunts were all in line with the dance of the vampire's ego and compulsion to play with its prey. With a quick flick of my wrist, I unsheathed one of my daggers from my garter belt and threw it at his face, not at all expecting it to land. It was a decoy as he countered it with his sword. It chimed and glistened in the distance from the rebound, and before he had time to move, I was below him, knocking his feet out from under him before the dagger even had time to clatter on the cemented ground.

I changed the grip of my sword, tilting it edge down and toward his heart. He grabbed it, black blood spluttering as he halted it with his strength, snarling at being bested. I couldn't jam it any closer as he hovered it above his chest. With his other hand, he thrust his sword and sliced toward my ribs, barely making a scratch as I twisted and tucked my wings behind me. I flapped my wings powerfully, forcing my blade back up and out of his grip that was so tightly bound around it. He dusted himself off, agitated by his hurt ego.

And here I thought Tythian might've tried a little more, but I now knew he was just playing with me. This vampire was strangely powerful, but he was outdated in a way as if he'd just been pulled out of a coffin and only learning to reuse his muscles. He had a deranged wild glimmer in his eyes and perhaps he might've once been lethal as the aroma around him portrayed, but he was nothing but a washed-up pawn, playing to Tythian's bid. Like they always were.

I deflected his sword, kicking into his side. I was faster and balanced, my strikes perfect in every way. He could only focus on the trail of his sword. My vampire self was irritated the moment it realized this fight was already fixed. This vampire might've once had potential. But inevitably, he was beneath me, and I was furious Tythian was still playing games. A sad trap that I had no doubt played a major role in his thinking. I just hadn't figured it out yet.

Unless he was set as a distraction, taking away from me the one thing I'd truly lacked all these years—time. That lit a defiant fire in my stomach. He'd separated us for a reason, and now I had to find out why. The vampire defensively hacked his blade, aiming for one of my wings and I was able to twist out of his trajectory. I had my sword upright, still guarding my front as I pulled out my remaining short blade that was hidden at my tail bone. I glided my sword against his, throwing him off-balance as I impaled his brain with the short blade.

His body went rigid. His body might've been able to heal, but not fast enough. I sliced my sword cutting through his neck, and with wicked satisfaction, watched as his head went sailing, eyes and mouth open in surprise. My short blade glimmered, catching onto light as I tasted the victorious spray of his blood on my lips. It was foul, but it was my claim to an uneventful fight—another vampire with tainted intent banished from this world.

I booted his stomach, speeding up the process of it naturally toppling over and decaying. I looked up into the high rooftops, staring at the two dull pink eyes that watched over me. Dillian's black hair rustled in the small breeze that swept through. He was dressed in black leather and a spiked collar that made him look more like a pet owned than some gothic punk. Everything about him was different, cold, and unrecognizable to the best friend I'd known all those years ago. This vampirism had taken everything from him that identified him as the warm-hearted hunter we'd all loved.

Halting me from stepping forward, I could sense Chase running toward me. If he got any closer, then Dillian would spot him if he hadn't already with that gift of his. His eyes that saw everything. His unreadable expression wasn't entirely inviting for a chat, but I wanted to corner him and gauge where his head was at. Even when I scanned my mind over his, it was an anguished calm oppressed by his own ability to hold down his emotions. It was completely adjacent to how he'd been as a hunter.

I sheathed my sword and yanked my short blade from the gooey mass. I wiped it over my leather sleeve and sheathed it at my tailbone as I ran toward Chase. The moment I intercepted him and the gargoyles, Lincon and Kasey, I traced the tug of Fire's link. She hadn't turned back around as I'd anticipated, she'd only run further into the city which meant possibly she was greatly outnumbered and couldn't deter.

I remained vigilant, ensuring that no one else was around who could sense Chase. I prepared to keep a fluttering distance between us, so I could outrun him and retrieve Fire without his aid or him being found out. But as the badass he was, he only pushed harder, as I reluctantly expected. Tell him to stay in place somewhere and he was twice as likely to leave.

Jerimiah and Darcy were first to follow and find me, no doubt at the tip of their barrier around Chase to ensure no one came in contact with him. But it still did very little to take away my nerves from anyone seeing him.

I was tormented by the presence that blocked Fire's path. *James.* What he had to do with the sabers and Tythian's little setup here was beyond me, but when I rounded the corner, I was fast to throw the final daggers in my garter, quickly hitting home into the available chests of sabers as they cornered Fire in a four-story building.

I sped past the sloppy decay of bodies and into the building with doors that had long ago rotted away. A smashing window and broken glass rained behind me as a saber had been pushed out from the second level. The lobby I ran into was cold and damp, a light drip consistently sounding as I followed Fire's tracks. On the other side of the building, I could sense James hovering, calculating his entrance as always. I reeled my vampire in who was already so disappointed by the uneventful fight and excited for one of my most anticipated ones.

Three sabers gave up on pursuing Fire and turned on me. I unsheathed my sword, hacking them down with precise skill, barely affecting my speed. I could sense Chase follow me into the old, crippled building. The others rounded it, fighting amongst those who continued to pursue Fire. They now broke out of their formation, scattering to attack.

The upheaval of dust from the recent activity in what was once a quiet and untouched place itched my throat. I ran up the stairwell, and the moment I reached the second level, splintering glass swallowed Fire as she jumped out of the window and onto the next rooftop with two sabers in pursuit. I intercepted another saber beheading it before it could jump out the window after her. The scraping of uncut nails flooded down the staircase as one lunged for my face, its open mouth and extended fangs giving me a foul smell and visual of the inside of its mouth.

Chase skidded in front of me, piercing his sword into its chest as it sagged over his shoulder with a short-lived choke. I was distracted by the entourage of numbers still pursuing us up the staircase as a definite click sounded through the room. A bomb blasted on the other side of the building, and it quickly exploded around us. I grabbed Chase by the coat, enveloping him with my wings as I torpedoed us through the window in a spinning motion, but it wasn't fast enough. As we attempted to escape the building, it crashed on top of us, crushing the rooftop and building beside us as well.

I waited for the crunch, hurt, and burn of the flames. When that didn't happen, I refocused my eyes that were disorientated by the quick-shifting metal and darkness around us. I was covered by a set of wings that weren't my own. Chase had shifted our grip, holding me instead, his calloused and rough hands bunching my wings behind me. The metal groaned around us, suspended on top of an invisible barrier that protected us. I couldn't see her, but I knew Kasey's gift was at work, preventing us from being crushed. These damn bombs, Fier loved so much.

I coughed and swished the dust about me with my wings, blasting them with billowing beats. They slickened the invisible barrier. Chase's chest was pressed against mine, so tightly that I had to lean back just so I could peer into his gray eyes that anguished over me. I wanted to tell him I was okay. I wanted to communicate to him telepathically, but his mind was still shut off from me. More effectively than words, I slid my hand between us and cupped his jaw.

He closed his eyes, a small tick passing through his jaw, savoring my touch. I didn't have to ask him why or even how he'd shifted our bodies. We always shielded one another like this. My oversensitive wings enjoyed the strength that strapped them down.

When his eyes flashed back open with that brilliant gray, I could sense he was thinking of letting me go. So instead, I tightened my grip around his hips, locking him into place. I was drawn in by his insufferable gaze. He wanted to pull away so badly but was inevitably just as magnetized as I was. Our bodies fit and were right for one another. Always had been and always would.

My heart pounded at our closeness and the touch of his bare skin against my leather. So beautifully close and *mine*. I stretched onto my tiptoes slowly, expecting sudden movement and rejection. But my body followed its only muse as I gently brushed my lips against his. His lips were soft with fragments of dust. I wanted them to be wet and cool as I licked my tongue over his bottom lip, ignoring the dirt on them. I shifted to catch his top lip: a small kiss, a gentle reunion.

The muscles in his arms flexed as he pulled me in closer, claiming my mouth and filling me with that soulful passion I'd dreamed of tasting for so many years. The elastic of our self-control snapped, and I wound my hands through his hair, reciprocating each and every push and lick—a taste and promise of many more to come.

He pushed me against the barrier, my wings curving awkwardly around me as he grunted into my mouth, my insides pooling and spreading warmth to my lower region. His knee nestled between my legs, and I ground into him, a small whimper escaping me.

Chase pulled away from me when a screech erupted, and large metal beams were being pulled away. I straightened my shoulders with a small grunt as the low light of night began to creep in, suddenly remembering where I was. I noticed the cool touch on my skin, realizing a singular tear had glided down my cheek. I quickly wiped it away, perplexed by my emotion that wanted to cry from the intimate reunion as much as our onlookers frazzled me in the midst of battle.

Thick tentacle like vines wrapped around the beams and debris, dividing them to make way. A small hole was formed, large enough for me to look out and notice Kasey, whose hand was raised in the air as she concentrated on our spot, focusing on her barrier. Wolves guarded her back, terrorizing the only few remaining sabers.

As the hole began to widen from the vines, I realized why this gift felt so familiar. Long waves of brunette hair pooled around her with fluorescent blue eyes painfully focused on the debris. *Julia.* The scraps shifted as more members pushed away the debris until there was enough space for us to crawl through. Carefully, Kasey controlled the movement of her barrier so it could mold itself around our exit point. If she were to drop it, we'd still be crushed.

I could sense Dillian watching on from a distance. I couldn't see him, but I could feel his attentive interest. I felt defensive, I wasn't sure whether it was for Chase or the reappearance of his former lover. But eventually, I felt him leave when the gargoyles began to approach his position.

I glanced back at Chase who had his hand extended out, insisting I went first, a heavy intensity washing through us. A small part of me wanted to stay in this little bubble, satisfied to have even another hour with him as we had now in exchange for anything else in the world. *But what a limiting thought that was*, I concurred.

I awkwardly crawled out, snapping my wings tightly. By the time I exited the mounted debris of what was once a four-story building, I noticed all the sabers had either been chased out or were dead. Scattered around Julia were my mother and fellow members of their rebellious group. Now this would make for some interesting chat.

In the distance, I could hear Lincon's delightful glee. "I have a present for you," Lincon cooed as he stepped between the hunters who ferally hissed and snarled at him. He didn't so much as bother to look at them, purposefully stepping on their toes in true Lincon fashion.

"Esmore," my mother said, grabbing my attention. "We need to talk. They attacked the city."

"I know," I said, startled by my mother's gaze until I realized what, or more specifically who she was staring at. Her lips thinned into tight lines as Chase crawled out of the hole. There was a thick tension amongst us as hunters, vampires, and wolves all sized one another up. My mother looked angry and disappointed by Chase's appearance, and I hated her for it. Did she want me to suffer as she did without her familiar? Surely, she understood the hurt. Wouldn't she want another day or even an hour with Cesar? I stood in front of him, my wings expanding to block her view from him.

"Wow, I know how to read a room, and this is tense. I'll just tie your present up and show you later," Lincon cooed, excusing himself and clicking at Kasey to follow. She looked back from him to me and then when Chase was fully away from the building, she pulled her hand back, the debris of the building groaning and collapsing on top of the roots and vines that had cracked through the road. Julia seemed relieved as she took a wobbly step back. Kasey looked relieved herself as she took a harboring breath. Both of the hunters previously acquainted briefed a satisfying glance at one another, appreciative of having worked so well together until Lincon snapped his fingers impatiently at Kasey once again.

Fire joined our party, heavily breathing as she sidled up to my side. I brushed my fingers through her thick fur, relieved she'd made it out with minor scratches and a filthy coat, icky with all the lives she'd no doubt taken to keep her own.

My mother was calculating and skeptical and almost stepped back into submission as another woman stepped forward. I'd recalled her from our meeting and exchange when she took Julia into her care. "Come," she instructed, pointing for us to follow and certainly not having her back to any of the vampires or wolves alike. The tension was palpable until I stepped forward, somewhat breaking it.

The moment I did, Julia jumped forward and into my arms, hugging me. "I never thought I'd see you again."

I was stifled by the greeting. Her head huntress reprimanded the emotional greeting but said nothing. My mother offered Chase one more unbelieving stare before turning her back and following her aligned leader. It was a disaster around us, the city in complete shambles and this was only the outskirts. I could only imagine what damage the central piece had taken amongst the battle. Smoke still billowed in the background. Another battle. More time wasted. Only but a game that Tythian was playing until we made our way to him. And all for what? Time to be wasted and for him to prepare, or was it all in the name of something else?

# CHAPTER 22

W E FOLLOWED THEM into a small, singular building with a neon sign that had been smashed in and vaguely resembled the word 'Bar.' Empty and broken bottles littered the floor. Small rodents and cockroaches scurried when the door was opened, allowing a minor split of light to seep into the haunted room. I'd since sent a few of my wolves to relay and inform the others where we were. For now, I wanted them to remain stationed while we sorted this mess out.

Two of the unfamiliar hunters stormed the room first, lighting a match and sparking flames on the old candles randomly positioned about the room. Wooden furniture had been turned over and broken shards crunched under my boots from the mass of litter the room had accumulated. Lamps had fallen from the ceiling and broken across the floor, and yet surprisingly, the long bar on the right remained intact, perhaps the only thing still in one piece.

Their head huntress scrutinized Chase, Fire, and me. We could trust her no more than she did us. Julia was scratching Fire under the jaw endearingly. And embarrassingly, Fire was lapping it up, even amidst the icy atmosphere.

My mother leaned against the bar, crossing over her arms as she ruthlessly stared down Chase, no doubt with Louise's prophecy playing in the back of her mind. And yet it wasn't Chase himself who'd burned down the city.

Chase leaned against the wall, closest to the entrance, crossing his bulky arms as he watched her in the same cool regard. Jerimiah and Darcy joined us to even out the numbers, and the others remained outside.

"Am I to believe it's a coincidence that the main Guild is attacked while you're on the outskirts?" the huntress asked in her objective monotone. I'd recalled that when we exchanged Julia over there was also a male with her. Maybe something had happened to him.

"Do you really expect me to give answers to a woman who hasn't even introduced herself?" I jutted out my chin. I didn't care what her name was, but I was making a point to remind her that although she might've led her own little faction, she had no control over me.

The woman brazenly stared me down, her gaze drifting to my mother who could do nothing to help her. She had, after all, raised me. "Morell."

"It's lovely to meet you, Morell," Chase said with a wicked charm. My vampire counterpart appreciated his cheeky antagonize.

Before she could spew venom, I intervened. I didn't want to be here any longer than she did. "Are you suggesting we had something to do with the ambush?" I asked harshly, and my wings flexed threateningly of their own accord. Whether she was part of my mother's alliance and group or not, I wouldn't accept such disrespect and speculation. I had bigger ambitions than making myself an even larger enemy of the hunters and I couldn't leverage ignorance if they tried to spread rumors or intercept us going forward.

"No, but the attack was sudden, and I want to know why?" Morrel hissed just as coolly in response.

Loud squashing noises echoed from outside, and Sabe barged through the doors with Louise tailing him. Chase watched him predatory-like, sizing him up as he passed through the room to take his center stage as usual. He was affronted when he had to walk around me. "Jesus, now we're dealing with big wing people," he hissed until he rounded me, and recognition clicked over. "I know you." He looked at my mother as if in confirmation. Yes, it wasn't the first time we'd come across one another. And I didn't much like him then, and I doubt I would be any fonder of him now. I wasn't so sure Sabe was a better leader than Michelle.

Although he had intentions to merge the Guild with their new ideals that much correlated with the hunter rebels in this room, I didn't have much hope for the species. For *my* species. We were as arrogant as we were foolish, and although we had to change with the times and away from the control humans still had over our manufactured belief and performance, I couldn't believe they'd stray so far away from their original purpose. Not all of them anyway.

And Sabe was in no way any different from all the head hunters before his time. He held the same arrogance as they all had. Respectively at least today he didn't hold his head high with that obnoxious charm that often encapsulated many.

He snapped his attention back to Morell. "Someone explain to me what the fuck just happened?" By way of their comfort within the space, I wondered if this was their usual meeting place where the few members of the rebel hunters met with them. Morell seemed unimpressed by his impudence. Louise was coated with black splashes of blood. Her eye patch was coated with a small lump of goop, no doubt from all the fighting they'd just gone through.

"That's what we're trying to figure out, Sabe," she growled out.

"I lost countless hunters today because of that freak storm that just caught us off guard, and then the sabers vanished as if they never existed. Poof." He paced back and forth. It was a similar tactic to how Fier had flushed out my own Hunter Guild. Except now it was far too easy to do so with Deemori's aid.

Louise was staring at me with her singular shifty eye taking in the size of my wings and then my familiar's. She was no doubt just as begrudging as my mother that he was alive.

I spoke up, there was no point in withholding information, especially as doing so could defame our intentions of passing through. "We were bypassing the area. We recently discovered the location of Fier's Vampire Council and ambushed him two days ago in Washington DC. We were able to dispose of the majority of his Council, however, Fier escaped."

"Escaped?" Sabe said ruthlessly. Chase pushed off the wall with a low growl that passed through the room in warning. I was warmed by the notion, knowing he had my back and how at ease I felt with him allowing me to take charge. Chase had come a long way as well. I'd learned to tolerate vampires in the same way he'd learned to tolerate hunters.

"Can't you just do your wipe the face of the earth gift shit," Sabe hissed, and Louise finally tsked at his insolence. He seemed to simmer down. Finding an overturned barstool, he flipped it and sat on it, his knee bouncing. Despite his new leadership role, he seemed reluctant to dismiss the veteran huntress. He now looked like a child, the barstool far too low for his bulkier frame. We were all still coming down from the high of battle, and he'd lost hunters today and was still on edge after the fight that had no real cause or end. And now he'd left his people all in the hope to find a glimmer of answers. But we'd lost numbers as well, although I hadn't the luxury of yet counting how many or how we'd faired.

"My gift doesn't work that way." I was reluctant to admit the truth, but if I didn't then they'd only consider me more suspicious, and besides, Louise had a knowing gleam in her eye. Her gift of foresight was a thorn in my side. "It has a temperament of its own. When I use it atomically it exhausts, and I need time to recharge. I was in Venice only a week ago and wiped out Antonio's Council there. Because of that, and what seems like ill-fated timing, I haven't been able to restore its strength. So no, I can't do my face wipey thing."

My mother's grimace was tight. Of course I knew more than anyone how easy this might've been to prevent if I *hadn't* attacked Antonio so early on, but that was the luck I had with time. I looked over my shoulder, finding calm in having Chase at my back. "We have suspicions that Fier retreated to Tythian's Council in Montreal. We also identified Connor, Deemori, and Dillian on the outskirts of the city, orchestrating the saber attack."

"Dillian?" Julia whispered hopefully with her hands pressed together in front of her mouth. I nodded, trying not to let the particulars of the situation bother me.

"So, it's very likely Tythian might've used this simply as a distraction because he knows we're now coming for him. There were a few other elements I'm not so sure on now regarding his tactic. He'd baited us with hunters who were led by James."

"James?" my mother murmured.

"And pray tell, who the hell is James?" Sabe said furiously.

"One of Campture's members, he had the gift to shift his skin into metal and shield himself. He disappeared shortly after the ambush and Campture's demise," my mother informed the others but kept her gaze intently on me. It lowered the uncomfortable tension in the room. And why was one of their own working alongside Tythian?

Chase finally spoke up. "Tythian's clever and he's persuasive. I worked with him for years, he articulates quickly, and his long-term game plans in the background serve for concern. He's very thorough and effective. Whatever win you felt like you might've had today should be considered minor. This was only a small game to him because he didn't really use any of his big players."

"There was a vampire who confronted me in the city. It felt as if Fire had purposefully been led to that part of the city because Tythian knew I'd follow. We were then divided by sabers and overlooked by Dillian and James."

"Who was the vampire?" Chase asked seriously.

"I don't know, it wasn't a long-lasting fight." We couldn't help but share a small victorious smile. "But it felt like it was just a small ploy. I think Tythian was definitely using it to delay our transit and more than likely gauge our numbers. I think the Hunter Guild was simply a distraction."

Sabe huffed, his chest puffing infuriated. Yes, how dare the *head* Guild be undermined and used simply as a distraction.

"We can't overlook this, Sabe," Louise finally spoke up. "Even with our association in secret, we as a Guild must act in some way. Once word gets out to other Guilds that we were attacked, it'll raise questions."

"Is that a premonition?" he asked.

"I don't need to have a premonition to know when our status will look weakened, boy," she chastised. "How far away is Tythian's Council?"

"Montreal," I said again.

Sabe tsked, biting the edge of his nail. He stood up from the chair, his bouncing knee now turning into agitated pacing once again. "I can't offer you anyone," he elicited. "It would be too soon to merge them with the rebels, and they're certainly a lifetime away from working beside vampires. And it's too far up North…too far away from our base," Sabe added.

Chase twisted a foul smile. "Is that why the Vampire Councils remained untouched for so many years? Because you couldn't be bothered going outside your guarded area?"

Sabe's expression turned into an angry scowl, and he shoved the chair back, smashing it against the wall. Great, another broken furnishing and a hot-headed leader. "Chase," I chastised him. But it was in his nature, in all the males who wanted to dominate the room and call attention to themselves. They couldn't help it, taunting at one another to assert their wittiness if they couldn't exemplify their burliness.

"We could still send a team," Morell cautioned. I found it interesting how they worked together in secret and were heard. I wondered if Sabe truly valued his new role or if he was simply a pawn in the hunter rebels' game.

"What did you have in mind?" my mother asked.

"You can't not act, Sabe. You've been attacked and are open to it happening again. Send a small team out to inspect their whereabouts but have them trace it back to Washington D.C. They'll come back to report what looked to be the remains of a recent fight."

"You want me to send my people on a wild hunt?"

"Well, you can't have them witness a combined force and effort of hunters, wolves, and vampires alike in Montreal, now could you?"

"You want to work with us?" I asked, surprised and mortified.

"*Want* is a very undesirable word, more out of necessity. We won't so much as work with you but can work in conjunction with you. Whether they came here to delay *you* or not, it's problematic that they know they can overpower and take down our defenses. Who's to say they won't do it again."

"We do," Chase interrupted. "We're going there to obliterate them."

"Mmmmm," Morell hummed. "And I won't believe that until I see it with my very own eyes."

Chase flashed a beautiful ruthless smile that showcased his fangs, haughty by her insinuation that we would fail. My mother shot me a frightful look. The veins in his gums and teeth…the hunters in this room knew what it meant.

"And are we avoiding the elephant in the room, such as why your familiar is alive and even more disgustingly, spiraling into a saber?" She pointed to Chase. In truth, she was reacting far calmer than I expected.

"It's irrelevant to you," I dismissed. "We have our task and don't get in our way. You're free to pursue whichever path you'd like, but if it crosses over with us we won't be so gentle."

"Esmore," my mother chastised. We'd been on basic terms with the members in this room. They'd been able to divert Michelle from focusing his attention on hunting me ever since Campture revealed who and what I could do. And we'd kept in communication. But I wouldn't be frowned upon nor let them look at my familiar so brazenly disgusted.

"We're not looking to become enemies with you, Esmore," Louise said with that all-knowing gaze.

"And nor are we trying to create anymore," one of the hunters who had lit the candle said. They couldn't hide their revolt as they stared at Fire. Julia seeped back toward the rebel hunters who had been her caretakers and home for the last ten years. The room was obviously divided. Where they thought they were the purity, we were left as the monsters.

"Esmore, think about this. It's Tythian," my mother said carefully. "You need more numbers and gifts would help. We can work in unison. But we too must act tactfully."

"And come together with the creatures of the night?" I scoffed.

"If it ensures a higher survival rate for my people, then yes," Morell said. "We're not like the old age and lectures, Esmore. Although there's still so much we don't understand, and I doubt we'll ever live in a world of unity, If there are agreements in place between leaders that can be trusted then I believe we can come to some sort of arrangement," she gritted out.

"You'll never trust us," Darcy hissed, and Jerimiah chastised him with a side glance. Morrell seemed irked that he'd interrupted us.

"I would trust you as much as you trust me. But we have something in common, we want Tythian's ruling Council disposed of. It's a win-win opportunity."

"Esmore, we're stronger together," my mother said sternly, and it irked me in the way she tried to dominate me with authority. But I could tell in the way that she looked at Chase that she didn't consider all of us stronger together.

"It's not only us this needs to be discussed with. We have another party involved who I doubt would enjoy working with you," Chase spoke up.

"Balzar and Cesar's remaining coven," I added to watch how my mother would react. As expected, there was very little change in her expression. How I'd envied her ability to be so cold, even if it ate at her inside.

"Then go to your people," Louise crooned. "But I can already tell you the outcome, girl."

"Much like how it was foreseen that *my* familiar was to wipe out New York. Funny how inaccurate that was," I snapped back.

A small vein at her temple pulsed. "But was your familiar not present during the attack. Time is fluid, girl, and ever-changing. As soon as one thing changes ever so slightly so do the co-ordinates of fate."

"Sounds like a pretty unreliable gift to me," I purred. My mother ground her teeth at my insult.

"You don't speak to her or any of us like that," Sabe growled. Chase took a step toward the burly man, which of course meant Jerimiah and Darcy were falling into the shadows of the edges of the room for a better angle if a fight were to break out.

"Go," Louise said easily, even though her eye remained on the two vampires shaping her up. "Go back to your group and see the number of deaths at your feet before you even stand before Tythian. Mark my words girl, you need us."

"I've never needed you," I hissed, irritated. The hunters always rubbed me the wrong way. Always assuming I needed or still wanted to be in their favor. And I didn't take kindly to my shortcomings being announced openly. I turned toward the door with one look back at Julia who had grown oh so beautifully. She still had her hands bunched together in that openly anxious way I remembered her. She hadn't changed all that much. Whereas Dillian had. I closed the swinging door behind me as if metaphorically blocking out the memories I'd shared with them. So much had changed and yet it seemed like my path was to continuously cross with the hunters even after hiding from them all these years.

# CHAPTER 23

I STARED DOWN at the rebel hunters outside who were perplexed by our ability to walk freely. I could say the same for them. Darcy and Jerimiah trickled out, and Chase was last to leave with an unreadable expression. It was highly likely my mother had said something to him on the way out, voicing her concern. The wolves growled and bared their teeth, warning the hunters to stay at bay until we were moving through the city, out of their reach. And then they silently dipped in and out of the streets scouting and ensuring we didn't catch attention from any nearby members of Sabe's Guild.

Perhaps Tythian had miscalculated his strategy. It was highly possible he'd also meant for us to oppose one another. If the sabers had caught both of our armies' attentions and we were lured into the city at a midpoint, we would've fought and taken one another out. The constant question suffocating me was Dillian's intentions in all of this. If he truly was loyal to Tythian, then that meant he'd report spotting Chase.

Jerimiah and Darcy flanked Fire, Chase, and me. It was a warm inclusion considering he was their rightful leader, but it felt like the old days, when they'd automatically blanketed that protection over me as well. The werewolves howled to one another in that sing-song way to alert the others of our arrival and deter any unfortunate near misses.

As instructed, Balzar waited with the others, taking point at the structure with his vampires while Chase's and my party were segregated as they cared for their fallen brethren. Before updating Balzar, a woman's wild scream caught my attention, and I darted toward my group first where the sound had come from. A few bodies were unmoving on the ground, both human and wolf form. I diverted from the deceased and tracked where the woman's scream had come from.

When she sucked in another sharp breath, trying to calm herself, I noticed her and the gushing wound. Her leg had been almost severed, hanging by flapping skin with a few chunks of remaining tissue and muscle attached. Two men catered to her, frantically trying to stop the bleeding. The foul stench of the blood sharply cut through the sweet, gentle kiss from the hunters' blood who'd died here as well. On the ground was a litter of massacred bodies with fatal wounds. One even hung limply over a tree branch, their Barnett bow dangling loosely in their hand. Their hair was a frizzled mess, and they had a smoky smell to their corpse much like their comrades around them. No doubt Iris had done some irreversible damage once he came to coherency.

"Esmore!" Titan gushed as she ran up to me. Had she still been a child I might've expected her to run into my arms, where I could curl my wings around her and tell her those nightmares will soon disappear. But now she was eye level with me, possibly to grow a few inches more. I scanned her briefly assured that besides a few light wounds that would soon heal—she was okay. Her mouth was coated in fresh red blood.

Chris hobbled over to her, a sizable gash at his ribs. "He'll be okay," Titan assured me. "It's faster to heal in wolf form." I pointedly looked over to the heavily breathing woman, perspiration appearing as she tried to focus on the men who helped her. Fire shifted into her human form to aid them.

"They snuck up on us with that mind gift," Iris said, cleaning his oversized hatchet with one of the dead hunter jackets. "Once we came too, it didn't take me long to *deter* them. Some ran, and others weren't so lucky."

"Any hostages?" I asked. Iris dipped his head in shame. That was a no then. But better them be alive than taking chances of trying to capture someone. "How many casualties?"

Tori's heavy boots crunched behind me. He seemed deflated from the fight or perhaps it was emotionally taxing for him to fight against those who used to be his own kind. Iris and I had accepted our fate, but I'd always noticed Tori's hesitation as if he was still holding hope that one day he might be able to return. "Eight dead. Seven severely wounded." *Damn.* "I don't know the numbers for the others, but it looks from a distance they've had a handful pinched off as well. But that's not what might grab your attention right now…"

I raised a disbelieving eyebrow. "That we've lost lives today?"

Tori briefed a glance at Titan, not wanting to say anything while she was attentive. She scrutinized him, looking repulsed that he was purposefully keeping her out of the loop, and huffed away steadfast. I could sense he wanted to chase after her to amend what had come across as cruel, but instead, he remained loyal to his true purpose and role. "It's who Lincon brought back…"

"*Who?*" I queried, recalling that he giddily announced he'd found me a gift. I could hear Chase and Balzar speaking as they walked my way. No doubt Chase had informed him of our conversation with the rebel hunters. We were at a standstill.

Tori seemed apprehensive to say it even out loud, and so he whispered ever so gently. "*James.*" I felt my eye twitch as I hid the remains of any expression that one name tortured me with. Finally, he was within my reach. Many wicked thoughts came to mind as to how I might treat him, what I would do to him, but all those dark thoughts would take days, weeks, maybe even months depending how long he'd last out.

"Esmore," Chase's voice snapped me out of my blood lust trance. He was slightly abashed by my heated expression. I would finally have vengeance. *We* could have revenge. It was Chase who held me as I cried, mortified and disgusted by the hideousness of James's crime and ideal of 'fixing' me. All those memories came flooding back. I wasn't so weak like I was those many years ago. James made the mistake of undermining me once again, and this time he would pay with his life.

"What damage did you take?" I asked Balzar.

"I lost five good soldiers." He tsked. "They came out of nowhere. Chase told me what happened. You've got to be kidding me. The hunters? I thought we were done dealing with them," he grumbled. I could barely focus on the conversation at hand, my thoughts flickering over to what I would do with James. I would reward Lincon handsomely for his capture.

"We can do it without them," Chase agreed.

"But are you willing to risk the rest of your group in doing so?" I asked. They glowered at me, and I already knew their answer. And was I really any different? I'd built this army specifically for this task. I watched Titan as she pulled bandages out of bags and hurriedly assisted Fire. Chris had since shifted into his human form and had loosely thrown pants on as he dragged one of the wounded wolves across to the log, lining up the wounded who still had a fighting chance. The wound at his ribs still bled but not enough to be of concern.

"You think we should let the hunters join us?" Balzar asked, disbelieving. It's not that I was necessarily agreeable to the idea, but when I looked around at my people, I found the edginess of my pride not as striking.

"Balzar, look at where we are," I argued. "I don't like it any more than you do, but you know better than most how Tythian works. Well, I mean we thought we did until he betrayed us. He'd been planning that for years. And it was no different now. He would've been planning this from the moment we went our separate ways alongside building his own Council. You didn't come to me for companionship. You needed numbers. So perhaps we need to put prejudice aside and consider it an element of surprise that Tythian might not expect. He thought the hunters and us would inevitably take one another out. I don't think he'd expect us to form a temporary alliance out of it."

Chase was intensely watching me, sensitive to my distracted thoughts. My tune had been completely different when I was discussing a treaty with the hunters. But as Louise said, I hadn't yet inspected the damage and amount of casualties.

Balzar grumbled his complaint. "I mean, I guess it's only for a few days. But can we really trust them?"

"Of course not," I said. "But we have no choice."

Quietly and looking at the ground, he asked, "Will your mother be there?"

Old faces were opening old wounds. I wondered how he viewed my mother, she was after all, Cesar's familiar. And she'd gone oddly quiet at the mention of Balzar's name too. We'd all parted that day having lost so much and they both deeply cared for the same man for different reasons. I wondered if that made them view one another any differently. I looked away, ashamed to look in Chase's direction. That day haunted all of us for similar reasons. Tragedy and loss overshadowed any edge or victory we had.

"We need to rest for a few hours," I said as I glanced back over to the line of injured soldiers. "Morell and the hunters will find us, and if not, we'll still move forward on our own. Until then I have somewhere else to be, and I want to remain undisturbed." I tried to open myself up to Chase, to speak with him telepathically but I came into contact with that thorny wall once again. Even after that moment we'd shared. He still had his guard up. "I'd like you to come with me."

Balzar looked between the two of us. I could tell there was much he wanted to say, but he closed his mouth and stormed back toward his coven. I thought Chase might argue with me, he certainly seemed reluctant to follow, but he simply pushed his hands into his pockets and nodded.

I wanted Chase with me as I confronted James, and although it might be selfish of me, considering I knew how it turned up emotional turmoil in Chase as well, our personal pains had become one another's. And this was as much a satisfying ending in revenge for him as it was for me. He'd known my pain and turmoil. And in a way I felt justified having him bear witness to my spiteful right. Time was against us, and I was satisfied I could at least give him this victory before… I refused to spiral down that intensified gloom of the reality we were in.

I signaled to Iris that I was leaving, and he watched on in silence. Tori grimaced and looked away, denying the truth of what was to happen. I'd waited for so many years for this. But Tori was still hesitant to fight against any hunter, no matter how loyal, and he'd looked up to James once.

"It would make it easier if you opened your mind to me, so I could tell you where we're going," I murmured to Chase who kept a distance between us as he trailed me. I could feel the anxiety roll off him in waves. He probably thought I was going to ask him about that kiss being trapped amongst the rubble. And we would have that conversation—there were many chats to be had. Because I knew deep down, no matter how much he kept his distance, his body could not lie to me. That moment was only an example.

"I can't do that," he said quietly.

"Can't and won't are two different things," I edged and didn't dare to look at him. I found the blemish of Lincon's mind in the woods and followed the trail. Soon I smelt the familiar scent of James. Once it bombarded and flared my nostrils, I turned to Chase. The primal nature rolled over his expression as he noticed it as well.

His eyebrows furrowed with a stern expression. Now was our time for some fun and I enjoyed the slither of my vampire coming to the surface as I approached the small nest Lincon had created in the woods. Kasey was leaning against a tree, nonchalant. She seemed, if anything, slightly tired from the day's events. I didn't think she had an attachment to James…not anymore. She tolerated Lincon's games and torture, much of which she'd witnessed as an inactive accomplice, but there was something different about this time. She'd killed many hunters by now. If not only for survival. But perhaps because she knew the havoc and torture that would befall James she seemed slightly 'off.' She wasn't aware of what'd happened that day—the event which escalated my hatred for him.

My hands were flexing back and forth into small fists, excited by the kill that was mine to claim. Pure hatred and adrenalin fueled me and yet the moment I saw James, in his metal form chained to a tree with multiple layers of thick chains tying him in place, part of my huntress was there. A small innocent and pure part of me that felt dirtied by his hands. I had once claimed to love this man in what felt like a lifetime ago. And yet he'd misused ideals to fix me. He began to create his own rules and narrative to fit the part so he could do horrendous things. I wondered at what point did he become so twisted in this bloodied world as well.

"James," I purred the moment I came into view. His head was slung forward, drool oozing from his mouth. He was slightly incoherent, but my voice cut through to him clearly at the same time that Lincon released his illusionist grasp.

"Esmore?" he said in a sodden voice that stifled my next step. He sounded as if he'd just come out of a nightmare, his tenderness grating on my vampire. How dare he seem small and pained after hunting me down for years. He had no right to act in such a way.

"Are you pleased," Lincon said with a skip in his step as he approached me. He seemed disgruntled by Chase's being here as well.

"Very," I said, not removing my gaze from James's head that bobbled around. "This pleases me greatly, Lincon." My voice didn't even sound like my own. I shut away the mixture of emotion that arose at the thought of James and let only my primal side take over. The darker side of my being who glorified in this kind of act as the executioner. Often my tasks and merit were for others, to protect them. But this was purely for selfish revenge. "Leave us."

"What?" Lincon demanded, flabbergasted. "But I—"

"Actually, you can watch, just don't let your presence be known," I corrected. I wanted this intimate kill for myself, excluding Chase who I wanted to be here. But as a reward, I would let Lincon watch. Where I would usually dismiss him, I decided this could act as a reward.

Lincon grinned from ear to ear and pretended to zip his lips and make a dash for it out of my immediate sight. Kasey naturally followed him, though she kicked off the tree slightly more reluctantly.

"Kasey," James groaned, pathetically. I wondered what terrible nightmares and illusions Lincon had implanted him with, perhaps it had much to do with our old days. And all that he'd betrayed for what? *To fix me*, as he'd once called it. I might've been the monster who'd come undone, but he'd certainly become insane. In reality, I didn't know which was worse. I watched Kasey from the corner of my eye. At the mention of her name, she seemed to pause momentarily. I then did look at her. All malice and vampire and I silently queried if she'd be so daring as to even try to step in my way. She rolled her eyes at me and walked off, finding Lincon where he no doubt found the best view.

I turned back toward James. There was a part of me that simply enjoyed staring at him, as he was now, satisfied that he looked so pathetic and out of sorts. But I waited until he came to clarity, the drool lessening slightly as his fluorescent green eyes struck up at me viciously. He reefed at his chains, but they were far too tight to even budge.

"YOU BITCH!" He spitefully spat. A brush of wind whistled past me as Chase sped past me, and out of pure rage backhanded him across the face. The sound of hand and metal hitting rung through in a tight blow. James began to laugh at its ineffectiveness until Chase stunned him with a mental jolt of pure horror. His expression changed quickly as his mouth opened and he silently gaped as if wanting to scream until he came back too. He snarled savagely again. Physical attacks wouldn't work on James, his gift made him too strong, too capable of repelling standard hits or elements. But that wouldn't serve him now. It might've once but no longer. And I somehow felt like I had even more strength with Chase being here with me now. I knew how much him being here spited James until the very end. The monster that I decided to bed with and chose over him was here to bear witness to his death.

"It's been a while, James," I purred with a seductive tone, not for him, but calling in the death that would soon follow. As if this was my cooing voice in a sing-song way that would be the last thing he'd ever hear. I only wished I'd have longer to toy with him. "You've been hiding from me for quite some time."

"Don't flatter yourself, you sick, evil, vile thing!" James snapped. Chase punched him in the nose, cracking the tree behind him into a definite split from the impact. It might not have hurt James, but it certainly left him stunned for a few seconds before he started laughing ridiculously. Chase was clever enough to know his methods weren't working. But if it brought him pleasure in striking at him in such a way— as much as it heated me between the legs to see him lash out—then we certainly had time to play. "You hideous bitch! Look at what he turned you into! I could've saved you! I could've fixed you!" he began barking like a madman with over a decade of hatred. His voice grated on me like nails dragging down a chalkboard.

"I've waited for this day in equal measure," I cooed pleasurably. "You just couldn't be a good boy, could you? A good little soldier was what you'd always been, abiding by the book and rules of the Hunter Guild. And now look at you, working with a Vampire Council. How the mighty have fallen," I taunted.

James hocked and spat on Chase's jacket. Instead of Chase, I now stood before him. I wouldn't let him so disrespectfully spit on my familiar, even if he could defend himself. I captivated him with my gaze. My predator inside wanting to tear him limb from limb within seconds. That gift of his would prevent it…but there were so many other ways to be unkind.

I slowly guided my hand toward his face, and he flinched at my closeness, a wave of mixed emotion rolling off him. Hatred and desire being the most prominent. Even after all these years he still wanted me to be his wife in a little cage. How deranged he'd become. I skirted my fingers along his jawline, disgusted that he thought it was a motion of endearment. I let my jittery gift seep out of my pores. It might've been weak, but it didn't mean I couldn't peel flesh from bone when I was touching him.

Slowly and painfully, it peeled through the metal of what was his skin, festering part of his jawline as he screamed from the painful torture. My smile widened as I released my gift, letting it take what it would until it receded out. It chewed away flesh and muscle, blood matted and oozing from the part that I'd just let *poof* into flickering ash. It dared to be so close to his lips. And now I was grateful that it hadn't. After all, I still wanted a polite conversation of course.

"Tell me, James, why were you working with Tythian?"

"You stupid bit—"

"Uh ah," I said, pressing my finger to his lips. Every part of me wanted to pull my hand away, feeling filthy from the touch alone. But I so relished in this, toying with him as I did. And I could feel the greedy rise from Chase, excited and brooding to dispose of him. We were in this together, cruelly defiling James, tipping the scale of leverage and power that he'd once held over me. "Unless you want these lips of yours torn away, you best be talking."

He gritted his teeth but angled his head away, now repulsed by my touch. Instead of wistfully taking away the rest of his face I decided to play. To terrorize him with truth, when for so many years he fed himself lies and fantasies. He'd always so desperately wanted me to settle with him, to become wife and mother, and to stand down from my true calling as a Token Huntress and warrior. I was nothing but a breeding mare in his delusion. He didn't care about me, he only cared about what he thought was his property, in the same sense it was just as sickening as that of the vampires. If I wanted to be so cruel, I could turn him, but even I wasn't so forgiving in being able to let him walk away, in any state. The only way I wanted him was completely and irrevocably dead.

"Did you know that Chase and I are married?" I asked him rhetorically. His head snapped up. "We exchanged vows and danced. He was such a better upgrade to you."

I could feel the anger rolling from James. It fueled me with delight. I was getting to him. Physical torture was only one way to break a person. But for someone who was so strong-willed, the best way was to destroy any hope and relinquish them to a pile of nothingness.

"Where you were so inadequate, Chase had more," I said, dipping my gaze to his crotch, a new wave of rage filling me as I remembered the last time he'd brought his cock near me. And it wasn't only in that, that James was inadequate, but in every way. But for any male, no matter what species, the comparison seemed to always stir a reaction.

"We've even spoken of having children, you know? To create more little monster babies."

"You vile bitch! Don't touch her!" James anguished with spit flying everywhere. Chase growled behind me, and I could sense the projection of his predator inside wanting to lunge and delve his fangs into his throat. But James was so dirty, we'd never be so inclined to touch this filth.

A wave of memory came back, of me crying on the floor in Chase's arms. After we'd rescued him from Fier who'd implanted that dammed disease in his mind, and I'd been rescued from Campture and James's lair…I was crying because I felt broken, filthy, and powerless. *James* had made me feel that way. I was a warrior, one of the best, a *Token,* and yet he'd been able to overpower me. I felt the calloused touch of Chase's fingers drift over mine and he intertwined his fingers as if he knew what I'd been thinking.

I looked over my shoulder, realizing he had, his mind was open to me. Only slightly, but it was there, taking on my lack of emotion that I was so heavily bottling up to get through this. He was there for that reminder and memory of the terrible things that had been done to both of us, and how we'd been there for one another. None of that changed now. My wing had curled around Chase's back as if protecting him thoughtfully while we addressed this monster.

"Don't fucking touch her!" James raged despite his predicament. It had been over a decade since we'd last seen one another and even longer since I'd told him that we were parting ways, and this was the state his hideous mind had turned. Sick, twisted, and utterly irrevocable.

"You don't speak to her," Chase said in a low, threatening voice. It took me all my might to keep my wall up because if I didn't I was scared I'd fall apart like an emotional dam. And besides, my vampire wasn't done yet, it still wanted to play. "You won't so much as even be able to look at her anymore."

"You piece of rotting shit! Tythian promised me her after all was done. And, oh boy, wait until he finds out that you're still alive. He's going to string you up and tear you limb from limb." James licked his lips looking at me like a madman. The stretch of his bloody cheek was spotting raw blood as he so passionately spoke.

"I told you," Chase said, stepping forward and letting go of my hand. I was sadder to feel his loss than him approaching my prey. *Our* prey, I had to remind my vampire self who greedily wanted this plaything all to itself. "You will not look at her." His shoulder blocked out my view, but in the way that James screamed and tried to break away from his chains, with the new array of enticing blood, I knew Chase was slowly and attentively gouging out one of his eyes.

James screamed, his monstrous below echoing through the treetops like music to my ears and yet it wanted to raise emotions that I truly didn't want to look further into. A small drop on the ground and then a second as Chase discarded them with as little as a second thought. I was distracted by Chase's mind, the understanding that he was diving into a darker part of himself. The form that would do anything to protect me and seek vengeance. It was as terrifying as it was mesmerizing. But I knew it would come with a cost—to him, to his mind, and the extension of his disease if he delved too deeply away from his humanity and all that made him good.

"Chase," I whispered past the screams that quickly turned to muffled cries. He reluctantly turned to me, and I caught a glimpse of those small black veins in his gums. It only dampened my mood. I had so badly wanted to torture James for years, and now that I was here, with it so closely in reach, it felt anticlimactic. The realization that I'd always known was by letting James haunt me in such a way I'd put him on an unreachable pedestal. I'd given him that power. And now I would take it back. For both Chase and me. Because it haunted him just as much that he wasn't able to protect me, just in the same way that I hadn't been able to protect him from Fier. It almost now felt fitting that we were in this situation with James. That we were able to confront this together.

I grazed my hand along his jaw, all anger and hatred for James seeping out of me as I could only adore the one man who truly fought for me. His hands had been bloodied so many times, and I wanted to prove that I could do the same for him. I rubbed my thumb over his jaw as his wounded gray eyes seemed to sap with all fury. It was unnecessary, this fight if it were to harm Chase in any other way.

I walked around Chase, my wings careful not to touch him as if he were a sensitive bomb. But I guided my hand down to his, to intertwine our fingers again. I could sense a few of the wolves coming toward us to inspect the new scent of hunter blood and screams. They'd seen my rage and fury all before. But they didn't have to see this open wound of

Chase's and mine. And it would be as if James had never existed by the time they got here. That for all his calculated doing, it was pathetic in every way. Tythian would have never held up his end of the bargain. James's desperation was pitiful.

I pressed the tips of my fingers to his chest, directly above his heart as I looked into his gaping eyes that bled out. He was grinding his teeth, waves of suffering and pain oozing from him.

"You should've found another path," I said quietly. "And you should've never made me feel powerless." I focused my gift sharply, as best as I could with my little control of its weak faltering presence. I willed it to eat away at his chest. To at least reach his heart. Surprisingly, my vampire subsided deep within my stomach, and I could feel the power of my huntress and Descendant, and the will of Chase behind me, flare an impactful wave of energy like a final splutter of vitality to feed my gift. It teetered from the chest, eating fast and hungrily, releasing me from this hold.

The chains slackened around the tree and what was once James's body flickered off into ash, catching on a breeze that hadn't always been there. Instead of feeling rage or triumph, I oddly felt saddened for the sickness that had taken James's mind to give him such a lonely path and ending. And I was disheartened for Chase and me, who had let this haunt us for so many years. I didn't understand why I suddenly felt so solemn with clarity around the situation. A lack of fight so to speak, but it was done. James was gone. And all this time he'd been so little when I reminded myself of the lie that I'd once been so powerless. I wasn't anymore. And I was supported. I turned to Chase once again, a tear daring to free from his eye. And I was loved. My own eyes began to tear as a wave of relief finally washed over me like I'd never known. He was gone, and a small part of me felt free again, when I hadn't known all this time, I'd felt like I was in chains. And I wanted to set Chase free in the same way.

He pulled me in, embracing me tightly as tears began to spill over my cheeks. I wanted to say something but knew my voice would quiver. "It's okay now," Chase ssh'd me as he soothed over my hair. His scent, masculinity and power rolled over me in waves as I began to sob, unknowing of the weight I'd been holding onto all this time. I'd prioritized everyone else, so it made it easy to try and forget. I thought I was stronger, a warrior, but right now it seemed like none of that mattered. And it took me only until now to realize I wasn't weak because of it, and it certainly didn't define me in any way. "You're okay," Chase whispered into my hair. I held him tightly, scared of when he would let go.

"Thank you for giving me this," I whispered hoarsely, hiding my face in his chest. He could've left me to deal with this on my own. No matter how hard he tried to avoid me, we were still in this together, and he wouldn't deny me at least this much.

I could feel his anguish at my words as if he were fighting against something else instead of just me. As we were now in one another's arms, this was easy, this was where we were meant to be. And yet, I could still feel how torn he was to let me go or stay.

I knew it was only a matter of time until he'd leave me again. So, I selfishly lapped in all that I could get, cursing the complications of our being together.

# Letting Go

*I let you, for so many years, hold such power over me.*
*I imagined this day when I would have my revenge;*
*To only realize it was unexciting and you were less than what I'd always remembered you to be.*
*I have been supported, loved, voiced, and protected-*
*By others and for myself.*
*And now I let go;*
*Because you should've never had such power over me.*

# CHAPTER 24

THERE WAS STILL much to be said between Chase and me, but we were both too exhausted to even begin to delve into our issues. It was nice to simply stand and be, putting aside our differences for this moment—for the truth and love we shared for one another at our core.

I could hear Lincon cursing and raging in the distance, pissed that the fun was over all too early. I'd set out to do exactly that, little did I realize I'd have an epiphany for something entirely different and it brought me greater peace. A few of the wolves were circling us, ensuring that I was safe. And strangely, I didn't want them to bear witness to my cruelty. They'd seen snippets of my vile nature before, but if I gave into it instead of relinquishing it, they might've seen something entirely different and ugly, a side to me they hadn't known before and was too often foreign even to me.

"I should get back to my coven," Chase said steadily after I was all cried out. I'd been silently clinging to him for some time now being comforted by his scent. This was right, and he was mine. And yet, I reluctantly peeled myself from him.

I looked up into his stormy gray eyes, refreshed from the savage darkness that only minutes ago consumed them. There was a defiant red slash of red across his cheek. I reached up slowly, scared I would alarm him, and wiped it away. He and I were both guilty of blood on our hands. "When will we have time to talk about us?" I asked quietly. Everything to do with Chase hinged on urgency. I was taunted by all the variables that at any point someone saw him, and I was certain Dillian had. I didn't want this space between us when I was so nervous about losing him and trying my best to feign that we had hope.

"Soon," he said carefully and pressed a small kiss to my open palm. "But for now, we have things to do." He slowly released his tight grip around me. Warmth filled where his once cold hands were, and I'd never felt colder. It was the most I could hope for from him considering how little we'd been able to converse these past few days.

I took a sharp inhale, which he watched considerately since the motion still fascinated him. I was *alive* and *breathing* with a beating heart. He'd missed out on all those years as I grew accustomed to the change once again instead of depending on my mother's fabricated heart. But it was tender to see that it was still a novelty for him.

"I should go," he said out loud as if reminding himself because we couldn't pull our gaze away from one another. Connection and longing. He turned and walked away, and I could do nothing but watch him leave.

The snap of a branch behind me was an obvious sign of Titan's intrusion, not that she'd tried particularly hard to hide her presence anyway. I was surprised she had a better sense of caution to wait until he had gone, even with little understanding of what had just transpired.

She crept out from the trees in her beautiful black-furred wolf form. I turned to her, straightening my shoulders. She shifted into her human form, those long muscular legs of hers striding toward me with certainty. Her face was smeared with dirt and blood. The child I'd once known was growing every day, and it reminded me that like I had let go of the terrors I'd let James hold over me, I'd have to let go of her, if only slightly as well. She was a woman now. Close to the same age as me when I'd been announced Token.

"Is everything okay?" she asked. I nodded curtly, giving one last look toward where Chase had left. The werewolves had since receded further into the trees, satisfied that Titan was now in range. "Is it true that we'll be working with the hunters?" she asked, somewhat disbelieving.

The hunters haunted the werewolves just as much as the vampires. Each Guild had their take on how they should be dealt with, and most actioned execution, just as much as they would on the vampires. But for some, they had also been allies.

"It's highly possible," I agreed. "How's everyone fairing?"

"We set up a few tents and have the wounded inside. We're watching them closely. Most should make it. But not all of them…" her voice dipped quietly.

It could've been more. Had it not been for those in our arsenal with their own ability to conquer mind gifts, it could've been an absolute annihilation. "Let the others know about the hunters and no one's to attack on sight. They're permitted to near our tents. Send a small group to keep an eye on the main Guild itself in New York to ensure large numbers don't scout toward our camp. It's going to be a long night."

She nodded curtly, and I could sense the assertive pride she harbored in being given a direct order. She shifted back into wolf form, giving a small howl that was reciprocated by the many that surrounded us. They immediately set into a different formation.

I walked back toward our camp, the repulsive smell of wolf blood flaring and burning my nostrils. It always made my stomach want to curl. Surprisingly, Lincon hadn't badgered me like I thought he would after taking away his fun so quickly, which only left me to worry what he might be up to instead, to fill what he probably considered a void right now.

I surveyed my platoon that quickly made sense of the chaos. I was thirsty after the fight and emotional weight and release of letting James go. I was ravished for a healthy feast and closed my eyes, trying to deter the slight ring that had begun in my ears from being so famished.

"Here," Kasey said from a nearby tree, in her usual position, lazily leaning against it. She offered me a small satchel of nuts and dried fruit. It wasn't blood, but at least it was something. I was wearily watching the others and decided it didn't hurt to have a handful. Everyone went about their own business, and I had to focus on the matter at hand of when the hunters would arrive and what we were to do next.

Instead of offering me the satchel, she shook a few into the palm of my hand that was still filthy with slick blood. I picked at one of the nuts, swishing it around my mouth with a dry disdain. No, it was the furthest thing from blood and the nutrition I truly desired. She crunched away, one by one without thought. I'd always appreciated her ability in being able to find food she could constantly snack on, even in environments when resources were low.

"I have to thank you," I said. It always felt so foreign to say the words out loud. As hunters, we weren't taught such courtesies. We were always to get in and get the job done. But it didn't mean I couldn't identify that Chase and I would've been in pieces if the building had collapsed on us.

Kasey dusted her hands free of the nuts. She chewed the last few pieces loudly before looking at me bored, and not expectantly that anything else was to be said. But reluctantly, calling against her own upbringing that was all too similar to mine, she said, "Well, I mean, someone has to haul your cocky ass out sometimes."

I looked up, trying to be distracted by the sky instead of giving her a small smile. It was the most I could expect from her. Day would break soon. I could feel it with the slight temperature drop. I surveyed her as she watched the others, bored, always keeping her distance from interacting. I still wasn't sure where Lincon had ventured to, but from time to time they preferred to have their own space. Her fangs edged over her lip that was constantly cracked because of the saber-like mutations. Unlike Chase, her gums were pink, with no black vein to be spotted.

I found it peculiar that she had no particular loyalty to me or James even when we'd all once been a part of the same Guild squad. I could never read Kasey, and she'd always been a thorn in my side in our younger years. But I dare considered, over time, and unfortunate events of keeping us together, we'd learned to tolerate one another. However, despite our differences, we could always count on one another during missions.

She seemed to feel so little when her twin sister, Kora, died and simply continued on as a quiet ghost that merely existed. She didn't despise nor enjoy anything…she was purely being until there was no more. And perhaps the reason she followed Lincon was simply because he was a man of action, no matter how vile, and through that she had a sense of living. I couldn't conclude whether that was the truth, but my idle curiosity had often swept over her. Ever since the government had changed her in such a way, I couldn't gauge much from her.

I threw back the nuts, trying to be appreciative of the offering instead of despising it for not being what I truly wanted.

"I'll be back. I need to hunt," I pardoned myself, and she shrugged as if my being there in the first place was a nuisance and my leaving meant very little.

At best, what I found was an owl, and it had very little to give regarding nutrition. I considered pillaging the hunter's nearby human camp, but weighed up the consequence in doing so. It would only cause a stir, and I couldn't get away with doing that on Sabe's territory after we'd just semi agreed to a treaty, even if it was with his secret rebel group. More importantly, I was supposed to lead by example. I'm sure many other vampires had the same nifty thought.

We'd lost two of our werewolves over the long night, the rest had begun to carefully heal, which left a sigh of relief over the camp. The wolves howled eerily throughout the night, singing a sad song for those who had fallen.

Although they'd erected a tent for my use, I didn't dare go into it. The space could be used for those who truly needed it, and I didn't want the sense of being cooped up. Instead, I often circled the area where we were resting, ensuring none of Tythian's army had returned to finish what they started.

I now balanced lightly on the top of a treetop, defying gravity as I watched the hunters in robes walk into the trees with two familiar scents belonging to my mother and Julia.

"Esmore," Titan said from below. I peered down at her, my wings blocking out the majority of the morning sun on my back and keeping my face shrouded in shade. "The hunters have reached our threshold."

I appreciated my old Barnett crossbow strapped over her back. It looked good on her as if it'd been made for her specifically. I swooped up, hovering along the treetops before elegantly swooping down beside her. Naturally, I was already aware of their presence but told her to fetch Balzar and Chase. But they most likely could already feel their oncoming crew.

I waited patiently for their arrival. I could feel the gargoyles shift closer, circling us. Fire crept out of the woods from the same direction in which Titan had left. She walked straight into my hand, brushing her head against my open palm. Her fur was matted with blood and filth from tending to the wounded during the night.

The hunters didn't attempt to conceal their appearance in any way, and my mother met me head-on. Without words, I turned my back on the group of thirty to lead them toward Balzar and Chase. They didn't have a large arsenal to offer, but it was a group of thirty with various gifts which often helped tip the scale. I wasn't surprised to see that Morell hadn't come herself. I imagined they had more numbers and were being conservative on who they were willing to spare. And because of our connection and history, it came as no surprise that she'd put my mother in charge. I was, however, surprised to see Julia attend. Her gift wasn't so much offensive, though she'd evidently helped us back with the building, but it wasn't designed to be used on such a large scale and sapped her energy and stamina quite quickly. But I imagined she had her own reasons for coming…the mention of Dillian being the main.

Chase and Balzar intercepted us from either side. Chase and I locked eyes and quickly looked away. My mother pulled back her hood as did the others following suit to show their faces. They varied in color, shapes, sex, and sizes. But they all carried that same stone-like expression. Just a number in the grand scheme of things to follow the purpose and cause. They might've considered themselves to be enlightened, looking forward to a new future, but I wondered how different that truly looked. Then again, I had faith in my mother choosing an ideal that was genuinely worth believing in, even if it was the only place she might've been welcomed after being banished by the Hunter Guilds.

My mother briefed another glance Chase's way, but her attention washed over Balzar for longer than I might've considered friendly. But they regarded one another much the same with old wounds and ties connecting them.

"We'll collaborate with you on this next mission," my mother announced, with no room for negotiation. "If any harm or curiosity comes from your covens, however, we will defend ourselves."

Balzar smirked and crossed his arms. "You just assume that you can waltz up and tell *us* how this is going down—typical huntress."

"Please don't misinterpret that I'm in the same status as I was when you last saw me, Balzar. I am not ranked beneath you in any way, and I certainly will neither take orders nor childish outbursts," my mother condoned. It was true that my mother had become rather impassive during her time within the vampire covens to appease Cesar's reign.

I raised my hand to Balzar, preventing him from saying anything further. This was going to be very far from friendly terms, like any treaty we'd ever had. But it certainly would have its advantages. And it wasn't like *I*, of all people, couldn't work with my own mother. At least I could keep a handle on that.

"Your group will run alongside mine. You're not to act impulsively. Whatever we do, we articulate together. No surprises on either end." I looked to Balzar and Chase included. "And we leave now."

I didn't want to waste time because every second lost was the possibility that Chase would be outed. And harsh decisions would have to be made, for those who were injured but could still run, they would join us. And those who weren't capable would be escorted back to our threshold. There would be no further deliberation.

My mother tersely inclined her head to agree. Finally, my gaze once again landed on the beautiful Julia. She'd been the one who'd gotten away, that we'd been able to free from the restraints of this life. And yet, she found herself back amongst it by personal choice. And I wasn't sure if I considered her the fool for it or endearing that I hoped it might be enough leverage to call Dillian in closer. It was a selfish thought, but we all had our ties to the past, no matter how hard we tried to run from them. And there was a very small line between love and hate.

# CHAPTER 25

THE VAMPIRES STARED begrudgingly into the distance with disdain at having to work alongside hunters who heeded them no attention with noses poised in snobbery, which only infuriated them more. The werewolves, however, despite their reputation were far more civilized. And I took pride in that. It was also practical that we were the ones to come between the hunters and the vampires because as it appeared now, we had more control and fewer hundreds of years of animosity, unlike the two other groups.

We followed Balzar who led with his gift but also took on my mother's recommendations so we avoided particular paths, ensuring we didn't run into any spotters from Sabe's Guild as we passed the New York territory. The city was no longer up in flame, and the sabers had since disappeared as if the moment Deemori was teleported away so was her gift and spell over them.

Titan was closely squeezed behind Tori in formation and whatever disagreement they might've had previously had been forgotten, or they'd taken the mature route to discuss it. It didn't go unnoticed by Chris who obviously kept his distance as if hurt by how quickly she'd forgiven him.

It would take us two days to reach Montreal, where we were sure Tythian would be waiting for us, dismissing the idea that he might meet us beforehand. I was certain he wouldn't run away. He'd never believed in such tactics when he so arrogantly believed in his own strength and clever mind. The reason he retreated that once was because Whitney was in danger. I growled at the thought of her. She'd once been pure, sweet, and gentle. One of the few humans whose deaths I'd mourned. But after he'd turned her, I could see she was devoid of all of those things. And I would return Tythian the favor consequently to what she'd done to Yolo and what they'd done as a unit together. If of course Balzar didn't reach her first.

The first half-day was eerily quiet…too quiet. We all expected something to jump out at any moment. Decidedly, we took a break by a small waterhole where the minority took the time to clean themselves after the previous night's fight.

My mother casually sauntered over to me, alongside Julia who took the liberty to join. She looked out of place, even now, even ten years on with a sure gleam of wisdom in her eye. The werewolves surprisingly made no fuse about them, as if knowing they were old friends. Most of them were acquainted with my mother. However, the other hunters who looked over at them indiscreetly were rewarded with snarls and fierce stares.

Titan paced back and forth, and when I pointedly looked her way, Chris tapped her on the arm. She perked up immediately. If she'd been in wolf form, I'm certain her ears would've perked up as well. I gestured for her to come over. Suddenly she rolled her shoulders like the soldier she was, and I couldn't help but find amusement in her action. It reminded me of a less subtle version of myself. Chris followed her. They'd seen my mother a few times throughout the year, but this was the first time they'd seen Julia who'd been abruptly torn away from them.

And that was the amounted impatience I could feel roll from the both of them. I wondered how they viewed Julia and if they recalled much of her at all. She flashed them her brightest smile, one that saddened me to see. It reminded me far too much of the reasons why Dillian had loved her. No matter how peculiar and verbally punished she'd been for being 'different' within our Guild.

"Do you two remember me?" she asked with admiration in her voice. "My goodness, I can't believe how big you've both gotten. Oh, my, and you have Esmore's old Barnett crossbow. I was wondering where that was, it had been such a staple item." For the first time in a long time, Titan appeared as a blushing child again. They were survivors in their own right, and although I'd adopted them, she was just as much a part of their safety in the early days amongst all the chaos that had happened.

Light growls erupted in the distance. "Two of the gargoyles are close by," Chris said nonchalantly. Obviously, one of the wolves had warned him so. I looked over to Iris who hiked a thumb over his shoulder, pointing me in the direction of the two who were shadily edging our camp's border. Two wolves were keeping them at bay while they eyed one another. Jerimiah and Darcy still looked appalled by their existence. Darcy waved me over with a half-assed smile as he timidly stared at the werewolf in front of him.

"Excuse me while you re-acquaint yourselves," I said to the others. "I'll be back shortly, mother," I added before she could argue her displeasure. Upon my approach, the wolves backed off slowly, but the growls remained. I could sense Fire sauntering up to me, checking up on me as she often did. "I'll be back, Fire," I added in earshot of her as well. Most of them seemed reluctant to let me go alone with the two gargoyles.

"Want to tell me what you two are doing summoning me in broad daylight?" I asked as I followed them.

"Trust me, I want nothing more than to be hanging upside down in a shady tree," Jerimiah divulged begrudgingly. Though I could tell he was calm in my presence, even if the heat was stirring him slightly crazy.

"He sounds like such an old hag these days, doesn't he? Give him and the rest of the gargoyles another ten years to slumber, and I swear their brains will solidify as well," Darcy joked. Jerimiah gave him a light-hearted growl in warning.

This was how I remembered the two, as old as time and joking around like two bickering hags. They were one of the few whose companionship I'd sometimes missed. "Want to tell me where you're taking me?" I asked. But I already had a rough idea as to who summoned me.

"Chase wanted to talk to you uninterrupted before we moved on," Jerimiah said somewhat formally.

"How's he going?" I asked. Darcy seemed surprised by my question, but the reality was, they'd spent more time with him than I had. I couldn't carefully watch him and gauge how the disease was affecting him as we moved on. They, however, were his personal guard.

"He's keeping it together," Darcy shamefully replied. I could sense the guilt roll off from them as if they felt responsible for his condition.

We were some distance from the camps now, and when my werewolves crept closer, I threw a sudden emotional surge into them to walk away. By now they'd become accustomed to my way of communicating with them. I couldn't speak wolf, but it was certainly an impactful form of communication.

They seemed to monitor from a distance, not stepping into the charted territory of the other camps. Jerimiah and Darcy stopped, motioning for me to continue walking while they shifted into gargoyle form. It felt refreshing to be away from the others with nothing but the forest around me and enough distance from the others where they could neither hear nor see us.

The dry foliage beneath me crunched. It might've been a hot day, but the earth had gone through strenuous, cold nights by the looks of its damp remains, and it was likely the further north we went we'd see snow.

Chase came into view, his back turned to me as he looked out to nothing in particular. There was a small broken down hut beside him, which once might've been an old house but had since received so much hardship that it was a pile of rotted wood soon to give the ground nourishment.

His hands were tucked into his pants, and his hair was unshifting. When he twisted, I was able to admire his abs and chest as they shifted to face me. The tug and pull of muscle and skin, delectably arousing.

"I wanted to talk before everything went down. It's the least we could do before… well, you know," he said somewhat disorientated.

I patiently waited for him to speak, but he seemed confused for words. So instead, I asked my most pressing question that affected me the most. "Why won't you open up to me?"

His stormy gray eyes struck me as hurt. "Because…you…"

"I know what I did was heinous, but I did it for you."

"It's not that," he quickly pushed to the side.

"Then what is it?" I quickly begged. Our words were coming hot and fast like it was the first honest conversation we'd had with one another since we'd been reunited.

"Can't you see?" he asked as if it were so obvious. "Esmore, look at me, my love." His tender endearment swelled my chest.

"I see you," I said, taking steps and closing the distance we'd created. It wasn't natural no matter how much we'd tried to erect walls against one another, we continued to inevitably fail.

"No, you don't. You see me as what I was but not what I am now."

I let out a small, haunted laugh as my wings spread in the way of example. I was many things too, but he'd always accepted me for that.

"You don't understand, Esmore. I'm disgusting. This disease, I can feel it squirming in my mind, trying, ready to take over as I keep it at bay. The reason I've been trying to keep a distance between us is because I don't want you near it." Because he felt filthy?

"Hey," I said, curling my fingertips around his and intertwining our hands. "We're in this together, remember." I felt guilty and had no right to claim such a thing considering all that I'd done to him. Selfishly for us. And I wanted to see him in all his forms as he had me. "I could never view you as anything other than what you are, Chase, my husband, familiar, and love. In sickness and in health, until death do we part. We promised that to one another, remember? Your disease is as much as mine."

He anguished and looked away as if fighting himself. "But what if it spreads to you?" he asked shamefully.

My heart sank. Had this been why he'd kept his distance? Even after all that I'd done to him, he was still worried about *me?* "I thought you hated me because of what I'd done…that—"

"I never hated you," he said breathlessly. "I could never hate you. I know why you did what you had to do. I just wished you hadn't. That I could've fought with you until the very end, maybe the last war would've turned out differently…I could've helped."

"Then I would've lost you too," I said, cupping his jaw tenderly. Without our minds being open to one another I could tell what he left unsaid. *That I'd only prolonged that pain and undoing.* "We're going to find a way to cure this, Chase."

He slowly dipped his head down, hesitation and defeat rolling off him in waves. I snaked my fingers to the back of his neck, pulling him toward me. Of course I wanted to kiss him. I wanted all of him, tenderly and fiercely and to claim him as mine all over again. I didn't care about the veins in his gums because the moment our lips touched that tender fire ignited through me and I could feel his stress recede from him naturally.

I kissed him slowly, half expecting him to pull away, but instead, it broke down his walls and reservations. We'd both been so hungry for this, trying to guard ourselves and perplexing emotions from affecting the mission. And we'd failed so miserably. We inevitably reacted to one another, constantly around one another as the sun and moon did in unison. We slowly buckled to the ground, our knees hitting the dirt as we gave in to one another. Bit by bit, he sparked back to life, his doubts sinking away. Our bodies intertwined closer, and as he dragged my lip out, pinpricking a tiny bit of blood, a small whimper crept out of me. Desperation, excitement, adoration—him. I simply wanted Chase.

"I can't be with you—"

"You don't have to be with me," I said, although I was lying to myself and denying how badly I wanted him inside of me. I wanted that physical connection. I *needed* him as much as I did my next breath. I parted my knees and dove my hand between my thighs. I palmed his already hard cock that was trying to split free from the restraining pants.

"Esmore," he growled, and the smell of him and his flushed breath on my face was intoxicating. I was so wet for him already, and even if I couldn't have him buried deep inside of me, filling my every urge and need that had been silenced for over a decade, I could still please him.

"Trust me," I whispered and unzipped his pants to spring his cock free. I admired it. It was more beautiful than I remembered. *He was more beautiful in person than any memory I savored.* I kissed him fiercely, taking his breath away, so there was no room for complaint. I wrapped my hand around his cock, hovering on my knees as I rolled back and forth over his shaft. I caught his next moan in my mouth, the taste of it ever sweet as my toes curled. We might not have been able to have sex, but it didn't mean I couldn't please him. As if catching on to my thoughts he unzipped my pants and cupped my warmth, all ability to refrain ourselves, gone. I groaned at the coolness of his calloused fingers as he shuddered with its familiarity. He began to circle my clit, and my breath became staggered as if waiting for every circle to come back around as it hit the spot that was already so quickly turning me into a frenzy.

I arched into him as I firmed my grip and slowed. I envisioned straddling him, my hips slowly finding movement as I rode his palm and fingers. I moaned again as I squeezed the bottom of his shaft harder and slowly pulled up. A low growl came from him, and he dipped one and then two fingers inside of me, his hand barely able to make enough room in my tight-fitting pants.

"Oh, Chase, fuck," I moaned with tears of pleasure. I placed my other hand on his shoulder to balance myself as I quickened the pace on his shaft. I was coming undone. I thirsted for him, my mouth parched as I internally begged to be able to have at least that small piece of him. I wanted him to fill my mouth and taste him.

I pulled back, my fangs edged and my gaze locked on his neck. *Esmore, I don't know…* he said telepathically. And my heart blossomed to hear him in my mind, to feel that warm connection opened to me once again. He was resisting because he still felt dirty. This disease was more apparent than it'd ever been before. It was once hidden, but now it was physically alive. And yet, no matter what way I looked at him, his larger fangs and black veined gums…I only saw him as beautiful. As my Chase. Nothing about him was filthy nor would it ever be and I wanted to reassure him of that until our very last breath. I would see him only for him and nothing else.

I felt whole again with him inside my mind, and his fingers delved deep into my liquid warmth. I was almost in every way being consumed by him. I could smell myself on his fingers, and the mix with his arousal was putting me in a state of desperate frenzy for more. He flooded me with images of every which way he could take me. I groaned at the satisfying indulgence. I wanted him, more of him, all of him, and if I couldn't have his cock diving ten inches into me then I at least wanted him in another way. Hastily, I drove my fangs into his neck, a trickle of blood messily oozing down his neck as he gasped in pure bliss with the crunch of his skin piercing and sharing his purest essence to me—feeding me in a way that only he could.

I moaned in bliss, aroused by the sound of my wetness sloshing in my pants by his undoing, so close to coming undone as stars danced behind my closed eyes. His taste, his everything was like a lightning bolt of ecstasy, thrumming through my veins and bringing me to life.

Chase bit into my neck, and a shudder went through me as I felt him drawing me into him. My hand quickened thinking about him and his pleasure as he drew from me. I whimpered into his neck, unable to hold back my own building pressure that was slowly drawing up my legs and forcing my toes to curl. *Chase,* I anguished as I came undone, like a bolt of lightning releasing from me and making me glow.

"Fuck," he grunted with his forehead pressed to my collarbone as my hand slid over his cock one more time before exploding, pulsing with power as I shook above him, convulsing in my own pleasure. It wasn't everything, but it was enough. I pressed my forehead to his, heavily breathing as I slowly guided my hand up and down his shaft, my hand sullied from his slippery pleasure.

He kissed my cheek, a light shudder still running through him. I felt exhausted and energized all at once. This was everything and yet still didn't feel quite enough. I gazed into his stormy gray eyes knowing that he felt the same. It was satisfying beyond measure, but I still wanted him.

*I know,* he said and kissed me, the mixture of our blood combining to make an alluring mixture that seemed to put me at ease. *I know.*

# CHAPTER 26

CHASE AND I had barely caught our breath when the wolves howled in the distance. By the rate of their communication, something was very wrong. I zipped my pants, blowing a stray strand of hair out of my face that had come undone from my plait.

"Something's here," Chase warned. "Wait here."

*Are you serious?* A half-cocked smile played at his lips as he kissed me on the lips.

*Of course I am,* he joked as he unsheathed his sword. I would never wait and play the damsel in distress. I unsheathed my sword, enjoying the smooth texture of its handle. A gunshot went off in the distance, startling me and a few birds who took to the sky in a panic. *Humans.* Chase and I synchronized silently. He went left, and I went right. I caught up to my wolves that were already on the front lines. Claus and Chris were in wolf form, leading a small pack, threading in and out in coordination.

Two humans boldly walked forward with guns raised. I could smell the fear and arrogance on them all at once. My nose flared with disgust as two foreign wolves jumped out from the sides, bee-lining me. Chris and Claus were fast to block them. Perhaps to them, I was a vampire, trained to one bite.

Another gunshot went off as the hunters aimed for the two werewolves already ahead of me. With lightning speed, I ran toward the humans, letting Chris and Claus deal with the wolves. I buckled the tips of their guns as they shot up, exploding into the air before the weapon was unrecognizable. I grabbed the first human by the throat, whose eyes bulged at the sight of me. I yanked the other human's gun from their hand when he aimed for my wing and crippled a tight grip around the first human.

"Where did you come from?" I asked him in my most intimidating voice. The human peed, the sickly warmth spreading down his leg. My two circling werewolves were intercepted by another two foreign wolves, all of which wore thick chained collars. A small yelp grabbed my attention as I noticed Chris on his back, but not for long as he scuffled back up, ripping at the wolf that was far larger than him in size.

The second human dropped a small ball. I flew out of its range expecting it to be a bomb, but instead, blue gas seeped from it, compromising my sight. I'd carried the human with me as he simply dangled while I dragged him this way and back. I depended on my sense of smell, twisting out of the way in time as another wolf jumped out from the smoke trying to bite me.

I heard another gunshot go off and dodged the bullet. But instead of a bullet that was easy to avoid, I was blanketed by small silver chains and wrapping. I immediately dropped the human, the sizzling and pain of silver weighing me down and burning at my wings—jolting my body awake. I flared my wings in an attempt to push the weighted silver away, but it already so quickly sapped my energy as I tried to squirm under it on the floor.

The whistle of an arrow shot past me, and then fresh human blood permeated the air as the gas slowly receded. I gritted my teeth angrily as I kept my anguish internal that I'd gone easy on the humans and now I was in this predicament. Another arrow whistled past as a wolf came into view. The arrow hit its bullseye in the skull as it tumbled over itself and landed straight in front of me. My remaining two wolves fought off the last one.

Chris and Claus were still preoccupied with the two who'd intercepted us earlier, and I could dauntingly feel the rise of another three government wolves coming our way.

"This shit must hurt, huh?" Titan asked, peeling back the silver netting. The immediate relief didn't last long as she offered me her hand with a small smile, Barnett bow cocked over her shoulder. I grabbed her hand, accepting the gesture.

"Don't get too cocky," I lectured her. "Where do you think you're going?" I asked, grabbing the boot of the human who'd tried to crawl away. When I yanked him back out of the remaining blue gas, his eyes were rolled into the back of his head, white paste coming from his mouth. "Fuck."

Titan hitched another arrow and shot at one of the werewolves who came streaming through the gas. The wolves naturally had a better sense of smell and appeared to be drawn toward me, no doubt because my vampire blood was like a beacon to them. I could hear rolling growls and ripping of flesh in the distance but could no longer see Claus, Chris, and the others wolves as the blue gas wafted around us.

I stood in place, my body slowly healing and stitching together from the burns across my skin and wings. I clutched onto my sword, closing my eyes and listening out for my approaching attacker. I could sense I was on one of the wolves' radars and they were hunting me. Titan shot another arrow, and a yelp erupted in the distance. I curved a sinister smile, impressed by her ability to use the bow I'd passed down to her so beautifully. She never missed her mark.

The werewolf lunged out of the smoke, and I sliced up, gliding my blade along its stomach to throat with a rasping noise as my sword scraped along its thick collar. The werewolf's contents fell to the ground, and I stepped back, bumping into Titan slightly to ensure its guts didn't mess my attire.

Another wolf lunged. I flicked out a dagger from my garter enjoying its weight on the tip of my fingers before I harpooned it, aiming for the wolf's forehead. Simultaneously, Titan released her bow. Kill shot. Both dove in between the wolf's eyes. We stepped to the side, ensuring its heavy weight didn't fall on either of us.

The smoke receded, and I quickly assessed the others. The two werewolves in front of me were tugging back and forth at the throat of the last government wolf to survive. Claus and Chris had dealt with their two, snapping and snarling with the only remaining one who gasped with a clawed gouge in its side. Whatever these wolves were on they seemed to have developed in even greater size. Whatever the human government was pumping them with it was unnaturally distorting them.

"Can you make it shift?" I asked Claus.

"They can't shift," Titan reported to me sadly. "The collars prevent them."

I almost felt sorry for the werewolf. I'd heard of how they now attacked, and my own had come across them twice while on their personal missions. But I'd never been confronted with a cluster of them myself.

"It's not sharing details from where it came from," Titan reported.

"Why?" I asked incredulously. Didn't it want us to free its brethren? Though with the feral crazed look in its eye, I doubted it had many humanly thoughts remaining.

"It says we betrayed our kind, and we're abominations for following you."

"But they're chained slaves to do the human government bidding," I said, disbelieving. Those who had escaped or been infected in the crossfire sought *us* out for a better life. Did not all of them think that?

"He's useless to us," Titan agreed to Claus who looked our way. From behind, Chris effectively closed his fangs, mauling his throat, and yanked. In the distance I could see four different colored clouds of smoke that were most likely meant to be used as the same camouflage that was used against me during the fight, which was embarrassing because I'd underestimated them.

If the position of the smoke indicated anything, they hadn't gotten close to the camp because they'd been intercepted. Titan slung her Barnett crossbow over her shoulder and walked over to Chris to assess the small wound on his leg. He bared his teeth at her, ashamed that he'd let the other wolf get a hit in.

Claus shifted. "They're getting bigger."

"Humans continuing their experiments no doubt," I added. He grimaced at what might've once been his brethren. "We should check up on the others." Chris sang out a victorious howl, which was met by others in the surrounding area.

*Are you okay?* Chase asked me, and I smothered myself in the cool wave of his voice.

*Yes. You?*

*Always,* he smoothed over and sent me an image of how I'd looked to him only minutes ago, sprawled in front of him, whimpering for more. Heat rose to my cheeks as I stiffened and walked faster.

"Do you think we're close to a Human Compound?" Titan asked as she sidled up beside me. Chris remained in his wolf form, keeping pace. Claus had since left, rounding up and checking on the others. I could hear the change in Titan's labored breath. No doubt because of the emotional connection she had to the Human Compound, it was, after all, her origin of birth and now one of many enemies she had to look over her shoulder for.

"It's possible, or they were just unlucky enough to stumble across us while we rested."

"Or they were led toward us," Balzar spoke over the top of us as we merged in the middle of our makeshift camp.

Fire was in her human form, naked, meaning she had no intention of staying that way for much longer. "They didn't break through the formation. We lost three wolves and six vampires. Well, five and counting…" she said, stepping to the side where one of Balzar's coven members rocked back and forth timidly, holding her arm that had already begun to fester from the wolf bite. *Shit.*

"Please, you have to help me somehow," she sobbed desperately. Clarissa silently sidled up behind her and with an indifferent expression, lopped off her head.

The covens broke into disarray. "You had no right!" Balzar spat angrily as the tension grew, but he tried to hold his coven back from the onslaught.

"I did what you hadn't been cruel enough to do. It was a kinder ending and you know it," she said nonchalantly. Her eyes creased into little slits as she watched him carefully. The two had spent time together, but it didn't mean they'd created any form of comradery, and she was causing a riot by acting out of line.

"Even so, it wasn't your place," Chase said, edging from the woods. She dropped her gaze embarrassed that she was being reprimanded. "I apologize on behalf of my member. But I agree it was the kinder thing to do."

Balzar's knuckles went white. He was a good soldier but not necessarily a coven leader. "And where were you two?" Balzar asked accusingly. "Oh, I see you were off doing the hanky-panky?!"

"Who even calls it that?" Titan asked, rolling her eyes as Chris shifted beside her.

"Hey," Balzar said, pointing his finger at her. "Don't forget that I'm still your elder, by like a lot. Show some respect."

"And just keep in mind that my one bite kills." She winked.

Chris smirked, looking away to try and hide his amusement.

"Stop arguing with the children," Clarissa crooned from the side as she dragged over a gasping human who'd taken a hard head injury to Spungee. His eyes bulged in excitement as he began suckling. "And besides, it's a blessing in disguise. Look at the snacks we've acquired." She acted as if she hadn't just been in the line of fire, disinterested in the tension that was rolling between the others.

"Stand down." Balzar grimaced as he looked at the blob on the ground. If she'd been a healthy vampire, the outcome would've been very different. But there was no changing her fate. Even so, it was unlike Clarissa to openly put herself but especially Chase in political jeopardy. Was it because she lacked in so much respect for Balzar?

Tori and Iris trudged through the woodland alongside Darcy and Jerimiah.

"The scent didn't lead to any close Compound," Iris reported. "I think it's by poor chance that they stumbled across us."

The others agreed. Well, wherever they'd been going, they'd never reach their post. And by the time the human government came looking for them, we'd already be gone.

"We should start packing up," my mother said, joining the circle. The hunters had mostly kept to themselves during the argument and confrontation. The humans hadn't even come close enough to see the bizarre mixture of our treaty.

I caught Chase's eye, and another small, lopsided grin spread across his face. I turned away, my cheeks blushing. How irresponsible we'd been, but we were so quick to lose ourselves to one another. I scanned his mind, reveling in the feel of him as I swam in his essence mentally.

But I could see it clearly, the disease that swept along his mind like a cancerous blanket, shifting back and forth as it ever so slowly ate away at him, even when he erected his own wall against it. I helped him, raising my own guard with him, which seemed to surprise him. But I could feel the tension release as he didn't so carefully have to focus on it by himself any longer.

I wasn't sure if it'd buy us time, but I would fight this with him until we found another way. And I'd remain with him, even when the walls began to crumble down—as long as he was open with me.

# CHAPTER 27

TENSIONS WERE RUNNING high amongst the group. Slowly, our numbers were being chipped away as was expected from covering such a considerable distance on foot. During the day we didn't have to worry ourselves with stray sabers, and we didn't catch wind of any more humans or the Compound they'd intended on returning to.

I could sense it remained on Titan's mind. She seemed distracted even when we ran in our unit. Had she been in her wolf form, I might've not noticed the expression that often perplexed her features when she was deep in thought. I could sense my mother and the other hunters on my left, keeping to our pace. We were secluded as we ran and so I waved a light tap on Titan's mind telepathically as we jumped over fallen trees and trampled tall dead shrubbery.

She seemed hesitant to let me in, as most did, and I still didn't particularly enjoy the intrusion. But I wanted her sharp and focused. Whatever was perplexing her now had to be pushed to the side, and I didn't want to call her out in front of the others. She wanted to prove herself and find her place amongst the pack. I didn't want to demean her chances in whatever that looked like.

*You're distracted*, I obviously pointed out.

She seemed reluctant to reply, hesitant to query her deepest concerns out loud. But she'd also always been very vocal in what she thought was right and wrong, so it only took a small amount of coaxing to get it out of her. *I don't like that they're collared and unable to shift. They've just trained them to be animals, taking away their humanity entirely. And they shouldn't be that big…it's not right.*

I'd gathered it had something to do with the humans and being the first time she'd taken down an outside werewolf—the same as her. But it certainly wasn't a side distraction I wanted her focusing on a day before we went into battle. Her moral dilemma would have to wait.

*It's not your battle,* I calmly cooed into her mind. She couldn't take on the world, even if she had the spirit for it. She was young. War would eventually wear her down as it did all of us.

*Isn't it? Just because I was so lucky to have been saved by you, Esmore, shouldn't there be someone else out there to do that for them?*

*Unless the human government attacks us personally, for now, there's no need to intervene.* What were we to do, wipe out the remains of the human government? Try to convert them into our own camps? It was no different from what the Vampire Council had done.

*That's rubbish and you know it,* she delicately said. *It's someone's responsibility to protect them. It was never your obligation to take us in. Or go against your own for us, but you did. How would this be any different? Once we're done here with the Vampire Council, we could focus our sites on—*

I cut her off, knowing I'd probably mentally hurt her. *You need to focus on the NOW, Titan. We're about to go into a war that some won't come out of alive. And this isn't the end. The Vampire Council still remains. Not all wrongdoings are our problem, Titan. And the sooner you learn this, the easier it will be for you to passage through this world. It has never been kind and nor do we need to be to any species, especially the lesser.*

*You contradict yourself. You say one thing, but your previous actions have done otherwise. We were never your problem, but you housed us werewolves.*

*I had my personal reasons.*

*I wasn't implying you were selfless,* she scoffed. And this time I did look over my shoulder pointedly with an icy glare at her snippet tone. She diverted her gaze. *I just want to do more. I don't want to stay in the castle when I know there's more out there—more of our kind. There has to be another way for them.*

I frowned, looking forward once again. I'd continuously been telling Chase there had to be another way. And no matter all the various thoughts that had plagued my mind the past decade, I came up short every time. Titan was young and perhaps I'd coddled her, she hadn't seen all the horrors of the world yet. Could she kill…yes. Was she crafted for this world…by my hand personally. But that big heart of hers could have damaging consequences. And yet, how could I reprimand her for it when she was right. My actions and words did contradict one another. I'd never considered myself a good being, and most of my actions had been based on survival or selfish reasons, and yet mostly it had always been on behalf of others.

*Just focus on the now.* I reminded her before closing our communication, relieved to be in my own head once again. And even then, what if the werewolves were too long gone to be saved? Would she only be met with disappointment? I was caught off guard by the nauseous wave of Kyran's presence. I skidded to a halt, signaling for the rest to carry on. Lincon, who was all too accustomed to his father's looming presence, sauntered over to me, Kasey at his back.

"This is unexpected," he deemed as he walked over to me. He had numerous holes in his clothes, no doubt from having close calls with weapons intimately brushing past his skin. He fed off the hope his enemies held when they thought they'd got him, and that's when he pounced, marveling in snuffing out that glimmer of victory they thought they had.

Fire hung back with us, guarding my back. I walked toward Kyran's presence. Why was he checking up on us, and what delightful animal form had he possessed this time?

"Oh, how tactless," Lincon mused. I spotted the small creature hanging upside down, surprised to see the nocturnal creature out in the daylight. The little black bat was hanging by the weak tree branch. The moment Kyran released his possession the little creature would no doubt have the fright of its life.

Its wide brown eyes were eerily watching us. I wondered what Kyran was thinking and why he continued to spy on us. Being in the castle and behind my mother's barrier didn't do anything to deter him from haunting my dreams, but he'd never been able to step foot in physically, even when possessing a small animal.

"I must confess, it's been some time since I last saw him. He's been surprisingly quiet as of late," Lincon crooned.

"The same goes for me," I grumbled. It was Lincon's screwed-up make-shift happy family, and it infuriated me that his father was still spying on *me* even after all these years. But then a sudden thought struck me. Kyran was something as old as time, especially when it came to the arrival of vampires in our world. I wasn't yet sold on the multi-dimension theory because I only ever believed in things when I saw them with my own two eyes. However, maybe his deranged brain had an answer as to how we could help Chase.

Lincon had once denied it, but it couldn't help to ask, I supposed. He was, after all, trapped in the bottom of the ocean somewhere. And the worst he could do was haunt me, which he'd already been doing for well over a decade. It was desperate times to be turning to him for advice, but I had nowhere else to go.

One of the werewolves howled in the distance, and Fire responded in equal measure. I always found it majestic in the way that she did. At times I'd forgotten that there was a woman deep inside.

She shifted into her human form as Lincon began to poke the little bat's chest. It silently received the bullying, begrudging him with a slitted gaze. A smile spread on his lips as he poked harder, the tip of his filthy nail digging in too harshly.

Fire looked away disgusted, and I turned my back. "Balzar's stopped. They're summoning us back." She shifted just as suddenly, offering one more wary glance toward the small bat that Lincon had begun to pick on.

"Lincon, leave it, we're being summoned." I looked into those brown bat eyes once more, a silent promise that I'd try to make contact with him soon. If Chase wanted to fight, then his existence would be exposed. Fier had to be taken out first, but even past that, we would only be buying ourselves time. I couldn't focus on anything past Chase.

When Balzar suddenly halted it worked like a domino effect. The separate platoons stopped, hiding amongst the trees and by the time I'd returned, the leaders had met in an open clearing occupied by rolling hills. My mother, Iris, Fire, Balzar, Chase, and I silently speculated the distant peaked mountains. It had significantly dropped in temperature the further we traveled.

"Tythian's teleported away from his threshold in Montreal. It's the first time he's moved in days."

"Where's he gone?" I asked.

"I don't fucking know," Balzar said, stressed. "But not close, west of us. We're talking days."

"It's possible he's confusing our tracking if he suspects we're focused on him. Is there any way he could know about your gift?"

"No," Balzar said firmly.

"He might continue teleporting around if he suspects as much. It's possible he's on the move for resources as well, or reinforcements," Chase theorized. "Can you get a lock on anyone else? Connor, Fier, Deemori, even Whitney?"

Balzar was exasperated, stressed by the moving target. It shouldn't have been Tythian we were locked on I now realized. He could, after all, change location on a whim.

"Are you sure Montreal is their base?" I asked impassively. A cold breeze swept through, and the dying colored leaves struggled against its might.

"Yes," he said absentmindedly, focusing as he used his gift.

"How do you know for sure?" I pressed.

He tsked angrily, staring at me broodily. "I have a source, okay?"

"And you don't think you should elaborate on that?" Iris pressed incredulously. My mother's gaze turned into small slits as she scrutinized Balzar.

Suddenly aware that he was being trialed he threw his hands up in the air, anguished, that fiery temper of his, flaring. He said, oh so quietly, almost ashamed, "It's Dillian."

"What?" I sharply quipped.

"Look, he didn't want me to say anything. And it's risking his life too, you know? How do you think I knew where the entry points to Fier's Council were?! But if anyone knew he'd been involved it would risk his life. Surely you can understand that?" His voice rose defensively.

Chase's jaw tightened as he looked away, abhorred by the information that had been kept from all of us. And it wasn't just any source. It was *Dillian*. The very same Dillian who just had involvement in the head Hunter Guild being attacked and watched from afar as I fought Tythian's chosen champion to bring my head on a platter. The very same Dillian who I was certain saw Chase… It suddenly dawned on me, if he had seen and he was in communication with Balzar…then maybe his loyalty did still lie with us. But after all these years could I really fall into believing that. I so badly wanted to, but I also hadn't spoken to my best friend for ten years to be certain about his alliances.

"And how do we know that this Dillian is honest and not setting us up?" Iris asked unapologetically. All eyes were on me, waiting to see how I would react.

"His intel about Fier's was accurate," Balzar said in his favor, which was still odd in itself because they'd never particularly got along.

"Remind me again how you two met?" I said, crossing my arms and taking a harsh cold breath.

Balzar threw his hands in the air with a curse. He rubbed his sharp jawline, trying to contain his frustration in explaining himself. "When I was hunting the hunter with this gift, our paths crossed, and we got into a little bit of a fistfight, then one thing led to another, and we realized we weren't necessarily on either side. He warned me to stay clear of particular posts and areas which Councils heavily dominated. It was just by chance our paths crossed. But he knew we'd seek out Tythian. I don't think he's ever been our enemy, Esmore. I think like a lot of us, his hands were forced in the last great war."

"Even then, how do we still know we can trust him? Maybe he's setting you up, after all, Fier did escape. And Tythian knew he was in danger. Somebody tipped him off," Iris gauged. He was neither for nor against Dillian who he hadn't yet met. He was simply weighing the pros and cons calculatingly.

"I'm certain he saw Chase in New York," I said as I tried to weigh my own logical sense into the mixture, with personal emotion and desire for Dillian to be on our side. "And nothing's happened. Obviously, he hasn't reported it, or Chase would be—" The words fell heavily in the air. His expression was saddened as I faced him.

*It's okay to say, Esmore,* he tried to comfort me. Except it wasn't okay to say out loud or internally. It was never okay to say.

"*Or* he has, and they're giving you space for hope to emotionally blackmail you on the day you do confront his army," my mother said coolly. I couldn't deny its possibility either. Another strong breeze passed through us, and we eyed one another. The facts were Tythian knew we were coming, and he would make the most of his time to prepare.

Chase pointed into the distance. "We're not going to come to a conclusion now, and if we do it'll be rash. There's an old ski resort lodging over there. We should rest and re-evaluate. Get a sense of where

Tythian's teleporting and how often. If it continues, we lock on one of the other members."

"And if he's hiding? And doesn't come back even if his Council's at risk?" Iris asked.

Balzar tsked. "Nah, he's many things, but he's not a coward. He'll be there. If only to gloat about everything that he's accomplished since his betrayal. I agree with Chase, maybe we should rest for the evening."

"We don't have time," I objected impatiently. I was almost embarrassed by my outburst. I felt like all we'd been doing was rest and wasting time.

Chase's gaze softened. "We have plenty of time." *My love, we can't rush into this recklessly because you're worried about what will happen to me. You have others to care for as well.*

I wanted to step away from him, disbelieving of how quickly he could disregard my desire to protect him. But I was even more ashamed in the truth of his words. I was so torn between my desire to protect him and the others. Time had never felt so palpable and against me like a drowning current, but the rest were in agreeance. It irked me because I'd become used to my power and authority in my domain, whereas out here, as I knew it would be, I was forced by the hand of the majority.

My mother's blistering stare rested heavily on me as if she were trying to figure out my very thoughts and plans. I matched her intense gaze. Such a shame she would never know, and I wasn't so willing to comply.

# CHAPTER 28

T HERE WERE GRUMBLES and complaints from Chase's coven about the incline of the mountainside though it didn't affect them physically in any way. They were just used to riling one another and feigning dramatics. Yet I could see that Chase found it amusing as if they were pretending they were still human.

The closer to the peak, the denser and cooler the air became. The large wooden oasis was surprisingly still in one piece, though extraordinarily dusty with glass littered on the ground from the years where nature hadn't been so kind. The smell of moss lingered in the air, but besides a few breakouts, it was still intact. It looked like a storefront with ancient treats and toys.

"Oh, my god, do you remember those?!" Darcy nudged Jerimiah as he collected a small white enclosed packet from one of the shelves. "Oh, man, I used to love these candies back in my day. Here, nibbler," he said, throwing a packet to Kasey. She snatched it from the air and coolly inspected the packet. "Don't worry about the expiry date, that shit lasts a lifetime, trust me."

"Darcy," Jerimiah growled contemplatively because he'd so quickly allowed himself to be distracted. Balzar's and my mother's groups remained outside inspecting the surroundings.

"Clear this way," Claus ordered his men down the corridor to inspect the numerous dusty rooms that once catered as accommodation in the ski resort. The werewolves filled the main room we inhabited, eyeing Chase's vampires who crept too close. Those who were in human form inspected the room with idle curiosity. Ironic that these were once their species treasures and treats and yet they had no recollection of generations that had passed. I examined the dusty shelves with scattered contents. I was surprised rodents hadn't infested the space after all these years.

Darcy dashed between the current of werewolves and vampires alike, receiving an elicited growl from both as he stood too close to them. "You're never going to guess what I just found!" he said childishly to Chase. He had a twitch of a smile. "I found a wine cellar."

One of Chase's eyebrows perked curiously.

"More wine?" I asked, shaking my head. Despite the seriousness of the situation, Chase always had the ability to lighten the mood. And it was almost like Darcy's youthfulness was replacing that of Yolo's.

"What do you want us to do?" Titan asked me stoically. The remaining few werewolves who hadn't spread out in the room and followed the vampires to inspect the interior were idly standing by. Iris looked misplaced beside her. Despite the height of the wooden ceiling, he always seemed too gigantic in enclosed spaces. Even the furred animals posted on the wall as trophies were second to attention when he stood in the same room.

I addressed Iris and Tori first, "Orchestrate security with the other groups. As for everyone else, rest while you can. If you require to hunt, do so, but detail where you're going and in what direction. And play nice with the others."

Chase had a cocked grin, bemused by my insinuation. Again, even though the situation was tense, he could melt my worries away. But as always, it was a cover-up, concealing what the underlying danger was.

My mother and Julia waltzed in with a minority of their hunters whose names I still hadn't cared to learn. The werewolves purposefully didn't divide to make room for them, and the chilly stares were reciprocated. Had it not been for the hunters' all-mighty self-importance, it might've been possible the hunters were first to cause strife amongst the camps. "The surrounding is uninhabited by vampires or sabers alike. We've created lookout posts, and Balzar's doing the same. Until we hear an update from Balzar on Tythian's location, we'll find quarters here and rest." She scanned the slightly lit room from where the sun was cascading in, illuminating the variating shades of differently shaped eyes. "I think it wiser that we keep a divide amongst the groups." It went without saying.

"Now, Trinity, that doesn't sound so fun, does it?" Lincon tsked with a Cheshire smile. Kasey threw back three of the green, mint-smelling lollies. She rolled them around in her mouth a few times as her expression changed ever so slightly while she tried to figure out if she liked the strong, sweet taste. She shrugged and popped another one into her mouth evidently satisfied with it.

My mother ignored Lincon. "I'd like to speak with you privately," my mother asked.

I internally grimaced. I'd known this 'chat' would be becoming. I would've preferred to hold it off. But I knew in the way that she stared at me that there was no option to walk away.

*Speak with your mother*, Chase encouraged. *And then afterward come find me in the cellar.*

I eyed him, keeping my eye roll at bay so my mother wasn't offended. He charmed a wicked grin, those enlarged fangs jutting out awkwardly. And yet, I found him adorable. As he always would be.

I walked down the hallway, my mother and Julia indicated. The others had been ordered to remain on standby. The first two rooms had already been inhabited. One of which the vampires gave haste to start courting one another. I felt internally pissed off, and I considered it had more to do with my own pent-up sexual frustration and jealousy than anything else. I opened the third door. It wasn't soundproof, if someone truly did want to listen in on our conversation, they were more than capable.

It was a small room, some kind of office space. It smelled of mold and rotten wood. The window had been smashed in and let years of moist weather decompose it slowly. I opted to lean against the wall beside the table that looked like it would collapse with the slightest of weight on it. Across from me, Julia idly inspected the worn bookshelf as she fumbled in her small satchel and pulled out a tightly bound ball of potent smelling herbs.

My face twisted in disgust as she plopped it in her mouth. "What was that?" I asked pointedly to her satchel of goodies. It hadn't gone unnoticed that Julia looked as if she'd hardly aged in the last ten years. Though as hunters, we had a longer lifespan than humans, usually it wasn't at a noticeable standpoint difference. Unless of course, your genes were mutated such as mine and immortality was a 'perk of the job' to being a revered monster.

She went sheepish as she tucked part of her fringe behind her ear. "It's umm, medicine?" Why was she saying it like it was a question? My mother leaned against the door with hands folded across her chest. Julia lost her squeamish aura and straightened after she gulped down what I imagined to be a very distasteful treat. Maybe Darcy should've thrown those sugary pills to her as well. "Since you relinquished me to the hunter rebels, I've worked really hard on becoming stronger and figuring out what else my gift might entail. It went with a lot of trial and error, but I realized my gift can not only enhance and develop plant growth, but also their properties. So, I started experimenting with different herbs and intent. I've since crafted numerous herbs for various ailments and performance enhancement." My mother seemed indifferent by the little herbed balls. I wasn't entirely sure how it worked. Julia had been labeled as one of the lowers within our guild because her gift didn't hold tremendous power or offensive ability. Anything past those particular skillsets was beyond my understanding.

"What's the one you just took now?" I asked skeptically.

She seemed reluctant to say. "I've made various ones. Some deter scent; others enable better sight in the dark; I've recently discovered one that can enhance a gift's power and magnitude for minutes, but it's still a work in progress, and as for the one I just took…it enhances longevity."

"Immortality?" I asked suspiciously. She certainly hadn't ever crossed me as someone who wanted to obtain such a thing.

"No, not immortality. Just self-preservation for longer." She seemed ashamed. But why would she want something so potent? Usually those who looked for a way to extend their life had a larger goal in mind and the doubt that their singular lifetime would enable them to acquire it. Unless of course, that particular goal was a certain immortal himself.

A spark of hope struck through me. "Could you create something to remove the disease from Chase's mind?" She seemed to squirm away from the question, and all my hope shattered to the floor.

"These have taken me years to master and even then…I wouldn't know where to start, Esmore. I fear there's not much time and as much as I would want to help you, I—" I raised my hand, cutting her off. I didn't need to hear anymore.

"I want to discuss your intention after this fight," my mother demanded, either inconsiderate to my previous conversation or saving me from the pitiful gaze Julia expressed.

"My intention?" I asked with a heavy undertone, warning her to be careful with how she was to articulate her 'concern.'

"It pains me to say it, daughter, but out of self-preservation you should try to keep your distance from Chase. If he's to turn at any second…"

My mother's words fell short, for once. Evidence enough that my expression must've been frightful. Even Julia looked down at the ground, probably wishing she hadn't followed my mother in.

"That's my familiar, and you already know this. Tell me, mother, how terribly did Cesar's death hit you? Do you even know the pain I face right now or is your heart too cold for even that?" My mother had wailed the day Cesar was murdered, and I had my own guilt considering it was me he was protecting. I never felt my mother blamed me, but she certainly didn't display any lingering loss or mourning for him after that day. Though displays of affection certainly weren't her strength.

"I know who he is to you, Esmore. But my role is to protect you. That's all I have concern for."

"I'm beyond the years of needing your protection, mother." And I could count on numerous fingers the number of times we'd protected one another. We were both casualties in this ongoing war. But my mother didn't come here to simply protect me. No, she was bound to come because her new superior had told her to, which meant there was more incentive than simply being my mother. Or she would've come alone, not with a handful of warriors. "Tell me, mother, what's the hunter rebels true intent with joining forces with us? I'm certain it's not simply to strike out a weed before it has time to grow. If it were, they would've already done so many years ago."

"We hadn't realized how toxic and active that weed was until it was spreading in our region," my mother quickly countered. I was becoming agitated by the metaphors.

"Metaphor aside. What other incentives are at play?"

"I came here to discuss Chase—"

"There's nothing to discuss," I defended sharply, my purple gaze blazing on her in intimidation. "I'll not have you dictate to me what should be done. I will not push him to the side. I swore vows to him that far outweigh any duty I've known prior. Even to you."

My mother stared at me diplomatically. Both of us preferred using our weapons and strength to conclude who was righteous decisively. But now, only a deep intensity through staring would do the trick.

Julia shuffled uncomfortably. "Our supervisors would like you to join us," she said. A defiant smirk titled my lips upward. My mother snapped her an unruly stare, but surprisingly, Julia found some resolve against her.

"You thought by coming and playing hero that I'd consider joining you?" I huffed out a pernicious chuckle.

"Don't be so conceited," my mother snapped ferociously. "We're here for the reasons we'd stated. But it's also my desire to have you join our cause. Esmore, the world is changing again, and we're on a movement to change how the Guilds will move forward and think. It won't be the same shackles that have tarnished our name and nobility. We'll finally be fighting for our own cause. No more Vampire Council and once we change the majority of Guilds' ideals and show them how to break away from our binding to the humans, we can overtake the human government and rule appropriately in a way where their kind can be restored."

"So, the masters become the slaves," I scoffed. "It's always about power, isn't it?"

"The world can never go back to as it once was. Whatever the human government is clutching on to, to revert this damage back to an era that cannot be restored. There's imbalance. If they continue building these werewolves like they have been for the last ten years, then humanity will be overrun completely, and then what happens to us?"

I suddenly realized what this was about. It wasn't the power they wanted, although that came naturally to the hunters' nature as well. It was about self-preservation, and apparently, the rebels were the only ones who had the longevity to see that. Or more specifically, Louise must've been privy to the future. And even then, I couldn't be sympathetic to their cause. My times of fighting for the hunters had ended a long time ago, and I had no intention of wielding my sword for them ever again. I'd found my family. The very one she was trying to pull me away from. And maybe I was ignorant and partial to the werewolves. But the ones who were housed within my castle had no intention of spreading their virus. They'd all suffered and were surviving as best as they could in this ill-fitted world.

"Do as you please, mother, but I won't be joining your cause." I headed for the door, but my mother made a point not to move.

"Where else do you have to go when Chase is gone?" my mother daringly asked. My sharp nails dug deep into my palms as I stifled control over my vampire self who adamantly wanted to lunge for her imprudence.

"Move aside," I carefully warned her.

"You only created this werewolf army to protect him. What's left to protect once the day and dust has settled, and you have nothing else?" The room rained down with an uncomfortable intensity as I let her words sink. I wasn't going to take her bait. I wouldn't react in the way she wanted me to. Because to fight this out would quench both of our blood-boiling tempers. And yet, she was still my mother, and I never wanted to lay a hand on her in such a way that dubbed her as my enemy.

I wrapped my hand around the door handle and yanked. She pushed off the door, still with arms folded. On the other side, Titan fell into me. She seemed shocked from being caught, and I couldn't even comprehend how childish her attempt to listen in was. She could've heard us just as easily by being in the next room over, but to press her ear against the door? Truly? Did she really lack this much subtlety?

"You're not going to leave us, right?" she asked cautiously. Bold of her to ask, considering she'd just been caught eavesdropping. I kept my composure, fully aware that my mother would've felt her presence and purposefully continued shaping the conversation. She was planting seeds of doubt and trying to separate me from the wolves.

"No, I'm not," I said, clicking the door shut behind me. Chris was leaning against a wall, further up the hall looking ashamed by her actions.

"But what Trinity said—"

"Don't worry about what my mother said. We only have one thing to focus on right now, okay," I said, placing my hand on her shoulder. Her kind appreciated physical contact, and I was certain this was the fastest way to put her at ease. "You two should go and hunt. Then get some rest." Everyone was tense, and I worried how long they might last before snapping that intensity onto one another. When would we attack? How far away were we? What did we have to look forward to?

My mother might've been right about a few things, and I oddly had a calm about me instead of being riled by the words she knew would sink in deeply later because I didn't want to imagine what a world without Chase looked like. And yet it had been all I could think about these past few days—torturing me like a rose being plucked petal by petal until the impending doom of nothing to remain.

# CHAPTER 29

I T DIDN'T TAKE me long to find Chase navigating the small wine cellar room. But instead of rummaging through the ghastly outdated bottles with his usual bravado, he clicked the door closed the moment I stepped in. He exhaustedly walked across the small room lined with glass shelves and leaned his back against the once polished wall. It was as if he was admiring them even in the stark darkness. But there was something comforting about being in the small, darkly lit room.

He closed his eyes, blocking out the noise of the outside world, and slid down the wall, reaching out to me. All of this was taking its toll on him. And it was as heartbreaking as it was encouraging that he still trusted me to see him like this—vulnerable and fatigued. He was bridging the gap between our mistrust and showing me his weakness.

I rested on my knees in front of him, somewhat delighted by the submissive pose. I pushed away the previous conversation with my mother. It had no space to fill my mind when I was already so fixated elsewhere. He wanted silence and rest, but I was still eager to talk with him. I had to have a plan in place, an option to out trump Tythian and Fier and whatever tricks they might've been up to.

"Say it, Esmore," he said with a small smile playing on his lips still with his eyes closed. He grabbed my hand and rolled his thumb over it, tracing the small bones of my fingers and palm.

Without hesitation, I blurted, "I think I should try to reach out to Kyran." Seeing him, well his possessed bat version, prompted me to think whether the old vampire might've had an inclination of how the disease could've been reversed.

"No," he replied tiredly but firmly. "A vampire like that is only self-serving. Whatever tidbit of advice he offers he'll expect a reward ten-fold. I'm assuming he still terrorizes you when you sleep?" My silence was enough of an answer.

"But he might know something. He might know how we can help you," I said, grabbing his hands and giving him my best efforts in a convincing plea. "I can handle Kyran, he can't reach me physically. There's nothing worse he can do."

"I don't like it," he argued in a frustrated tone.

"And nor do I." I wasn't going to misconceive that it was comfortable by any means. But I was desperate.

"I just don't want this consuming you. We should enjoy the small moments while we have them, Esmore. I know you can feel and see this disease growing. We both can," he said, disgustedly. His gray eyes flashed open, filled with so much anguish, so different to the mischievous gleam usually in them. He looked down at my hand sentimentally. "You know, I dreamed of you often while I was frozen." I felt a pang of guilt roll through me. He pulled me in awkwardly, hugging me and ensuring to wrap his hands under my wings, having sensed my shame. My cheek was pressed to his chest, and I relinquished my guard to wrap my hands around his waist. "I often dreamed of us. What it might've been like after the war. Living together, flying together, having all of eternity to tease and taunt you, to make love to you and claim you as mine over and over again as if it were the first time I'd ever laid eyes on you."

A sad smile changed my expression. I'd much fantasized the same. I could see how easily he redirected our conversation from Kyran, but this time I would let him get away with it because I was more captivated by what he'd envisioned. What there might've been for us, besides all these games and bloodshed.

"I was jealous, you know? When I saw your castle. The werewolves, the family you'd created without me. I'd never been able to give you that.

Ever since our coming together, we've only known how to fight for survival and shifted from place to place, hidden and out in the open all in the same. I was petty that I hadn't been able to provide you with that security."

I rested my hand around the back of his neck, patting him reassuringly. "I'd never once thought of it like that. The castle never felt like a home, Chase, not truly. Not without you. It has always been a place that I created, waiting for the day when you'd returned. I just ran out of time to make sure it was safe."

He hugged me tightly, not daring to say the words out loud. *You can't protect me from the world, Esmore.*

The pit of my stomach sunk. No matter how many times he said it, I didn't want to believe it. I couldn't stand to hear the defeat in his voice. He was cleverer than this. We both were. *We had to find another way.* I wanted to give him something, anything that would entail a spark of hope.

"Do you want to fly together? It doesn't hurt you in any way calling upon the Descendant, does it?" I enquired. Chase had never been able to control the gift until now. And it still felt peculiar being able to rely on it. But if it offered us the good fortune to finally be able to fly as equals together, then that was a magical experience I wanted to share with him.

"It doesn't hurt, my love. It more so exhausts me. But I would give a lifetime of energy away to be able to have one chance to fly with you, Esmore." He pressed a kiss on the side of my mouth, and a sweet smile crossed my face, I couldn't hold in my endearment for him. I stood up, taking his hand. "Then let's fly."

I led him down the corridor, ignoring the multiple conversations happening behind closed doors. The night sky was dark and cloudy as were the corridors and crevasses of the ski resort.

When we walked out into the main room, I noticed that a handful of the bagged lollies Kasey had taken a shine to had gone missing. Iris was standing by the door, peering outside when I addressed him. "We're going to be gone for a little while." He looked over his heavily muscled shoulder, his gaze dipping to our entwined hands, and offered a curt nod. I often wondered what he might've looked like before Tracey had permanently fiddled with his looks and build. Did he even remember what he'd once looked like anymore?

I further surveyed the room, looking for Fire and Titan. I scanned for their minds, not finding them within range. "Where are Fire and Titan?" I couldn't find Tori's or Chris's minds for that matter either.

"They're out hunting while they're off shift from patrolling. And for how long should we anticipate your departure?" he asked nonchalantly.

*What is he, your secretary?* Chase provoked as he sized the large vampire with mixed emotion. He envied Iris for being by my side these past ten years. I wasn't familiar with the term 'secretary' but imagined it was something berating for the warrior that Iris was.

"We're not running away, Iris," I edged with a hint of degrading sarcasm. He sighed, frustrated, but watched on elsewhere as he kept an eye on the house of misfits.

It was unreasonable of me to escape while there was so much tension. But I'd also implemented members such as Iris for a reason. And I would take all the moments with Chase alone that I could. That wasn't to be further questioned. They could see just by looking at him that he was edging toward becoming something that could never return. These might've been my only few days left with him, for all we knew. And that weighed on me heavily.

The night air was chilled, the shift in breeze promising a storm soon to come. My wings flexed of their own accord, excited to feel the air bristle between the feathers. Feeling free and mighty in their domain.

I looked at Chase expectantly as he removed his beloved jacket that had already taken such a beating from the last time his wings sprung free, and the amounted years of deterioration before that. And yet he still treated it as if it were a prized possession. He slung it over the edge of a wooden railing and caught the eye of one of Balzar's guards. "You make sure no one takes that or I'm holding you personally accountable."

I couldn't help but let a small laugh out which in return had the corners of Chase's eyes crinkle into an embarrassed smile. He thought my laugh was a beautiful thing, like a bird waking up to the sunrise and welcoming the new day. Balzar's vampire nodded curtly, too scared to defy him.

I admired Chase, feeling the sensational swell in his stomach as the power reached into his back and powerful big wings sprouted. It was an instant delivery of pain, but he shuddered with its aftermath. I could sense the disease swelling with it, but Chase quickly barricaded it from spreading any further. It was like cages against cages, and yet he'd still managed to let me in so we could communicate like we always had.

His wings were beautiful, a replica of mine but only larger, fitting for his bigger build. He looked stronger. *Felt* stronger. He brushed through his shoulder-length black hair as he posed like a beautiful statue flexing his muscles. Another small laugh evoked from me, and I could sense Iris's attention. Had I ever laughed in front of him before?

"My lady?" Chase charmed with raised eyebrows and a dorky gesture. "Shall we?"

"Don't slow me down," I appraised as I harpooned into the sky. I flew higher and higher into the stormy clouds that were layered with thick condensation. He separated the clouds behind me, keeping pace as he swiveled back and forth getting used to the movement. Where I had to learn of my own accord, he had the advantageous intel of how to maneuver his body because I'd already learned how to do so, and also his muscle memory. His body had done this before, for years, even if he had no recollection of that time. A time when Tythian had saved him. How very differently their paths were crossing now.

I weaved up and down and then finally plateaued beneath the clouds for a beautiful aerial view of the landscape below. Even though it was dark, I could still make out the shapes and movements as vampires hunted in the night and werewolves circled the premises. The moment one spotted me they howled, and the message carried on throughout them in a sing-song way. Naturally, they were keeping track of my whereabouts. It was the most privacy I could atone for.

*You're well cared for,* Chase commented as he listened to their blissful howling song.

*I'm well-guarded. But the only one who can care for me is you, Chase.* I could sense his delight and pride in that and then followed with a hollow sadness. How anguishing this was to go back and forth.

The wind bristled through my feathers as if cleansing me from the day. I was still exhausted from the silver that sapped my energy, and the burning sensation seemed to linger as a reminder not ever to be caught again. Those humans were becoming craftier, and maybe my mother and Titan were right in their own regard…perhaps attentions should be turned to them next. But I was defiant against turning it into my fight. Would I turn against all of the world because it felt right? I had to draw the line somewhere.

*Down there,* Chase chimed. I followed his direction, spotting a slow-moving, furry creature.

*What's that?* I asked inquisitively. I could hear Chase chuckle down the line.

*That, my beautiful huntress, is dinner. And also known as a black bear.* He swooped low. The creature had no idea what was happening before it was too late. Chase pounced on its back, his large wings curling around it as he took claim to his prey and dove his fangs in, injecting his venom. Within seconds the bear was paralyzed.

As majestic as the creature was, it was certainly old as well. It was a surprise it'd lasted this long, but perhaps it'd found a location that was rarely visited until now. "They got you with silver today, didn't they?" he asked carefully as he encouraged me closer. "I think we could both do with a light snack."

"I don't think there's anything 'light' about that creature." He let out a hearty laugh that filled me with warmth. It reminded me of the old carefree Chase. But that had never been entirely accurate either. He'd had plenty to worry about, he'd simply run away from them until he had to face them head-on.

I bent over the bear as he did and followed suit, biting into the bear's blubbery neck, wanting to spit the texture of its matted fur away. I much preferred drinking from humans, at least their skin was smooth to the touch. Animals, not so much nor as nutritional. But with the added blend of Chase's venom running through its veins it gave me a slight buzz.

The creature's breathing became shallower. It was beautiful, and perhaps we could've let it go. But it felt almost cruel to let it back out into this world. It would certainly find a less humane ending than being euthanized in such a way. And for what? All so we could walk for another day longer. I pushed that thought away. I'd come to terms long ago with my thirst and dependency. I wouldn't fall back into the pit hole of ridiculing myself because of my very nature.

Chase was watching me as I had the last bite, draining it completely dry. The bear was slowly falling into an easy forever silence. "You still have issues with feeding?" he inquired. I felt the rest of the animal's life force drain from it. When I pulled away the chilled air hitting my sensitive fangs, I licked over my lips, savoring the last of it, feeling slightly more rejuvenated.

"Not at all."

He didn't entirely believe me. It had taken me years to recondition myself and tell myself it was okay, as opposed to the raising I had as a huntress. I possessed two conflicting natures and had to find a middle ground. Sometimes guilt did flair up, but I didn't let it badger me for long because there was a long list ready to swallow me whole if I let it.

"You know, something doesn't quite add up for me in all of this," Chase said openly.

"What's that?"

"Tythian, he knows you're on your way now to confront him. It's unlike him to wait until we're knocking on his door." We were far enough away from the others not to be overheard, and I realized he was confiding in me, most likely away from my mother and Balzar's opinion.

"You know him better than most, you worked closely with him. What do you think he's up to?" I asked. Even I couldn't gauge Tythian's thinking. He was calculated and cool. He rarely let emotions flair his execution which made him lethal.

"I don't know," Chase said honestly. He paused, raking through his black hair as he looked down at the dead bear. He was hesitant which only concerned me further. Besides personal grudges and power gain, was it possible Tythian had other incentives? During our last war, he'd insinuated that Chase had the potential to be their ultimate power and threat. But I also felt as if Chase might be hiding something from me.

"What if he's re-evaluated the situation and thought of your power and making it into his?"

"What?" I exasperated. "That's nonsense. Tythian wants to break my neck not harvest my gift."

"You undervalue your ability, Esmore," he said seriously. "Maybe he's hesitating because he doesn't know if he'll be able to control it. It's most certainly a power that should only be controlled by a huntress. And even then, it took you some time to get used to it."

I could sense his mind ticking over in thought, and yet he still tried to conceal them from me. "What is it, Chase?"

"You're not going to like what I suggest," he said sheepishly, and I could tell it was grinding on him to even ask me. What could be so bad? "I think we should ask your mother to remove your heart."

"What?!" I drew out the word very carefully. "You can't be serious." He knew what it meant to me. How unbalanced I was without it. And without it the source to my gift would vanish.

"Just until after the fight. You can't use your gift as it is now, and if there is the slightest chance that he might try to monopolize your gift, he won't be able to take it. This isn't like our last fight with Oppollo where we had the element of surprise with your power." No, but it had served its purposes many times over ever since. I'd become something to be revered and feared from reputation alone.

"Absolutely not. It'll only turn me into a mutilated huntress again without it. I can't believe you're serious." My eyes had bulged in disbelief, and I felt so shaken to the core that he'd even request this of me. I pulled away when he reached his hand out. I re-evaluated the trees around us as if this might be one of Lincon's illusions.

"Just please hear me out," he begged uncomfortably.

"I wouldn't ask this of you," I retorted.

"No?" he asked, raising his eyebrows and now his calmness had spiked. "Would you not say it's the same as asking me to step out of a fight? Or even taking my rights away for ten long years?"

I felt the sharp pain of his words and threw my hand in the air. How many times would we go around in circles? "I'm not arguing with you."

"Esmore, please," he said, crumbling and forcefully collecting my hands so I'd pay him attention. "I don't want to fight you. You're the last person I want to fight. You left the empty box where your heart had once been stored with me. I held that for the last ten years as you froze me in time to keep me protected. Please don't devalue its sentiment. Your heart was with me. I'm your most trusted resting place. Please trust me on this. I just want to take the risk away and the added security that you'll be fully immortal again."

"Unless I'm beheaded," I corrected.

He stroked the side of my hair, desperately as if it were our last night together. "I won't let anyone do that to you."

My heart and connection with my huntress was the one thing that kept me sane. It grounded me in a sense to turn away from the instinct to turn into a monster on every whim.

"I know it's a lot," he agreed. "But I want you to seriously think about it. You know I wouldn't suggest it otherwise unless it was for your own safety. I just don't want to leave anything to chance when it comes to Tythian's scheming ways."

I wanted to argue with him as much as I did kiss him. *Then I'll kiss you,* he purred into my mind. It curled my toes and prickled along my skin, sweeping the tension out of me. No matter how crazy his request, I wanted him in earnest—always. His tongue swept over mine, demanding and pleasurable all the same as the residue of the animal blood tangled. He crumpled his hand into the back of my hair, looming over me as he dominated me entirely. My legs became weak and trembled as I gave in to the desire—*the need to have him fill me.*

He ground his hard shaft against me, and my world crumbled. I groaned into his mouth, my heart pounding to have his friction against me. He whirled me against a tree and slammed my back against it, completely dominating me. He molded his hand into my pants, his delicate finger swirling as he sent me flashes of images of us fucking in the sky. His wings dipped around me as if protecting me from being watched by any onlookers because I was only his to be enjoyed.

His images riled me, and I had to fasten my hand to his chest to take in a shaky breath. "Chase, we can't," I squeaked, but oh how I wanted to. We were only days away from the soon-to-be war. I wanted nothing more than to have him inside of me. I could sense how desperately he clung to the importance of being with me. But I was so scared of what my gift could do to him. He placed his hand over my beating heart, transfixed by its sound that reached our sensitive hearing. We'd never been together like this.

"I think we should," he disagreed.

"Are you crazy?" I asked before the immediate thoughts of being with him, that skin-to-skin friction and passion in all the right places flared my desire. How cruel of him to even suggest it when he knew it was so far out of our grasp. "It'll kill you, Chase. You won't be able to control my gift."

"We can and, Esmore, I'm already dying," he said sadly. I flinched under his words as he pulled his hands out from my pants and all the throbbing of desire perplexed me as it remained. "I'm sorry," he said quietly, and I could sense him weeping inside. "I'm already dead." He tried to twist with a cruel smile. My face slackened as he broke in front of me. He turned so I couldn't see him. I jerked back his elbow, twisting to see his face. Tears dotted his eyes, and my heart broke painfully in two.

"I can lock your gift away. I can control it when it's needed. Just like I am this disease. I can protect you," his voice wobbled. Tears streamed down my face as all the pain and anguish he felt mixed with my own as reality broke open like a dam. He'd already given up.

"You can protect me without this gift, Chase. It's me who needs to protect *you*," I said, cupping either side of his face and trying to speak reason into him. I wanted to put him together. Tell him the right things so he would be okay. But his pain and suffering were only a reflection of my own. And we'd both been in denial. He was sick. Very sick. And those saber-like pointed fangs were only a startling reminder.

"Esmore, please," his voice rasped. "I doubt your gift will affect me unless I trigger it like I do the Descendant, and even if I do…I don't know how to explain it, but there's a tranquility about sitting on the edge of your humanity. It's like everything that's been out of my control has suddenly snapped into order. Even if it does trigger, I'll have you to guide me. And if nothing else, if it does immediately take effect…maybe it's a sooner mercy."

"Don't say that." I wanted to remain inside my nurturing denial. Tears continued to stream as he tilted my chin up.

I was still baffled enough that he was daring to ask this of me. But I didn't want to see him cry anymore or anguish over the pain that we mirrored. We needed this for reasons that went beyond physically molding. We were made for one another, we knew that. But I dared to inhale him in the same way he needed me. And how could I deny him? All my strength relinquished. I would give him the world and if all he asked was for one night with me, then be damned the consequences. I wanted to be selfish for this once. I gently kissed him, sending all my love down our line. I let out a hearty warm breath, flushing his face, wishing that it was enough. But it never was, not when we knew how perfectly fitted we were for one another. A kiss was no longer enough.

Of course, I wanted to share every part of me with him, but I felt and tasted my gift's destructive nature on a daily. I didn't consider him weak by any means, but he'd only learned to control the Descendant while on death's door of his humanity. How would receiving my gift push him?

*Please, Esmore, I need this,* he begged. I wanted to be the wiser person for it. And that by being with him in this way could jeopardize everything we'd worked hard to protect…and yet I couldn't deny him. Fighting against being with Chase was like denying the fact that I felt like I was drowning at the bottom of the sea. It was weighted, insufferable, and I needed him like I needed my next breath.

I let all complaints and discipline snap free. I kissed him gently, rolling my tongue over his as he so preciously returned the favor. He was my salvation, and I would selfishly claim it now. He pressed me against the tree again, all resistance snapping loose. He dominated me entirely, kissing along my jawline until his fangs sunk deep into my neck. I arched back into it with a reactive hiss. The smell of my blood aroused me as I rubbed the bud of my heat against his slick hand that rolled over effortlessly.

I fumbled for his belt, letting his cock fly free and palmed its length almost whimpering that I'd finally enjoy its size once again. "Pants," he ordered. With efficiency, we both pulled off our pants while sharing playful kisses. The moment we'd removed them he wrapped his arm around my waist and harpooned us toward the sky. The cool air was refreshingly liberating. My wings flexed to naturally take flight but trusted in his strength to guide us.

His tongue wrapped around the already closed wound on my neck as he licked the salty and remaining blood. I palmed his cock and shuffled my weight, enabling myself to straddle him from below. My heart raced with adrenalin with the knowledge that if his iron grip were to release me, I'd fall through the night sky.

I rolled the edge of his painfully hard shaft over my wet lips, my eyes rolling in the back of my head, just by the anticipation alone. His wings breezed through the air steadily, every beat eliciting an electrifying jolt.

*You're so beautiful,* he confided, having the urge to push back my cascading hair. I looked into those stormy gray eyes, entirely absorbed and adored my familiar, my love, this husband of mine. And only a moment of pause flickered through my mind before he took matters into his own hands.

He forcefully pushed himself into me. My legs buckled tighter around him as I exhaled to take in his size. I was almost too tight to fit him. It'd been too long since having him home, and yet my body pumped with the thrilling euphoria. He edged out slightly and thrust again. His wings beat in sync jolting him angularly into me.

The cool air brushed past my naked skin, kissing it as I focused on the warmth of him filling me. Suddenly he dove for the ground, the size of him somehow filling me to a new heightened pleasure. My animalistic groan was stifled by the roaring wind. He held me tightly, spinning us. I had my arms wrapped around his shoulders, my legs tightly bound around his waist as we felt like a star shooting through the night sky. We were one. Together and powerful.

The ground crept closer jubilantly as we free fell. His wings flattened, and he sharply shot back up. Noises couldn't even escape as the amounted rapture and pressure anchored him inside of me. The change in air pressure concocted a lightheadedness that went beyond any pleasure I'd known.

His free hand brushed along the edges of my delicate feathers, rumbling a compulsive sensitivity through me as he plateaued in the sky once again. I was slick with evolving pleasure as I reached out and slithered my finger over the smooth texture of his wings. His back arched slightly as he rocked out and back into me. *Oh,* he said, realizing how sensitive they were and what he was actually doing to me.

He guided us to a cliff edge, still impaling me as he gently landed. His knees buckled, the thick muscle and tension in them meatily dropping to the ground. I rocked back and forth on him as he held me up. One strong arm holding me in place, the other helping him arch backward.

I rode him, my wings hotwiring with sensitivity as the breeze rustled through them now, sending tingles throughout my body, making me feel like I was lighting up. I clutched onto his thick thigh for support as I bit down on my lip to prevent all the weird and wonderful noises that wanted to erupt from me.

"Fuck," he breathed harshly as I sped my hip movement up, the perks of partially being a vampire with speed. A twitch ran through his jaw as he clutched tighter to my hips, his grip bruising. I was heightening myself, that impending light so close to erupting. I went harder faster, claiming him so desperately. I wanted my scent on him afresh and my juices flowing over him. *Mine.* I breathed, bubbling over the edge, my toes curling as I clung to that sensation for as long as I could. I would hold out until he gave in first.

"Always," he breathed. His grip was almost bone-snapping as he cursed out loud and I felt the fulfilling twitch of his cock pumping into me which sent me into overdrive. My body flared with pleasure, toppling over like a wave as all tensions released from my body. I curled into him, my breath labored as I sporadically twitched with each pulsing wave of come-down pleasure.

Chase's hand flattened over my chest, listening to my beating heart. He rested his head against my shoulder, deflated for numerous reasons. It was wondrous, everything I'd been holding out for in the last ten years. I curled my hand over his, focusing on the ugly disease of his mind. It seemed that my gift had no trigger worthy responses which was a relief. I dipped my head, pressing a small kiss to the corner of his mouth, catching one of his large extended fangs. I loved him wholeheartedly— even as he was now.

His fingers trailed over my wings, and a sharp overstimulation rumbled through me with another afterthought explosion. I playfully slapped his hand away bewitched by his cocky grin. He'd known what he was doing. "You need to let a girl recharge."

I could feel his cock hardening inside of me once again. "Lucky for me, you're no girl, Esmore," he growled with a sinister smile.

# CHAPTER 30

I T TOOK US some time to circle back and find our clothes. And even when we did, Chase decidedly pinned me against another three. We just couldn't keep our hands off one another, liberated by passion and claim. When we'd finally shuffled our pants back on, my legs and heat bruised and satisfied all in the same, panicked howls erupted in the distance in warning. Something was happening. Chase and I both took to the sky, sweeping through the chilled air before the storm finally showed itself. A ruckus began outside the lodgment as vampires and wolves panicked around the entrance and flooded into the main room. I couldn't sense any attackers, and yet everyone seemed to be in disarray.

We gently landed on the wooden balcony. Chase's wings crumbled back as they morphed into his body once again. He collected his leather coat throwing it on as if it was essential to whatever we were about to walk into.

"What's happened?" I demanded from the vampire closest to the door. Before I even reached the threshold to open the door, Titan burst through. Her sudden appearance caught me off guard before realizing her anger was directed at me. She plowed into me with full force, grabbing my shoulders and toppling me over the porch's wooden rails. We wiped out chunks of splintered wood as we rolled down the staircase and she snapped and snarled, acting more wolf than her current human form.

When she went for my face, I curled my weight under her, kicking into her stomach and pushing her over. I rolled into a crouch, trying to figure out why she was in such a vengeful spirit.

"Titan!" Tori screamed from behind as the others trailed our movement in complete bewilderment. Fire leaped down the broken staircase to intervene, but I raised my hand to her. Whatever this fight was about, this was between me and the girl.

Dry tears streaked her face as she curled her lips back, growling as if her canines were on show. The gleam of the Barnett crossbow I'd honored her shone behind, but she didn't dare pull it out on me. No, the intent in her eye was to kill. Menacing and barehanded.

"You killed him!" she snapped. "It was you all along!" Sudden realization dawned on me as one of my many wrongdoings found its way back to me. There was no doubt in my mind as to who she spoke of. Titan now knew about Sydney, her father. But how? Who told her?

"I took you in to protect you, that much isn't a lie," I said coolly.

"Protect me?!" she squealed as if the pain were far greater than any physical shift she'd managed. Her heart bled into a harrowing howl as her anger took over. "I hate you!" She lunged for me again. She used her blunt dirty nails, trying to claw at me. It was animalistic, her mind scattered as she tried to confront me. I elbowed her stomach enough to wind her and stepped out of the way from her wobbly legs in case she fell forward.

She let out a harrowing gasp as she tried to hold her standing position. Her knees buckled. "I never intended to hurt him," I said in a low whisper, conscious of all the vampires, hunters, and werewolves alike who watched on. Fire was pacing back and forth, eager to intervene but quick to object to anyone else who stepped closer.

"He's dead…" she squeaked out, "because of you. You turned him and then killed him!" She took a gulp of air as her lungs finally permitted the suction. The moment she did, she shook off her Barnett crossbow, shifted into her werewolf form, clothes ripping apart with muscle and skin. She leaped for me as anger pooled from her in waves.

Canines snapped at me as I uppercut her jaw in an attempt to stun her. But she took it without a flinch, clawing down my arm in respite. The sting of it ignited my survival instinct as I pitied her all the same. I deserved this. And yet, I couldn't give her the satisfaction of taking her full wrath out on me. I had so many onlookers, I couldn't give her the reprieve she so wanted without looking weak.

My left hand stung from the gaping gashes, and I savored their feel because I knew deep down, I deserved this wrath and pain. She was entitled to it, if not more. She aimed for my thigh. I crashed my elbow down on the top of her head, she knelt into it, taking most of the blow as her canines dragged down my leg. I twisted out of her way before she could crunch those powerful jaws over my leg. I wrapped my arms around her throat as I twisted and sat on her back, enforcing my weight and power to make her buckle as I choked her out.

She twisted, snapped, and snarled, her power surprisingly stronger than I'd ever know it to be as she awkwardly twisted and latched onto my arm. A sharp pain shot through me as I kept my grunt internal. She rolled me onto my back, my wings painfully and awkwardly pinned beneath me from her weight. But I refused to release her out of the chokehold I'd managed around her thick throat. I arched my fangs into her neck, reaching through the thick fur, and injected my venom, the cool serum taking only seconds to stop her thrashing into a weighted mass.

I flicked her over and looked her dead in the eyes as they frantically darted back and forth panicked. Blood oozed down my arm and leg as I mournfully watched her. The werewolves were pacing back and forth, uncertain as to who they should be eager to defend. And part of me hoped they would side with her but would continue to serve me until the mission was complete. The onlookers were silent, and I could feel the shame roll from Tori and infuriation from Chris.

"I never meant to hurt your father. I respected him greatly, and it's been one of my greatest shames," I said honestly. "It was when I'd first been turned, and I ignored the advice of others and lost control to my bloodthirst. I never meant for it to happen."

"Is that why you took us in?" Chris demanded, his chest rising and collapsing in fury as he spoke on Titan's behalf. "For pity? To try and amend your wrongdoing?"

I stared him down. Tori remained silent beside him, his gaze fixed on Titan. He hadn't known of this secret, most didn't. But I imagined it might've crossed his mind before. Perhaps this only solidified his theories.

*Others are watching, my love,* Chase reminded me. I'd already looked less them impressive because I let Titan get a few hits in. Had I been a full-blooded vampire, her bite and graze would've been the end of me. And maybe she'd been hoping the same.

"Take care of her." Was all I said to Tori and Chris. Tori flashed to her side in an instant. Chris, however, remained with chest puffed out. I could feel the heat radiate off him in waves of fury as he contemplated taking me on.

"I will not be so gentle with you," I said in a lowly warning. It saddened me to see the hilt of the sword plastered to his back, the one I'd sourced for him personally. Though I might've taken them in because of my guilt for what I'd done to Titan's father, Sydney, I'd grown fond of the two in earnest.

Fire stepped in front of me, her low growls rumbling through as she eyed him, and I couldn't tell if they were communicating or not. But he eventually gritted his teeth and looked away ashamed that Tori was now carrying Titan instead of him. I imagined he always felt that little bit not good enough. Not strong enough, not brave enough, not enough for *her*. Maybe one day he'd make a good Alpha, but he'd have much to learn and become to ever even stand a chance against me, if that was ever at all possible.

"Who told her?" I scanned the faces finding the two I'd suspected first. *Balzar and Lincon.* Balzar was there when we'd returned Sydney to Cesar's coven and realized the consequence of me turning him into a vampire such the likes of Spungee. He'd witnessed what I'd done. Lincon, however, hadn't, yet his craftiness and ability to find out everything was unparalleled.

Balzar was furious by the unsaid accusation. "Well, perhaps if you two weren't off frolicking, you might've been here when Tythian decided to give us a little greeting."

I was about to defend Chase and my decisions until the realization that Tythian had been here dawned on me. And by the way everyone else looked about frantically, there was no denying Balzar's words. I froze and scanned the area as far as I could go. My gaze immediately caught Chase's as I feared if he truly had arrived, if he'd noticed Chase's presence.

Fire shifted into her human form, and one of the hunters looked away disgusted. How prudish their kind had become at the sight of a naked body. "It's true, Esmore. I was with them. He was with Connor. The moment they appeared, Connor dealt with Tori and me using his gift. And then Tythian spoke sweet nothings into the young one's ears and teleported before anyone could make sense of what happened or anyone else could arrive."

My heart pounded through my ears. *They were here.* They knew where we were and toyed with us. All for what? To create friction between me and Titan by telling her the truth of her father's death? They could've killed Tori and Fire and so many more before we'd become aware of their trespassing, so why didn't they? Were Chase and I far enough away for them not to have felt his presence?

Now I understood why everyone had gone into panic mode and were pooling into the cabin. Tythian was completely in control of the maneuvers, and no one had any inclination as to what he was up to. He was trying to break us apart. And as I searched the various species before me, who were all unsettled and eager to fight amongst themselves, I realized he was so easily putting another wisp of doubt amongst our weak treaty. Was he doing it on a whim, curious as to whether they would turn on one another with such high tension?

"We need to relocate," one of the hunters advocated. My mother was standing on the porch, closest to where we'd broken the old wood, with hands crossed over her chest. She side-glanced the hunter who'd suggested out of turn.

"No," Balzar shook his head, "he got what he came for. He won't come back tonight."

"And what was that?" one of his vampires demanded.

Balzar eyed me. "Panic. And to let us know that he's watching us. He knows where we are."

"But how? Trinity has her gift concealing our location," the same hunter advocated, and this time my mother did pin them with a lethal stare.

"Only if everyone stayed within the circumference," Balzar pinned Lincon and Kasey with a glare. Lincon's wide grin guiltily shaped the culprit. And he couldn't give a damn. "Or we have an insider." Whispers began suspiciously rolling around one another.

"Those two vampires were acting suspiciously," one of the hunters deemed arrogantly.

"Are you kidding me?!" Two of Balzar's vampires turned savagely. "It's called having sex, you should try it sometime to pull that pole out of your ass."

"Yea!" one of their counterparts barked.

"I still can't believe we're dealing with amateurs," Clarissa coldly undermined as she tucked Spungee in closer to her, aware of the growing tension and that a fight was about to break out.

"Enough!" my mother advocated.

"No! We've had enough of you filthy hunters and wolf freaks that are totally into bestiality!" another vampire shouted.

"What did you just say?!" Claus demanded and his temperament snapped like a rubber band as he lunged forward, sinking his fangs deep into the piece of wood the vampire quickly collected to protect himself. Chaos had erupted around us as the different groups pushed and shoved at one another arguing. Gifts went alight as the hunters turned on the vampires and were not at all shy to turn their bright gazes toward the werewolves as well.

"Enough!" I demanded, but no one listened. The gargoyles had circled around Chase in their cemented form, fending off the werewolves who bit and clawed at them, unable to leave a mark no matter how powerful their canines. One of the instigating vampires was hiding behind Chase, who strung him up without remorse, throwing him into the pit after initiating this fight. We needed to stop them, even Balzar seemed perplexed as he yelled for his coven to stand down. My mother had no control over her hunters who were ignorant to 'defend' themselves.

"Lincon! Silence them!" I demanded. He lit with excitement after being so disheartened because everyone actively avoided him in the brawl. Kasey stood in the doorway, stepping out of the way as two opposing vampires from Chase's and Balzar's covens rolled out the front door. She threw back one of the candies animatedly as she watched Lincon do what he did best.

Everyone who'd previously been a problem stopped, and small whimpers eerily descended over the camp. The gargoyles moved uncomfortably as Lincon sheltered them from his mass illusion. My mother, Balzar, Kasey, Chase, Iris, Fire, and I had all been censored from his gift. He began to chuckle to himself, enjoying their pain. Had I half a sense, I would've asked him to exclude the werewolves, but I was too focused on putting a stop to their antics. This was exactly what Tythian wanted.

"Your hunter started this!" Balzar accused my mother. Remorsefully, I'd noticed Julia was caught horrifically in Lincon's illusion amongst the others.

"Your vile followers were trying to bite into my people and—"

"Enough!" Chase bellowed, and fear seeped into everyone's bones. Even Lincon twisted his neck awkwardly as he demanded attention. "We need to separate the groups until they've settled and we need to move on. If Tythian knows where we are it means at any time, he can direct an attack. Balzar, do you still have a lock on him?"

Balzar reluctantly turned his focus away from my mother. "He's back in Montreal."

"Is it possible he's dangling himself in front of us to taunt us?" Fire acquired.

"It's highly probable. But what other choice do we have?" Chase elicited. "We move forward."

My mother brooded but didn't disagree. "Are you going to be able to?" Balzar asked Chase. You two have claimed one another again, haven't you? What does that mean, that you're going to blow up like she did with her gift?"

"That is none of your concern," Chase growled, and I saw the flash of fear roll through Balzar squandering him to silence. A scream broke out as one of Chase's coven finally cracked under the pressure of Lincon's mass illusion.

"Lincon, down," I commanded.

He gave me a wide-eyed expression that the wolf pups often twisted on their parents when they were told they couldn't play anymore. "Lincon," I reprimanded him again. He let out an anguished sigh and finally let them go. Everyone sagged back into consciousness, a wave of confusion rolling through them. I noticed two blobbed masses where wolves had bitten vampires amidst the chaos.

The others stared at one another, restricted in movement by their own fear after being under Lincon's prying fingers in their minds again. This is what Tythian intended. A divide, and his presence slipping in could so easily craft it. But instinct didn't gravitate toward another traitor. And I wasn't often wrong.

*It looks like Tythian isn't lying low anymore. He's making his move personally,* Chase elicited.

It wasn't like Tythian was lying low to start with, except now he had made it personal. "We need to move out."

"Everyone prepare your group separately. We leave in less than an hour. I fluttered over the steps with ease making my way to Tori and the other two. They needed to be ready as well, despite personal grudges. I left the aftermath to Iris and Fire. Balzar shouted at his coven to patrol once again, fanning them out before catching up to me. Not all members had survived their chaotic brawl, and the tension of distrust and disdain for one another was reeking from them.

"Is he going to be all right?" Balzar followed me down the hallway to where Tori and Chris were watching over Titan. I didn't inject her with much venom, and because of her fast-pumping heated blood, it would've started wearing off by now. "Esmore. I asked if he's going to be all right."

I spun on him, realizing he was peering over my wings to make sure I heard *and* saw him. "I don't know, Balzar!" I said offensively but nor did I want to justify our actions to him. Was any of this okay? But what would he know? He'd never had a familiar. He didn't understand the potency of its grasp. Balzar's hittable face was ultimately enticing. But Tythian's intrusion wasn't his fault, and I needed him in action to get our asses into gear and toward Montreal. Tythian had been so close. What if he'd sensed Chase? What if he goes back and tells Fier? What if at any moment Chase were to change?

"I'm not your enemy, Esmore," Balzar quietly said.

"No, your fucking brother is!" The thought jarred me that he'd sense Chase, debilitating the time we'd have left together. Reality snapped back together like a vice around my throat.

He grabbed my arm jolting me back. "Hey, that's not fair," he condoned. I reefed my arm back, fighting against my natural instinct to put a blade to his throat. I wasn't in my right mind. "I don't want him to get to Chase either, Esmore. You know he asked me to end him if you couldn't."

My face slackened. Of course he did, and I wanted to spite Balzar for using it against me as an example of the trust my familiar had in him. I shook my head and spun on my heels again. "Just have everyone prepared to leave." I tried to narrow my focus, avoiding all the invading terror and thoughts. I had to prepare Titan even when she despised me. A part of me considered it was safer to leave her behind, not that she would listen even if she didn't still respect me.

I kicked in the door. Chris jolted and snarled at my aggressive entrance. Titan had shifted back into her human form, and they'd thrown an old blanket over her naked body. She was sitting up against the wall glaring at me, eliciting that if her body moved of her own accord, she'd attack me all over again.

"We're moving out. I don't have time for this conversation. Put your pride aside, and once the job is done then you can do as you please. If you dare throw a knife at my back, either of you," I pointed to Chris and Titan, purposefully segregating Tori. He was under my command. Even if he was fond of her, he'd never betray me. "I will kill you."

I turned and walked away, licking over my fang as Tori broke into a run after me. "Wait, Esmore! Are you really just going to leave it like that?"

I grabbed the corner of his shirt and slammed him against the wall. I was sick and tired of stepping around everyone's *feelings*. The moment that raw realization crept up on me, I dropped him, hideously distracted by his taken aback expression.

*My love, don't punish them for what's happening, and don't close off your emotion.*

*You asked this of me earlier, did you not?* I snapped, cursing myself immediately for turning on him. But he sent down love and tenderness, pressing past the hideous molten disease so he could still have space for us to communicate.

*I asked you to remove your heart for your own protection. Those are two different things, and you know it.*

I hated that he was right and didn't want to take any responsibility for the chaotic pressure and thoughts rummaging in my mind. I was so *angry* and sad. And if I didn't act now, if I wasn't walking toward something, I knew I'd fall apart.

"If Tythian sensed Chase while he was here…" I said, steering my tone away from any giveaway that I was a shambles inside, though I imagined no one missed it. "We need to move. I can't—" I pointed to the room behind him where we'd left the others. "I can't deal with that as well right now. I need your help to control this situation, please. Just give me some time. Just keep her away from me and safe until then. And then I'll deal with my consequences after."

Tori softened. And I hated even more that he pitied me so.

"I'll keep her at bay, Esmore," Tori promised. I knew what it might cost him, that it might drive a wedge between their trust. That Titan might assume he betrayed her to defend me. But I knew after watching Tori protect her for so long that was far from the case. He cared too much. I curtly nodded and headed for the door. They could carry her until she was able to run of her own accord.

As I walked out into the chilly night, I searched the grounds. Everyone was distributed, but I could sense that they were gearing to go. *Has anyone told you how sexy you are when you're on a mission,* Chase purred.

He waltzed out of the shadows with his hands tucked into the pockets of his pants. Jerimiah and Darcy broodily trailed him on either side. I couldn't share the same flare as Chase tried his usual light-hearted humor to dispel the thick tension. He looked scary, monstrous even. And yet, all I could see was the man I loved, slowly dying and acting as if nothing had happened.

*And here I was thinking how sexy you looked wrapped up in protection paper and blankets well away from this fight,* I replied tediously. I tried to strike humor, but it had never come to me so easily.

His laugh rolled through me, naturally easing the tension in my body. *Not a chance, my love. Come on, everyone is almost ready to leave.*

He held out his hand, and I was by his side within seconds clutching it almost desperately. *Relax,* he reassured me. *I'm not going anywhere—yet. You have an army to lead, don't give them a moment to consider your responsibility otherwise.*

Clarissa crept out of the woods, Spungee not far behind her, his neck clicking awkwardly as it always did. "Chase, everyone is ready to move on." She adored him, not romantically but in admiration for who he was and the power he contained. And that still radiated from him despite the evil that lay inside. His coven was still willing to fight alongside him. I considered that most would bail the moment they went for one another's throats. But what kept them together was their own personal desires for revenge. Everyone had lost someone or something valuable to them because of the discord and last war, and it all pointed in one direction now.

They could walk away if they truly wanted to. They could become rogue and never look back. Iris was waiting patiently in the lead where Tori usually positioned himself. My warriors weren't backing down, and it encouraged me to hold the same strength. It was time I sent Tythian a reminder that he toyed with the wrong huntress.

# Chapter 31

W E'D MANAGED A half days' run before coming across the next small township. Chase was irritated far more than usual by the sun, and although he wouldn't admit it or raise the need for concern, I purposefully kept us in the trees, and he silently thanked me. Closing the distance during the day took away their advantage of using sabers against us. Our course was still on track for Montreal where Tythian had returned.

Titan had since recovered and was guided toward the back of the pack, with numerous members between us. Not much had been said, but I could tell in the way Fire purposefully positioned herself between Claus and the pack, instead of by my side, that she was monitoring them carefully. It wasn't that I thought they'd betray me for finding out I'd turned and killed Titan's father. Besides, it was far before any of them had joined my army. But it was yet again another frightful truth that I wasn't one of them, and I considered that to have been a factor that was often overlooked. Our make-do housing dynamics were shifting, and although I couldn't premeditate what would happen after this fight, I considered that it would definitely change the inhabitants when we returned to our 'home.'

Nightfall was to soon fall upon us in the next hour, and despite the endurance all the species had, the hunters were most sensitive to the temperature change of night, and its chilly front as dusk approached.

The town we neared had been abandoned for the longest time. It was surrounded by peaked mountains which acted as a lovely cover-up, and we asserted a group of guards higher in the mountains in case anything decided to descend. After creating a formation of guards, the groups divided and spread out through the township. Upon our entrance, a black crow squawked to grab my attention. I clenched my fists, my knuckles turning white perplexed by the knowledge that Kyran was still watching us.

"Shoo!" One of the vampires ushered it away, none the wiser by the presence of who possessed the crow. Surprisingly, it did flap away into the distant white snow.

The town was oddly eerie. All of the buildings had an abandoned, long ago lost feeling, but for some reason, this one had a rotten decay about it, the smell stifling, without so much as a body to be seen.

"It smells rank here," Balzar complained, covering his nose with his forearm in an attempt to do what we were all trying to endure. My werewolves whined with their ears pinned back, their far superior sense of smell almost crippling them.

"We should walk around the town instead of through it," Clarissa suggested with her Lolita-styled dress and sleeve covering her nose. Spungee clutched to her long black dress like a whining babe.

"Maneuvering through the mountains will delay us," my mother articulated, seemingly the least responsive to the smell, but I knew that was her well-trained experience to not show weakness.

"Aww, is the little princess feeling sick?" Balzar teased Clarissa which earned him a tedious stare, considering he was doing no better.

"Balzar, somethings up here," one of his comrades called out.

Balzar cursed, "What now?" We dauntingly followed him. The small wooden cabins contained the remains of sleet and snow. The howling wind whistled through the open and worn-down roofs. I noticed marks on the ground as if numerous people had been taken and dragged from their homes. The footprints had only been made recently.

*They're fresh,* Chase observed, verifying my thoughts. A small sobbing noise caught my attention as I narrowed down on the small beating heart in one of the cabins. *A human woman was here.* I signaled Tori to inspect the particular cabin, and a wave of excitement and curiosity rolled out throughout the vampires who wondered if this might be their next feast.

Tori pulled out the reluctant teenage girl who was shivering and cold in her woolly attire. She smelt of urine and fear as she closed her eyes, shaking terrified.

"What the fuck is that?" Balzar asked, catching my attention. I drifted my gaze from the girl, who was drunk in fear and out of her wit's end. She looked like the carnage of someone who'd spent far too long housed in Lincon's illusions.

We inclined forward, coming to a stop behind Balzar who inspected a pile of distorted figures. It was a mass grave. The top layer appeared to be humans, freshly killed. The layers beneath were a stench of something far more sinister.

"Girl, what happened here?" my mother addressed the teenage human. She flinched and trembled, still somewhat coherent. Tori's grip might've looked loose, but there would be no escaping for her.

The mottled gray color of the bodies looked like they'd begun to be bitten by the frost. The smell was a torturous odor in the center square. One of the vampires inspected closer under Balzar's order, creeping toward the closest as he lifted the thin woman's arm.

*I don't have a good feeling about this,* Chase said, unsheathing his sword. Cautiously, a few others did the same. I dipped into my small satchel on the side, stroking my golden claws that I'd use if needed.

"They're definitely dead," the vampire who inspected them choked out. Vampires didn't breathe, but they were still sensitive to scent.

"No shit," Balzar barked back. "What do you think?" he asked, twisting to face us.

"It moved!" the vampire yelled back, retracting a step.

"Wha—"

In a flash, the vampire disappeared into the mob of bodies. Everyone took a mortified step back as the vampire's scream splattered into silence and his rotting corpse combined with the others. The mass pile shifted under the low tune of a whistle.

The human girl screamed, trying to block her ears from the low whistle. Everyone unsheathed their weapons. My gold claws were already on as that ominous sensation in the town rose.

Another wave of tension rumbled through as Whitney teleported in with Connor and Dillian on either side. Two vampires jumped for them but were quickly flattened to the ground by Connor who looked down at them like scum.

"Hiya, kids!" Whitney mocked in a voice that was higher pitched than I'd recalled it in her human life. She still wore a floral dress that cascaded around her loosely; her long blonde hair was in two ponytails as she charmed a tantalizing smile.

"Dillian," Julia rasped as she seemed to lose self-awareness in our current predicament. The moment his name left her lips his attention snapped to her. He looked back at me angrily as if it were my fault that she'd come.

Iris's lightning struck at where they once stood as they teleported behind the mass of corpses, standing on top of one of the crumbling roofs.

"Oh my, looks like her familiar's still alive after all. I wonder what Fier might have to say about that?" Whitney toyed with a sinner's smile. "I'll let you both deal with this." I could feel a surge of power shift through her, and that low whistle screened the entire township. She immediately teleported out.

The figures rolled to standing. Though the bodies on top might've been fresh, the ones beneath were far from. And of all different species. An assortment of wolves, small wildlife animals, and humans staggered to a stand with stiff movement.

Balzar went into a frenzy, his focus on his brother, Connor, as he dodged through the dead puppets before they advanced with stifling speed on the rest of us. Balzar quickly skirted into the ground, huffing into the melted snow as Connor used his gift on him but looked displeased the moment he and Lincon made eye contact. Lincon had been one of the few who could counter Connor's mental gift and make him scream for it.

Everything erupted so quickly, the lamented puppets, which hosted fatal wounds leaped for the closest moving thing near them. Iris passed another lightning strike, distracting Connor who jumped behind the building. Titan shot an arrow, protecting Balzar's back as he came to consciousness again.

Dillian's gaze remained on Julia until he had no choice but to retreat from the attackers. Two undead jumped at me, the woman's hair plastered to her bashed in head by the blood that had seeped from the wound, in what looked to be days old. Tori pushed the girl back into the cabin to protect her, unsheathing his blade.

The undead woman lunged for me, a small knife that she might've tried to defend herself with once being her only means of a weapon even now. Their speed and strength surpassed any expectation of a living human and even when I reefed out her heart—contemplative that the same laws applied as that of the vampires—she continued moving, undisturbed. I twisted out the knife's way, using my wing to backhand the other male who attacked me.

"Take out their legs!" I heard Chase command his coven. I noticed Julia skirting through the sides, hiding as she drew closer toward where I sensed Dillian retreating.

Lincon was cackling like a madman as he continued hacking the undead into tiny pieces. Despite being in the midst of battle, others actively avoided getting in his way as he wildly and savagely swung about the sword he'd found, which meant those who pursued Connor had no chance, even if they did have a mental guard of some kind.

I cursed, torn to track Iris and Balzar or Julia who was floundering on her own. *Stupid girl.*

I let out a low whistle, commanding Fire to my side. I took to the sky, sweeping over the disastrous scene. Even if they were undead and brainless they were actively standing against us physically. I tried to sweep a wave of panic over them, to slow them momentarily but not even that worked. Which meant any mental gift wouldn't work against them.

Fire dodged between their masses, snapping her fangs into a small fox that attacked her. It still flustered in her mouth, nipping at her. She threw the half-decayed body across the partially snowed ground. Its ribs were awkwardly sticking out through matted fur as it immediately lunged for another vampire.

Julia ducked in between homes and into the west forest. There was a clear divide in which way Connor and Dillian had gone. They were targeting the few soldiers who had gone ahead of us as scouts, who were now returning and being attacked one by one. They knew they were outnumbered, and this was only a preliminary attack from the army Tythian had at his disposal. But now the *dead* as well?

They were picking at our numbers, one by one. Connor was dodging Iris's attacks as lightning strike after strike landed on the side of the mountain, aiming for him. Balzar struggled to keep up as he searched for answers and vengeance for Yolo's death. Connor might not have put the blade through him, but he was an accomplice and helped Tythian all these years.

Dillian, however, was drawing a much smaller crowd into the forest. The moment he and Julia intercepted, I swooped low and stood in front of her, blocking his view of her.

"No, Esmore, it's fine!" Julia anguished as she tried to step around me. I slammed a wave of fatigue through her, forcing her next step to stumble before she'd realized what I'd done. But it wasn't her response and reaction I was keeping an eye on. It was Dillian's. He seemed unfazed as he looked at me with those hollow, bland pink eyes.

"You shouldn't have come here," he said. His gaze darted beyond me as he quickly pulled back his bowstring and set loose to the bow. I could hear in the distance the vampire who'd come to support Julia and I drop into an amounted mass of goop as Dillian's aim hit home.

"Dillian," Julia said weakly from behind, and I could sense the twist of emotion within him. Interesting, perhaps not as cold as he'd presented himself all those years ago. Or maybe these years had brought some of him back as his feral vampire nature settled over time.

I cautiously remained in front of her. Not simply to protect her because I was certain he wouldn't harm her, but because me blocking their reunion was upturning more from him than I'd expected. Maybe there was more of Dillian still in there.

"You should return to your familiar. Now that Whitney knows Chase is alive, she'll report it to Tythian and Fier. I doubt you'll have much time together," Dillian warned. My anxiety grew. *I knew that.* But maybe if he could tell me more, then I could actually do something about it.

"Do you know how I can fix it?" I asked quietly, embarrassed by my own hopelessness.

His stark attire had evolved over the years. Now he truly looked the part with his multiple earrings that often scared the humans at face value. But he'd always been the kindest of the hunters—second to Julia of course.

"Not that I've overheard," he pointedly said. He twisted, shooting another arrow into the distance, so far that I couldn't even see where he was aiming. "Don't come to Montreal. Tythian's recently acquired this power. The one to turn the dead into his puppets. Take your armies and flee while—"

I scoffed at him, and his gaze glazed with an arrogant demeanor. "It's a bit late to be worried about us now, wouldn't you say?"

A tick went through Dillian's jaw as he straightened in resolve. "I did what I had to, to keep Tori and you alive for another second. Do you think I've enjoyed being a pawn? You don't know the things I've been forced to do or the wrath I've endured for being an outsider. How I was treated as someone who was constantly shadowed by my affiliation with you. I did what I had to, to make sure everyone remained safe. We all had our parts to play," he said as he looked away when Julia stepped out from the shadow of my wings.

"Dillian." Her small voice was like honey against his anguished, graveled tone. "Thank you."

He looked up at her, disbelieving and deflated. Even I twisted to get a better look at her. I was so used to others' malice and manipulation that when I saw sincerity at its finest I backed away from it. She was like light to my darkness. Where I had killed and conquered for my place and power, she had slowly worked with the small gift she had, patiently waiting for the day when she could be reunited with Dillian. Maybe this *was* the reason she'd joined our mission with the intent to see him again and took the opportunity when it presented itself—even if it risked her life.

"I know you did this to protect the others," she said sincerely. He watched her movement as if she were a feral animal about to attack him. As if she herself were one of the undead, about to be puppeteer by someone else's motive. A small bud pierced the skin of the inched snow bedside him and continued to grow. He watched it, mystified. It reached his hip level when a vibrant purple flower bloomed. Anguish and pain rolled off him in waves as he stared at the flower. Whatever its sentiment or value…it was twisting a transfixing nostalgia through him. "I told you I'd come back for you," Julia said with a small smile. From beneath her leather shirt, she pulled out the small ring that Dillian had once shown me in his excitement to propose. That was before any of this had escalated and we were on the run from the Hunter Guild. The easy and naïve life we'd once lived.

It had my hand gravitating toward and wanting to smooth over the lock of Chase's hair in my pocket. Though we weren't able to exchange rings, we held our sentiments elsewhere. And besides, I was branded by the blue gemmed necklace balancing between my breasts.

"You don't know the things that I've done," he hauntingly said to her. My own heart churned as I saw the Dillian I'd known and loved. My best friend who'd fought and laughed by my side for years. After my grievance of never thinking he was still in there after being turned, he was slowly creeping back. The cold stature of when he was first reborn, breaking to birth the real version of him. For how long had he trapped his emotions and sincerity to play out the role he'd had to assume within Tythian's Council?

"It doesn't matter to me. I only care about you. And you did what you had to, to come back to me," Julia said patiently. "I was never going to give up on you."

Fire caught up to me, and I stepped in front of Dillian's trajectory as he aimed his bow and arrow. I shook my head. He seemed torn. Continue his duties and pledge to Tythian or come back to the old? To return to his family?

A lightning bolt struck the side of the mountain, and the earth beneath us shook. I could hear the ground croak in pain. I caught Julia as she stumbled unbalanced by its shake. Behind us, an avalanche erupted, pouring down the side of the mountain and toward the town.

*Shit.* When I turned to face Dillian, he'd vanished. The purple flower gone as well. "Come on," I ordered Julia as I ran back toward the others. I was grateful I didn't have to drag her alongside me. "Look after her while I get an aerial view," I ordered Fire.

I jumped through the treetops, aware of Dillian as he circled back toward Connor on the mountainside. The town was flooded by snow. Only its edges unaffected. From what I could see, the majority of everyone got out.

I could sense Whitney teleporting in as she took Dillian and Connor back with her. Perhaps the undead weren't smart enough to outmaneuver an avalanche. I found Chase, my heart racing as I considered the likelihood of what was about to happen. *They knew about Chase.*

I dropped into the soft snow, my attention immediately drawn to the human teenage girl who had once been the sole survivor who acted as a distraction. She wasn't so fortunate now as her dead body was half-covered by snow. But that hadn't been what ended her, the snow bled red around her from the numerous wounds in her upper back where most likely one of the undead had found and dragged her out.

Chunks of the undead were littered across the snow. The small fragments still disturbingly moving as best as they could, even without having an attached body. One hand and arm continued to drag itself toward Jerimiah, who looked at it grotesquely and chopped it into finer pieces.

"No!" Lincon screamed, trying to swim back into the weighted snow. "NO! They can't be gone already?!"

"Lincon!" Kasey growled, throwing a rock into the back of his head. He toppled over with it, deflated that his fun was gone. He sobbed into the snow, dramatically pained that they'd leave him like this.

"Tythian must've known we'd come through this way," Balzar growled. His spiked gloves were coated in red from warding off the undead and a few fine specks of black blotches. Perhaps he'd been able to get a hit in on Connor after all, but I knew for a fact that he wasn't dead. I'd sensed the moment they'd teleported out. Perhaps Whitney hadn't gone all that far after all considering her impeccable timing to take them back when the avalanche began. Her undead puppets were no longer of use to her.

"They saw him," Clarissa said in her dreary monotone. "What do we do now?"

"It's okay," Chase ushered to his coven who looked pissed off that they'd been bested. Everyone was.

"What, now we're fighting against the undead?!" one of the hunters demanded from my mother, unperplexed by Chase's situation. I walked over to him, shamefully checking over his fangs to make sure they hadn't enlarged in any way or the disease in his mind hadn't spread.

*Esmore, it's okay. What will be will be.*

*It's not okay, Chase,* I said in a warning tone. I didn't want him telling me that I was silly for holding concern.

Most of my werewolves had survived. Despite striking down a few of our members, the undead had no special ability or gift that we'd witnessed besides being ridiculously strong and fast.

But the larger problem was what Tythian had in mind for this new found 'gift' of his. If they purposefully constructed this pile to simply trial it against us, then what had time permitted them to build in Montreal?

The top bodies had been killed only in recent days. How had we not caught wind of such a gift until now? I wished I'd had longer with Dillian. If I'd been thinking more clearly, I might've been able to ask him where Tythian even acquired such a power.

Chase stammered, and a wave of nauseous pain channeled through our link and slammed into me. My natural instinct was to release our bond, but instead, I held on tight. "Chase!" He dropped to his knees, a rumbling of intensity spreading over his mind as that thorny disease began to spread further. A line of drool hung from his mouth, and he tried to catch himself as his knees buckled beneath him. I wobbled from my own undoing and pushed Clarissa and Spungee out of the way, thoughtfully protective and scared that they might turn on him any second.

I clung onto him, aiding him as we tried to push away the disease as it swarmed him.

*No, no. Stay with me,* I was mentally slapping him to stay alert. He could fight this. He was better than this foul goop that was trying to rot his brain. I pushed against it, the lightness of my huntress being drawn as a natural beacon against the darkness that webbed against his humanity. Urgency pounded through me as the sensation of talons tore into my mind. I mentally stood by him, hand in hand trying to fortify a wall and prevent the spread of the disease. My sight was hazing in and out as I noticed the few droplets of blood that had splattered on my thighs. My nose was bleeding as I shook him physically and mentally to fight this evil. I wouldn't let them take him!

With all my focus on Chase and keeping him out of peril, I was too late to defend myself against the back of my mother's sword, smacking into my neck. I crumpled into Chase, keeling forward and unconscious. Dark. Emptiness. Alone.

# CHAPTER 32

"WELL, WELL, WELL, *what a delightful surprise."* Kyran clapped. *My eyes burst open in the dusty old throne room. The room was foreign to me, yet Kyran seemed right at home as he sat cross-legged on a throne with a tilted crown atop his head. He ogled the dreary room as I did.*

*It was big, meant for audiences and staff. And all that remained was the singular throne.* "This used to be my brother's throne. He sometimes had me sit on it for ruling kingdom stuff, and it was such a bore," *Kyran droned.* "You wouldn't believe how selfish the people of our court could be." *He charmed a wicked smile, delightfully so because there was no doubt that he was the most selfish person of all.* "But we all have our own duties to uphold, don't we?"

*His smile was as patronizing as it was terrifying. I pushed myself off the ground, discovering my weak legs couldn't find enough strength to even stand. I remained keeled over but offering him my most defiant glare. I felt weak here. My gaze caught the mirage of my wings pinned to the wall behind him. I looked over my shoulder, unbalanced by their disappearance. I hadn't once retracted them over the last ten years and had to fight through the unsettling detachment, reminding myself this was all but a dream. A crafty place for Kyran to torment me.*

"They're beautiful, aren't they?" *he asked sincerely.*

*"Just try in the real world, Kyran, I dare you," I provoked. Because I knew he couldn't. He was trapped in his own menacing torture. His smile only grew wider. His blue eyes held that crazed look about them. Constantly in a feral state as Lincon often paraded when he went into a blood frenzy. Kyran was a maniac. A beautiful one at that. The dark angel of our kind, one might even dare say, if it wouldn't feed his ego so prominently.*

*"Looks like you're in some terrible timing and luck." He pouted. "Is there perhaps anything I can do to help?"*

*I remembered Chase's words. He didn't want to make a deal with this archaic vampire because it left too much room for consequence. But Chase wasn't here, and this 'meeting' wasn't exactly planned, considering I didn't anticipate my mother turning her weapon against me. Suddenly I became aware of why I was here in the first place. Chase.*

*"Don't worry," Kyran mused. "He's still alive. Barely, but you know how it is. Transforming into a saber kind of kicks the life out of you." Another dashing tight smile. But I could feel the hold on his temperament loosening like he was getting sick of his own long-winded game. "Anything I can do?" he asked again.*

*I leaned back, my spine feeling like a loose, watery substance. It was bad enough I was on my knees before him, but I put every effort into being able to at least sit upright. "What can a vampire in a coffin at the bottom of the sea possibly do for me?"*

*Now he flexed his fingers back and forth angsty as if I was wasting his time.*

*"I do come from the old world, child. Who's to say my knowledge wouldn't surpass such a small 'inconvenience'?" he inquired. I demobilized my expression. Lincon was certain Kyran didn't know anything, but then again, he could be bluffing.*

*"You know of Fier's gift?"*

*"Well, I certainly know his gamble. But yes, I also know his trick. A tough one that and from my understanding un-revocable."*

*My jaw clenched, a tick flexing through it. Why was I even listening to him? He knew nothing, and he came here to gloat, wasting even more of my precious time.*

*"But perhaps I know someone who can? If you were able to release me in time?"*

*I let out a haughty laugh, my own craziness filling me. Is this what my life had come down to? Playing catch and release with the villains of our world? He would ask that of me even without a favor he could return. And even if I did, it wouldn't serve me in any positive light. He would create chaos in this world the moment he was released, and perhaps it's what was needed. And I couldn't help but be bitterly compelled toward the idea if the world was so cruel as to take my love away from me.*

*Kyran's patience was growing thin. He swished against the marbled floor grabbing my throat and dangling me in the air like I weighed nothing. I tried to laugh if only to piss him off, but he crushed my windpipe so tightly that only a small gasp managed to escape.*

*"You have the audacity to laugh at someone so great before you?" he enquired, loosening his grip only slightly because he genuinely wanted a response. Up close, his skin was so porcelain smooth. His features so immaculately placed that it was as if he were created from marble.*

*"You can do nothing for me, Kyran, unless you have a way to save my familiar," I hauntingly wheezed out. I didn't have the will to fight him. In this dream place there was no point. He controlled all of it.*

*His eye twitched. "And what will you do if your familiar doesn't make it through? Will you still fight?"*

*His blue eyes were intense, putting me in a light daze or perhaps that was the lack of oxygen reaching my brain. I trod my feet lightly in the air, trying to scrape them against the marble floor. This seemed unusual for Kyran, and I couldn't gauge his angle. When I didn't reply he pressed his face closer to mine. The tip of his nose touching mine. I was about to head-butt him when his next words halted me. "I want Tythian dead, girl."*

*He dropped me to the ground, and I slithered, gasping desperately for my breath as he walked away.*

*"Why do—" my voice broke. I took a shaky and torturous breath.*

*"My reasons are no concern to you. I just want the assurance that if I can't have my revenge personally, you will do so for me. And when you do, pierce him in the heart and give him my regards."*

*Before I could question any further, he waved his hand about. The room became distorted, and I felt like I was freefalling into darkness.*

I jolted back into my body and gasped for breath as my hand inevitably went to my throat. Thick burning chains restricted my hands as I lurched forward without impact. I was bound by the wrist and ankles by thick tentacle-like vines that seemed to grow through the compacted snow.

Chaos had erupted around us as the different groups pushed and shoved at one another arguing. Chase was lurching forward, his head hung as he was mounted with vines in the same way. He was still conscious but weak. *So very weak.*

The gargoyles had circled us in their cemented form, safeguarding if anyone else attempted to make a move on us. The werewolves surrounded us guarding against the mixture of Balzar's coven and hunters who demanded Chase's execution.

"Stop!" I needed silence to try and orientate myself. My head and neck throbbed from where my mother had struck me. I tried to lean into Chase, with all my might pulling at the unmovable vines, and tried to press through the ringing in my ear. All of it was a blur as I ached in misery for Chase to lift his head—to show me that he was okay.

"Hi there, Esmore, just noticed you're in a bit of a pickle," Lincon said, crouching beside me. He seemed to have appeared out of nowhere. The two gargoyle warriors who he'd put under illusion were flabbergasted about how he got through their barrier until they'd realized what had happened. Kasey was nearby, erecting her barrier around us. I felt unbalanced and disorientated. Something was off, and I was certain it was all to do with Chase. I just needed to see his face. I needed to make sure he was okay.

"Cut down these vines!" I snapped at Lincon, infuriated that he was still exuberant even now. He whistled at me and defensively raised his hands before efficiently slicing them down with one of Kasey's knives. The moment I was set free I scampered over to Chase. His weight titled forward as one of the gargoyles cut him loose.

The others argued and fought amongst one another. "Shut them up!" I demanded of Lincon as I curled my hand under Chase's chin to see his face. "Chase?!" He didn't respond. When I lifted his chin, it revealed his fangs had gotten longer and thicker. Black squirming veins protruded around his eyes. His nails had elongated into claws. *No, no, no, no.*

Everyone who'd been a problem prior stopped and small whimpers eerily descended upon the camp. The gargoyles moved uncomfortably as Lincon sheltered them from his mass illusion. He began to chuckle to himself, enjoying the suffering of others.

"Chase," I rasped. My nose had stopped bleeding as he groaned and I braced myself. I couldn't kill him. He couldn't ask that of me. This wasn't real.

*Esmore,* he shallowly said down our link. I cowered into a sob, bunching myself into his lap. His hand curled on the back of my head, brushing through my hair, cautious of his sharp nails. We hadn't lost the fight yet. I collected his hand, kissing it. Reconfirming that no matter what his appearance or ailment—I loved him.

"I love you," I squeaked as I looked up at his washed-out gray eyes. *What had they done to him?* This wasn't like a saber, yet it was at the same time. Was this the result of him fighting it or were they playing with us?

He looked sad as he smiled. "And I you. I'm sorry," he said, depleted.

"You have nothing to apologize for. Hey, I'm not going to leave you. Your battle's mine, remember," I said more so for my own clarity. He was still with me, right? He was holding on until the end. How torturous was this for him? Was I cruel for asking such a thing of him? But we could face this, we could find another way. Of that, I was sure.

He cupped my face serenely. "Until death do us part." My eyes filled with tears.

"I don't know what to do," I said pathetically. What was I to do for him? How could I fix this? I felt so depleted and empty. Like the moment I'd pull away from him the vortex of emotion would leave me stark in a darkness I'd frequented too often. I remembered this feeling, but it wasn't yet dawning on me what had transpired.

"Ssh, you don't have to do anything, Esmore. This is what it is. And we move forward anyway."

"No, we can't! You can't fight like this!" I continued to frown, my own disorientation heavily lying on me.

He smiled serenely, and it scared me too much how he could immerse himself in the notion of doting and letting go of me at the same time. I felt it. I could see it. "This is who we are, Esmore. Those were your words exactly."

"But this is different."

"No, it's not," he gently said and pressed a small kiss to my forehead. I felt the color drain from my face. His fangs were cool as they brushed against my skin. Too big. They were too unnatural and yet it made me clutch him tighter. They weren't allowed to take him away.

"We should run away," I said quietly under my breath, ashamed if anyone heard how desperate I sounded. And at that, he let out a small chuckle. One that conflicted me emotionally as I wanted to laugh away my woes too.

"I've always wanted to run away with you. From the very start," he teased. "But this is too far gone. I've only ever seen Fier work his gift within the same room. Perhaps the distance is what stopped the transition entirely. Or it's because we're fighting it together, and for that, I thank you." We were equally holding up the last of his mental stronghold. It was melted away in places where the disease was seeping in. Where he couldn't reach, I was trying to fortify myself to protect him. As one we were, more intimately than I ever knew were possible. But it still wasn't enough. The disease would still make its way in. It already had. "I don't have much more time, Esmore. We need to end this fight. I'm so sorry for betraying your trust."

"I don't understand," I confided intimately. Until I realized the shallow and panicked breaths I'd been taking fell short. They were an imitation. I slowly shoved back from him, my hand reaching to my chest and acknowledging its silence. My expression twisted, mortified. I turned to my mother who was stuck in Lincon's trance.

"I suspected that if you tried to help me as the disease transitioned, it might take you with it as well. I had your mother promise me she'd intervene in the only way I knew how to protect you."

My mouth went agape, but no words came out. "How could you?" I trembled with disbelief. I could feel the confusion leeching out of me, leaving behind the open wound and void of what I was. Without Chase's presence and his touch, I was only this thing that knew cruelty, order, and possession. I was the same monster I'd hated from all those years ago.

"No," I said selfishly. *I'd rather go under with you than be this empty thing.* I was scared to keep my distance from him, knowing the further I'd step away from him the more apparent my emotionless soul would be. And although my gift had been weak, I felt alone without its jittery presence. I felt stuck in time, only my vampirism keeping me entitled to the world as a shell. He relieved a sad smile and took hold of the blue gemmed necklace at my chest that replicated the blue gem of his earring. His. I was his.

I was lost for words, searching for my beating heart. But my mother was efficient, and her gift already concealed its whereabouts or who might've held it, if they hadn't already hidden it. I did a headcount in disarray but couldn't account for those who'd been lost in the fight. I searched the backs of Chase's gargoyles. Had they been in on it? Just as I had betrayed Chase, had Jerimiah and Darcy been in on this, conspiring against me? A scream broke out as one of Chase's coven finally cracked under the pressure of Lincon's mass illusion.

"Esmore, please. Let me do this for us. I'm okay. I'm ready to fight. And you're safe. From not only Tythian, but anyone else who tries to oppose you. Let me do this for you."

I was tearing with mixed emotions as if trying to cling to their remains.

"This is who we are, Esmore. Until we're not," he reminded me. To not…meant to die. I pressed down the lump in my throat, suddenly aware of Jerimiah and Darcy who were painfully watching us. Their condolences oozed from them and how I hated their sympathetic expressions looking at us so pitifully. We'd fought so hard to protect him and for what, to extend time only for this?

I straightened my shoulders, pulling the blue gemmed necklace out of his grip. I stood, my head still aching and squandering my perfect balance. Even if he had asked my mother to do so for precautionary reasons, it didn't make me any less vexed by it. "Lincon, down," I commanded. I walked over to my mother, feeling with each step my defiance creeping in with a raw blemish of only what was to remain.

When my mother came to coherency, I struck her across the face. Her face shifted only slightly by my hit that would've left her ears ringing. Had it been for any other reason, she would've fought back. But she had now defiled my body twice without my permission. She sided with my love behind my back and now hid it away from me. Perhaps it was a returned favor considering what I had done to Chase. But it didn't burn my spiteful spirit any less.

"If this is the creature you wanted to come forth," I coaxed her, my voice grave in contained rage. "Then congratulations, you've succeeded."

"Esmore," Tori said, stepping forward cautiously. My icy glare pinned him, and Titan's pitiful dagger-like gaze had nothing on the undercurrent of death I promised as I eyed every single one of them. It was so quickly overturned that I felt the difference drain from me until that pain and sadness seemed to trickle bit by bit. It didn't take away the suffering because with Chase so close I still knew and felt that. But they'd unsheathed me as a weapon yet again, and anything that would happen now was beyond any of our control.

"We're moving forward. If anyone has any issues with that then stay behind. And if anyone *dares* try to take claim to Chase's coven, they'll have to go through me," I warned. I wasn't disillusioned by his current state. Though he might've still been physically fit, surprisingly. Some might still consider him in a vulnerable and compromising position. And although they'd shown their loyalty many times over, it was in their nature to try and gain power at any advantage they could.

"And me." Balzar sidled up to my side, eyeing Lincon filthily for ensnaring him in his illusions before addressing the others.

My mother and I stared at one another measurably, her cheek reddening by the second.

"Where's Tythian now?" Chase asked, slowly pushing himself up. A few of the vampires took a step away, uncertain about his transformation. He was a thread away from being turned into a saber completely.

Balzar grimaced at the sight, but held out his hand to help him up. Chase clasped it in comradery, evidently grateful for the brother he'd found in him. It offered a fluttering reminder of when Yolo had still been alive, and Chase had favored him in a similar way. "Montreal with the others."

Without a second glance, I hastened in that direction, leaving behind the littered bodies snowed under in a town that I would never think of again.

# THE PASSAGE OF WAR

*I was crafted for only this.*
*To fight.*
*To survive.*
*And to sacrifice myself for what was known as a greater cause.*
*But in the folds of the darkness — I found something light.*
*He called it love. I called it curiosity.*
*We came from a different time, and yet we found middle ground.*
*We fought side by side and rediscovered the world as if it were new.*
*But one thing remained, besides our inner demons we were still*
*forced to slay.*
*This war of ours was hideous and only stole those who we cared for.*
*There is no victory in this.*
*Never-ending and all soul-consuming.*
*Until there is nothing.*
*But I beg of you, to whom it may concern.*
*Please let him stand. And I pray, don't let me watch him fall.*
*Please find a safe passage for him. Or I will give you nothing at all.*
*And if you do, I'll give you myself and carnage in return.*

# CHAPTER 33

A THIN LAYER of snow encapsulated the city as dusk set in. The worn-down retired Ferris wheel we stood atop gave us a heightened lookout. Well back in the distance, our armies waited for our intel and signal. Chase and I had carried Balzar and my mother, flying over the small river to land stealthily on top of the decaying rusty wheel that somehow was still vertical even after all these years.

We'd witnessed numerous vampires patrolling as we flew overhead. My mother used her gift to conceal our scent and Lincon was nearby using his illusions on the patrolling officers, making them ignorant to our arrival.

The others knew we would come. And despite that knowledge, Tythian's patrol officers seemed causal as if he was coaxing us in, arrogantly indifferent to our invasion. But there was more peril to be had, and Balzar was the first to address it.

"It reeks here too." Balzar grimaced as he held a cloth over his nose. It smelt of the undead and throughout the city were accumulations of bodies. Even Tythian's Vampire Council members actively avoided them.

"Where are they?" I asked Balzar, whose eyes blazed with ill intent. He pointed to two separate buildings that were ground level.

"Tythian's on the right with Fier. Whitney, Connor, and Deemori are over there. Not that it accounts for anything because the moment we execute action, they'll split and teleport all over the place." I grumbled my complaint about the webbed landscape. Had my gift been restored and thriving it would take me only a decisive second to obliterate everything in range before they'd even known what had happened. Much in the same way that Fier monopolized Washington DC, Tythian had also spread out his Council in Montreal.

Chase balanced on the peak of the circular enclosure, his wings slightly hunched over as he assessed the area silently. If only Chase knew how to use my gift on such a wide-scale landscape. But even if he did know, triggering it would most likely kill him in the process. And even at the suggestion, he'd probably throw himself toward it which is why I kept the thought to myself.

He knowingly looked over at me, aware of my rising temper. If only I had more power and my gift hadn't been taken. I would've finished this in a matter of seconds. But I supposed that would've only taken away my fun.

I sensed the power radiate from the city. Like the vampire I'd faced in New York, Tythian had undoubtedly recruited strong vampires as he took the remains of Oppollo's Council. And on top of that, there were those pesky blue robe wearing vampires who were formerly his assassins. They were a handful on their own to challenge, and the average of our warriors wouldn't be able to face them. They'd just cut through them too easily. The likelihood of my werewolves surviving a platoon of them coming out unscathed was unlikely.

A whistling arrow sunk deep into the metal of the capsule I balanced on. We quickly unsheathed our weapons, alarmed by its suddenness. I couldn't see the perpetrator, but the arrow was of the same style that Dillian preferred. Attached was a note. I crouched down, tearing the note off.

*Fier's set bombs along the rivers. Keep Julia out of this.*

"And where's Dillian?" I asked curiously. None of our eyesight was as keen as his. And although Balzar couldn't see him, he pointed in a direction. I sense he's on a rooftop over there. I scrunched up the note.

"Fier's set up bombs along the river's edge. We'll use the werewolves to sniff them out to avoid them."

"It'll cost us time," my mother said.

"Yes, but at least our warriors will have arms and legs attached when we charge in," Chase argued.

"How do we ensure none of them escape? Tythian and Whitney can teleport out at any time," Balzar considered. This was endgame. We couldn't chance their disappearance once again.

"They probably depend on it. They might already be aware of my gift's fatigue, but there's no way they could be certain. Surely they would've put radical procedures in place trying to counter that, so perhaps we might have a slight edge. And they don't yet know that my hearts been removed," I said, begrudging. "They want us here. It's endgame for them too. That's why they've made it look so inviting for us just to waltz in. And now that Tythian has such a gift…he's arrogance has overridden his sensibility." I understood this notion personally.

"Don't underestimate him," Chase warned me, and I let out a snarky hiss. I certainly wasn't someone who was going to underestimate him, not after all he'd taken from me. But I would make his demise as painful as possible. A wicked smile stretched over my face, my vampire self rising to the occasion as my eyes flared into their bright purple.

"To ensure they stay and play, we make sure the one thing he cares about most is anchored here. We go after Whitney."

Chase was judging my malicious and wicked intent, and I almost siphoned pride in it. This is what you made me, you knew the consequence of what would happen. And I felt even viler than the times before, considering I'd now found balance within myself for the last ten years. And now, there was nothing but a gaping hole that could only be fixed with one thing—blood lust.

Multiple strategies had gone through my mind about how to best approach Tythian's trap, but all fell considerably short of the one we'd ended up with. And although I wasn't particularly fond of our collaboration and that it divided Chase and me initially, I had to succumb that it was the most calculated movement.

"But I don't want to go with Balzar!" Lincon sulked.

"Oh, stop your whining, we're all going, you idiot," Titan snapped. We'd decided it was best if Balzar and my platoon squared off Connor, Deemori, and Whitney while my mother and Chase deliberated Fier and Tythian. I didn't like the divide, but it had to be done. If we went in as a whole, we'd be surrounded. We'd be overwhelmed with the amounted sabers and undead who were attacking us, let alone those who orchestrated them. They were the ones we had to prioritize as targets.

I'd gifted Chase and my mother a few of my werewolves to assist them in sourcing out the bombs along the river to avoid them. With my mother's gift, she was able to conceal Chase's presence until Tythian and Fier physically spotted him. Though I doubted he'd care much for coverage now.

I wanted to throttle him for taking the lead. But he'd only deplore that I was doing the same.

*This will work,* Chase promised me as we set into formation. I was aware of Titan's leer in the background, and my vampire self encouraged the girl to attack me, just to diffuse some of my own hungry jitters. A very tiny part of me continued trying to remind myself what I might've felt, and I tried to mirror its example.

Whenever I spoke with Chase telepathically, I was first addressed by the gooping disease that I detested so much. I was so angry. *You're asking me to watch on as you walk into your death. But pay heed, Chase, if you don't make it out then neither will I,* I threatened.

I could feel his calm and soothing effect rub over me like a balm. I wanted to roll in it, the gentle caress of what was something more connected than I was. *You will make it through. No matter what. I'll make sure of it.*

I was so infuriated. How could he say that to me when I'd fought and gone through all this effort to keep him alive! And then I was only infuriated further that self-sacrificial thoughts were all that consumed me. As if we were trying to one-up one another in a wild declaration of love. I loved him. I knew that much, but I couldn't connect any rational thought because all I wanted to do was *fight.*

Chase inclined his attention toward Titan, Chris, and Tori as if they were one of the examples as to why I had to live on. I shunned him. Yes, I had an attachment to the younger ones, but this was war, and he knew the statistics of how many of us might walk out, especially with the stakes so high. There was no life beyond this, none of which I could see. It came down to now, and I would fight to my glorious content in hopes it would protect as many of them as possible. But I'd given up on any sense of reward if Chase himself had already given up. Chase swept another wave of serenity through me, trying to balance the crazed thoughts that danced about. But to see him fight would be just as beautiful.

I pushed away the gruesome expectation and let the vampire come to play. The wave of promised death and tantalizing my prey came with a beautiful cost. I didn't have to think about anyone else because I dared to focus on only one thing. *I'll kill them all.*

"Are you ready, Esmore?" Balzar asked me. White puffs of smoke billowed from my platoon's mouths. Some of them were in their werewolf form. Their clothes flung over the tree branches for when they would return. *For those who would return.*

"Do we really want to do this?" one of them asked. He was still clothed with a backpack. Twelve of the members were still in human form, carrying bags of silvered chains, one of which was Titan as well with her Barnett crossbow and arrows strapped across her chest and hip.

"You know they'll come for us sooner rather than later. If we want it to be safe for our loved ones, we have to," one of the other women encouraged him. A damped mood licked the air, and I growled at its festering smell.

"If anyone is having a change of heart, then I recommend you stay behind," I tried to say calmly though my vampire wanted to snap their jaws shut forcefully for wasting such breath on an ill sentiment. "You are all warriors. *My* warriors. You came here to fight and think of nothing else."

"It's just that easy, huh?" Titan begrudgingly said. The wolves looked between her and me, and I crept toward her dubiously. I still had the slight advantage of height and peered down on her, my wings flaring slightly to embody my obvious intimidation and power.

"Take your shot, child, but you'll only get one. Or shrivel into line so I can actually get the job done. Besides, this isn't a place for children so if you're going to act like one, step to the side," I taunted, so easily distracted.

"Esmore," Chase cautioned. Droplets of raging tears budded in her eyes. "Ignore her, Titan, she's not herself in this state."

"No, this is exactly who she is," Titan said with a wobbly voice as her hand clenched tightly around the strap of the Barnett crossbow.

My vampire purred with delight. At least she understood that much. "Then, shall we?" I asked Balzar. Iris and Fire formatted behind me, which instructed the others to step into formation.

I sashayed across to Chase, grabbing the back of his neck as he dropped his forehead to mine. I was ballooned with the mixture of emotion, sidestepping their waves. My vampire entity wouldn't have even the slightest involvement of their distraction. "See you on the other side," I said before pulling away from him. I could sense his outstretched hand calling me back for comfort, but I ignored it. I would succeed at my task and then meet with him before he did anything stupid. Anything that I might've done myself.

# CHAPTER 34

I T DIDN'T ADD too much time to detect and avoid the bombs, thanks to the werewolves' keen sense of smell. Lincon effectively used his illusion on nearby vampires who were on patrol, shading us out of sight. Now that we were within the city and closer to Tythian's patrolling vampires, I realized what I'd consider to be a nonchalant attitude from a distance was actually a giddiness for the fight to come. How unsightly for them to think so highly of themselves when they were only pawns in his game. And yet their nature called forth a certain victory about them in the same way that I knew my own.

I was conscious of the footprints we were leaving behind in the thin layer of snow behind us. Eventually, someone would come across it, giving us the upper hand for only a few minutes until we were found out, but that's all we needed. The moment we gave the signal, the others would make their move. I was conscious of the sabers who lingered in the streets, loosely laid out around Deemori ready for her beck and call. It also served as a reason why we kept Chase as far away as possible from her so she wouldn't take control of him. Besides it being a Vampire Council, the sabers would've acted as a natural buffer to any outsiders. Most avoided cities because they were often infested with sabers. And unlike where most Councils tried to hide their location discretely, Tythian was in plain sight. He'd long given up the times of hiding as he so much despised Cesar for.

"Are you ready to play your part?" Balzar asked Lincon, begrudging that he had to speak to him directly and that a huge part of our entrance involved Lincon, which of course only fed his ego and flair for theatrics.

Lincon shifted into Tythian. And although he hadn't physically changed, to our eyes he had. And the moment we stepped into the oversized warehouse those who were inside would be equally tricked. The night was stark, offering the familiarity of darkness. I signaled the werewolves to surround the warehouse we were slowly honing in on. Balzar's vampires lurked, some pouncing on top of the rooftops as we listened in.

I wanted to keep everything that was about to transpire contained inside. If we drew them out here, it gave them more room to counter and control the space and their sabers and vampires to surround us easily. But if we could prevent them from intruding outside, we'd have more time to execute our mission. I hadn't yet seen any blue-cloaked assassins, but it didn't mean there weren't any close by. They were, after all, in the art of concealing their presence. They were seen before they were heard and that was only when they wanted to be.

Balzar wrapped his hand around Lincon in what looked to be silver. And naturally Lincon flared with grits and groans as if the silver were sapping away his very life force. Although it would've pained him so, I had the certain sense that he was enjoying its torturous burn.

And then we had to take into consideration that across multiple streets was a small burial of the undead. And although they weren't moving now, we had to assume the moment we tripped our arrival they would. Everyone fanned out into position. We had to keep them in the warehouse and the others out no matter the cost.

Iris sidled up to me, focused on the warehouse in front of us. He didn't want to be involved with our mission, instead he wanted to go directly to Tythian to claim his vengeance once promised for killing his former Council leader, Tracey. The sooner we disposed of those within here, the sooner we'd move on to the main prize. But it didn't lessen my greedy aspiration of beheading the three vampires in here who deserved their sentencing in equal measure.

I signaled Iris to illuminate his signal. Everyone prepared themselves as Balzar, Lincon, and I strode up to the two-bay door. An eerie silence settled over the space as Iris flared the sky with blue lightning. The moment it hit the ground with a grumbling wave we burst through the door in the same way I imagined the others to descend upon Tythian's location. The hunters' gifts would keep Tythian and Fier at bay for some time until we could fight by their side.

Iris's lightning crashed into the warehouse doors, splintering it into thousands of pieces that began a fiery blaze. Instantaneously, sabers began to drop from nearby rooftops and streets. Titan was at my back, circling her silver chains, ready to capture Whitney, our prize.

Kasey erected her gift around Connor and Deemori trapping them. A glower of saber eyes pierced back from the darkness, perched on multiple levels within the warehouse at our hasty entrance. The room had various rows of bare shelving, and with the smell of blood and gore, it noticeably was housed as something utterly different from its original purpose. Whitney teleported out, fleeing immediately until she flashed back after noticing Lincon who kicked and screamed a little less dignified than what Tythian might actually act out.

Whitney might've been powerful, thanks to the gifts her familiar had blessed her with, but she was still young and naïve to the games of warfare. And it was Tythian's mistake for not having her so close by even with the knowledge of our coming. Titan lassoed her silver chains toward Whitney, who smoothly dodged them and snarled at the others. The few werewolves who swarmed in were quickly knocked to the ground as Connor fiercely pioneered against them, his icy blue eyes bulging as he used his gifts on them. Kasey was squeezing her hand in an attempt to squash Connor and Deemori who bunched together, their bones crushing, but it did nothing to loosen Connor's focus. No, it'd have to be something far more drastic than that. Lightning struck at them as Kasey dropped her shield to allow the shot to blow them apart, just before a saber pounced on her and she pulled out her two knives to defend herself.

"Tythian?" Whitney quivered.

"Now," I goaded Titan. Chris and Tori covered her back as numerous sabers avalanched down the aisles. I torpedoed toward Whitney, confronting her head-on. Titan's strong arm and throw twisted the thick silver chain beside me like a slithering line that I latched onto mid-air. I couldn't hold it for long which is why I waited until the very last moment.

Whitney's doe-like eyes widened as she realized too late what was happening because she'd allowed herself to be so distracted by Tythian's capture. My fingers coiled around the end of the thick silver. My immediate instinct was to reef my hand away as my hand burned and sizzled. I wrapped the chains around Whitney with lightning speed, hooking it around a wooden post and kicking her off the second level she'd been standing on. The chain hooked tightly around to give Titan leverage as two other werewolves shifted into their human forms to pull at the other end of the chain, helping hold Whitney in place. She hung, her legs dangling above the ground as she thrashed and squealed with her arms strapped tightly to her side.

Lincon's illusion dropped as he shifted into his second phase and Connor's face slackened in rage. Lincon had been the only one who'd been able to stop Connor's gift, and they immediately went into a battle of wits.

"You tricked me!" Whitney squealed. A large bang rocked the ground coming from somewhere else in the city. I couldn't even believe what I was looking at and the difference of who she was compared to the human I'd recalled her to once be. Tythian had once vowed to protect her virtue as a human, but the raging vampire dangling like bait was far from that vision he'd held.

Balzar launched himself at her, and I toppled over the edge to intervene. "What do you think you're doing?" I snaked on him. The plan was to use her as bait against Tythian, her death served no greater purpose right now.

"She killed Yolo!" He flared with rage. And no matter how easy it was to use her to enable the large incentive to question his brothers who so greatly betrayed him, his vengeance couldn't step past the easy claim and prey of dangling bait. One that would compromise our mission completely and I wouldn't let him take.

"Don't make me do this, Balzar. Remember what happened last time," I purred, reminding him of the time my hand had been joyfully playing with his heart. Sabers dropped down heavily around us, and without hesitation, he punched through them with his studded gloves while I opted for my beautiful golden claws. Deemori was guiding them into two distinctive directions. To guard and protect Whitney, and to come between Lincon and Connor, giving him pockets of time to catch his breath as he continued coming out of a torturous daze. Lincon ruthlessly ripped through the sabers bare-handed, his wicked laughter cackling through as he pulled them limb from limb.

Tori and Deemori were circling one another, the anticipation of who would lunge first being their only break as she tried desperately to focus on Connor at the same time. Even after all these years, acknowledging one another as familiars they hadn't claimed the other physically. They'd always kept one another at an arms distance but had they shared their gifts it might've made them a more formidable team—a missed opportunity of power in my opinion.

Disarray began to flood in as the chaotic energy of the night sprung free. The low bearing whistle began to sing its tune, forcing Fire's ears to pin back as she side-stepped the saber who tried to bite into her. I pegged one of my daggers at its head, toppling it over. Her quick gaze was appreciative enough when the whistle dropped in tone.

"Do you really think you can keep me here?!" Whitney screamed like a spoilt child while the rotting smell of decay and lifeless limbs grew stronger. I countered Balzar as he lunged for her again and grabbed him under the shoulders, flinging him to the side of the warehouse. He broke through the wall, puncturing a hole where I could peer outside. Those lifeless dolls with rotting flesh were accumulating around the warehouse as expected. "Tythian will find out—"

I struck her against the jaw, the defining crunch of bone satisfying me like a tantalizing stroke against my skin. "Let's just say your love is too preoccupied to care." She tried to thrust back and forth, a small sob mumbling from her as she gave in to the silver's grimacing pain.

"I was once dying slowly from inside, of course I have a tolerance for pain, you wench!" She hissed.

"Really?" I purred, evoked by her recollection of being a human. I yanked on the remaining silver chain thrusting it into her mouth and making her choke as she screamed from sizzling pain. A hearty laugh escaped me as I enjoyed watching her try to fight its burn. She snapped shut, her small pinprick fangs piercing my hand as she was forced to bite down on the silver that I fed her.

Two sabers dove for me. I whisked away from Whitney and peeled back one of their faces with my claws, raking my grip along its backbone. The second leaped for my wing, and I caught it by the throat before its filthy fangs could touch them. I reefed out its heart throwing it at Whitney, finding a moment of humor at her upheaval. Her mouth was bloody and scorched with marks that would take longer to heal than most.

Lightning went ablaze in sharp shoots as Iris fought the majority of the sabers and undead that swarmed the warehouse, effortlessly using his gift and oversized hatchet simultaneously. I had the sense that Balzar was perhaps too preoccupied with those swarming him to return.

"She doesn't move," I ordered the three werewolves who were holding Whitney's chains. I turned my back to aid Lincon and Tori when Titan slackened her hold on the thick silver chain and shot an arrow with her Barnett crossbow at me. I tilted my head slightly, growling at the arrow that had splintered pieces of my hair. The arrow ricocheted off metal and was thrown into a different trajectory. The blue-robed assassin Titan aimed for had been aiming to cut the thick chain.

But now that he'd been spotted, he descended to fall upon me. I smashed a wave of shock through him, startling him mid-air. I aimed for his chest as he fell, but he was quick to recover from my mental attack. Instead, his sword glided against my own, deflecting it and squaring me off. Facing him and that hideous mask only brought memories of days long gone when we'd once worn the same hideous attire. And I very much existed to exterminate this lasting piece of Oppollo's Council and reign. His greatest assassins would fall before me like their master had done.

The air began to ferment with mixed odors of blood and decay. Screams and war cries assembled as the battle continued to erupt around us. The assassin was more patient than most vampires, articulated in their execution like a fine brushstroke of a long-lost art form.

Connor's low yelp caught my attention at the same time Balzar busted back through the wooden panel headfirst and tackled the assassin who squared me off, quickly flipping him over. Four of my werewolves now guarded Whitney, ensuring no one else tried to cut her down. Her head was limp as she dangled weakly.

"Connor!" Deemori screamed in her thick accent as she dodged Tori's next attack. Dry black blood splattered as Tori came between her aiding her familiar.

With Balzar's attention on the assassin, I took to Lincon. He didn't need assistance, but there was one question I wanted to ask Connor before I ripped his heart from his chest.

I flew across the room, launching him into the numerous shelves and using his body to deter anything from hitting me personally. I lavished in the sound of crunching bone and speared him into a fallen pole. The pole pierced through his abdomen, the point of the blunt instrument out of his arms reach. He'd have to pull along the pole to unhinge his body from it.

He was still in a mere daze as Lincon skipped from side to side as he approached us. I could hear Deemori screaming his name, the sabers suddenly only interested in our direction. They piled in as Tori continued fighting Deemori to prevent her from reaching him.

"Lincon, I don't want to be interrupted," I purred pleasurably. He'd taken most of the fight out of Connor who groggily looked about. Lincon seemed displeased to let go of his plaything but excited by his job well done and the handfuls of sabers who pooled in to attack him. He snaked a smile.

"Oooh, Incy, wincy, spider…" he began to count as he ripped an arm from one of the sabers. Like a flash of light, he zoomed through them, his singing enthralling to my blood lust, thrumming to the beat of my own elicited desires.

Connor's icy blue eyes snapped back into focus when he heard Deemori's shrill scream. I felt the force of his gift against me, excruciating pain stabbing part of my brain through my nose. But it didn't have the potency like it once did. Lincon truly had done a number on him. I enjoyed the taste of my blood dripping into my mouth as I turned his mental gift upon him.

The problem with mental gifts and games was it also left one exposed to another mental user. And Connor wasn't at his best, which put me in place to be the prosecutor. His mind was open to me. I didn't need to knock on it for permission, but I wasn't here to speak telepathically. No. Connor and I had shared this private bond before, and I was enthralled to be a part of the illusions Lincon had set upon him to weaken his stature so.

His little sister was screaming out his name, begging for his protection. It was the same memory of his human life as his home was set in flames and he walked in to witness his murdered family.

*The humans are the monsters,* he elicited groggily into my mind, admitting defeat the moment he knew I was in his mind instead of him having the advantage.

"I pity you. You were nothing but a foot soldier to Tythian," I said out loud, excited by this little private game I was allowed to have in the corner of the warehouse. If he felt remorse, I could not sense it, nor was he willing to admit he was a puppet. "I have but one question to ask you," I purred, aware of my slackening time to play. I had somewhere else to be, and that gentle reminder was tugging at me to be done. "Why did you help him after he murdered Yolo? He was your brother too."

I was conscious of Balzar standing behind me. Surprisingly, Lincon had let him through in his sing-song way. Finally, Balzar would get his answer or any form of closure that he might've been searching for from the brothers who had betrayed him and were accomplices in Yolo's death.

Connor dropped his head defeated, and I thought he wouldn't even offer us that much. But reluctantly, he spoke, and I felt like the weight of his words would soon ask for a favor in return. "I've never fit in anywhere. Tythian was the only one who'd given me any kind of purpose."

"And how that's failed you now," I rendered.

"Wait," he gasped. "Please…Deemori…I promised I'd find a way to turn her into a saber and set her free. I beg you, Esmore, have Fier change her. She was only involved with all of this because of me."

"You're awfully chatty for once," I coldly said, considering he was mute at the best of times. I was almost disappointed by our exchange. How mighty and powerful, he had once been revered. But when I turned my gaze upon them as my enemy, I realized it didn't take all too long to overpower them, and much of that had been managed because of those who I'd accumulated around me. Those who were sneered at by the likes of Connor, Tythian, and Fier were ironically now part of their downfall. There was no added value he could offer me.

I turned away and offered Balzar the right to his brother in whatever way he saw fit. I was impressed by Lincon's handiwork. He was hanging upside down from the roof, ripping one of the sabers apart as their body sloshed into decay and sprinkled the black muck to the floor. It had been the last of them, and he was still singing that crazed melodic song in his mother tongue. My purple gaze landed on Deemori who screamed, throwing herself toward Connor blindly.

They may not have mated, but they were fated and had grown attached to one another over the last decade. And I wasn't so much a masochist that I took pride in watching two familiars ripped apart when I felt the cruelty of my own fate.

"You stood by as he died!" Balzar yelled angrily and punched Connor in the face. Blue lightning sparked the outside like a wild furnace as Iris slaughtered through his obstacles. Deemori had no more sabers to call forth, or if she had, they'd be defending her. The warehouse was now a decomposing ground, littered with the remains of their soldiers.

Tori leaped with a deadly sequence, and I did nothing to stop him. Unfortunately, Deemori had chosen her fate by association. And a small part of me, perhaps if I was still considerate of either of them, might've halted him and considered the possibility of fulfilling Connor's wish. But I cared more for Tori's conquer than of her demise. She was just an obstacle in my way.

"No!" Connor screamed, pressing his mental pain and anguish into our minds. But it was immediately glossed over by Lincon who transfixed on him once again, only allowing him a fleeting moment of coherency to watch Tori's sword slice through Deemori's neck, sending her head flying through the air.

Her outstretched hand sagged like the rest of her. Connor screamed, trying to pry himself from the pole and that's when Balzar struck him like lightning, his hand crumpling into his brother's chest. "I'm sorry, brother," he said as he yanked it out. "But it is personal." Because as Connor had webbed a bond with Tythian, Balzar had the same with Yolo, and they'd stolen that from him.

I whistled, signaling the few who were to follow me that it was time to move on. But just before I left, I would ensure to wreak havoc on the majority of those who opposed us. If I left without doing so our members would be overrun. And I wasn't in the form to leave them at a disadvantage when I had such a prize tied up here.

# CHAPTER 35

I'D ORDERED KASEY and Lincon to guard Whitney. If Tythian were to teleport in, I knew he'd have a hard time getting through their gifts. He couldn't teleport into Kasey's erected wall, and so she'd solidified it around both her and Whitney who was too weak to fight. Lincon, however, paraded in the remains of what was left to kill as the rest of us vacated the warehouse. We'd conquered our first mission, now on to phase two.

Outside, the warehouse was brimming with glorious disaster. Buildings had been set alight, and the speed and strength of which everyone fought was at a devastating but ever so delicious rampage. One of my werewolves yelped as a blue-robed vampire pounced on him, biting into his neck. Titan shot an arrow at his chest, piercing its target. Chris leaped and guarded the wolf's hind while he staggered back onto his feet.

The undead was a mirage of stifling speed and their numbers vastly overpowered ours. My wolves had been doing a good job to hold them back, but it still wasn't enough. Iris descended blazing lightning bolts upon them. It stunned their smoking forms long enough that he'd then hack his oversized hatchet, splitting them in half. Large pools of black goop glazed the ground from all the sabers and vampires alike that had been killed. But the werewolves had taken a heavy blow on their side as well. Crumpled werewolves were scattered amongst the fighting, some being trampled on amongst the heated bloodshed. Their deaths were the price of capturing Tythian's most prized possession.

Titan was devastated as her gaze frantically took in the bodies. This was the reality of what she wanted. To be treated as an adult and a part of the carnage—none of this could be unseen.

I curled my fingers, my temperament heating with desire. And now it was time to leave some carnage of my own. I vanished in a flash, slicing my beautiful golden and bloody claws against the vampires first. Iris was following me as he cleaned up the mess of the undead, properly hacking them to size as I glided amongst the vampires who served as a greater challenge.

"Get that one! That's her!" one of the vampires commanded, and I brimmed with joy allowing them to circle me in a sense of triumph. I was even intrigued to see how long it might take one of them to attack me as they silently goaded one another to go first. A few blue-robed vampires with masks pushed past their formation, pushing the younglings back. So, the assassins remembered from our last battle, if not by name alone. *Excellent.*

Two sprung for me, skirting around Iris's thunderbolts with beautiful efficiency. Since both charged me with a sword, I decided to pull my own out. I stopped the first one with my blade, one-handed. And then stopped the second one's sword with my golden claws, clamping it so perfectly that it didn't even slice the interior of my hand. I couldn't see their expression or how they might've realized their inferiority, but a gleam of mischief sparked in my purple hazed eyes.

I wasn't the same warrior they'd attacked all those years ago. I pushed back the one who held the sword, gutting the vampire whose sword I still held. I swept my blade up, slicing off his hand and claiming his sword. It was a different weight from my own, but I quickly adjusted as my wings balanced my beautiful swings. The first assassin leaped for me, throwing three daggers at me. I dodged two of them and deflected the third, angling it so it darted for the second assassin's eye. It split the mask, a definite *crack* sounding as it clutched at the dagger that was meant to embed into his brain. He'd caught it only just in time but not enough to protect his mask that split into two.

I deflected the first assassin's sword, carrying him over its weight. They were highly skilled and yet…so inferior. I plunged my blade into his chest. Reefing it out and quickly beheading the assassin who still hadn't managed to pull out the dagger embedded in his skull. He'd tried to jump out of the way, but there was nothing to counter my speed. I was a deadly blade that had waited for this very night, and I would take my revenge and pleasure.

Despite the fear that reeked from them, the other vampires jumped in unison. I spun and jarred with the two swords acting as extensions of my arms with beauty and grace, dancing to the thumping of a war song that only I could hear. And their screams and pops of black blood were my satisfying encore.

Finding my final prey, I pierced it through the back of the heart, its frightened screams gurgling into mush. Black blood splattered across Titan's face as she'd been fighting the very same vampire and I'd selfishly staked my claim. When it sluggishly moped to her feet we were at eye to eye, her eyes turned into small slits as she stared me down. I was stickily covered in blood, my wings thriving in the thick molasses of all those I'd killed.

"Geez, Esmore, what have you become?" Balzar breathed from the sideline.

"Capable," I replied with a feral smile. It unnerved Titan as she trembled before me. I could smell the palpable tang of fear. Yes, I was the monster who'd killed her father. And they'd seen me fight before. Not like this. Not when I had no reason to hold back. I was giving myself completely to this fight. The difference was they all fought because they had somewhere to return. I was fighting to watch how much blood I could shed and set Tythian's world ablaze. There was nothing for me after this so I would make my face memorable. I would be the last sickly creature they would see in this world passing them onto the next.

I threw the ownerless sword and sheathed my own. Squirms of the undead continued to crawl around from being so precisely hacked by the others. They continued to swarm in small spurts, but Balzar's coven and the werewolves were now leveraging at an advantage again.

"It's time for phase two," Iris condoned. I agreed and walked past Titan, still eyeing her as she stood frozen in her spot.

Claus shifted quickly into his human form. "We've got it here. We'll make sure no one else steps into the warehouse," he promised. Good. As was his role. Although Lincon likely wanted intruders to break through just so he could play.

"I'm coming too!" Titan burst into life.

"Don't start this," Tori said quietly to her. "Stay on your mark."

"Yea, kid, this is for adults only," Balzar remarked, signaling to a few vampire members who were to carry on phase two with us. Fire led a team of six werewolves.

"But—"

"We all have our role to play," I reminded her. "And yours is here." She'd done well to survive the first wave. But the next phase was beyond her. I took to the sky. *We're coming now.*

*Oh fabulous, I've been munching on popcorn waiting,* Chase remarked though the communication was strained, either from fighting or the disease was taking its toll and I wondered if it only grew stronger in the presence of Fier. *Did all go to plan?*

The city below had set to flame. Nothing was to remain of the city or Tythian's reign. We'd conquer his armies and his home. He'd let us walk straight up to his door, so arrogantly and that had been his mistake.

*Whitney's been captured. Connor and Deemori have been disposed of.*

He was hesitant to reply. *You killed them?* he asked quietly. Of course we had, that was the plan we'd intended. Anyone who'd sided with Tythian wasn't to be shown remorse.

*Yes. Where's Tythian?*

*Being entertained by your mother and the hunters, but I don't know if they'll be able to hold him back much longer. The silver should keep Whitney from reaching out to him, and Iris's signal ensured your mother used her concealing gift on her location.*

The first initiation had gone to plan. Chase was fighting in the shadows, and from here I could see his coven slaughtering through the undead and blue-robed vampires. Chase was central, easily and god-like slicing through them. I wanted to sweep down to fight alongside him and partake in that lucrative dance together, but I had to set my sights on one more before meeting Tythian head-on.

Fire and the werewolves trailed me as I swept through the city, searching for Fier. Balzar, Iris, and the others continued on as they went to assist the hunters. Balzar and Iris would have their hand at killing Tythian, and I was ordained the pleasure to set my sights upon Fier one more time.

I got a whiff of Fier's scent and took a sharp lean left, my wings gliding me to the open space where he was waiting for me. It was a park of sorts, reminding me of where it had all begun when Whitney had been used as bait in San Francisco in a decrepit old park. Perhaps he was feeling nostalgic as to where he wanted to end this. No more hiding but out in the open and may the best vampire win.

I descended, aware of Fire leading her werewolves to fight against the multiple undead whose attention I'd grabbed and had begun following me. In a glorious entry, I broke the surface of the ground, defiant cracks opening as a thrill ran through me for showcasing my strength.

"Wretched woman," Fier spat from across the dead grass in the abandoned childrens' playground.

"You look good in blue," I insincerely complimented with a smile. He was wearing Tythian's colors. Embarrassment from his own coven falling and having to run with his tail between legs to a fellow Council.

He returned the venomous smile. "Not as fitting as Chase looks as a saber, right?" He cocked his head to the side contemplatively. My now black slicken claws dug into my palms producing droplets of blood. "This is, after all, your fault. Remember, little golden bird, if he hadn't defected to protect you, he'd still be fighting by my side in true form instead of chasing around a pair of tits all day long. How humiliating!" he seethed.

His gaze caught the long pointed golden claws now covered with an array of colored blood. "You—" His words fell short as pure rage enveloped him. He recognized the weapons perhaps Chase's mother had once described to him. But their symbolism was enough to drive him over the edge. I was wearing the token weapons of his deceased familiar—Chase's mother. And I found it only fitting that he died by them.

That bubbling sensation began to rise in my lungs as water foamed from my mouth. Ah, he was trying to torture me again with one of his hindering gifts he'd found so useful the last time we'd met. Water began leaking from his mouth as he stared me down with an eternity of hatred. Had he been focusing or even aware of his disadvantage in this fight, he might've realized that I had no beating heart or functioning lungs to drown in. Perhaps Chase's demand to remove my heart wasn't so unsolicited.

I exploded into action, crossing the distance between us, his surprised expression was marvelous to bear witness to. I aimed my clamped golden claws at his chest, and he deflected me with a gust of wind. I curled into a ball, my wings protecting me as I was pushed back.

"Oh, what another beautiful fucking trick!" he exclaimed. "Just die already!"

How lovely it was to be so passionately hated. Blast after blast of wind continued smashing into me, pushing me across the grass and toward the buildings. I could hear a low howl in the distance, notifying others that one of my seven wolves had been taken out.

I rolled to the side, jumping away from his next two slashing winds that split buildings apart. Water still dribbled from my mouth, the internal sloshing throwing off my balance and taking me time to adjust to as I moved. I pegged two daggers toward him, of which he only deflected one—the one aimed at his pretty face. The other hit home in his foot. It wasn't a deadly target but served another purpose. Winding Fier up would make him sloppy, and that's what I was doing to draw him out.

"I took great pride in turning him!" Fier shouted in an attempt to throw me out of my controlled malice. And it was working. Chase might've not yet been fully turned. But there wasn't a way to revert it and it was all because of Fier.

I felt my body build in strength and wild rage as I continued circling and irking him. He gestured both his hands forcefully toward me, trying to embed two clean slices into my wings. "Where's your oh so special gift now, bitch?"

I flared my speed, embodying the most powerful version of myself, when all my entities came together controlled by my blood-thirsty vampire. I punched him in the face, grabbing hold of his hair and reefing it back as he seemed surprised by my speed that outmatched his keen gaze to track me. He might've been older in years, more experienced in war. But he was not me unleashed.

"That mouth of yours has always been so irritating," I purred, grabbing his tongue and stringing my nails along it to rip it out. He gurgled under black blood as a clean slice of wind cut open my abdomen and pushed me back. I held onto my stomach, holding everything in place. It just as quickly stitched itself together which drew out another smile from me.

His next words came out in a strained lisp as his tongue grew back. "Just you watch. Tythian and I will kill you and your mutts and restore our reign."

My laugh was sinister as I pointed around us. "Look around you, Fier. If Tythian cared for you, then where is he now? Where are your men,

Fier? All of them have fallen. You're an offensive sight to those who call themselves a powerful vampire." I drove in the words that I knew would hurt his ego the most.

"A Council Leader does not need to be defended!" he shrilled.

Chase's voice drifted over smoothly. "Which is why you ran with tail between your legs last time."

I hadn't heard any more howls from my wolves which meant very likely Chase had helped them on his way over here to even the numbers, in the same fashion that I had done back near the warehouse.

Chase stood on the nearby rooftop, his destroyed leather coat flapping in the wind as he hauntingly looked down on Fier—embodying his superiority. Fier was baffled, his mouth agape.

"I turned you!" he shouted. "I felt the disease consume you, and the deed was done! What cheap trick is this?!" he snarled.

Lightning flashed in the distance. It was Iris's warning signal to let us know that Tythian had teleported and was on the move. They might've been able to entertain him, but it was always probable he'd move, no doubt trying to find Whitney.

"I owe you a favor." Chase glowered with all sinister intention, and I felt my core spread with desire for him. Oh, how we'd enjoy this kill together. A howl called out in the distance as Chase jumped off the building, his beautiful wings torpedoing toward where Fier stood.

In sync, I ran for him, thrumming with delight as I envisioned his doom while Chase and I tore him apart and bathed in his blood together. Dust assorted itself around him, concocting a whirlwind. Black blood began to stuff his nose as Fier tried to strain his gifts to keep us out. The wind sliced in separate directions but Chase and I were certain to reach him. When the winds suddenly dropped, Chase and I collided. Chase was quick to hold me as we swung in the air, anchoring ourselves to the ground. Across the field where I had once been standing, Tythian stood with Fier by his side. Titan and Chris were chained in thick metal.

"Don't move," Tythian said with a cool tone, but the rage currented his gaze. "You have something of mine. And I have something of yours." He looked disgusted but not surprised to see Chase standing beside me. "It just seems like neither of you knows when to call it quits."

"Lincon giving you trouble again?" I sneered, knowing too well he wouldn't have been able to get through their defenses. He jolted Titan and Chris who were in their human forms. They both exhaustedly hung over the chains unable to speak. Their blood grossly fermented around them and Chris's naked body glistened with it.

"I never had to enter that putrid warehouse because I wanted to show you what crafty little creations I'd managed when I visited these pups last. Surely you didn't think I'd just gone to tell her the truth of her father's death. Come now, I thought you'd known me better than that."

Chase's grip tightened around me. *Don't do anything rash,* he warned and sent me calming waves which naturally irked my vampire counterpart. Those pups were *mine*. And with the cool gaze Tythian had on us, I knew something sinister came this way. Another howl erupted in the distance as that odious whistle perforated the air and Tythian's eyes turned into small slits.

# CHAPTER 36

LIGHTNING FLASHED THROUGH the sky as Iris warned our groups of danger and its direction toward exactly where we stood. I could hear Fire and her small group snarling close by trying to edge their way closer toward us. It wouldn't be long until Balzar tracked Tythian to where we stood. Tythian tightened the chains, their little whimpers straightening my spine. The inside of the chains were spiked and embedded into their stomachs. Even if they were to shift, it'd split them open, and their healing wasn't as instantaneous as the vampires.

Chase's firm grip was what kept me in place. "What did you do to them?" I gritted out.

Tythian's icy gaze landed on me. Our hatred had mutually festered over the last ten years.

"I'd considered what more I could do to make this more personal. Besides taking your familiar away from you, who somehow seems to still be alive." He side glanced Fier who looked as if he wanted to defend himself. But it was apparent to everyone that it'd still taken effect. Chase was impartial to the features of a saber. All that was different was those black vein-like tentacles around his eyes and mouth as he fought to keep the slither of humanity that remained. "Who else could I have taken to drag you through consistent pain, I'd wondered. I mean, after all these years this is what you cared about most, wasn't it? Your noble inclination toward playing the role of hero and protector. And then it dawned on me. The little pups that you brought into the big bad vampire lair those many years ago, of who you turned your back on your own kind to protect. They would be a good start."

It went without saying that I'd never considered Cesar's coven my 'place' or vampires my own kind. Tythian was dressed neatly as he'd always been, his blond hair tidily slick. His cool icy blue eyes watched us carefully. "So, I decidedly played with their fates, and it was all too easy, really. I wondered what Fier's saber-like gift might do to the likes of your little beasties. And when I targeted them at the edge of the forest I had him whisper sweet things into their ears so the moment I decidedly clicked my fingers they would shift into heinous creatures, worse than what they already were."

Titan and Chris's eyes groggily widened as they stared into the master of their fate. Chase continued to hold me back, his strength at full which only satisfied Tythian further.

"Fier wasn't there!" Tori panted harshly. He'd gotten here sooner than anyone else, coated in blood from what I imagined to be the many he'd cut through to find Titan the moment Tythian had taken her. Screams and noises surrounded us as the war continued raging only blocks away.

"No?" Tythian asked humbly. "And what would you know? Who would you have seen while having your face in your knees keeled over in pain as Connor repeatedly bled out your brains?" I could sense my mother and the fellow hunters creeping silently on rooftops and in between buildings. My mother was using her gift of concealment, and it was only because I'd detected her mind that I was aware of her edging ambush.

"How'd you know where we were?" Chase asked calmly, but his expression was as slicing as any blade he'd wielded before.

"I don't think you're in any position to ask questions," he sneered.

"Oh, and you think you are?" I cockily replied. "Tell me, how much of Whitney do you think is left?"

He jarred the bladed chains making a point, yelps coming out from both of them as it sliced further into their stomachs.

"I could as easily tell Lincon to hurt Whitney in so many ways. So, you best loosen your grip on them or we'll tighten our own."

"Bring her here now!" he demanded losing patients, startled by his own outburst. He was usually so calm and collected. "Or I will show you very quickly what fates I have install for your little mutts."

"Esmore," Titan whimpered with strong resolve. "Kill him. It doesn't matter what—" Tythian reefed the chains again. And despite all the pain and hurt I had caused her, she looked at only me as if I were their only hope. That low whistle began to ring out, synchronizing with a stampede of undead that came in our direction. How far did his whistle reach? Was he calling bodies from the nearby mountains and even farther beyond? Or had he been storing them in his city purposefully for this fight?

My mother and her hunters were on standby, waiting for an opening. I had to find a way to separate Tythian from the pups. Lightning struck between where Fier and Tythian stood, and they just as quickly teleported out. Chase pounced as Balzar and Iris announced themselves from the shadows. A cluster of undead broke through the streets, and the hunters advanced into a bloody collision.

When Tythian teleported back with Fier who looked motion sick, the wolves were no longer in his possession. *He'd hidden them.* I slammed a sense of urgency into Balzar who quickly explained to Tori the location he suspected they'd been taken to.

Blue-robed vampires, and the undead broke into the center like a wild stormy night terrorizing the sea. Waves of them poured into view and the frequency of Tythian's whistle enhanced. They were somehow adapting, becoming faster and stronger as gifts and blood were sprayed as the hunters parlayed with them, simply in an attempt to keep them back.

"Joining with the hunters," Tythian said disapprovingly to Chase. "As if taking a huntress for a familiar wasn't bad enough." Chase and Tythian collided at midpoint in the air. Tythian was spiriting in as Chase continued to pound his heavy wings, intercepting every second hit of Tythian's as he appeared out of thin air.

A gust of wind pushed me back, segregating me from Tythian and Chase's fight. "Oh no, your fight's with me," Fier barked angrily. He swept blade-like winds toward me, provoking my full attention. Iris shouldered the majority of the undead, hacking them into pieces while he absentmindedly trailed Tythian's movement waiting for an opening where he could strike. This was his vengeance, and I was partial to ensure he wouldn't make the mistake of striking Chase instead as I trained my gaze on numerous fights including my own.

I slammed an overbearing sense of grief into Fier, crippling him for a moment as he left himself open and I closed the distance between us. If I removed him, then there wouldn't be a chance for the pups to shift if he'd already implanted such a thing unbeknownst to them. I dodged his powerful waves creeping closer toward him until I delightfully found an opening. "You did this!" I snarled, slashing down his front with my nails dragging along the flesh of his face. He smirked as if I'd taken some sort of bait. Suddenly a snake wrapped around me and bound my wings to my body tightly.

My body was being crushed as the scaly creature tightened its grasp. "Now look at what you've done!" Fier screamed crazily. One of his arms had slackened into a long-bodied snake attached to his body. I'd been wary of Chase's warning about Fier's many gifts including some of which he couldn't control or use because it would have consequences on his own body as well. I wondered if drawing the power of this snake-like gift was a permanent fixture.

I felt the hair on my neck prickle as Chase skirted into view, defending my back as Tythian simultaneously tried to behead me. Chase ground his sword against Tythian's, deflecting him and grabbing hold of his shoulder so he could teleport out with Tythian.

I screamed wildly at the binding strength of the snake. *How infuriating.* I pushed my wings out, proudly urging my strength to burst alight. If only I'd been able to depend on my gift! But the Descendant pushed through, stretching the snake's death grip and slowly edging it looser.

Fier crazily laughed, his intention clear that he would try to behead me with his gift. I tugged on my link with Fire urging her assistance. I only needed to shake him off. The snake caught me off guard, and I wouldn't let it happen twice.

Without delay, Fire bounced between two of the undead as she snapped toward Fier who shrieked. His snake hand slithered away, still thick and scorching to the touch and what appeared to not be retractable. It wasn't his arm anymore as the ugly snakehead hissed where a hand should've been. It hissed and bopped of its own menacing intent, but I was certain if Fire were to bite him, he'd still die within minutes from the infection.

I unsheathed my sword, two undead pouncing for me as I sliced through them with ease. Fier jumped back, trying to create distance between him and Fire as she weaved from side to side dodging his striking winds. The snake that acted of its own accord advanced on me again. This time I did smirk, coming face to face with the ugly thing. My wings slowly stretched out, restoring the damage it had once elicited. It might've prevented me from flying for some time, but I wouldn't need my wings for this. Fier was a madman, trying to hide amongst the undead to escape as my shadow cast over him frightfully. Fier had outgrown his days.

He tried to retract the snake, but it was now a creature of its own ill intent, nurtured by the desire to feed off power. I skirted to the left, dodging as it impaled its face into the ground, rock splintering from the impact. It tugged Fier slightly forward as he screamed miserably at his inability to control its weight and pull of his body. *Vampires couldn't control all gifts that they leached from hunters.*

I unsheathed my sword, slicing across its body, zigzagging it into chunks as it burst into a festering mess of flesh. I knocked Fier back and placed my foot on his throat. He erected a whirlwind around us, and it began slicing upward, painfully chipping away at my wings as I closed them in tightly to my body. His shoulder wasn't healing or reproducing an arm, and I realized pleasantly that the gift had been unrepairable after all.

My hair was tangling in upheaval as I finally tasted my sweet, sweet victory and plunged my golden claws into his chest cavity. He squirmed, desperation in his eyes as I watched those few moments of realization and death descending on him draw closer.

"I've waited for this for a very long time," I purred cunningly. Both of his legs desperately turned into snakeheads, and they twisted to bite into my wings, trying to drag me back. I kept my grip tight, dropping my knees to straddle either side of him, and clenched my other hand firmly under his neck to keep me anchored to him. "You hurt the one person I cared about most."

He sneered, all venom lacing his last words. "You will both die."

"Maybe so, but not before you." I ripped out his heart, the black goop fresh in my hands as a defiant snap of his fingers was the exit to this world. The snakes sagged into black goo as the wind died. I frowned at the echoing noise of his click.

"Esmore!" Titan's harrowing scream defiled my ears as I searched for her. "Es—" I ran in her direction, spotting Tori first who was climbing the side of the building to get to her. He jumped from window sill to window sill as they contorted uncomfortably in their chains. Chris choked out blood as he tried to swing toward her. She screamed again, a gurgling cry as the sounds of snapping bone began. *No. Not them too.*

I leaped into the sky, plunging into the side of the tower so forcefully that it groaned and began to topple over onto the next. I sliced at the chains that dangled them from the side of the building. Tori caught Titan mid-air, falling to the ground with her and landing safely. I grabbed Chris, untying the binding as his body rapidly contorted and his eyes began to glaze.

*No. No. No.* I forced myself into both of their minds, slamming them with wave after wave of adrenalin. They had to fight this.

"Stay back!" I said to Tori as he unchained her. They were fighting it, but when they changed they wouldn't recognize him, and they would turn on him. Fire rounded me, another two shifting into their human forms to grab the children.

My mother seemed to have appeared out of nowhere, placing her hand on both of their foreheads and forcing them into a dead-weighted coma. Much like I'd frozen Chase, this would only work temporarily. Tori sliced through oncoming undead like his life depended on it. More than that because the most precious thing to him was bundled in a coma and being taken away as they hurried them to safety.

I looked into the sky, barraged by my fury. *He did this.* Chase and Tythian continued fighting overhead. The tether between Chase and I ebbing in and out as he fought against his self-control and restraining the flaring disease.

Julia screamed, an undead who was dragging itself across the ground without its bottom half was vengefully tugging on her ankle. She toppled over, her vines weakly able to assist as her stamina fleeted. Another two jumped for her. I torpedoed toward her, slicing the two undead into four pieces, my sword work like a beautiful dance. When I turned back to make sure she'd gone unharmed she wasn't to be seen. I traced her lack of scent since she'd been consuming those herbal balls. When I finally tracked her, she was backed into a corner, Dillian facing off the undead as he chopped them down and protected her.

A vampire shot two arrows toward where Tori and Fire ran into the distance with the pups. With clean precision, Dillian flung a dagger embedding it into the vampire's skull. The action wasn't missed by Tori who deflected the two arrows that'd been fired. A moment of serene appreciation passing between the two old friends.

Within a flash, Tythian teleported in beside Dillian, his displeased grimace entailing the expected treachery. I ran to intervene as Tythian sliced his sword through his neck. A shard of crystalized ice shot across the ground and supported the side of his neck, in the same fashion Cesar had once done for me. My mother gasped at the invasive pain when it spread up and claimed her leg and side of her ribs.

"No!" Julia belatedly screamed as wild vines wrapped around them, protecting her and Dillian in a ball as the undead pounced on them. Tythian next appeared beside my mother and was thrown off by Chase who punctured his sword into his chest, catching Tythian off guard. Chase was faster, stronger, and I realized with fear as the world began to tilt…losing himself.

Hunters circled my mother, protecting her as she was frozen in position. "Just chop the leg off!" she screamed.

"You won't make it!" another one of them yelled back. "You'll lose too much blood!"

When they reappeared, Tythian slammed Chase into the side of a building, crunching wings and bone. Lightning struck at the sword protruding from Tythian's chest, electrifying him. He fell to the ground flipping himself over into a crouch. Whatever the lightning had done to him, it immobilized him momentarily. The moment he hit the ground, trying to shake off its aftereffects, I was upon him. His siphoning whistle bombarded my ears as the undead targeted me, intervening and falling over one another to overwhelm me.

I felt Chase's anguish and pain trickle through our line as he tried to break through their mass to get to me. I sliced through the avalanche of undead soldiers, bitterly frustrated by their interference. I could feel Chase's mind drifting as I incrementally cut away the masses to get to him, watching my back as I turned it on Tythian.

"Ah-ah," I heard Lincon tsk from across the center. Alongside his appearance I caught a whiff of Whitney's scent and the undead hastily stepping aside, giving me enough of a glimpse to see the undead bouncing off Kasey's shield as Lincon carried Whitney over his shoulder, still tangled in silver.

The sword that had been embedded in Tythian's chest clanged to the ground as he pulled it out and teleported, projecting off her shield in the same fashion. One of his blue-robed assassins caught him, ensuring his knees never touched the ground. A mound of four dead werewolves was splattered around that assassin. Balzar leaped from the sidelines, taking the close proximity advantageously to attack Tythian. When he did, Tythian teleported out, reappearing and backhanding him so hard across the face that he bounced across the ground and slammed into the building across the space.

"Hey, Esmore!" Lincon shouted marvelously. "I found out some interesting things while I had some fun with this little miss. And do you know what appeared in her illusions and fears? No?! Okay, then I'll tell you!" Tythian was frozen in place, the desperation in his eyes scattering as he tried to find a way to reach her. "She feared that my daddy bear would come and hunt them down! What a small world?!"

*Kyran?* "You're involved with Kyran?" I edged toward Tythian. But how and why? Kyran was sinking at the bottom of the sea. And then it dawned on me. I'd met with Fier a few times on the dreamscape, and they had always been because Kyran initiated them. Was it probable I wasn't the only one he was communicating with him in such a way?

Tythian snarled, unable to find a solution as to how he could get through to Whitney. I felt Chase's scream down our line as he grew savage, his lips peeling over his enlarged fangs and his pinpoint focus trained on Tythian. He was trying his best to hold on.

*Stay with me,* I repeated, but that hole where we communicated was slowly closing up, and I hauntedly realized I was about to lose him entirely as he internally fought against himself. This fight had strained him, and he was at his limits.

"Did you really think you were the only special one?" Tythian gritted as he felt as if he were forced to talk if only to keep Whitney alive. I could sense a few of his members use mental attacks against Kasey's shield. None of which would reach her or Lincon.

"That's how you acquired the gift?" Balzar said coldly as he stood up, shaking the dirt and debris. I was confused as to how he came to that conclusion.

"I needed something to give me the upper hand," Tythian gritted out furiously as if speaking with his long-lost brother was a burden. As if he'd only ever been an inconvenience. "And no, I didn't speak to that filth directly, it was orchestrated through Fier who suggested we find his 'Sasha Darling' who'd created such a hunter with a gift to raise the dead.

It wasn't easy getting my hands on the hunter, but when I did, I understood how this power could help my cause.

"Foolishly, Fier's implication and promise to Kyran was to retrieve him from the bottom of the sea. When I'd found that out in only recent days, I'd refused. The world doesn't need such maddening chaos, and I don't need another adversary. And now I've landed a wonderful little bounty from Kyran whoever might be willing to gamble with him."

*He stole from Sasha?* I was certain if that was the truth then even if we hadn't found him, she would've eventually hunted him down for doing something so bold. And now, it made sense to me as to why Kyran wanted him dead. Not because he stole from her, no he would've planted that seed. But because he probably wanted something in return that Fier and Tythian could not favor or accomplish. Kyran wanted out, and yet now he still lay in a box at the bottom of the ocean. Fier had promised something on both their behalfs and now Tythian wasn't able to deliver.

"What, you needed even more power after destroying our family?!" Balzar screamed angrily. Tythian teleported, and Balzar shifted only just in time to counter the fatal blow. The side of the building collapsed by the strike as Balzar sunk into the crowd of vampires, trying to catch his footing. Tythian was old and calculated. Strong and fast all the same, and he'd had hundreds of years to hone his gift and craft.

"Family!" Tythian spat. "All Cesar wanted was vengeance, a pathetic notion."

"No different to now," Balzar bespoke.

Tythian let out an ingenious laugh. "Why? Because I want you all dead? The means to it doesn't bother me in the slightest. You're all but a nuisance in my grand plan. What?! Did you think I merely wanted power over the Vampire Council? It just shows how small you think." His hand swooshed in rage. "I will use this power to wipe out everything that ever lived on this filthy world. I can raise more than any known great army!" he declared as that haunting whistle began to raise even the deceased werewolves to do his bidding. I snarled at his cockiness to use my own members against me and disrespecting their death in such a way.

"You've gone crazy!" Balzar yelled back. "What will you do? Kill everyone?! For what?"

"To clean the world of this forever war. And the only way to do that is to clean the slate entirely," Tythian said coolly. "All of you must go."

The irony in it that we had been after the same thing all this time but paved our different ways forward. Where he was inclined toward genocide, I'd been motioning toward rebirth. And Kyran had effectively helped him with a gift that could assist him in that cause whereas I was naturally born with such a powerful gift. He'd been jealous of my natural-born talent and taking Chase away from him, that's what had made it so personal. And yet, no matter how clever Tythian might've once been, he was a madman, now fearing the shadow of Kyran ever meeting the light of day. Funny how twistedly we were all connected except I'd learned to be the shadow. Sinisterly another realization dawned on me.

"It was Kyran who told you where we were," I gritted out, understanding his hand to play. Because Kyran was always keeping tabs on us. That's how they'd found us at the ski resort.

Tythian sneered a distasteful smile. "And you! You've been nothing but a nuisance to my plans since the moment you arrived," he pointedly said to me. "I had planned to unleash Chase upon the world once again. Once he lost control to the Descendant I would set the world ablaze, and you took him away from me! Look at what I had to do because of it!"

A piece of his hair had fallen out of its usual slicken appearance. He looked like a crazed madman, and I couldn't help but creep a smile. Ah, and there was the vampires' nature, so encouragingly in denial of their part to play. That he could never be at fault, no matter how calculated and ensured there was always someone else to blame. He thought he was fighting for a greater notion. But he was just like the rest. He only wanted power and to throw it around and bask in his own magnificence. Tythian wasn't special. He didn't care about this city, nor his people. Everything was a tool. Except for one.

"Tythian, I'm sorry," Whitney sulked.

"It's okay, my love. I'll—"

Lincon plunged his hand into Whitney's chest with a gracious smile. "You hurt the pup, I quite liked her," he said, referring to Titan, and pulled Whitney's heart out. Kasey stepped back, making sure not to dirty her shoes as the silver chains flopped to the ground.

"Tyth—" Whitney's gurgling scream came undone as her body decayed immediately and a moment of silence stilled the air as everyone realized what had been done, and the undoing of Tythian was about to unleash.

# Chapter 37

I INTERRUPTED TYTHIAN, bountifully aware that he'd slash down everything in his path as he lost himself in a frenzy. His gurgling cry was a drum in my blood fully aware of his newly heightened devastation. I collided with him, my wings wrapping around us as we spun, entrancing into a spin. He thrashed inside my cocoon until he teleported out, springing on my back and piercing a sword into my shoulder. I twisted out of its way, taking the brunt of its graze down my front as I embedded my fingers into his stomach, trying to travel up.

We flashed from landscape to landscape as he tried to shake me off. The nauseating swirl of his gift was catastrophic as I dizzily held on. When we landed once again a clunk of metal was descending upon us. When I didn't dare to move, even if I were about to be squished, he teleported out, preventing his own demise.

His hand wrapped around mine as he tried breaking my wrist while I squirmed it painfully inside, twisting it into a bloody mess. I fought off his other hand, hitting him with wave after wave of paralyzing shock. A clean slice swept down my front and chopped off my hand as I pulled back stifled by the sudden change. My arm squirted messily with blood, and my feet dragged along the dirt as I skirted back, still shocked by what had happened.

We were back within the center, and one of his assassins had countered our timing, severing my hand and freeing him. I was overwhelmed by a fabricated darkness of pain as a rapid razor tried to sever my link to Chase, sawing in what felt like the slowest of motions to split us apart permanently. The disease was crippling him, finally finding enough leverage in his haste of anger and pain to finish the job it'd set out upon him.

Tythian teleported, his intent clearly to show up beside Chase next. An eye for an eye. A familiar for a familiar. A lightning bolt struck at Tythian when he appeared, throwing him into a nearby wall. Balzar punched into his face, breaking bone beneath his bloodied gloves, stunning him.

I buckled to my knees, my run turning into a crawl as the insufferable pain of those tentacle-like claws dug in, and I tried my hardest to pry open my connection with Chase as I felt the light at the end of the tunnel dim. I couldn't speak with him anymore, his presence dimming into an abyss. I wasn't bothered by my hand taking time to heal and regrow because its pain was irrelevant to what I was feeling now. "Chase," I choked, suddenly coming to a paramount stop as I set my gaze upon him.

The undead tried to reach him, but his coven fought them off, his gargoyles protecting him in their most stifling formation. "Chase," I gasped as his eyes flashed open into a sunken black. Emptiness looked back at me. I couldn't sense or hear him. His scent had changed as if entirely cloaked by whatever this creature was that had taken him over.

His hand shifted on the sword he was still holding, and in a swift movement he swirled it and aimed it at his chest. *No!* I screamed, prying open the only speck of light I could find in our link, flinging myself into it, and trying to make him stop as I physically jumped for him but not in time to stop him from piercing his own chest.

A bright golden light sapped my vision until I became accustomed to its unnatural glow that was unparalleled to anything in our world. Slowly, the two hands holding mine stretched into strong arms and continued rolling up to the bare chest I'd known and loved for years. Chase politely smiled back at me, his blue dangling gemmed earring striking against the stark brightness of this place. There was nothing, only him and I.

*You shouldn't have followed me in,* he sadly empathized. I tightened my grip on his forearms, scared that he would try to push me out. No, we were in this together. *It will take your sanity with it.*

And although I heard his earnest warning, I could also hear the polite thank you so he didn't have to endure this alone. For all we knew, we were already trapped in this place, our bodies doing as they pleased in reality. But what if this was our new reality? A place of silence for only him and me. I certainly had no complaint about this sudden easiness and calm.

He folded the inside of my palm to his lips, kissing it gently. *I tried to avoid this,* Chase admitted as he bubbled a memory into my mind. Something he'd kept hidden. It wasn't a memory, no, it was something that was shown and shared with him. It was a private discussion he'd had with Louise after we'd spoken to the Hunter Guild at New York. She'd shared with him one of her many premonitions.

In various outcomes, they were all the same. I was bled dry by Tythian twice. Fier once. Against all odds, it was just a bombarding shamble of the many ways I would die. If they did acquire my gift, it was total genocide because a vampire without connection to a huntress counterpart couldn't control my gift's mass or fury. I watched on as my gift annihilated the existence of all species and swept the world into anew. Tythian would've been granted his wish. Chase had taken that burden from me, trying to remove its danger. How I'd spited him for it, and yet he did all that he could to protect me.

*Well, I suppose they didn't expect it to end like this then,* I said somewhat comforted by his actions. Perhaps this was always what was intended. As Louise had confided, future and fate always changed. And part of me felt relieved that we'd carved our own way—even if it was in death.

*There's still time for you to go back,* Chase encouraged. Very slowly and lacking in pain, two great wings sprouted from our backs. I wanted to cry in the relief that mine had returned to a blinding white. Their original form as the Descendant had claimed me—pure and huntress. It was only because of the vampire within that they'd changed accordingly. *I'd changed.* I'd allowed the power and twisted world to consume me.

Chase's black wings were distinguishingly beautiful, and I couldn't help but think it metaphorically represented when we first met in what felt like a lifetime ago. We were opposing creatures, and yet here we stood now—united.

*I'm not going back without you,* I promised. This was my oath to him.

*I'm so tired,* he admitted. He dipped his forehead to mine. This place was so serene and quiet. Nothing to fight. No inner turmoil. Tranquility deserving even for us.

*So am I,* I admitted. *Maybe it's okay this once to stop. This doesn't have to be our fight anymore.* How many years had Chase been fighting? How long would we constantly be pitted in a war that was never our own to begin with? We were just casualties in the animosity between humans and vampires. It was our time for peace. And I envisioned that towering shrine back in my homeland Guild where we'd turn the hunters' bodies to ash and keep them safe, thanking them for their service. I don't know what was to come of my body…but it didn't matter, not if I still had Chase like this.

Chase let out an exasperated sigh. *That's just not good enough.*

The retraction of the bright light sapped us back toward the screaming and chaotic groans of buildings collapsing. The sound of war crept up as I tried to convince Chase one last time that it was our time where we could have such peace. But he dragged us back.

*One last shot, my love. What else do we have to lose?*

A pang of fear eluded me, scarce that was the only time we'd be offered such serenity together. What if by resurfacing to the living, we wouldn't have a second chance. But I wouldn't say no to Chase either as he smiled so gently, reassuringly that all was going to be okay. But I was certain he was about to lull me into a false sense of security just to ensure that I survived.

The cold air hit me first as I jolted back into my body. I was on top of Chase, from where I'd evidently thrown myself over to protect him. I could still feel the disease's might as it spread over into my mind with no other reasonable cause other than being familiars and my refusal to let go.

Chase's body jolted bizarrely as tiny little sparks began to erode my skin. The handle of his blade was still in his hand, but his blade had disintegrated. My gaze darted about him as I realized what was taking hold. He'd triggered my gift, and it protected him before he killed himself. *Chase,* I tried to call him out down our line, but I could only hear my voice echoing. He was unresponsive, and I couldn't see past that black mass that had eroded his brain. His wings were crumbled between his shoulder blades as they evaporated into nothing as the gift ate them away. Painful strips peeled away from my skin as I tried to wake him, to pull him away from this nightmare, begging for him to return to me. *Please.*

"Julia, that's enough! You'll die!" I heard my mother scream out in warning. She was letting Dillian feast off her, and she was too weak to fight back any longer. He was draining her completely as he took nourishment from her to regain his strength and help restitch his neck.

"You will know my pain too!" Tythian tormented vilely. "You both just wouldn't die!"

My erratic thoughts were alarmed, thinking of all the visuals about how this gift would be used through a vampire—total extinction. "Chase," I repeated desperately, slapping his face slightly. "Chase, come back?" I was unbalanced. If he couldn't control it, it'd wipe everyone out, giving Tythian the exact result he wanted.

Tythian teleported, closing in on us. When he swept to our side, I grabbed the sword he tried to attack Chase with, slicing down my inner palm as I clutched it, my golden claws scraping alongside its metal. Chase's gift encircled Tythian's face defensively like a swarm of angry bees pushing him away. I could sense a spark of Chase returning to me, but like a newborn bud, unfurling to see the first ray of sun. He wasn't coming back to me soon enough. *Chase, my love, you have to stop. You can control this.*

All fighting spirit was sapped from me, and the painful torment of skin and muscle stripping away almost became irrelevant as I only focused on him. The gargoyles were pushed further away, not daring to remain close enough to its integral licks.

Tythian's hysterical laughter found its way back to me as he realized what was happening. Although Tythian found it served a purpose to destroy his family bonds, he'd turned into a madman since, an embarrassment of the tactful vampire he'd once been. I wondered if he regretted his lust for power that took him away from the web of a family that would keep him sane. And I felt hopeless to think of the cheerful Whitney who bubbled with optimism I never understood in this world during her former life as a human, only to be nurtured by this form of Tythian. Did he hate himself for it?

His laughter dulled with sudden coherency as a lavish weight of lightning struck around him and pinned him to his spot. Iris's height grew behind him as he whispered into Tythian's ear, "This is for Trinity." He clamped his hands down on Tythian's head, a stream of lightning running through him as he painfully crippled and tore his head from his body. My hand that his stomach had once swallowed hit the ground in goop, a small tinkle eluding from my golden claws.

Tythian's body sagged into a lump, and I sagged with quiet relief, knowing the fight was over. Though many bodies around us continued to fight and the undead was still unruly. Who knows what damage they'd spark if they continued on?

"Esmore?!" Balzar screamed from the distance. He watched Chase and me through the wavering miasma that pulsated further and further out. My hand had stopped bleeding but hadn't yet begun to heal, not when my body was trying to restore itself as Chase stripped it bare.

I tapped on Balzar's mind, asking for permission to communicate telepathically. He opened to me immediately. *Retreat. Take everyone from here, Balzar.*

*What do you mean? We can't leave without you two!*

*It's not going to hold. You all need to run. Now!* The final was a command. I'd already given myself to the idea of dying here today, and although I didn't have my heart to blazingly understand the full pain of that, I found comfort in falling to my knees beside the man who I loved in a well-fought war. Because we were in this together and I would go down with him, there was no other place for me to be. If Tythian's goal had been genocide, I found it only ironic that I harbored the very gift he truly desired. It was forewarned that my gift could be used for either good or evil. And I found its potency only laughable as the one I loved most was burdened by it. No one should manage this power in a starved world.

Balzar was reluctant to leave as I sent a wave of urgency to him and everyone else within the vicinity. I lingered my thoughts on Tori who was already on his way with the pups and Fire who protected them. She wanted to return to my side, and I urged her a reminder of her place. She was to do as I bid, not as she wanted to do so freely. There was no reason for her to die by my side as well. I pushed against Iris who hacked away my mother's leg, her scream deafening as he threw her over his shoulder. I was grateful to him for holding out my wishes. He then moved on to break apart Julia and Dillian.

"No!" Julia weakly screamed, near unconscious as her hand slithered out of Dillian's as she was ripped away. Dillian had at some point stopped feeding from her, but she was delirious with how much blood she'd lost, and I felt the bitter tang of revolt ooze from him as he hated himself for what he'd done. It only saddened me that nothing could be done for

Dillian. His neck was frozen with my mother's gift. Where she'd saved his life, she'd also trapped him.

*I'm sorry,* I whispered into his mind which was surprisingly already open to me as his dull gaze looked at me sadly.

*You have nothing to apologize for. And I'm sorry it ended this way for you too.* He closed his eyes, and I could feel him coiling into himself mentally, prepared for the same death that I anticipated. I didn't want to intrude on his lasting thoughts and memories of Julia. The miasma from Chase continued to spread as his bleak black eyes stared through me. I placed my hand on his chest, envisioning him without this cursed face or expression.

He'd wanted us to come back to this fight, and I'd complied only to find it'd all been in vain. For destruction. Even the undead peeled apart, aware of the greater danger that threatened them. The few of Chase's coven who tried to step in and help were immediately incinerated and turned to ash.

My red raw muscles were bleeding in blotches as my wings crippled from the wave of miasma. "Chase, my love," I said, pressing a small kiss on his lips. "Let's try our best to control its magnitude." I wanted the others to escape and for this gift to have a limit even though it would take us both down with it. I opened my mind wide to him, like throwing my arms in a welcoming hug. The spreading of the disease easily crept over, giving me that last moment to speak with him as we became one.

*You can control this.* The disease fluctuated the moment I communicated to him, filling in the space I'd used even to create the thought. But it was fitting. It was a part of him and now filled me. We'd share this nothingness together as the outside world burned around us. I could feel his power, our gift, sweep over the undead as they tried to crawl away. I tried my hardest to shield Dillian, focusing on contorting this gift to obliterate his frozen status or wrapping around him so the mass of our power didn't take him.

We focused on our comrades, conjoining our efforts to ease their passage out of the city. I brushed my mind against the two pups who were frozen in their shifting status as the disease tempted to take them over. It was bittersweet to let Titan go. For all the pain I'd caused her, I hoped she lived a long life, one that lacked in the pain and suffering I'd inevitably dragged her into. I reached out as if to kiss her mentally, seeing her off. The twist of Chase's gift infused in the notion and I felt the light dance of it spark around her mind banishing the taint as if it were never there.

The black swell of the thorny roses embedded into me as I could only think of one thing. *Chase. Chase. Chase.* I tried my hardest to help him manage the gift. To insist on how he could whip it back instead of allowing it to continue spreading like a sickening haze across the land. I dropped my heavy head on his shoulder, aware that most of my face had been peeled away. But in this pain and suffering, I still felt warm and connected because I was *him*. If only he'd respond.

I could sense him, underneath so desperately wanting to fight it and be with me. A bubble of our gift arose, cutting through the disease so we could have that—a moment of serenity as we held hands somewhere, maybe in the now or maybe in the afterlife. The disease bubbled away, eroding the sickness that had consumed us, giving us total clarity.

We were together, and the infinite world around us blew apart as Montreal fell and we were in the center. Together. Alone. And possibly forgotten. The heavy intrusion of this disease released our minds and gave us the moment we deserved. To envision holding one another in serenity and realizing we'd achieved what we'd set out to do. No fighting. Just us. The sprinkle of physical dissolve reminded me that we were being left behind in the real world as his use of the gift suctioned back in, and we fell—one last time.

# EPILOGUE

## TITAN

I T HAD BEEN three weeks since our return from Montreal. I was standing in the room that was once Esmore's. How I loathed her, in part for what she'd done to my father and in equal measure for leaving us behind. She'd promised I'd have my revenge and despite how strong she was, she'd managed to get herself killed. All for the sake of the love she had for her familiar. And that irked me even more because a small part of me had always grown up on the notion that she was invincible. But equally as much as I spited her, I hoped she'd finally found the peace she's always wanted with Chase.

If I was being honest with myself, I despised her as much as I had admired her. All of my memories and the reason why I was still alive were because of her. And it made me feel all that much weaker that I still had to depend on her in such a way. As Tori had told me, before the two sunk into the calamity of their own gift they'd blessed both Chris and me—eroding away the disease within in our minds. A part of me was furious that they hadn't managed to do the same for themselves. But a lingering sense told me that maybe they had. After all, it's not like their bodies were to be found, and if anyone was able to defy death, it was certainly those two. And in the way the others said very little in its regards as the wolves mourned for their loss, I considered the possibility that they knew better and something was being left unsaid in the palpable tension.

A light tap on the door interrupted my thoughts. I could smell Tori before he'd let himself in. At least that was one thing she'd left me. At least I still had *him*. My hand skirted along the chair she'd so often sat in, staring out into the night sky, of what I imagined to be her guilt and longing for Chase. My shoulders slumped as much as I hated them for dying in the atomic blasting of Montreal and losing to their own gift and power, I couldn't help but wish such an unwavering love was set out in my fate as well.

A small part of me queried as to whether they'd actually died. After all, they'd seemed so unstoppable. And equally strange, after her demise, Fire was never to be found again. Likely, because she'd always followed her master whether dead or alive. Even with that unyielding loyalty and knowledge, it didn't make the halls feel any less empty.

"Titan," Tori said, waiting for me beside the door. "It's time." A small part of me queried if she had survived, would Tori have chosen her over me. He'd always been her loyal soldier, but my heart lurched at the thought of anyone taking him away from me, and a selfish part of me wished he was only loyal to me, especially now that Chris had chosen to abandon me.

I sighed gravely. "I know." Chris said he'd leave upon dawn and as a small light skimmed the trees past the castle, I knew it was time. But I didn't want it to be goodbye. I couldn't fathom that he was actually deserting us. We'd been together since childhood, and a small part of me wanted to go with him, excited by the sound of adventure. But an even greater inkling was that I was to stay and fill a void that would take time to grow into, I thought as I looked at Esmore's empty chair.

Tori and I silently walked down the quiet hall to the alcove of the entrance. Iris was already waiting, standing alone with his oversized hatchet strapped to his back. "He just went looking for you," he said. Which meant Chris wouldn't take too long to return. He'd never leave without saying goodbye.

We'd argued over his decision for many nights. He felt inferior for not being able to protect me in Montreal, even though I lectured that wasn't his role and reminded him we'd both been hurt. And for whatever reason, Iris agreed to train him as they went on foot across the land searching for new places and perhaps to reunite with familiar faces. I didn't want him to go—he was plenty strong enough for me. But he just couldn't handle his own inadequacy as he decided on his own to leave. Everyone was abandoning me.

His smoky scent hit me before his bulked arms crushed me across the chest and he hugged me from behind. I closed my eyes, my fingers lightly dancing across the veins in his forearms. He and I had a close call with death. And I was grateful we'd recovered from the dark and lonely place Tythian had twisted us into.

I was just as guilty for not protecting him as he was me. But it didn't mean he had to leave, not like this. I wanted to go with him, but my place was here with the pack. I wanted to learn all that I could from Claus and the other warriors to become stronger and understand my higher calling.

"Don't do anything reckless while I'm gone," he purred into my ear. I nuzzled myself into him, memorizing his scent so I'd remember the moment it caught wind to return.

"Now, what fun would that be?" I replied. I could feel his mischievous smile as I twisted to look up at him. I didn't want him to go. He'd been my safety net for so many years.

He rustled around in his pocket, pulling out a jaded red necklace. "I know we promised to celebrate our eighteenth in some outlandish way and I'm sorry I won't be here for it." He circled around me, clipping it at the back. The edges were ragged but beautiful. "But when you're celebrating look up into the sky and know that I'm thinking of you on that day. Well, every day until I return stronger to protect you properly."

I caught his hand after he fastened the thin rope tightly around my neck, the necklace acting more like a high collar. "You don't need to go. No one is asking you to leave," I urged.

He gave me a small smile. "I need to do this for me, Titan. But I'll return." He grabbed the edge of my fingers and lightly placed a kiss along my knuckles. It sent a confusing hot flush over my skin. Before I could say anything he swept me into another big hug, kissing the top of my head. "Just be safe and don't be rash in moving against the humans."

Many of the werewolves had woken to see him off, most in their wolf forms, which the majority of us were most comfortable in. "Then don't take so long." I pouted. He smiled and let me go. He and Tori exchanged a courteous nod and roguishly hugged one another.

"Look after her."

"I'll protect her with my life," Tori replied.

I punched them both in the arm which they rubbed childishly. "You two know I can damn look after myself, right?"

"Yes, the oh so fierce, Titan," Chris patronized, rubbing my hair. I slapped his hand away, and his sad smile reminded me once again that this wouldn't be our every day anymore.

"It's time," Iris encouraged. Chris shuffled the bag on his back.

"Until I see you both next time," he said, staring at me with an expression I didn't quite understand. The outside world was full of monsters as we'd discovered in Montreal, but even past that there was more to come. I could sense it. Though Esmore might've passed into the afterlife and her war dealt with it, it didn't remove the reality that humans still lived, experimenting on our kind. And someone had to set them free.

Chris hesitantly turned and began walking, following his new sensei. The wolves surrounding sang to him. The song of which was a kind departing truth that we wished him well and hoped to see him soon. That our ancestors before us would watch over him and protect him against monsters. To anyone else, they heard the wolves' cry. But I heard their words and song about departure and promise. And strangely, my heart sang its own, pleading with him to soon come back into my arms and to never let him go. But I knew it was selfish of me to ask him that when he had his own free will. And if he were to grow stronger, then so would I.

"Oh no! Iris, you didn't hug me goodbye?!" Lincon demanded. He had blood all over his face from goodness knows what he'd massacred. For the most part, he knew that the humans who lived here weren't to be eaten. But it didn't make his nature any less disturbing. But I'd been desensitized to his actions after growing up with him for so many years.

"You're such a mess, Lincon, at least clean your mouth," I said, watching the other two walk into the forest. "And besides, Iris never liked you, you do understand that, right?" Although I was certain Lincon was oblivious to all rationality.

"Ooh, grouchy little wolf when her buddy abandons her." Lincon pouted. I cut him a gutting stare, and he laughed holding his belly.

"Don't you have anywhere else to be, Lincon?" I queried. Of all the vampires to be left with, I know Claus was least happy to have him remain but had no idea how to be rid of him. Even though Claus was our new leader, it was obvious he couldn't oppose Lincon. None of us could. He was as old and powerful as the dust settling on the land—maybe even more.

"Oh, little wolf, but you don't know what fun is going to trail you," Lincon mused. "But you must remember if you bore me too much I'll leave."

"Pfft," I said transparently, seeing him for what he was and why he was staying. We'd often played pranks on others together, which were often taken too far, and naturally, Esmore reprimanded me for following his lead. But I wasn't a child anymore, and I could follow my own intuition. "As if you'd leave the fun and intention to annihilate the human government."

His smile widened in that crazed expression he often had. Kasey was munching on an apple behind him, forever his shadow. I never understood their relationship. It certainly wasn't of the romantic type. And I could only vaguely remember her twin sister before she'd killed herself. But that was her business. I had no right putting my nose in it.

I stared back toward the silhouette shoulders of my best friend departing. I shifted, my clothes stretching and ripping apart around my new form. It might've been a tad rash, but I didn't care because I wanted to sing to him and say my farewells until next we would meet. I encouraged my father to look over him and all the family we'd known and loved who were high in the sky to protect him from any evil he may pass, until he returned once again—safely in my arms.

# ESMORE

I WAS HANGING upside down with my legs strapped over the tree as my braid fell toward the ground. "I really don't see how this brings you so much joy," I said to Darcy who hung upside down on the tree beside me.

He charmed a boyish smile. "I don't know what to tell you. When you see the world so many ways, don't you think it gives you a different perspective?"

My eyebrows furrowed. "You're kind of weird, you know that?"

"I don't need to hear that from you of all people," he replied. Chase's chuckle enveloped me as he walked toward us. Then again, maybe every perception of Chase could be enjoyed.

"I leave you for an hour, and this is what I return to," he said, crossing his arms over his chest.

"It teaches you for leaving me then, doesn't it," I replied, my words muffling as he leaned up to kiss me. His tongue glided along mine, licking the top of my mouth. His calloused hand grabbed hold of my arm and yanked. He as quickly caught me in his arms. A slight head spin occurred giving me a light thrill.

"Hello, wife," he purred. I pushed back part of his black hair that had drifted with the wind concealing his beautiful face. His blue gemmed earring sparkled in the day's light. "Shouldn't you be seeing off our guests?"

"Are they leaving already? I thought they might be sleeping in," I sarcastically said.

*You think you're so funny,* he chimed down our line embracing me with all the light and love he had in the world, all selfishly for me.

*I was just getting an aerial view to make sure they were safe to leave.* He felt the leather holes in my back to confirm.

*You need to be more careful of ruining your clothes. We're not attached to the mainland anymore. It might be harder to find you a shirt.*

*Oh, the hardship. Then I might have to walk around shirtless,* I toyed as I stood up and began walking away. He slapped me on my ass.

*Only I'm to see you naked,* he growled, and it went without saying. He was the only being I wanted to stare at me with that heated expression. It felt refreshing not to carry my wings with me anymore. I'd worn them almost as a barrier between me and the others. A constant reminder that I was different and a beacon of my power for anyone who opposed. And now I didn't need that. I had no one to challenge and no need to hide behind my blatant display of power. I could just be me and retract the Descendant, thanking it for its years of service and hopefully it would now slumber forevermore, never having to be called upon again.

I'd become so accustomed to them over the decade that not having them left me unbalanced for the first few days, but now I felt lighter like I'd finally enabled myself to take a weight off my shoulders. And now I felt complete with my beating heart that my mother had returned to me yesterday. I placed my hand on my chest, relieved that I was one piece again.

Fire sidled up to my side, and I brushed my fingers through her fur. She looked the cleanest she had in years from all the leisurely time she'd been taking by the water. Admittedly, this lifestyle would take some getting used to—for all of us. The remains of Chase's coven chose to stay by his side even though only a handful made it out alive. All of the gargoyles had and were planted around the island, guarding the new place we called our home. They were in their gargoyle form, ready to serve when needed but grateful they were finally able to rest once again.

Darcy and Jerimiah often conversed with us, not entirely ignorant of our new world. And besides, I think they liked us. Thanks to Balzar's tracking skills, he was able to escort my mother to find us from the mainland with only a few hours required with boat and oar. I'd been grateful to his skill that could track us, quickly identifying that we'd survived even though it remained secret. But he'd honored me in being able to say goodbye to my mother properly and have my heart returned.

My mother walked out of the guest hut. We were still in transition of creating cabins across the island giving everyone space. And my mother had offered to use her gift to conceal the island. Because of the fatigue it set on her hiding such a large piece of land, I'd suggested she stay the night before her travels back to the hunter rebellion.

"Daughter," she announced when she saw me.

"Mother," I said just as dryly. Although we didn't see eye to eye on my decision to remain hidden on an island after feigning my death, I decided what was best for me and Chase, not my mother, even if it was just for now. He and I were killers. Naturally born for war and programmed for the fight. And although that sometimes plagued my thoughts of how we would adapt without it, I also found an amounted relief to know that I wouldn't be pushed and shoved in a direction someone else wanted me to go. And that those who I wanted to protect most wouldn't be manipulated simply because of this gift I harbored.

Because of the devastation left behind in Montreal and the numerous hunters who became casualties for it, we'd be hunted more than ever. For the time being, maybe even forever, we wanted a moment of peace. We'd waited a long time for this. Where every waking moment wasn't focused on the next life we were to take. And although I was going against my programming, I felt liberated and finally free. Like these wings had a purpose besides being a fine weapon.

I was sad to relieve my duty to the werewolves. But there was no place for me there anymore. After Titan had found out and despised me so, my disappearance was the most I could offer her as a sense of peace, and Tori was the added gift. And besides, if I'd stayed, she'd never grow into her potential of being Alpha and all that she was destined to become. She could never thrive in my shadow. I was grateful before we were seen that I could dissolve the disease in their minds—my last parting gift to offer them a fruitful life.

That was when I realized I could use that same precision to erase Chase's disease. It saddened me to realize the gamble I played because if it didn't work, turning the gift on him might've left him brain dead, but it was no different from being mindless as a saber. I had the pups to thank for that, for making me realize with their liberation of the disease that the whole time we'd had the answer to his illness. We simply needed to find a way to insert the key into his lock. And now it seemed as if nothing had happened. That we hadn't lost ten years and he acted like his normal, cheeky self without a care in the world.

A sacrifice we had taken was Tori. But in that last fight as he so bravely fought for Titan's life I knew then that although loyal to me because of our history and hierarchy, his heart lay somewhere else and I hoped this acted as fine a gift as any other. And he was one of few who knew of our survival. Like my mother, Balzar passed on the message offering Tori his ultimatum. He could stay with the werewolves or return to us. I favored that he stayed with Titan. At least I knew she would be looked after properly and I hoped Tori found whatever it was he searched for after all that had been taken from him.

"I still don't like it," my mother grumbled with arms crossed. How many times had we come to this crossroad? We didn't often agree on much, but we would fight for one another to the death. And had she the option to have an oasis with Cesar, even if it were short-lived, I was certain she might've contemplated it. Though her rigidness would probably never allow her to have so much happiness. I was lucky enough to have a familiar who reminded me how much I deserved to spend a moment in the light instead of drowning in the darkness.

"I love you too, Mom," I said sympathetically. Her breath hitched.

"Why do I always feel like I'm saying goodbye to you," she berated.

"Because you are. You know we can't come back, the moment we do we'll be hunted down. Sabe might've been able to pull away interest from my activities the last decade but Chase turning on the hunters when he atomically went boom will not be pardoned. Not everyone made it out alive. And it'll only incriminate you if you continue to associate with us."

We had our separate paths and duties. Together we had finished only one war. But there were plenty more to come. And I wanted nothing to do with them. I'd already lost much of my humanity by all the blood on my hands. And although my mother had fought many more years than I had, she hadn't vanished cities at a time. This gift was beautiful and mine, but I'd used it for so many disastrous pillagings before I learned the secret of its equal blessing.

"Oh, don't be so sheepish," Clarissa dryly remarked behind us. She was talking to Balzar who was grossed out by Spungee rubbing adoringly against Clarissa's breasts.

"It's just weird, woman," he barked back.

"Oh, how I can't wait until you take your leave," Clarissa purred. Cesar's coven had depleted to nothing and Balzar disband the remains wanting no part of his ties to the past. Before finding us, he returned to Yolo's grave for days, deciding on what he should do next. He was the only brother to remain of the four. From the conversation we'd had last night, it was evident he still didn't know where to go.

"You should stay with us," Chase offered. "You're always welcome. I could always go with another fine wine drinking partner." Balzar twisted his face in disgust. It somewhat only felt natural for Balzar to stay. We'd had our differences, and there was that one time he'd attacked Dillian and Julia, and I almost killed him as well. But since fighting together we'd come to learn to trust one another. I never thought I would one day form any kind of bond with Cesar's sons.

Balzar was a fighter. But like all of us, he'd also been fighting all his life, and I wondered if he condoned our lifestyle choice or was disgusted by it. Balzar looked to me, his face twisting with contemplation.

"Just don't piss me off," I remarked. A dashing smile spread across his face.

"Someone has to keep your combatant skills up to par," he replied. And I realized he was hoping for an invitation to stay, because where else did he have to go? "Well, I suppose I could stay for a little while until it becomes too boring around here."

"I object." Clarissa frowned.

"Oh, come on, don't be like that." Balzar slung his arm over her shoulder, and Spungee immediately bit it, riling with jealousy. "Ouch, it actually fucking bit me!" Clarissa patted Spungee's head as she flung Balzar's arm off her with a hmph.

"Are you sure this place will be peaceful?" my mother queried.

"Well, I suppose it's going to be slightly livelier now. If it gets too much, we'll just throw him into the sea," I added.

"Hey!" Balzar crooned. "Why am I already being ganged up on?"

My mother and I ignored him. "There's something else I wanted to leave with you, although I hope it'll never have to be used again," my mother said, shuffling through her bag. She pulled out the wooden box sealed with the vined roses and heart in the emblem. The very box that had concealed my heart and gift for years.

"I won't ever need this again," I replied, but she firmly tried to place it into my hands.

"I know I'm not often good with words, Esmore," she began to say before locking up. I had seen my mother cry for my benefit a few times in my life and I had seen her fight for me even harder. And in conclusion, I knew that this box, to her, didn't represent my oppression but to the lengths of which she would protect me. Even if it meant hiding me on an island from those who would hunt me down, even when it went against her very nature and personal mission. This embossed box was what she had to offer me, to remember her, as if I could ever forget. But I curled my fingers around it, accepting her sentiment.

I wrapped my arm around her pulling her in for a hug. It was always awkward and uncomfortable, but she lightly pressed an arm around me, contemplative that this might be the last time. The reality was, I was an immortal thanks to my counter vampirism part. My mother, however, would age.

"I love you too, Esmore," she breathed, pressing a small kiss to my temple. She pulled away, wiping over her leather shirt as if it were now dirty or she'd crinkled it by the physical contact. "You look after her," she pointed her finger at Chase. "Or I'll hunt you down myself."

Chase gave her his cockiest grin as he leaned against a tree. "How a good game of cat and mouse tempts me so."

*Chase,* I grumbled. My mother was not known for having a sense of humor and he knew that. Her eye twitched at his sentiment, but she curtly nodded and made her way toward the edge of the island.

"You know, I thought she might consider staying," Dillian's voice rung out. Julia's and his hut was closest to ours though still miles apart. I couldn't see Julia but knew she was about, most likely nursing the garden she'd started since the day we'd arrived. Fire, her, and I were the only ones who could eat any kind of food, but she was adamant to continue her herbology and maintain taking her bitter-smelling balls of herbs to slow down her aging and deter vampires from her huntress scent. And so far from what I'd seen, it'd worked. Although I couldn't help but consider how much of a turn-off that might've been for Dillian during sex when he wanted to bite.

*Dirty fiend,* Chase chastised me. I could feel his suave smile as I replied to Dillian. "And miss the chance to fight? Whose mother are you talking about?"

A small smile pressed on Dillian's face, and it warmed my heart to see. He wasn't back to himself entirely. No, the colder exterior was now part of who he was. But I imagined in time and reunited with Julia, he'd possibly find a pathway to peace and perhaps even joy.

"Walk with me?" Dillian asked. And how I'd longed to be asked that question from my best friend for so many years.

We'd quietly walked across the small grove where we could watch as Julia frolicked in her garden and Dillian unblinkingly stared at her adoringly. It relieved me to see the spark of life in his gaze once again. And I had much to praise and thank Julia for. For saving my best friend even when risking herself. Although silent, she'd always been strong.

"It kind of feels like full circle, doesn't it?" he rhetorically asked, leaning back on his elbows as he looked up at the overcast day as if it was sun beaming down on him instead. Here on this island, there wasn't fog or mist in the mornings. It felt free and detached from all that we'd known on the mainland.

"In what way?" I asked, following suit and stretching out as well. It felt bizarre to lay out in such a leisurely fashion. I was no longer weighed down by my decisions costing everyone their mortality or humanity. My power resided within me, satisfied by the break and my vampire self found an escape route. Instead of drumming for bloodshed we'd put my familiar to good use fulfilling my lustful desires instead.

"Remember when we used to sit on top of the wall at the Guild? We were so naïve back then," he contemplated out loud. Had we ever known what was to come, I dare say we would've called it a lie. And I certainly couldn't have expected to be what I was, or falling in love with the enemy, or my best friend being turned into a vampire.

"We were but children," I replied. I had always thought of myself so highly being ordained as a Token Huntress at eighteen. I'd been one of the best and thrived to grow stronger, but I'd never prophesized it would lead me to all of this and risking my life daily for a very different cause.

He put his hand on mine, and I found those gentle eyes that belonged to my best friend who sat upon that wall with me, helping me cover my fluctuating and unbeknownst anger. That listened to me as I crooned about my unsettling understandings and who'd risked his life for me time and time again. "I don't blame you for what happened to me," he said earnestly. "It wasn't your fault that I was turned. You went through similar hardship, and I never understood it. I even became wary of you. A part of me even believed that being turned was a punishment for not being there to fully help you. I'd been useless until I was turned."

"You've never been useless!" I exclaimed.

He relieved another calm smile. "Much in the way that you tortured yourself Esmore by throwing yourself into danger. I also did the same thing, hoping to find a way to return the favor to help you. You set Julia free. And I only ever followed Tythian to protect Tori and in the hope to one day help you. But the things that I've done... The blood on my hands..."

I curled my hand around his. "I understand." I understood more than anyone what he was going through and the accounted crimes committed.

A cause of issue being a part of me sinisterly enjoyed it. And that was a part of me I'd accepted and faced my demons with. I realized now that Dillian still had a long time to go. And once again I would depend on Julia, her kind and gentle soul to save my friend. Because I couldn't defend him for his actions and he'd never listen. But the person he wanted forgiveness from was the woman we watched over now, collecting herbs with a twinkle in her eye. Had I been able to give him any future it would've been them together and able to have a child, something they'd wanted for years. And earnestly, I was sad that they had to settle for less. But at least they had each other.

"We all have time," I said thoughtfully. "To measure our sins and then release them one at a time. But also remember we were but innocent of this war and world as well. And if I beat myself up every day for all the wrong I'd committed I wouldn't be able to take my next breath. And that's why I have Chase, and you have Julia, to remind us that even we are deserving of such salvation."

His face crumpled with an array of confused emotions. He wanted to beat himself up for all his crimes. He had been, after all, the kindhearted one of us both. But now I had time to help him heal. Both he and Chase had been returned to me, and even if they hadn't, I would've given my body and soul to bring them back. Because they meant to me more than life, and I would never take that for granted.

*And you are the world to me as well, my love, my wife, my familiar,* Chase soothed, his warmth filling me from the inside. And then an erotic image flashed through my mind. I bit down on my lip and pulled my hand away from Dillian, flushing with heat. I wanted to smack Chase over the head, maybe wanting to frolic with him first and then reprimand him for catching me off guard in such a moment.

"Go," Dillian said, shaking his head with a small smile. "I don't have to be a mind reader to know. You two have all of eternity together and yet look at you both, like ravished beasts."

I embarrassingly heated red and complied, walking away to search for Chase. Maybe this island wasn't a big enough space to prevent everyone hearing us. But I certainly wasn't changing my agenda. I'd never take my time with Chase for granted again, and it turned out what made me feel closest to him was…well, him inside of me.

*Oh no, the big bad vampire is coming to eat me,* Chase squealed like a girl in my mind.

*I'm so going to throttle you!*

*Or how about you put your fists to another use,* he purred and sent me an image of my soft hands curled around his cock, just how he liked it.

My heat and core were flashing hot as he pulled me amongst the trees and wrapped my legs around his waist. "I've been jealous of everyone having your attention all day," he purred, licking down my neck, ready to mark it again for his fill. His fangs grazed delicately against my throat sending a consistent pulse between my legs, which was met with the grind of his hard cock between pants.

"And how shall I be punished?" I breathlessly said.

"For all of time," he replied, leaning back to look into my purple eyes which he so loved. "You are to be my sex slave for all of time."

I heartily laughed. "If I must," I said before grabbing him with both hands and kissing him wildly. My Token. My forever. My immortal love. We finally have time.

*Thank you so much for reading my book. If you enjoyed this book, I'd love to hear your honest thoughts in way of a review. It not only helps support my writing but also gives me important feedback on how you felt and connected with the world and characters. I love connecting with my readers and would appreciate if you could take two minutes to leave a review or rating. Thank you so much and I hope you are having a wonderful day!*

# About the Author

Kia grew up in the Darling Downs Region in Queensland, Australia. Graduating High School, she pursued a career in freelance journalism. In 2014, having always had a passion for writing fiction, she decided to follow her dream of becoming an accomplished author.

Now living on the Gold Coast, Australia and travelling every spare minute she gets, Kia is constantly searching for new inspiration for her writing and filling her heart with adventure, one country at a time.

# OTHER BOOKS BY KIA CARRINGTON-RUSSELL

***Mad Hatter Vampire Prince:***

A PREQUEL NOVELLA TO THE TOKEN HUNTRESS SERIES.
CAN ALSO BE READ AS A STANDALONE.

Kyran Klaus is the prince of Grand Klaus, his reputation honoring him the title of the Mad Hatter Vampire Prince. Crazy, deadly, lustful, and utterly bored with life.

Sasha Pierce is one of a kind. Having been experimented on by her mother as a child, she's become a human weapon who's looking for answers beyond the walls where her kind aren't enslaved to vampires.

When the Mad Hatter Prince takes a sudden interest in Sasha and her work, she scarcely begins to cover her tracks and hide her secrets. What she doesn't anticipate is being a pawn in his most sinister performance yet.

Disturbingly Wicked! This novella is not for the fainthearted. Lust, Gore, Wit, and Malicious Humor. Prepare to be deliciously tainted.

## Token Huntress

Being born a hunter, Esmore has been raised with one purpose, to hunt and kill the vampire race that destroyed the world as it was known. At eighteen, Esmore's a Token Huntress in her Guild, surpassing her mentor's expectations of her, despite having no magical ability, like all hunters before her.

During a raid in the once iconic San Fransisco, Esmore's team is ambushed, and a mysterious vampire that she is drawn to captures and takes her to the Vampire Council as a prisoner. Her captor- Chase, a lethal, immortal, sexy, and charming vampire who will stop at nothing to claim her as his familiar.

While in captivity, Esmore learns information that makes her question everything she's been taught.

Now in the year 2341, Esmore fights for her survival. But who exactly is she fighting against? The very people who nurtured her, or the evil she's supposed to hate?

## The Shadow Minds Journal:

In this world, there are creatures lurking in the shadows. As a child, I once played with them. As a teenager, I began to fear them and became victim to their attacks. As an adult, I now realize that no matter how much I try to escape the grasp of this world, I was inevitably born into it.

Now reborn as a Guardian in the year of 2986, Vivian Lair must uphold the treaty between Angels and Demons on the human world and city of Shabeah. Contracted to seven demons who she can shift into while taking direct orders from the Underworld Lord, Haymen, it wasn't exactly her ideal rebirth. Involving herself with the Angel of War, Gabe is even worse.

Still fighting those who try to possess her during her sleep, Vivian must now record and try to hunt the Volv through the Shadow Minds Journal. Now stuck between the hatred and lust of two of the most powerful entities in all worlds, Vivian is involved inevitably in the upcoming conflict.

*Blood. Lust. War. She must kill before being killed.*

### *My Escort Collection:*

A collection of the Best Selling contemporary series that includes: My Escort, My Exception and My Expectation. Clover is personal assistant to Debra Coorman, the merciless boss of Candice fashion magazine. The bright lights of New York are dim for Clover, who is tormented by a work schedule like no other. Debra is relentless in her determination to demean Clover. For once, Clover dares to play Debra's games, and intends to prove her wrong at the next glittering event. With mixed emotions, Clover contacts a male escort, Damon. If his velvet voice over the phone is anything to go by, Clover knows her money will be well spent. But when Damon appears at her door, something unexpected happens. The taunts and the games begin. Who is truly going to win at this game?

### *Aroused: Taming Himself*

"Remember my name because you will be begging me for more. This is my promise to you."

Meet Hayden Zilch: entrepreneur, sports manager, investor. Cocky, tantalizing, and an utter womanizer. He is a man who loves pleasuring women. He can show you a world you have only fantasied about.

So what happens when this sex-mad womanizer decides to finally find The One?

Starting off with a list of five women, Hayden sets out to learn the difference between lust and love. His adventures have him laughing, crying in pain, and begging on his knees as he battles to tame himself. Can Hayden really control himself around these five beautiful temptresses?

*Taming Himself is the first in this five-book series which tells the story of Hayden's search for both love and pleasure.*

## *Phantom Wolf*

*A book that is so dynamic and can pull my emotions free so easily is a 5 star novel.*
★★★★★ *- Paranormal Trance Reviews*

Sia is a Phantom Wolf. Neither dead nor alive--and rotting from the inside--she is on the edge of her curse. Once a Phantom Wolf has been created, they hunt their blood pack and slaughter all their loved ones. Except for Sia, who woke years after her death to find herself rampaging through the land on a lonely path.

She continues to run from the rival pack that hunts her because she is a Phantom Wolf. Attracted to a scent, Sia finds her old best friend, who is now a grown woman. Having once saved Keeley, Sia takes the role of protector yet again, despite Keeley's involvement with the mysterious Alpha, Kiba, and his kin brother, Saith. An ambush separates the pack and the four of them blindly fight the new warriors that attack them: desperately needing to find out where the attacks are coming from, as Sia has vowed to protect Keeley. But at what cost?

Now being chased, Sia finds herself conflicted by the mortal and spirit world while trying to protect her kin. Sia must confront her fears, as well as the human lover who killed her many years before. It is not only survival Sia contends with, but her own façade that must be broken so that she may find peace within herself once more.

## *The Three Immortal Blades*

Contains the entire Award Winning Collection. Karla Gray is an ordinary young woman that is taken from her mundane life into a world of blood lust as she begins to struggle with a unique ability. Karla is a Shielder; an exceptional fighter born with the rare ability to project a Shield for protection. However, Shielders are not the only kind that possesses such a talent. The Shielders battle a war that has been raging for centuries against Starkorfs, who harvest humans and Shielders alike to obtain a near immortality. Alongside the charming Lucas and selfless Paul, Karla must unravel the purpose of her curse and battle an unknown presence manipulating her thoughts; a mysterious woman who may be dormant for now, but has every intention of possessing Karla- mind, body, and soul. Within this new reality that Karla faces the search for the Three Immortal Blades begins.

www.ingramcontent.com/pod-product-compliance
Lightning Source LLC
Chambersburg PA
CBHW020334120726
47904CB00002B/407